The Little Paris Bookshop

Nina George

W F HOWES LTD

This large print edition published in 2015 by
W F Howes Ltd
Unit 4, Rearsby Business Park, Gaddesby Lane,
Rearsby, Leicester LE7 4YH

1 3 5 7 9 10 8 6 4 2

First published in the United Kingdom in 2015
by Abacus

A CIP catalogue record for this book is available
from the British Library

ISBN 978 1 51000 351 4

Typeset by Palimpsest Book Production Limited,
Falkirk, Stirlingshire

Print ... bound ... Great Britain in
by TJ International Ltd, Padstow, Cornwall

I dedicate this novel to my father,
JOACHIM ALBERT WOLFGANG GEORGE,
known as Broad Jo.
20 March 1938 (Sawade/Eichwaldau)–
4 April 2011 (Hamelin).

Papa,
you were the only person who read everything
I ever wrote from the moment I learned to
write. I will miss you at all times. I see you in
every ray of evening light and in every wave of
every sea.
You left in midsentence.

NINA GEORGE,
January 2013

Dedicated to the departed.
And to those who go on loving them.

CHAPTER 1

How on earth could I have let them talk me into it?

The two generals of number 27 Rue Montagnard – Madame Bernard, the owner, and Madame Rosalette, the concierge – had caught Monsieur in a pincer movement between their ground-floor flats.

'That Le P. has treated his wife shamelessly.'

'Scandalously. Like a moth treats a wedding veil.'

'You can hardly blame some people when you look at their wives. Fridges in Chanel. But men? Monsters, all of them.'

'Ladies, I don't quite know what . . .'

'Not you of course, Monsieur Perdu. You are cashmere compared with the normal yarn from which men are spun.'

'Anyway, we're getting a new tenant. On the fourth floor. Yours, Monsieur.'

'But Madame has nothing left. Absolutely nothing, only shattered illusions. She needs just about everything.'

'And that's where you come in, Monsieur. Give whatever you can. All donations welcome.'

1

'Of course. Maybe a good book . . .'

'Actually, we were thinking of something more practical. A table, perhaps. You know, Madame has—'

'Nothing. I got that impression.'

The bookseller could not imagine what might be more practical than a book, but he promised to give the new tenant a table. He still had one.

Monsieur Perdu pushed his tie between the top buttons of his white, vigorously ironed shirt and carefully rolled up his sleeves. Inwards, one fold at a time, up to the elbow. He stared at the bookcase in the corridor. Behind the shelves lay a room he hadn't entered for almost twenty-one years.

Twenty-one years and summers and New Year's mornings.

But in that room was the table.

He exhaled, groped indiscriminately for a book and pulled Orwell's *Nineteen Eighty-Four* out of the bookcase. It didn't fall apart. Nor did it bite his hand like an affronted cat.

He took out the next novel, then two more. Now he reached into the shelf with both hands, grabbed whole parcels of books out of it and piled them up beside him.

The stacks grew into trees. Towers. Magic mountains. He looked at the last book in his hand. *When the Clock Struck Thirteen*. A tale of time travel.

If he'd believed in omens, this would have been a sign.

He banged the bottom of the shelves with his fists to loosen them from their fastenings. Then he stepped back.

There. Layer by layer, it appeared. Behind the wall of words. The door to the room where . . .

I could simply buy a table.

Monsieur Perdu ran his hand over his mouth. Yes. Dust down the books, put them away again, forget about the door. Buy a table and carry on as he had for the last two decades. In twenty years' time he'd be seventy, and from there he'd make it through the rest. Maybe he'd die prematurely.

Coward.

He tightened his trembling fist on the door handle.

Slowly the tall man opened the door. He pushed it softly inwards, screwed up his eyes and . . .

Nothing but moonlight and dry air. He breathed it in through his nose, analysing it, but found nothing.

—'s smell has gone.

Over the course of twenty-one summers, Monsieur Perdu had become as adept at avoiding thinking of—as he was at stepping around open manholes.

He mainly thought of her as—. As a pause amid the hum of his thoughts, as a blank in the pictures of the past, as a dark spot amid his feelings. He was capable of conjuring all kinds of gaps.

Monsieur Perdu looked around. How quiet the room seemed. And pale despite the lavender-blue wallpaper.

The passing of the years behind the closed door had squeezed the colour from the walls.

The light from the corridor met little that could cast a shadow. A bistro chair. The kitchen table. A vase with the lavender stolen two decades earlier from the Valensole plateau. And a fifty-year-old man who now sat down on the chair and wrapped his arms around himself.

There had once been curtains, and over there, pictures, flowers and books, a cat called Castor that slept on the sofa. There were candlesticks and whispering, full wine glasses and music. Dancing shadows on the wall, one of them tall, the other strikingly beautiful. There had been love in this room.

Now there's only me.

He clenched his fists and pressed them against his burning eyes.

Monsieur Perdu swallowed and swallowed again to fight back the tears. His throat was too tight to breathe and his back seemed to glow with heat and pain.

When he could once more swallow without it hurting, Monsieur Perdu stood up and opened the casement window. Aromas came swirling in from the back courtyard.

The herbs from the Goldenbergs' little garden. Rosemary and thyme mixed with the massage oils used by Che, the blind chiropodist and 'foot whisperer'. Added to that, the smell of pancakes intermingled with Kofi's spicy and meaty African barbecued dishes. Over it all drifted the perfume of Paris in June, the fragrance of lime blossom and expectation.

But Monsieur Perdu wouldn't let these scents affect him. He resisted their charms. He'd become extremely good at ignoring anything that might in any way arouse feelings of yearning. Aromas. Melodies. The beauty of things.

He fetched soap and water from the storeroom next to the bare kitchen and began to clean the wooden table.

He fought off the blurry picture of himself sitting at this table, not alone but with—.

He washed and scrubbed and ignored the piercing question of what he was meant to do now that he had opened the door to the room in which all his love, his dreams and his past had been buried.

Memories are like wolves. You can't lock them away and hope they leave you alone.

Monsieur Perdu carried the narrow table to the door and heaved it through the bookcase, past the magic mountains of paper onto the landing and over to the flat across the corridor.

As he was about to knock, a sad sound reached his ears.

Stifled sobbing, as if through a cushion.

Someone was crying behind the green door.

A woman. And she was crying as though she wanted nobody, absolutely nobody, to hear.

CHAPTER 2

'She was married to You-Know-Who, Monsieur Le P.'

He didn't know. Perdu didn't read the Paris gossip pages.

Madame Catherine Le P.-You-Know-Who had come home late one Thursday evening from her husband's art agency, where she took care of his PR. Her key no longer fitted into the lock, and there was a suitcase on the stairs with divorce papers on top of it. Her husband had moved to an unknown address and taken the old furniture and a new woman with him.

Catherine, soon-to-be-ex-wife-of-Le-Dirty-Swine, possessed nothing but the clothes she had brought into their marriage – and the realisation that it had been naïve of her to think that their erstwhile love would guarantee decent treatment after their separation, and to assume that she knew her husband so well that he could no longer surprise her.

'A common mistake,' Madame Bernard, the lady of the house, had pontificated in between puffing out smoke signals from her pipe. 'You only really get to know your husband when he walks out on you.'

Monsieur Perdu had not yet seen the woman who'd been so coldheartedly ejected from her own life.

Now he listened to the lonely sobs she was desperately trying to muffle, perhaps with her hands or a tea towel. Should he announce his presence and embarrass her? He decided to fetch the vase and the chair first.

He tiptoed back and forth between his flat and hers. He knew how treacherous this proud old house could be, which floorboards squeaked, which walls were more recent and thinner additions and which concealed ducts that acted like megaphones.

When he pored over his eighteen-thousand-piece map of the world jigsaw in the otherwise empty living room, the sounds of the other residents' lives were transmitted to him through the fabric of the house.

The Goldenbergs' arguments (Him: 'Can't you just for once . . .? Why are you . . .? Haven't I . . .?' Her: 'You always have to . . . You never do . . . I want you to . . .') He'd known the two of them as newlyweds. They'd laughed together a lot back then. Then came the children, and the parents drifted apart like continents.

He heard Clara Violette's electric wheelchair rolling over carpet edges, wooden floors and door-sills. He remembered the young pianist back when she was able to dance.

He heard Che and young Kofi cooking. Che was stirring the pots. The man had been blind since birth, but he said that he could see the world through the fragrant trails and traces that people's feelings and thoughts had left behind. Che could sense whether a room had been loved or lived or argued in.

Perdu also listened every Sunday to how Madame Bomme and the widows' club giggled like girls at the dirty books he slipped them behind their stuffy relatives' backs.

The snatches of life that could be overheard in the house at number 27 Rue Montagnard were like a sea lapping the shores of Perdu's silent isle.

He had been listening for more than twenty years. He knew his neighbours so well that he was sometimes amazed by how little they knew about him (not that he minded). They had no idea that he owned next to no furniture apart from a bed, a chair and a clothes rail – no knick-knacks, no music, no pictures or photo albums or three-piece suite or crockery (other than for himself) – or that he had chosen such simplicity of his own free will. The two rooms he still occupied were so empty that they echoed when he coughed. The only thing in the living room was the giant jigsaw puzzle on the floor. His bedroom was furnished with a bed, the ironing board, a reading light and a clothes rail on wheels containing three identical sets of clothing: grey trousers, white shirt, brown V-neck jumper. In the kitchen were a stove-top coffee pot, a tin of coffee and a shelf stacked with food. Arranged in alphabetical order. Maybe it was just as well that no one saw this.

And yet he harboured a strange affection for 27 Rue Montagnard's residents. He felt inexplicably better when he knew that they were well – and in his unassuming way he tried to make a contribution. Books were a means of helping. Otherwise he stayed in the background, a small figure in a painting, while life was played out in the foreground.

However, the new tenant on the third floor, Maximilian Jordan, wouldn't leave Monsieur Perdu in peace. Jordan wore specially made earplugs with earmuffs over them, plus a woolly hat on cold days. Ever since the young author's debut novel had made him famous amid great fanfare, he'd been on the run from fans who would have given their right arms to move in with him. Meanwhile, Jordan had developed a peculiar interest in Monsieur Perdu.

While Perdu was on the landing arranging the chair beside the kitchen table, and the vase on top, the crying stopped.

In its place he heard the squeak of a floorboard that someone was trying to walk across without making it creak.

He peered through the pane of frosted glass in the green door. Then he knocked twice, very gently.

A face moved closer. A blurred, bright oval.

'Yes?' the oval whispered.

'I've got a chair and a table for you.'

The oval said nothing.

I have to speak softly to her. She's cried so much she's probably all dried out and she'll crumble if I'm too loud.

'And a vase. For flowers. Red flowers, for instance. They'd look really pretty on the white table.'

He had his cheek almost pressed up against the glass.

He whispered, 'But I can give you a book as well.'

The light in the staircase went out.

'What kind of book?' the oval whispered.

'The consoling kind.'

'I need to cry some more. I'll drown if I don't. Can you understand that?'

'Of course. Sometimes you're swimming in unwept tears and you'll go under if you store them up inside.' *And I'm at the bottom of a sea of tears.* 'I'll bring you a book for crying then.'

'When?'

'Tomorrow. Promise me you'll have something to eat and drink before you carry on crying.'

He didn't know why he was taking such liberties. It must be something to do with the door between them.

The glass misted up with her breath.

'Yes,' she said. 'Yes.'

When the hall light flared on again, the oval shrank back.

Monsieur Perdu laid his hand briefly on the glass where her face had been a second before.

10

And if she needs anything else, a chest of drawers or a potato peeler, I'll buy it and claim I had it already.

He went into his empty flat and pushed the bolt across. The door leading into the room behind the bookcase was still open. The longer Monsieur Perdu looked in there, the more it seemed as though the summer of 1992 were rising up out of the floor. The cat jumped down from the sofa on soft, velvet paws and stretched. The sunlight caressed a bare back, the back turned and became—. She smiled at Monsieur Perdu, rose from her reading position and walked towards him naked, with a book in her hand.

'Are you finally ready?' asked—.

Monsieur Perdu slammed the door.

No.

CHAPTER 3

'No,' Monsieur Perdu said again the following morning. 'I'd rather not sell you this book.'

Gently he pried *Night* from the lady's hand. Of the many novels on his book barge – the vessel moored on the Seine that he had named *Literary Apothecary* – she had inexplicably chosen the notorious bestseller by Maximilian 'Max' Jordan, the earmuff wearer from the third floor in Rue Montagnard.

The customer looked at the bookseller, taken aback.

'Why not?'

'Max Jordan doesn't suit you.'

'Max Jordan doesn't suit me?'

'That's right. He's not your type.'

'My type. Okay. Excuse me, but maybe I should point out to you that I've come to your book barge for a book. Not a husband, *mon cher* Monsieur.'

'With all due respect, what you read is more important in the long term than the man you marry, *ma chère* Madame.'

She looked at him through eyes like slits.

'Give me the book, take my money, and we can both pretend it's a nice day.'

'It *is* a nice day, and tomorrow is the start of summer, but you're not going to get this book. Not from me. May I suggest a few others?'

'Right, and flog me some old classic you're too lazy to throw overboard where it can poison the fish?' She spoke softly to begin with, but her volume kept increasing.

'Books aren't eggs, you know. Simply because a book has aged a bit doesn't mean it's gone bad.' There was now an edge to Monsieur Perdu's voice too. 'What is wrong with old? Age isn't a disease. We all grow old, even books. But are you, is *anyone*, worth less, or less *important*, because they've been around for longer?'

'It's absurd how you're twisting everything, all because you don't want me to have that stupid *Night* book.'

The customer – or rather noncustomer – tossed her purse into her luxury shoulder bag and tugged at the zip, which got stuck.

Perdu felt something welling up inside him, a wild feeling, anger, tension – only it had nothing to do with this woman. He couldn't hold his tongue, though. He hurried after her as she strode angrily through the belly of the book barge and called out to her in the half-light between the long bookshelves: 'It's your choice, Madame! You can leave and spit on me. Or you can spare yourself thousands of hours of torture starting right now.'

'Thanks, that's exactly what I'm doing.'

'Surrender to the treasures of books instead of entering into pointless relationships with men, who neglect you anyway, or going on crazy diets because you're not thin enough for one man and not stupid enough for the next.'

She stood stock-still by the large bay window that looked out over the Seine, and glared at Perdu. 'How dare you!'

'Books keep stupidity at bay. And vain hopes. And vain men. They undress you with love, strength and knowledge. It's love from within. Make your choice: book or . . .'

Before he could finish his sentence, a Parisian pleasure boat ploughed past with a group of Chinese women standing by the railing under umbrellas. They began clicking away with their cameras when they caught sight of Paris's famous floating *Literary Apothecary.* The pleasure boat drove brown-green dunes of water against the bank, and the book barge reeled.

The customer teetered on her smart high heels, but instead of offering her his hand, Perdu handed her *The Elegance of the Hedgehog.*

She made an instinctive grab for the novel and clung to it.

Perdu held on to the book as he spoke to the stranger in a soothing, tender and calm voice.

'You need your own room. Not too bright, with a kitten to keep you company. And this book, which you will please read slowly, so you can take

14

the occasional break. You'll do a lot of thinking and probably a bit of crying. For yourself. For the years. But you'll feel better afterwards. You'll know that now you don't have to die, even if that's how it feels because the guy didn't treat you well. And you will like yourself again and won't find yourself ugly or naïve.'

Only after delivering these instructions did he let go.

The customer stared at him. He knew from her shocked look that he had hit the target and got through to her. Pretty much a bull's-eye.

Then she dropped the book.

'You're completely nuts,' she whispered before spinning on her heel and tottering off, head down, through the boat's book-filled belly and out onto the embankment.

Monsieur Perdu picked up the *Hedgehog*. The book's spine had been damaged by the fall. He would have to offer Muriel Barbery's novel for a euro or two to one of the *bouquinistes* on the embankment with their boxes of books for people to rummage through.

Then he gazed after the customer. How she fought her way through the strolling crowds. How her shoulders shook in her suit.

She was crying. She was weeping like someone who knows that this small drama is not going to break her, but is nonetheless deeply hurt by the injustice of the here and now. She had already suffered one cruel, deep blow. Wasn't that enough?

Did this nasty bookseller really need to rub salt in her wound?

Monsieur Perdu suspected that on her personal idiot scale of one to ten, she ranked him – the paper tiger idiot on his stupid *Literary Apothecary* – about a twelve.

He agreed with her. His outburst and his high-handed tone must somehow be related to the previous night and to the room. He was usually more sanguine.

He was generally unperturbed by his customers' wishes, insults or peculiarities. He divided them into three categories. The first category comprised those for whom books were the only breath of fresh air in their claustrophobic daily lives. His favourite customers. They were confident he would tell them what they needed. Or they confided their vulnerabilities to him, for example: 'No novels with mountains, lifts or views in them, please – I'm scared of heights.' Some of them sang Monsieur Perdu children's tunes, or rather growled them: 'Mm-hmm, mmh, dadada – know that one?' in the hope that the great bookseller would remember for them and give them a book featuring the melodies of their childhood. And most of the time he did know a book to match the songs. There had been a time when he sang a lot.

The second category of customers came aboard *Lulu,* the original name of his book barge in the Port des Champs-Élysées, because they had been lured there by the name of the bookshop: *la pharmacie littéraire,* the *Literary Apothecary.*

They came to buy wacky postcards ('Reading kills prejudice' or 'People who read don't lie – at least not at the same time') or miniature books in brown medicine bottles, or to take photos.

Yet these people were downright entertaining compared with the third kind, who thought they were kings but, unfortunately, lacked the manners of royalty. Without saying '*Bonjour*' or so much as looking at him as they handled every book with fingers greasy from the chips they'd been eating, they asked Perdu in a reproachful tone: 'Don't you have any plasters with poems on them? Or crime-series toilet paper? Why don't you stock inflatable travel pillows? Now that would be a useful thing for a book pharmacy to have.'

Perdu's mother, Lirabelle Bernier, formerly Perdu, had urged him to sell rubbing alcohol and compression stockings – women of a certain age got heavy legged when they sat reading.

Some days he sold more stockings than literature.

He sighed.

Why was such an emotionally vulnerable woman so eager to read *Night*?

All right, it wouldn't have done her any harm.

Well, not much.

The newspaper *Le Monde* had feted the novel and Max Jordan as 'the new voice of rebellious youth'. The women's magazines had worked themselves into a frenzy over the 'boy with the hungry heart' and had printed photo portraits of the author bigger than the book's cover. Max Jordan always looked somewhat bemused in these pictures.

Bemused and bruised, thought Perdu.

Jordan's debut novel was full of men who, out of fear for their individuality, responded to love with nothing but hatred and cynical indifference. One critic had celebrated *Night* as the 'manifesto of a new masculinity.'

Perdu thought it was something a bit less pretentious. It was a rather desperate attempt by a young man who was in love for the first time to take stock of his inner life. The young man cannot understand how he can lose all self-control and start loving and then, just as mystifyingly, stop again. How unsettling it is for him to be unable to decide whom he loves and who loves him, where it begins and where it ends, and all the terribly unpredictable things in between.

Love, the dictator whom men find so terrifying. No wonder that men, being men, generally greet this tyrant by running away. Millions of women read the book to find out why men were so cruel to them. Why they changed the locks, dumped them by text, slept with their best friends. All to thumb their nose at the great dictator: *See, you're not going to get me. No, not me.*

But was the book really of any comfort to these women?

Night had been translated into twenty-nine

languages. They'd even sold it to Belgium, as Rosalette the concierge had been keen to note. As a Frenchwoman born and raised, she liked to point out that you could never know with the Belgians.

Max Jordan had moved into 27 Rue Montagnard seven weeks ago, opposite the Goldenbergs on the third floor. He hadn't yet been tracked down by any of the fans who pursued him with love letters, phone calls and lifelong pledges. There was even a *Night* Wikiforum, where they swapped their news and views about his ex-girlfriends (unknown, the big question being: was Jordan a virgin?), his eccentric habits (wearing earmuffs) and his possible addresses (Paris, Antibes, London).

Perdu had seen his fair share of *Night* addicts in the *Literary Apothecary*. They'd come aboard wearing earmuffs and beseeching Monsieur Perdu to arrange a reading by their idol. When Perdu suggested this to his neighbour, the twenty-one-year-old had gone deathly pale. Stage fright, Perdu reckoned.

To him, Jordan was a young man on the run, a child who had been proclaimed a man of letters against his will – and surely, for many, a whistle-blower on men's emotional turmoil. There were even hate forums on the Web where anonymous posters ripped Jordan's novel apart, made fun of it and advised the author to do what the despairing character in his novel does when he realises that he'll never be able to master love: he throws himself from a Corsican cliff top into the sea below.

The most fascinating things about *Night* were the author's descriptions of male frailties: he wrote about the inner life of men more honestly than any man had done before. He trampled on every one of literature's idealised and familiar images of men: the image of the 'he-man', the 'emotional dwarf', the 'demented old man' and the 'lone wolf'. A feminist magazine had given its review of Jordan's debut novel the appropriately mellow headline MEN ARE HUMAN TOO.

Jordan's daring impressed Perdu. Yet the novel still struck him as a kind of gazpacho that kept sloshing over the edge of the soup bowl. Its author was just as emotionally defenceless and unprotected: he was the positive print of Perdu's negative.

Perdu wondered how it must feel to experience things so intensely and yet survive.

CHAPTER 4

Next Perdu served an Englishman who asked him, 'I recently saw a book with a green-and-white jacket. Has it been translated?' Perdu figured out that it was a classic that had been published seventeen years back. He sold the man a collection of poetry instead. Afterwards, he helped the deliveryman transfer the crates of books he had ordered from the handcart onto the boat, and then gathered a few recent children's books for the somewhat frantic teacher from the primary school on the other bank of the Seine.

Perdu wiped the nose of a little girl, who was absorbed with *Northern Lights*. For the girl's overworked mother, he wrote out a tax refund certificate for the thirty-volume encyclopedia she was buying in installments.

She gestured towards her daughter. 'This strange child of mine wants to have read the entire thing before she turns twenty-one. Okay, I said, she can have the enclyco . . . encloped . . . oh, all these reference books, but she won't be getting any more birthday presents. And nothing for Christmas either.'

Perdu acknowledged the seven-year-old girl with a nod. The child nodded earnestly back.

'Do you think that's normal?' the mother asked anxiously. 'At her age?'

'I think she's brave, clever and right.'

'As long as she doesn't turn out too smart for men.'

'For the stupid ones, she will, Madame. But who wants them anyway? A stupid man is every woman's downfall.'

The mother looked up from her agitated, reddened hands in surprise.

'Why didn't anyone ever tell me that?' she asked with the flicker of a smile.

'Do you know what?' said Perdu. 'Pick a book you'd like to give your daughter for her birthday anyway. It's discount day at the *Apothecary*: buy an encyclopedia and we'll throw in a novel.'

The woman accepted his fib without blinking and sighed. 'But my mother's waiting for us outside. My mother says she wants to move into a retirement home and that I should stop taking care of her. But I can't. Could you?'

'I'll look after your mother. You look for a present, all right?'

The woman did as he said with a grateful smile.

Perdu brought a glass of water to the girl's grandmother out on the embankment. She didn't dare venture across the gangway.

Perdu was familiar with such distrust from elderly people; he had many customers over seventy whom

22

he gave advice to on dry land, on the very same wrought-iron bench where the old lady was now sitting. The further life advanced, the more protective the elderly were of their good days: nothing should imperil the time they had left. That was why they no longer went on trips; why they felled the old trees outside their houses so they didn't come crashing down onto their roofs; and why they no longer inched their way across a river on a five-millimetre-thick steel gangway. Perdu also brought the grandmother a magazine-sized book catalogue, with which she fanned herself against the summer heat. The elderly lady patted the seat beside her invitingly.

She reminded Perdu of his mother, Lirabelle. Maybe it was her eyes. They looked alert and intelligent. So he sat down. The Seine was sparkling, and the sky arched blue and summery overhead. The roaring and beeping of traffic drifted down from the Place de la Concorde; there was not a moment of silence. The city would empty a bit after 14 July, when the Parisians set off to claim the coastline and the mountains for the duration of the summer holidays. Yet even then the city would be loud and voracious.

'Do you do this too sometimes?' the grandmother suddenly asked. 'Check on old photos to see whether the faces of the deceased show any inkling that they will soon die?'

Monsieur Perdu shook his head. 'No.'

With trembling fingers dotted with liver spots, the lady opened the locket on her necklace.

'This is my husband. Taken two weeks before he collapsed. And then, all of a sudden, there you are, a young woman in an empty room.'

She ran her index finger over her husband's picture and tapped him gently on the nose.

'How relaxed he looks. As if all his plans could come true. We look into a camera and think it will all carry on and on, but then: *bonjour,* eternal rest.'

She paused. 'I for one don't let anyone take photos of me any more,' she said. She turned her face to the sun. 'Do you have a book about dying?'

'Many, in fact,' said Perdu. 'About growing old, about contracting an incurable disease, about dying slowly, quickly, alone somewhere on the floor of a hospital ward.'

'I've often wondered why people don't write more books about living. Anyone can die. But living?'

'You're right, Madame. There is so much to say about living. Living with books, living with children, living for beginners.'

'Write one then.'

As if I could give anyone any advice.

'I'd rather write an encyclopedia about common emotions,' he admitted. 'From A for "Anxiety about picking up hitchhikers" to E for "Early risers' smugness" through to Z for "Zealous toe concealment, or the fear that the sight of your feet might destroy someone's love for you".'

Perdu wondered why he was telling a stranger all this.

If only he hadn't opened the room.

The grandmother patted his knee. He gave a quick shudder: physical contact was dangerous.

'An encyclopedia of emotions,' she repeated with a smile. 'I know that feeling about toes. An almanac of common feelings . . . Do you know the German writer Erich Kästner?'

Perdu nodded. In 1936, shortly before Europe sank into the black-and-brown gloom, Kästner had published a *Lyrical Medicine Chest* from the poetic medicine cabinet of his works. 'This volume is dedicated to the therapy of private life,' wrote the poet in the foreword. 'It addresses – mainly in homeopathic doses – the minor and major ailments of existence and helps with the "treatment of the average inner life".'

'Kästner was one reason I called my book barge the *Literary Apothecary*,' said Perdu. 'I wanted to treat feelings that are not recognised as afflictions and are never diagnosed by doctors. All those little feelings and emotions no therapist is interested in, because they are apparently too minor and intangible. The feeling that washes over you when another summer nears its end. Or when you recognise that you haven't got your whole life left to find out where you belong. Or the slight sense of grief when a friendship doesn't develop as you thought, and you have to continue your search for a lifelong companion. Or those birthday morning blues. Nostalgia for the air of your childhood. Things like that.' He recalled his mother once confiding to him that she suffered from a pain for which there was no antidote. 'There are women who only look at another woman's shoes and never at her face. And others who always look women in the face and only occasionally at their shoes.' She preferred the second type; Lirabelle felt humiliated and misjudged by the former.

It was precisely to relieve such inexplicable yet real suffering that he had bought the boat, which was a working barge then and originally called *Lulu*; he had converted it with his own hands and filled it with books, the only remedy for countless, undefined afflictions of the soul.

'You should write it. An encyclopedia of emotions for literary pharmacists.' The old woman sat up straighter and grew more lively and animated. 'Add "Confidence in strangers" under C. The odd feeling you get in trains when you open up far more to someone you've never met than you ever have to your own family. And "Grandchildren comfort" under G. That's the sense that life goes on . . .' She fell silent, far away.

'A zealous toe concealer – I was one. But he liked . . . he liked my feet after all.'

As the grandmother, mother and girl said their good-byes and went on their way, Perdu reflected that it was a common misconception that book-sellers looked after books.

They look after people.

★　★　★

When the stream of customers abated around midday – eating was more sacred to the French than state, religion and money combined – Perdu swept the gangway with the stiff broom, disturbing a nest of bridge spiders. Then he saw Kafka and Lindgren sloping towards him beneath the avenue of trees that lined the embankment. Those were the names he'd given to the two stray cats that paid him daily visits on the basis of certain preferences they had developed. The grey tomcat with the white priest's collar enjoyed sharpening his claws on Franz Kafka's *Investigations of a Dog*, a fable that analyses the human world from a dog's perspective. On the other hand, orange-white, long-eared Lindgren liked to lie near the books about Pippi Longstocking; she was a fine-looking cat who peered out from the back of the bookshelves and scrutinised each visitor. Lindgren and Kafka would sometimes do Perdu a favour by dropping off one of the upper shelves without warning onto a third-category customer, one of the greasy-fingered type.

The two well-read strays waited until they could come aboard without fear of big, blundering feet. Once there, they rubbed themselves against the bookseller's trouser legs, mewling gently.

Monsieur Perdu stood totally still. Briefly, very briefly, he let down his guard. He enjoyed the cats' warmth and their softness. For a few seconds he abandoned himself, eyes closed, to the unbelievably soothing sensation against his calves.

CHAPTER 5

The cats slunk off into the half-light to search the galley for the tin of tuna Perdu had already set down for them.

'Hello?' called Monsieur Perdu. 'Can I help you?'

'I'm not looking for anything,' croaked Max Jordan.

The bestselling author stepped tentatively forward with a honeydew melon in each hand. His obligatory earmuffs were riveted to his head.

'Have the three of you been standing there long, Monsieur Jordan?' asked Perdu with exaggerated sternness.

Jordan nodded, and a blush of embarrassment spread to the roots of his dark hair.

'I arrived just as you were refusing to sell my book to that lady,' he said unhappily.

Oh dear. That was rather bad timing.

'Do you really think it's that terrible?'

'No,' Perdu answered quickly. Jordan would have taken the slightest hesitation for a yes. There was no need to inflict that on him. What was more, Perdu honestly didn't think the book was terrible.

'Then why did you say I didn't suit her.'

'Monsieur . . . um . . .'

'Please call me Max.'

That would mean that the boy can call me by my first name too.

The last one to do so, with that chocolate-warm voice, was—.

'Let's stick to Monsieur Jordan for the moment. Monsieur Jordan, if you don't mind. You see, I sell books like medicine. There are books that are suitable for a million people, others only for a hundred. There are even medicines – sorry, books – that were written for one person only.'

'Oh, God. One person? A single person? After all those years of work?'

'Of course – if it saves that person's life! That customer didn't need *Night* right now. She couldn't have coped with it. The side effects are too severe.'

Jordan considered this. He looked at the thousands of books on the freighter – on the bookshelves, on the chairs and piled on the floor.

'But how can you know what a person's problem is and what the side effects are?'

Now, how was he to explain to Jordan that he didn't know exactly *how* he did it?

Perdu used his ears, his eyes and his instincts. From a single conversation, he was able to discern what each soul lacked. To a certain degree, he could read from a body's posture, its movements and its gestures, what was burdening or oppressing it. And finally, he had what his father had called transperception. 'You can see and hear through most people's camouflage. And behind it you see all the things they worry and dream about, and the things they lack.'

Every person had a gift, and his happened to be transperception.

One of his regular customers, the therapist Eric Lanson, whose surgery was near the Élysée Palace and who treated government officials, had once confessed to Perdu that he was jealous of his 'psychometric ability to scan the soul more accurately than a therapist who suffers from tinnitus after thirty years of listening'.

Lanson spent every Friday afternoon at the *Literary Apothecary*. He relished Dungeons & Dragons fantasy, and would attempt to elicit a smile from Perdu by psychoanalysing the characters. Lanson also referred politicians and stressed members of their administrative staff to Monsieur Perdu – with 'prescriptions' on which the therapist noted their neuroses in literary code: 'Kafkaesque with a touch of Pynchon', 'Sherlock, totally irrational' or 'a splendid example of Potter-under-the-stairs syndrome'.

Perdu saw it as a challenge to induct people (mainly men) who had daily dealings with greed, abuse of power and the Sisyphean nature of office work into the world of books. How gratifying it was when one of these tormented yes-men quit the job that had robbed him of every last drop of singularity! Often a book played a part in this liberation.

'You see, Jordan,' said Perdu, taking a different tack, 'a book is both medic and medicine at once. It makes a diagnosis as well as offering therapy. Putting the right novels to the appropriate ailments: that's how I sell books.'

'I get it. And my novel was the dentist when the lady needed a gynecologist.'

'Er . . . no.'

'No?'

'Books are more than doctors, of course. Some novels are loving, lifelong companions; some give you a clip around the ear; others are friends who wrap you in warm towels when you've got those autumn blues. And some . . . well, some are pink candy floss that tingles in your brain for three seconds and leaves a blissful void. Like a short, torrid love affair.'

'So *Night* is one of literature's one-night stands? A tart?'

Damn. An old rule of bookselling: never talk to authors about books by other writers.

'No. Books are like people, and people are like books. I'll tell you how I go about it. I ask myself: Is he or she the main character in his or her life? What is her motive? Or is she a secondary character in her own tale? Is she in the process of editing herself out of her story, because her husband, her career, her children or her job are consuming her entire text?'

Max Jordan's eyes widened.

'I've got about thirty thousand stories in my

head, which isn't very many, you know, given that there are over a million titles available in France alone. I've got the most useful eight thousand works here, as a first-aid kit, but I also compile courses of treatment. I prepare a medicine made of letters: a cookbook with recipes that read like a wonderful family Sunday. A novel whose hero resembles the reader; poetry to make tears flow that would otherwise be poisonous if swallowed. I listen with . . .'

Perdu pointed to his solar plexus.

'And I listen to this too.' He rubbed the back of his head. 'And to this.' Now he pointed to the soft spot above his upper lip. 'If it tingles here . . .'

'Come on, that can't be . . .'

'You bet it can.' He could do it for about 99.99 per cent of people.

However, there were some people that Perdu could not transperceive.

Himself, for example.

But Monsieur Jordan doesn't need to know that right now.

While Perdu had been reasoning with Jordan, a dangerous thought had casually drifted into his mind.

I'd have liked to have had a boy. With—. I'd have liked to have had everything with her.

Perdu gasped for air.

Something had been out of kilter since he had opened the forbidden room. There was a crack in his bulletproof glass – several hairline cracks – and everything would be smashed to pieces if he didn't regain control of himself.

'Right now, you look very . . . underoxygenated,' Perdu heard Max Jordan's voice say. 'I didn't mean to offend you. I merely wanted to know how people react when you tell them, "I'm not selling you this – you don't go together."'

'Those ones? They walk out. What about you? How's your next manuscript coming on, Monsieur Jordan?'

The young author sank down, with his melons, into one of the armchairs surrounded by piles of books.

'Nothing. Not a line.'

'Oh. When do you have to hand it in?'

'Six months ago.'

'Oh. And what does the publisher think of that?'

'My publisher has no idea where I am. Nobody does. Nobody must find out. I can't cope any more. I can't write any more.'

'Oh.'

Jordan slumped forward and laid his forehead against the melons.

'What do *you* do when you can't go on, Monsieur Perdu?' he asked wearily.

'Me? Nothing.'

Next to nothing.

I take night walks through Paris until I'm tired. I clean Lulu's engine, the hull and the windows, and I keep the boat ready to go, right down to the last screw, even though it hasn't gone anywhere in two decades.

I read books – twenty at a time. Everywhere: on the toilet, in the kitchen, in cafés, in the metro. I do jigsaw puzzles that take up the whole floor, destroy them when I've finished and then start all over again. I feed stray cats. I arrange my groceries in alphabetical order. I sometimes take sleeping tablets. I take a dose of Rilke to wake up. I don't read any books in which women like—crop up. I gradually turn to stone. I carry on. The same every day. That's the only way I can survive. But other than that, no, I do nothing.

Perdu made a conscious effort. The boy had asked for help; he didn't want to know how Perdu was. So give it.

The bookseller fetched his treasure out of the small, old-fashioned safe behind the counter.

Sanary's *Southern Lights*.

The only book Sanary had written – under that name, at any rate. 'Sanary' – after the erstwhile town of refuge for exiled writers, Sanary-sur-Mer on the south coast of Provence – was an impenetrable pseudonym.

His – or her – publisher, Duprés, was in an old people's home out in Île-de-France enduring Alzheimer's with good cheer. During Perdu's visits, the elderly Duprés had served him up a couple of dozen versions of who Sanary was and how the manuscript had come into his possession.

So Monsieur Perdu kept on searching.

For two decades he had been analysing the rhythms of the language, the choice of words and the cadence of the sentences, comparing the style and the subject matter with other authors'. Perdu had narrowed it down to eleven possible names: seven women and four men.

He would have loved to thank one of them, for Sanary's *Southern Lights* was the only thing that pierced him without hurting. Reading *Southern Lights* was a homeopathic dose of happiness. It was the only balm that could ease Perdu's pain – a gentle, cold stream over the scorched earth of his soul.

It was not a novel in the conventional sense, but a short story about the various kinds of love, full of wonderful invented words and infused with enormous humanity. The melancholy with which it described an inability to live each day to the full, to take every day for what it really was, namely unique, unrepeatable and precious; how that dolefulness resonated with him.

He handed Jordan his last copy.

'Read this. Three pages every morning before breakfast, lying down. It has to be the first thing you take in. In a few weeks you won't feel quite so sore – it'll be as though you no longer have to atone for your success with writer's block.'

Max thrust his hands, still holding the two melons, apart and shot him a look of terror through the gap between them. He couldn't help bursting out: 'How did you know? I really cannot stand the money and the horrible heat of success! I wish none of it had ever happened. Anyone who's good at something is hated – or not loved in any case.'

'Max Jordan, if I were your father, I'd put you over my knee for saying such stupid things. It's a good thing your book happened, and it deserved the success, every last hard-earned cent of it.'

All of a sudden, Jordan glowed with proud, bashful joy.

What? What did I say? 'If I were your father'?

Max Jordan solemnly held out the honeydew melons to Perdu. They smelled good. A dangerous fragrance. Very similar to a summer with—.

'Shall we have lunch?' asked the author.

The man with the earmuffs did get on his nerves, but it had been a long time since he had shared a meal with anyone.

And—would have liked him.

As they were slicing the last of the melons, they heard the clatter of smart high heels on the gangway.

The woman from earlier that morning appeared at the galley door. Her eyes were red from crying, but they were bright.

'All right,' she said. 'Give me the books that are kind to me, and to hell with the men who don't give a damn about me.'

Max's jaw hit the floor.

CHAPTER 6

Perdu rolled up the sleeves of his white shirt, checked that his black tie was straight, took out the reading glasses he had recently started wearing and with a deferential gesture, escorted the customer into the heart of his literary world: the leather armchair with a footstool in front of a large plate-glass window that framed a view of the Eiffel Tower. There was, of course, a side table for handbags too – donated by Lirabelle. And next to it, an old piano that Perdu had tuned twice a year, even though he couldn't play it himself.

Perdu asked the customer, whose name was Anna, a few questions. Job, morning routine, her favourite animal as a child, nightmares she'd had in the past few years, the most recent books she'd read . . . and whether her mother had told her how to dress.

Personal questions, but not too personal. He had to ask these questions and then remain absolutely silent. Listening in silence was essential to making a comprehensive scan of a person's soul.

Anna worked in television advertising, she told him.

'In an agency with guys past their sell-by date, who mistake women for a cross between an espresso machine and a sofa.' She set three alarm clocks every morning to drag her out of a brutally deep sleep – and took a hot shower to get warm for the coldness of the day to come.

As a child, she'd taken a liking to the slow loris, a provocatively lazy species of small monkey with a permanently moist nose.

During childhood, Anna most liked wearing short red lederhosen, to her mother's horror. She often dreamed of sinking into quicksand in front of important men, dressed only in her vest. And all of them, every last one, were tearing at her vest, but none would help her out of the pit.

'No one ever helped me,' she repeated to herself in a quiet, bitter voice. She looked at Perdu with shiny eyes.

'So?' she said. 'How stupid am I?'

'Not very,' he replied.

The last time Anna had really read anything was when she was a student. José Saramago's *Blindness*. It had left her perplexed.

'No wonder,' said Perdu. 'It's not a book for someone starting out in life. It's for people in the middle of it. Who wonder where the devil the first half went. Who raise their eyes from the feet they'd been eagerly placing one in front of the other without looking where they've been running so sensibly and diligently all this time. Only those who are blind to life need Saramago's fable. You, Anna, can see.'

After that, Anna had stopped reading; she'd worked instead. Too much, too long, accumulating more and more exhaustion inside her. So far, she had not once succeeded in including a man in one of her advertisements for household cleaners or nappies.

'Advertising is the final bastion of the patriarchy,' she informed Perdu and the rapt Jordan. 'Even more than the military. Only in publicity is the world as it always was.'

Having offered up all these confessions, she leaned back in her chair. 'So?' her expression said. 'Can I be cured? Give me the plain truth.'

Her answers didn't affect Perdu's book selection one bit. They were merely meant to familiarise him with Anna's voice, its pitch and her way of speaking.

Perdu collected the words that stood out from the stream of everyday expressions. The shining words were the ones that revealed how this woman saw and smelled and felt. What was really important to her, what bothered her and how she was feeling right now. What she wished to conceal behind a fog of words. Pains and longings.

Monsieur Perdu fished out these words. Anna often said: 'That wasn't the plan' and 'I didn't count on that.' She talked about 'countless' attempts and 'a sequence of nightmares.' She lived in a world of mathematics, an elaborate device for ordering the irrational and personal. She wouldn't allow herself to follow her intuition or consider the impossible possible.

Yet that was only one part of what Perdu listened out for and recorded: what was making the soul unhappy. Then there was the second part: what made the soul happy. Monsieur Perdu knew that the texture of the things a person loves rubs off on his or her language too.

Madame Bernard, the owner of number 27, transposed her love of fabric onto houses and people; 'Manners like a creased polyester shirt' was one of her favourite sayings. The pianist, Clara Violette, expressed herself in musical parlance: 'The Goldenbergs' little girl plays only third fiddle in her mother's life.' Goldenberg the grocer saw the world in terms of flavours, described some-one's character as 'rotten' and a job promotion as 'overripe'. His youngest girl, Brigitte, the 'third fiddle', loved the sea – a magnet for sensitive dispositions. The fourteen-year-old, a precocious beauty, had compared Max Jordan to 'the sea view from Cassis, deep and distant'. The third fiddle was in love with the writer, of course. Until very recently Brigitte had wanted to be a boy. Now, though, she desperately wanted to be a woman.

Perdu swore to himself that he would soon take Brigitte a book that could be her island haven in the ocean of first love.

'Do you often say sorry?' Perdu now asked Anna. Women always felt guiltier than they ought.

'Do you mean: "Sorry, I haven't finished what

I wanted to say" or more like "Sorry for being in love with you and only giving you headaches"?'

'Both. Any request for forgiveness. Maybe you've got used to feeling guilty for everything you are. Often it's not we who shape words, but the words we use that shape us.'

'You're a funny bookseller, you know that?'

'Yes, I do, Mademoiselle Anna.'

Monsieur Perdu asked Jordan to haul over dozens of books from the Library of Emotions.

'Here you go, my dear. Novels for willpower, non-fiction for rethinking one's life, poems for dignity.' Books about dreaming, about dying, about love and about life as a woman artist. He laid out mystical ballads, hard-edged old stories about chasms, falls, peril and betrayal at her feet. Soon Anna was surrounded by piles of books as a woman in a shoe shop might be surrounded by boxes.

Perdu wanted Anna to feel that she was in a nest. He wanted her to sense the boundless possibilities offered by books. There would always be enough. They would never stop loving their readers. They were a fixed point in an otherwise unpredictable world. In life. In love. After death.

When Lindgren then jumped onto Anna's lap in one audacious leap, and made herself comfortable, paw by paw, purring loudly, the overworked, love-crossed and conscience-stricken advertising executive reclined in her chair. Her tense shoulders slackened, her thumbs unfurled from her clenched fists. Her face relaxed.

She read.

Monsieur Perdu observed how the words she was reading gave shape to her from within. He saw that Anna was discovering inside herself a sounding board that reacted to words. She was a violin learning to play itself.

Monsieur Perdu recognised Anna's flickering of joy and felt a pang in his chest.

Is there really no book that could teach me *to play the song of life?*

CHAPTER 7

As Monsieur Perdu directed his steps onto Rue Montagnard, he wondered how Catherine must find this supremely quiet street in the middle of the bustling Marais. 'Catherine,' murmured Perdu. 'Ca-the-rine.' Her name tripped lightly off his tongue.

Absolutely incredible.

Was number 27 Rue Montagnard an unpleasant exile? Did she see the world in terms of the stain of her husband's abandonment since he'd said, 'I don't want you any more'?

It was rare for someone who didn't live here to wander into this neighbourhood. The buildings were no more than five storeys high, and each façade was painted a different pastel shade.

A baker, a wine merchant and the Algerian tobacconist lined the street further down Rue Montagnard. The other buildings contained flats, medical practices and offices, all the way to the roundabout. And there was the realm of Ti Breizh, a Breton bistro with a red awning whose savoury pancakes were soft and tasty.

*   *   *

44

Monsieur Perdu set down for the waiter Thierry an ebook reader that a hectic publishing salesman had left behind. For avid readers like Thierry, who would have his nose in a novel even between orders, and had a crooked back from hauling books around ('I can only breathe if I read, Perdu'), these devices were the invention of the century; for booksellers, one more nail in their coffin.

Thierry offered Perdu a glass of *lambig*, Breton apple brandy.

'Not today,' Perdu declined. That's what he said every time. Perdu didn't drink alcohol. Not any more.

That was because whenever he drank, each sip opened a little further the breach in the dam, against which a foaming lake of thoughts and emotions was pressing. He knew; back then he had tried drinking. Those were the days of smashed furniture.

Today, however, he had a special reason for refusing Thierry's offer: he wanted to deliver the 'books for crying' to Madame Catherine, the former Mme Le P., as quickly as possible.

The green-and-white awning of Joshua Goldenberg's corner shop protruded next to Ti Breizh. Goldenberg stepped out in front of Perdu when he saw him coming.

'Say, Monsieur Perdu,' Goldenberg began, somewhat embarrassed.

Oh no, he's not going to ask for some soft porn now, is he?

45

'It's to do with Brigitte. I think my little girl is, um, turning into a woman. That causes, er, certain problems, you know what I mean? Do you have a book for that?'

Luckily, this wasn't going to be a man-to-man talk about one-handed reading material. One more father in despair over his daughter's puberty and wondering how he could tackle the sex-education stuff before she met the wrong man.

'Come along to the parents' clinic.'

'I'm not sure. Maybe my wife should . . .'

'Okay then, both of you come. First Wednesday of the month, eight o'clock. The two of you could go out to dinner afterwards.'

'Me? With my wife? Why?'

'It'd probably make her happy.'

Monsieur Perdu walked off before Goldenberg could back out.

He will anyway.

Of course, there would only be mothers at the clinic when it came down to it – and they wouldn't be discussing their sexually maturing offspring. Most of them were actually looking for sex-education manuals that could teach their husbands some basic female anatomy.

Perdu tapped in the code and opened the front door. He was less than a metre inside when Madame Rosalette came barrelling out of the concierge's flat with her pug under her arm. Edith the pug clung on sullenly beneath Rosalette's ample bosom.

'Monsieur Perdu, you're back at last!'

'New hair colour, Madame?' he asked as he pressed the button to call the lift.

Her hand, red from doing household chores, flew to her bouffant hairstyle. '*Spanish Rosé*. A tiny shade darker than *Sherry Brut,* but more elegant, I think. How observant you are! But I do have something to confess, Monsieur.'

She fluttered her eyelashes. The pug panted in time.

'If it's a secret, I promise I'll forget it immediately, Madame.'

Rosalette had a chronological streak. She enjoyed registering her fellow citizens' neuroses, intimacies and habits, plotting them on a scale of decency, and knowledgeably passing on her opinions to others. She was generous in that regard.

'You're so naughty! And it's really none of my business if Madame Gulliver is happy with these young men. No, no. It is . . . there was . . . well . . . a book.'

Perdu pressed the lift button again.

'And you bought this book from another book-seller? Forgiven, Madame Rosalette, you're forgiven.'

'No. Worse. Dug it out of a crate of books in Montmartre for all of fifty cents. But you said yourself that if a book's over twenty years old, I should pay no more than a few cents for it and rescue it from destruction.'

'Right, I did say that.'

What's wrong with this treacherous lift?

Now Rosalette leaned forward, and her coffee-and-cognac breath mingled with that of her dog.

'Well, I'd rather I hadn't. That awful cockroach story! The mother chasing her own son away with a broom. Horrible. I was cleaning obsessively for days. Is that typical of this Monsieur Kafka?'

'You've summed it up well, Madame. Some people have to study it for decades to get the meaning.'

Madame Rosalette flashed him a blank but contented smile.

'Oh yes, the lift is out of order. It's stuck between the Goldenbergs' and Madame Gulliver's again.'

It was the sign that summer would come over-night. It always arrived when the lift was stuck.

Two at a time, Perdu bounded up the stairs, which were covered with Breton, Mexican and Portuguese tiles. Madame Bernard, who owned the building, loved patterns; they were the 'house's shoes and, as with women, shoes are a sign of character'. Seen from this perspective, any burglar daring to enter would have assumed from the staircase that number 27 Rue Montagnard was a spectacularly fickle creature.

Perdu was nearing the first floor when a pair of satin mules the colour of golden corn with feather pom-poms on the toes stepped decisively onto the landing and into his line of sight.

On the first floor, above Madame Rosalette, lived Che, the blind chiropodist. He often accompanied

Madame Bomme (second floor), who used to work as a secretary for a famous fortune-teller, to do her food shopping at Goldenberg's (who lived on the third floor) and carried Madame Bomme's bag. They shuffled along the pavement together – the blind man arm in arm with the old lady pushing her wheeled Zimmer frame.

Kofi – which meant 'Friday' in one of the indigenous languages of Ghana – had showed up at Rue Montagnard one day from the outskirts of Paris. He had dark skin, wore gold chains over the top of his hip-hop hoodies and a gold earring in one ear. A good-looking boy, 'a cross between Grace Jones and a young jaguar', was Madame Bomme's opinion. Kofi often carried her white Chanel handbags and attracted suspicious looks from ignorant passers-by. He did caretaking jobs, or made figures from raw leather and painted them with symbols that nobody in the building could understand.

Yet it was neither Che nor Kofi nor Madame Bomme's wheeled Zimmer that now hove into Perdu's path. 'Oh, Monsieur, how lovely to see you! Listen, that *Dorian Gray* was a very exciting book. How nice of you to recommend it when *Burning Desire* was out of stock.'

'I'm pleased to hear it, Madame Gulliver.'

'Oh, after all this time do call me Claudine. Or at least Mademoiselle. I don't stand on ceremony. That *Gray* was so amusing, it only took me two hours. But if I were Dorian, I'd never have looked at that picture. It's depressing. And they can't have had Botox back then.'

'Madame Gulliver, Oscar Wilde spent six years writing it. He was later sentenced to prison and died a short time afterwards. Didn't he deserve a little more than two hours of your time?'

'Oh, poppycock. That won't cheer him up now.'

Claudine Gulliver. A spinster of Rubenesque proportions in her mid-forties, and a registrar at a major auction house. She had to deal with excessively rich, excessively greedy collectors on a daily basis – strange specimens of the human species. Madame Gulliver collected works of art herself, mainly gaudily coloured ones with heels. She had a collection of 176 pairs of high heels with a room of their own.

One of Madame Gulliver's hobbies was to lie in wait for Monsieur Perdu and invite him on one of her excursions, or tell him about her latest continuing education courses or the new restaurants that opened in Paris every day. Madame Gulliver's second hobby was reading the kind of novel that starred a heroine who clung to a scoundrel's broad chest and resisted long and hard before finally he powerfully over . . . er . . . powered her. Now she twittered, 'So, will you come with me tonight to—'

'No, I'd rather not.'

'Hear me out first! The university jumble sale at the Sorbonne. Lots of long-legged female art graduates breaking up their group housing, and dumping their books, their furniture and, who knows, their lovers.' Madame Gulliver arched her eyebrows suggestively. 'How about it?'

He imagined young men crouching among grandfather clocks and boxes of paperbacks with Post-it notes on their foreheads saying such things as: 'Used once, almost new, barely touched. Heart in need of minor repairs'; or 'Thirdhand, basic functions intact.'

'I really don't want to.'

Madame Gulliver gave a deep sigh.

'Good gracious. You never want anything; have you ever noticed that?'

'That's . . .'

True.

'. . . not because of you. Really it isn't. You're charming, courageous and . . . er . . .'

Yes, he was rather fond of Madame Gulliver. She seized life with both hands. More of it than she probably needed.

'. . . very neighbourly.'

Heavens. He was so rusty when it came to saying something nice to a woman! Madame Gulliver began to totter down the stairs with a waggle of her hips. *Clack-slap, clack-slap* went her corn-gold slippers. When she reached his step, she lifted her hand. She noted that Perdu shrank back when she reached out to touch his muscled arm, and instead laid her hand resignedly on the banister.

'Neither of us is getting any younger, Monsieur,' she said in a low, husky voice. 'We're well into the second half.'

Clack-slap, clack-slap.

Perdu raised his hand involuntarily to his hair, to the spot on the back of the head where many men developed a humiliating bald patch. He didn't have one – yet. Yes, he was fifty. Not thirty. His dark hair had grown silvery, his face heavily shadowed. His tummy . . . he pulled it in. Not bad. His hips bothered him: every year a thin extra layer. And he couldn't carry two crates of books at once any more, dammit. But all of that was irrelevant. Women no longer eyed him – with the exception of Madame Gulliver, but then she viewed every man as a potential lover.

He squinted up at the landing where Madame Bomme would be lurking to snare him in conversation. About Anaïs Nin and her sexual obsessions – at top volume since she had mislaid her hearing aid in a box of chocolates.

Perdu had organised a book club for Madame Bomme and the widows of Rue Montagnard, who hardly ever received a visit from their children and grandchildren, and were withering away in front of their televisions. They loved books, but more than that, literature was an excuse to get out of their flats and hand around colourful ladies' liqueurs for close examination and tasting.

The ladies generally voted for erotic books. Perdu delivered this kind of literature inside more discreet jackets: *Alpine Flora* wrapped around Millet's *The Sexual Life of Catherine M.*; *Provençal Knitting Patterns* for Duras's *The Lover*; *Jam Recipes from York* for Anaïs Nin's *The Delta of Venus*. The liqueur researchers were grateful for the disguises; they were wary of their relatives who thought that reading was an eccentric hobby for people who were too snobbish to watch television and that eroticism was unnatural in women over sixty.

This time, however, no Zimmer frame blocked his path.

On the second floor lived the pianist Clara Violette. Perdu heard her practising Czerny runs. Even scales sounded brilliant under her fingers.

She was considered one of the five best pianists in the world. Yet fame was denied her because she couldn't stand to have anyone in the room when she played. In the summer she gave balcony concerts. She would open all the windows, and Perdu would push her Pleyel grand piano over to the balcony door and place a microphone beneath the instrument. Then Clara would play for two hours. The residents of number 27 sat out on the steps in front of the house or set up folding chairs on the pavement. Strangers would crowd the tables at the Ti Breizh. When Clara came out onto her balcony after the concert and bowed with a shy nod, she reaped the applause of nearly half the population of a small town.

Perdu managed to make it the rest of the way upstairs without further interruptions. When he reached the fourth floor, he saw that his table had disappeared; maybe Kofi had lent Catherine a hand.

He knocked on her green door and realised that he had been looking forward to this moment.

'Hello,' he whispered. 'I've brought some books.'

He put down the paper bag against the door.

As Perdu stood up, Catherine opened it.

Short, blond hair; mistrustful, but with soft, pearl-grey eyes beneath delicate eyebrows. Her feet were bare and she was wearing a dress with a neckline that gave a faint glimpse of her collarbone. She was holding an envelope.

'Monsieur. I found the letter.'

CHAPTER 8

Too many impressions at the same time: Catherine – her eyes – the envelope with the pale-green writing on it – Catherine's closeness – her scent – the collarbone – life – the . . .

Letter?

'An unopened letter. It was in your kitchen table, in the drawer, which was completely sealed with white paint. I opened it. The letter was lying under the corkscrew.'

'No,' said Perdu politely, 'there wasn't a corkscrew.'

'But I found . . .'

'No you didn't!'

He didn't mean to be so loud, but neither could he bring himself to look at the letter she was holding up.

'Forgive me for shouting at you.'

She held out the envelope.

'But that's not mine.'

Monsieur Perdu retreated backwards to his flat.

'It'd be better if you burned it.'

Catherine followed him across the landing. She

looked him in the eye, and a searing flush burned across his face.

'Or throw it away.'

'But then I might as well read it,' she said.

'I don't care. It's not mine.'

Catherine continued to stare at him as he pushed his door shut, leaving her standing outside with the letter.

'Monsieur? Monsieur Perdu!' Catherine knocked. 'Monsieur, it's got your name on it.'

'Go away. Please!'

He had recognised the letter. The handwriting.

Something shattered inside him.

A woman with a head of dark curls pushing open a compartment door, first gazing outside for a long time, then turning to him with tears in her eyes. Striding through Provence, Paris and Rue Montagnard, before finally stepping into his flat. Taking a shower, then walking around the room naked. A mouth drawing close to his own in the half darkness.

Wet, water-wet skin, water-wet lips taking his breath away, drinking his mouth.

Drinking and drinking.

The moon on her small, soft tummy. Two shadows in the middle of a red window frame, dancing.

How she then covers herself with his body.

—is sleeping on the divan in the Lavender Room, as she called the forbidden room, rolled up in her Provençal patchwork quilt, which she had sewed during her engagement.

Before—had married her vigneron, and before . . .
She left me.
And then left me a second time.

—had given a name to every room they had met in during those five short years: the Sun Room, the Honey Room, the Garden Room. They were rooms that meant the world to him, her secret lover, her second husband. She had named the room in his flat the Lavender Room; it was her home away from home.

The last time she'd slept there was a hot August night in 1992.

They had showered together; they were wet and naked.

She had caressed Perdu with her hand, cooled by the water, then slid on top of him and, raising his two hands in her own, pushed them down onto the sheet-covered divan. She had fixed him with a wild look and whispered, 'I'd like you to die before me. Will you promise me that?'

Her body had taken his, more unbridled than ever before, while she moaned, 'Promise. Promise me!'

He promised her.

Later that night, when he could no longer see the whites of her eyes in the darkness, he had asked her why.

'I don't want you to have to walk from the car park to my grave on your own. I don't want you to have to mourn. I'd rather miss you for the rest of my life.'

'Why did I never tell you I loved you?' whispered the bookseller to himself. 'Why didn't I, Manon? Manon!' He had never confessed his feelings. So as not to embarrass her. So as not to feel her fingers on his lips as she whispered, 'Shush'.

He could be a stone in the mosaic of her life, he thought at the time. A beautiful, sparkling one, but a stone all the same, not the whole picture. He wanted to do that for her.

Manon. The vibrant, never-dainty, never-perfect girl from Provence, who spoke with words that he felt he could grasp with his hands. She never planned; she was always entirely present. She didn't talk about dessert during the main course, about the coming morning as she was falling asleep, about meeting again when saying good-bye. She was always in the now.

That August night 7,216 nights ago was the last time Perdu slept well; and when he woke up, Manon was gone.

He hadn't seen it coming. He had thought it over again and again, had sifted through Manon's gestures and looks and words – but had found no possible clue that could have told him she was already leaving.

And wouldn't come back.

Instead, a few weeks later, her letter.

This letter.

He had left the envelope on the table for two

nights. He had gazed at it as he ate alone, drank alone, smoked alone. And as he wept.

Tear after tear had run down his cheeks and dripped onto the table and the paper.

He hadn't opened the letter.

He had been so tired back then, from crying and because he could no longer sleep in the bed that was so big and empty without her, so cold. He was tired from missing her.

He had thrown the letter into the drawer of the kitchen table, angrily, despairingly and above all unopened. To join the corkscrew that she had 'borrowed' from a brasserie in Ménerbes and spirited away to Paris. They had come from the Camargue, their eyes bright and almost glazed from the southern light, and had stopped off in the Luberon, in a guesthouse that clung to a craggy slope with a bathroom halfway down the stairs and lavender honey for breakfast. Manon wanted to show him everything about herself: where she came from, the kind of country that was in her blood; yes, she'd even wanted to introduce him to Luc, her husband, from afar, on his tall tractor moving along the grapevines in the valley below Bonnieux. Luc Basset, the vigneron, the winemaker.

As if she wanted the three of them to be friends, and each to grant the other their desire and their love.

Perdu had refused. They had stayed in the Honey Room.

★   ★   ★

It seemed as though the strength was bleeding out of his arms, as though he could do nothing but stand there in the darkness behind the door.

Perdu missed Manon's body. He missed Manon's hand against his buttocks as he slept. He missed her breath; her childish grumbling when he woke her too early in the morning – always too early no matter how late it was.

Her eyes watching him lovingly, and her fine, soft, short, curly hair when she snuggled up to his neck. He missed all these things so much that his body would twitch as he lay in the empty bed. And every day when he awoke too.

He hated waking up to a life without her.

The bed was the first thing he smashed, then the shelves and the footstool; he cut up the carpet, burned the pictures, laid waste to the room. He got rid of every piece of clothing, gave away every record.

The only thing he kept were the books from which he had read to her. He had read aloud every evening – lots of verse, scenes, chapters, columns, short extracts from biographies and other nonfiction books, Ringelnatz's *Little Bedtime Prayers* (oh, how she'd loved *The Little Onion*) – so that she could drop off to sleep in this strange, barren world, the chilly north with its frozen northern folk. He couldn't bring himself to throw those books away.

He'd used them to wall up the Lavender Room.

But it wouldn't go away. The damn missing simply wouldn't go away.

He'd only been able to cope by starting to avoid life. He'd locked away the loving with the missing deep within. Yet now it swept through him with unbelievable force.

Monsieur Perdu staggered into the bathroom and held his head under a stream of ice-cold water.

He hated Catherine, and he hated her cursed, unfaithful, cruel husband.

Why did Le P.-Dipstick have to leave her now, without giving her so much as a kitchen table as a send-off? What an idiot!

He hated the concierge and Madame Bernard and Jordan, Madame Gulliver, everyone – yes, everyone.

He hated Manon.

He flung the door open, his hair soaking wet. If that's how that Madame Catherine wanted things, then he would say: 'Yes, dammit, that is my letter! I just didn't want to open it at the time. Out of pride. Out of conviction.'

And any mistake was reasonable if backed up by conviction.

He had wanted to read the letter when he was ready. After a year. Or two. He hadn't intended to wait for twenty years, and to become fifty years old and peculiar in the meantime.

At the time, not opening Manon's letter had been the only safe option, refusing her justification the only weapon he had.

Definitely.

If someone left you, you had to answer with

silence. You weren't allowed to give the person leaving anything else; you had to shut yourself off, just as the other person had closed her mind to your future together. Yes, he had decided that was the way it was.

'No no no!' cried Perdu. There was something wrong with this; he sensed it, but didn't know what. It was driving him mad.

Monsieur Perdu strode over to the opposite door.

And rang the bell.

And knocked and rang the bell again, after a suitable pause, for as long as it would take a normal person to emerge from the shower and shake the water out of her ears.

Why wasn't Catherine there? She had been a minute earlier.

He rushed back to his flat, tore the first page out of the first book that came to hand on one of the stacks, and scribbled:

I'd like to ask you to bring the letter around, no matter how late. Please don't read it. Sorry for the inconvenience. Regards, Perdu.

He stared at his signature and wondered whether he'd ever be able to think of his first name. Every time he thought of it, he heard Manon's voice too. The way she sighed his name. And laughed. Whispering, oh, whispering.

He squeezed in his initial between 'Regards' and 'Perdu': J.

J for Jean.

He folded the piece of paper in half and stuck it to Catherine's door at eye level with a bit of tape. The letter. Either way, it would be the kind of helpless explanation that women give their lovers when they've had enough. There was no need to get worked up.

Of course not.

Then he went back to his empty flat to wait.

Monsieur Perdu felt suddenly and truly alone, like a stupid little rowing boat on the mocking, scornful sea – without a sail, a rudder or a name.

CHAPTER 9

As night took flight, abandoning Paris to a Saturday morning, Monsieur Perdu sat up, back aching, took off his reading glasses and rubbed the swollen bridge of his nose. He had knelt there for hours over the floor puzzle, noiselessly pushing the cardboard pieces into place so as not to miss the sound of Catherine moving about in the other flat. Yet it had remained completely silent over there.

Perdu's chest, back and neck hurt as he took off his shirt. He took a cold shower until his skin went blue, then it turned lobster-red as he rinsed himself with hot water. Steam rose off him as he strode over to the kitchen window with one of his two towels slung around his hips. He did some press-ups and sit-ups as the coffee pot bubbled away on the stove. Perdu washed his only cup and poured himself some black coffee.

Summer had indeed descended on Paris overnight. The air was as warm as a brimming teacup.

Had she left the letter in his letterbox? After the way he had behaved, Catherine probably never wanted to set eyes on him again.

Clutching his towel by the knot, Perdu walked barefoot down the silent staircase to the letterboxes.

'Now listen here, that's no . . . Oh, is that you?'

Madame Rosalette, wearing a housecoat, peeked out of her lodge. He sensed her eyes running over his skin, his muscles and the towel, which felt as if it had somehow shrunk.

Perdu felt that Rosalette really did linger a bit too long. And was that a satisfied nod?

He hurried upstairs with burning cheeks.

As he approached his door, he spotted something that hadn't been there before.

A note.

He unfolded the piece of paper in a rush. The knot gave way, and his towel fell to the floor. However, Monsieur Perdu was hardly aware of the bare backside he was parading to the staircase as he read, with increasing irritation:

> Dear J.,
>   Please come around for dinner this evening. You will read the letter. You must promise me that or else I won't give it to you. Not sorry.
>   Catherine
>   PS: Bring a plate. Can you cook? I can't.

As he worked himself into a rage, something incredible happened.

The left-hand corner of his mouth twitched.

And then . . . he laughed.

Half laughing, half stunned, he muttered, 'Bring a plate. Read the letter. You never want anything, Perdu. Promise me. Die before me. Promise!'

Promises – women always wanted promises.

'I'm never promising anything ever again!' he called into the empty staircase, naked and all of a sudden furious.

The response was unfazed silence.

He slammed his door behind him and was delighted with the noise it made. He hoped that the huge bang had startled everyone from their beds.

Then he opened the door again and, slightly sheepishly, picked up his towel.

Wham! a second slam of the door.

By now they must all be sitting bolt upright.

As Monsieur Perdu made his way along Rue Montagnard at a smart pace, he seemed to see through the fronts of the houses, as if they were open dollhouses.

He knew every library in every house. After all, he was the one who had compiled them over the years.

At number 14: Clarissa Menepeche. Such a delicate soul in a heavy body! She loved the warrior Brienne in *A Song of Ice and Fire*.

Behind the net curtains at number 2: Arnaud Silette, who would like to have been alive in the twenties. In Berlin. As an artist. And a woman.

And opposite, at number 5, sitting ramrod straight at her computer: the translator Nadira del Pappas.

She loved historical novels in which women dressed as men and outgrew their limited opportunities.

And upstairs from her? No more books. All given away.

Perdu paused and looked up at the front of number 5.

Margot, the eighty-four-year-old widow. She'd been in love with a German soldier who was the same age she was – fifteen – when the war robbed them both of their youth. How he had wanted to make love to her before he returned to the front! He knew that he wouldn't survive there. How ashamed she was to undress in front of him . . . and how she now wished she hadn't been ashamed! Margot had been regretting the missed opportunity for the last sixty-nine years. The older she got, the more the memory waned of that afternoon when she and the boy had lain quivering alongside each other, holding hands.

I see that I have grown old without noticing. How time has passed. All that damn lost time. I'm scared I've done something terribly stupid, Manon.

I've grown so old in a single night, and I miss you.

I miss myself.

I no longer know who I am.

Monsieur Perdu ambled along. He stopped in front of Liona's wine shop window. There, reflected in the glass. Was that him? The tall man in the conventional clothes with this unused, untouched body; stooping, as though he longed to be invisible?

When he saw Liona come forward from the back of the shop to give him the usual Saturday bag for his father, Perdu recalled the many times he had passed by and refused to step inside for a quick glass. For a chat with her or one of her customers – with friendly, normal people. How many times in the last almost twenty-one years had he chosen to walk on by, rather than stop, look for friends, approach a woman?

Half an hour later Perdu was at the Bassin de la Villette, standing at a table in the Bar Ourcq, even though the bar wasn't technically open yet. This was where the *boules* players parked their water bottles and their cheese-and-ham baguettes. A short, thickset man looked up at him in surprise.

'What are you doing here so early? Has something happened to Madame Bernier? Tell me, is Lirab—'

'No, Maman's fine. She's ordering around a regiment of Germans who want to learn conversation from an authentic Parisian intellectual. Don't worry about her.'

Father and son fell silent, united by the memory of how Lirabelle Bernier used to explain to Perdu as a schoolboy over breakfast the distancing elegance of the German subjunctive compared with the emotional nature of the French *subjonctif*. She spoke with a raised forefinger, whose gold-polished tip lent extra emphasis to her words.

'The *subjonctif* is the heart speaking.'

Lirabelle Bernier. His father now addressed her

by her maiden name, after having first called her Mrs Mischief and then Madame Perdu.

'And what message did she send you with this time?' Joaquin Perdu asked his son.

'That you should go to see a urologist.'

'Tell her I'm going. She doesn't have to remind me every six months.'

They had married when they were twenty-one to annoy their parents. She, the intellectual from a household of philosophers and economists, who met an ironworker – *dégoûtant,* disgusting. He, the working-class son of a police constable father and a devout factory seamstress mother, getting together with an upper-class girl – class traitor.

'Anything else?' asked Joaquin, and took the bottle of muscatel wine from the bag Perdu had set down in front of him.

'She needs a new second-hand car. She wants you to look for one, but not some weird colour like the last one.'

'Weird? It was white. Your mother. I ask you—'

'So will you?'

'Of course. The car salesman wouldn't speak to her again?'

'No. He always asks for her husband. It drives her nuts.'

'I know, Jeanno. Coco's a good friend of mine. He plays in our three-man *pétanque* team – he throws well.'

Joaquin grinned.

'Can your nice new girlfriend cook, Maman asks, or are you going to eat at hers on 14 July?'

'You can tell your mother that my so-called nice new girlfriend is an excellent cook, but our minds are on other matters when we meet.'

'I think you'd better tell Maman yourself, Papa.'

'I can tell Mademoiselle Bernier on 14 July. She does cook well. Surely brains with tongue.'

Joaquin almost split his sides laughing.

Ever since his parents' early divorce, Jean Perdu had visited his father every Saturday with some muscatel wine and various questions from his mother. Then every Sunday he would visit his mother to convey her ex-husband's answers along with an edited report on his father's health and relationship status.

'My dear son, when you're a woman and you get married, you enter irreversibly into a supervisory position. You have to keep an eye on everything – what your husband does and how he is. And later, when children arrive, on them too. You're a watchdog, a servant and a diplomat rolled into one. And something as trivial as divorce doesn't end that. Oh no – love may come and go, but the caring goes on.'

Perdu and his father strolled along the canal a little way. Joaquin, the shorter of the two, had an upright, broad-shouldered gait in his purple-and-white-checked shirt, and cast longing glances at every single girl they passed. The sun danced in the blond hairs on Joaquin's ironworker's arms.

He was in his midseventies but acted as if he were in his mid-twenties, whistling hit tunes and drinking to his heart's content.

Beside him, Monsieur Perdu stared at the ground.

'So, Jeanno,' his father said abruptly, 'what's her name?'

'Sorry? What do you mean? Does it always have to be a woman, Papa?'

'It's always a woman, Jeanno. Nothing else can really knock a man out of sorts. And you look seriously out of sorts.'

'In your case that might be down to a woman – and usually not just the one.'

Joaquin beamed. 'I like women,' he said and drew a cigarette packet from his shirt pocket. 'Don't you?'

'Yes, I do, kind of . . .'

'Kind of? Like elephants: nice to look at but you wouldn't want to own one? Or are you a man's man?'

'Oh, come on. I'm not gay. Let's talk about horses.'

'All right, son, if you want to. Women and horses have a lot in common. Would you like to know what?'

'No.'

'Fine. Well, if a horse refuses, you've phrased your question wrongly. It's the same with women. Don't ask them: "Shall we go out to dinner?" Ask: "What can I cook for you?" Can she say no to that? No, she can't.'

Perdu felt as if he were back in short trousers. His father was actually teaching him about women now.

So what shall I cook for Catherine this evening?

'Instead of whispering instructions to them like you would to a horse – lie down, woman, put your harness on – you should listen to them. Listen to what they want. In fact, they want to be free and to sail across the sky.'

Catherine must have had enough of riders who want to train her and consign her to the cavalry reserves.

'It takes only one word to hurt a woman, a matter of seconds, one stupid, impatient blow of the crop. But winning back her trust takes years. And sometimes there isn't the time.'

It's amazing how unimpressed people are by being loved when it doesn't fit in with their plans. Love irks them so much that they change the locks or leave without warning.

'And when a horse loves us, Jeanno, we deserve that love as little as when a woman does. They are superior beings to us men. When they love us, then they are being gracious, for only rarely do we give them reason to love us. I learned that from your mother, and she's right. Sad to say, she's right.'

And that's why it hurts so much. When women stop loving, men fall into a void of their own making.

'Jeanno, women can love so much more intelligently than us men! They never love a man for his body, even if they can enjoy that too – and

72

how.' Joaquin sighed with pleasure. 'But women love you for your character, your strength, your intelligence. Or because you can protect a child. Because you're a good person, you're honourable and dignified. They never love you as stupidly as men love women. Not because you've got especially beautiful calves or look so good in a suit that their business partners look on jealously when they introduce you. Such women do exist, but only as a cautionary example to others.'

I like Catherine's calves. Would she enjoy introducing me to someone? Am I . . . intelligent enough for that? Am I honourable? Do I have something that women value?

'A horse admires your overall personality.'

'A horse? Why a horse?' asked Perdu, genuinely irritated. He had only been half listening.

They had turned a corner and were now standing back near the *pétanque* players beside the Canal de l'Ourcq.

Joaquin was greeted with handshakes, and the *boulistes* spared a nod for Jean.

He watched his father step into the throwing area, go into a crouch and swing his right arm like a pendulum.

A cheerful barrel with an arm. I've been lucky with this father. He always liked me, even if he wasn't perfect.

Iron hit iron: Joaquin Perdu had skilfully struck out one of the opposing team's *boules*.

A murmur of applause.

73

I could see her and cry and never, ever stop. Why can I be so stupid that I don't have any friends left? Was I afraid they'd leave one day, like my best friend Vijaya did back then? Or afraid that they'd laugh at me because I never got over Manon?

He looked at his father and wanted to say, 'Manon liked you. Do you remember Manon?' However, his father was already turning towards him: 'Tell your mother, Jeanno . . . no, no. Tell her there's nobody like her – nobody.'

A look of regret flashed across Joaquin's face that love couldn't stop a woman wishing to string up her husband because he was a serious pain in the neck.

CHAPTER 10

Catherine had inspected his red mullets, the fresh herbs and the cream from broad-beamed Normandy cows, then held up her small new potatoes and cheese, and gestured to the fragrant pears and to the wine.

'Can we do something with this lot?'

'Yes. But one after the other, not together,' he said.

'I've been really looking forward to this all day long,' she confessed. 'And dreading it a bit too. How about you?'

'The other way around,' he replied. 'I've been really dreading it and looking forward to it a bit. I have to apologise.'

'No, you don't. Something's gnawing at you at the moment, so why pretend it isn't?'

As she said this, she tossed him one of her blue-and-grey-checked tea towels to use as an apron. She was wearing a blue summer dress and tucked her towel-apron into her red belt. Today he could see that her blonde hair was tinged with silver at the temples and that the former confusion and terror had left her eyes.

Soon the windowpanes had misted up; the gas flames were hissing under the pots and pans; the white wine, shallot and cream sauce was simmering; and in a heavy pan the olive oil was browning potatoes sprinkled with rosemary and salt.

They were chatting away as if they'd known each other for years and had simply lost touch for a while. About Carla Bruni, and about how male sea horses carried their young around in a pouch on their stomachs. They talked about fashion and about the trend for salt with added flavourings, and of course they gossiped about their neighbours.

Heavy and light topics such as these came to the fore as they stood next to each other at the stove, the wine and the fish before them. With every sentence, it seemed to Perdu as though Catherine and he were discovering a communion of souls.

He continued working on the sauce, and Catherine poached one piece of fish after another in it. They ate straight from the pans where they stood, as she didn't have a second chair.

She had poured the wine: a light, golden Tapie from Gascony. And he had drunk it, with cautious sips.

That was the most astonishing aspect of his first date since 1992: he had felt intensely safe from the moment he entered Catherine's flat. All the thoughts that usually pursued him could not accompany him into her territory; some kind of magic threshold kept them at bay.

'How are you spending your time at the moment?' asked Perdu at one point after they had dealt with God, the world and the president's tailor.

'Me? On looking,' she said.

She reached out for a piece of baguette.

'I'm looking for myself. Before . . . before what happened, I was my husband's assistant, secretary, agony aunt and admirer. I'm now looking for what I was capable of before I met him. Or to be more precise, I'm trying to see whether I'm still capable of it. That's what's keeping me busy: trying.'

She began to scrape the soft white part out of the crust and roll it between her slender fingers.

The bookseller read Catherine like a novel. She let him leaf through her and look through her story.

'Today, at forty-eight, I feel like I did at eight. I used to hate being ignored – and yet at the same time I was distraught if someone actually found me interesting. And it had to be the "right" people who took notice of me. The glossy-haired rich girl whom I wanted to be my friend; the kind male teacher who was struck by how modestly I hid my wonderful light under a bushel. And my mother. Oh yes, my mother.' Catherine paused. Her hands kept kneading the bit of baguette.

'I always wanted to be noticed by the biggest egotists. I didn't care about anyone else – my dear father; fat, sweating Olga from the ground floor – even though they were much nicer. But I was embarrassed when nice people liked me. Stupid, eh? And I was the same stupid girl during my marriage. I wanted my moronic husband to notice me, and I took no account of anyone else. But I'm ready to change that. Would you pass me the pepper?'

She had formed something out of the bread dough with her slender fingers: a sea horse, which she now decorated with two peppercorns for eyes before handing it to Perdu.

'I was a sculptor. Somewhere along the line. I'm forty-eight, and I'm learning everything again from scratch. I don't know how many years it's been since I last slept with my husband. I was faithful, stupid and so awfully lonely that I'll gobble you up if you're nice to me. Or kill you because I can't bear it.'

Perdu was utterly stunned to be alone with a woman like this.

He was lost in contemplation of Catherine's face and head, as though he were allowed to crawl inside her and look around for any interesting things that were hanging about in there.

Catherine had pierced ears, but she wasn't wearing earrings. ('His new girlfriend wears the ones with the rubies now. Shame, really: I'd have loved to cast them at his feet.') She sometimes touched the hollow of her throat, as though searching for something, maybe a necklace that the other woman was now wearing too.

'And what are *you* up to at the moment?' she asked.

He described the *Literary Apothecary* to her.

'A boat with a low-slung belly, a galley, two sleeping berths, a bathroom and eight thousand books. It's a world apart from our world.' And an arrested adventure, like any moored ship – but he didn't say this.

'And the king of this world is Monsieur Perdu, a literary pharmacist who writes prescriptions for the lovesick.'

Catherine pointed to the parcel of books that he had brought her the previous evening. 'It helps, by the way.'

'What did you want to be when you were a little girl?' he asked before his embarrassment could get the better of him.

'Oh, I wanted to be a librarian. And a pirate. Your book barge would have been exactly what I needed. I would have solved all the world's mysteries through reading.'

Perdu listened to her with growing affection.

'At night I would have stolen back from evil people everything they'd tricked the good ones out of with their lies, leaving a single book that would cleanse them and force them to repent, turn them into good people and so on – of course.' She broke into laughter.

'Of course,' he fell in with her ironic tone. That was the only tragic thing about books: they changed people. All except the truly evil, who did not become better fathers, nicer husbands, more loving friends. They remained tyrants, continued to torment their employees, children and dogs, were spiteful in petty matters and cowardly in important ones, and rejoiced in their victims' shame.

'Books were my friends,' said Catherine, and cooled her cheek, which was red from the heat of cooking, on her wine glass. 'I think I learned all my feelings from books. In them I loved and laughed and found out more than in my whole non-reading life.'

'Me too,' murmured Perdu.

They looked at each other – and then it simply clicked.

'What does the J stand for?' asked Catherine in a huskier voice.

He had to clear his throat before he could answer.

'Jean,' he whispered. The word was so unfamiliar that his tongue collided with his teeth.

'My name is Jean. Jean Albert Victor Perdu. Albert after my paternal grandfather, Victor after my maternal grandfather. My mother is a professor, and her father, Victor Bernier, was a toxicologist, a socialist and mayor. I'm fifty years old, Catherine, and I haven't known many women, let alone slept with them. I loved one. She left me.'

Catherine studied him intently.

'Yesterday. Twenty-one years ago yesterday. The letter is from her. I'm scared of what's in it.'

He waited for her to throw him out, strike him or look away. But she did none of those.

'Oh, Jean,' she whispered instead, full of compassion. 'Jean.'

There it was again.

The sweet sound of his own name.

They looked at each other; he noticed a fluttering in her eyes and felt himself growing softer too, letting her enter and understand him – yes, they pierced each other with their gaze and their unspoken words.

Two small boats on a sea, both thinking they'd been drifting alone since they'd lost their anchors, but now . . .

She ran her fingers fleetingly across his cheek.

The caress struck him with the force of a slap – a wonderful, marvellous slap.

Again. Again!

Their bare forearms brushed as she set down her wine glass.

Skin. Downy hairs. Warmth.

It wasn't clear which of the two was more startled – but both of them immediately realised that it wasn't the strangeness, the sudden intimacy and the touch that was startling.

They were startled by how good it felt.

CHAPTER 11

Jean took a step until he was standing behind Catherine and could smell her hair and feel her shoulders against his chest. His heart was racing. He laid his hands incredibly slowly and extremely lightly on her slight wrists. He embraced her softly and ran his thumb and fingers up Catherine's arms in a circle of warmth and skin.

She gasped, a tightly clasped birdcall of his name. 'Jean?'

'Yes, Catherine.'

Jean Perdu felt a tremor run through her whole body. It came from her very centre, below her navel, a trembling and a rolling. It spread like ripples on water. He hugged her from behind, holding her tight.

Her body was shaking, betraying the fact that it had been a long time, a very long time, since she had been touched. She was a bud trapped inside a calloused husk.

So lonely. So alone.

Catherine leaned back gently against him. Her short hair smelled good.

Jean Perdu touched her even more lightly, just

stroking the tips of the little hairs, the air above her bare arms.

It's so wonderful.

More, begged Catherine's body. Oh please, more; it's been so long, I am thirsting. And please, no, not so hard. It's too much, too much. I can't stand it! How I've missed it. I could cope with missing it, until now. I was so hard on myself. But now I'm cracking, I'm trickling away like sand, I'm vanishing. So help me – carry on.

Can I hear her feelings?

The only sounds coming from her mouth were variations on his name.

Jean. Jean! Jean?

Catherine let herself fall back against him and surrendered to his hands. Heat coursed through his fingers. He felt as if he were hand and cock and feeling and body and soul and man and every muscle at the same time, all concentrated in each fingertip.

He touched only what he could reach of her bare skin without moving her dress. Her arms, which were firm and brown where they emerged from her sleeves; he encircled them repeatedly, and moulded his hands to them. He stroked her nape, dark brown; her throat, delicate and soft; her magnificent, sweeping, hypnotic collarbone. He did this with the ends of his fingers, the tip of his thumb; he followed the contours of her muscles, both hard and soft, all with the tip of his thumb.

Her skin grew ever warmer. He felt the muscles

swelling underneath, felt Catherine's whole body gaining in vivacity, suppleness and heat. A dense, heavy flower emerging slowly from its bud. A queen of the night.

He let her name roll off his tongue.

'Catherine.'

Long-forgotten emotions shook off the crust of time inside him. Perdu felt a tautness in his lower abdomen. His hands had a better sense now not only of what they were doing to Catherine, but also of how her skin responded, how her body caressed his hands in return. Her body kissed his palms and his fingertips.

How does she do that? What's she doing to me?

Could he carry and lay her down where her trembling legs would be able to rest, where he wanted to explore how her skin felt on her calves and behind the backs of her knees? Could he conjure further melodies from her?

He wanted to see her lying there in front of him, eyes open, their gazes interlocking; he wanted to touch her lips with his fingers, and her face. He wanted her whole body to kiss his hands – every part of her body.

Catherine turned around, eyes the grey of rain-laden storm clouds, wide, wild and turbulent.

Now he lifted her up. She melded herself to him. He carried her into the bedroom, rocking her gently on the way. Her flat was the mirror image of his own. A mattress on the floor, a clothes rail in the corner, books, reading lamp – and a record player.

His own reflection greeted him in the high windows – a faceless silhouette. Upright, though. Strong. A woman in his arms – *and what a woman.*

Jean Perdu felt his body shaking something off. An emotional mustiness, a blindness about himself. A desire to be invisible.

I am a man . . . again.

He laid Catherine on the simple bed, on the smooth white sheet. She lay there, her legs together, her arms by her sides. He stretched out on his side facing her, watched how she breathed and how her body trembled in certain places, like the after-tremors of tiny earthquakes under the skin.

In the hollow of her throat, say. Between breast and chin, below her neck.

He leaned over and placed his lips on the trembling. That birdcall again.

'Jean . . .'

Her pulsations. Her heartbeat. Her warmth. He felt Catherine streaming into him over his lips. Her scent, and how his muscles contracted. The heat she was radiating caught a flame in him.

And then – *Oh! I'm dying!* – she touched him.

Fingers on fabric, hands on skin. She had run her hands up along his tie and burrowed under his shirt.

As her hand made contact with his skin, it was as though a very ancient sensation was rearing its head. It was spreading, filling Monsieur Perdu from inside to outside, and rising higher and higher, into every fibre and cell, until it reached his throat and took his breath away.

He didn't move, so as not to disturb this wonderful, awe-inspiring, absolutely captivating sensation; he held his breath.

Lust. Such desire. And even more . . .

But he forced himself to breathe out slowly, as slowly as possible, so as not to betray how paralysed with delight he was, and not to potentially unsettle Catherine by his overwhelmed stillness.

Love.

The word bubbled up inside him, along with a memory of this feeling; he noticed water filling his eyes.

I miss her so much.

A tear rolled out of the corner of Catherine's eye too. Was she weeping for herself? Or for him?

She withdrew her hand from his shirt, then unbuttoned it from bottom to top and took off his tie. He sat up, half over her, to make it easier.

Then she put her hand behind his neck. She didn't press. Or pull.

Her lips parted to form the tiny slit that said, 'Kiss me'.

He traced Catherine's mouth with his fingers, running them again and again over the various textures of softness.

It would have been easy to carry on.

To bend his head and bridge the remaining distance. To kiss Catherine. The game of tongues, turning novelty into familiarity, curiosity into cupidity, happiness into . . .

Shame? Unhappiness? Arousal?

Reach under her dress, gradually unclothe her, first her underwear, then the dress – yes, that's how he'd do it. He wanted to know she was naked under her dress.

But he didn't do it.

For the first time since they had touched, Catherine had shut her eyes. At the very moment her lips were opening, her eyes closed. She had shut Perdu out. He could no longer see what she really wanted. He sensed that something had happened inside Catherine; something was lurking there to do her harm.

The memory of what it was like to be kissed by her husband? (And wasn't that an awfully long time ago? And didn't he already have a mistress then? And hadn't he said things, terrible things even then, such as: 'It's disgusting when you're ill' or 'If a man doesn't want a woman in his bedroom any more, then the woman is partly to blame'?) Was her body recalling how much it had been ignored – no more tenderness, no caresses, no loving words? The memory of being taken by her husband. (Never so she got enough; he shouldn't spoil her, he said. Spoiled women didn't love the same way; and what more did she want anyway? It was already over for him.) The memory of the nights when she had doubted whether she would ever be a woman again, ever be touched again, ever be thought beautiful, ever be alone with a man behind closed doors?

Catherine's ghosts were there and they had brought his to the party too.

'We're no longer alone, Catherine.'

Catherine opened her eyes. The storm in them had subsided from a silvery glint to a fading picture of surrender.

She nodded. Tears filled her eyes.

'Yes. Oh, Jean. That idiot appeared at the very moment I was thinking, "At last. At last a man is touching me as I always wished to be touched." Not like . . . well, that idiot.'

She turned on her side, away from Jean.

'Even my old self. The stupid little submissive Cathy. Who always sought to blame herself when her husband was so repellent or when her mother ignored her for days on end. I must have overlooked something . . . neglected something . . . I hadn't been quiet enough, not happy enough. I hadn't loved him and her enough, otherwise they wouldn't be so . . .'

Catherine was crying.

At first she cried softly, but when he wrapped the duvet around her and held her body tightly in his arms, his hand softly cupping the back of her head, her sobs grew louder. Heartbreaking.

He felt how, in his arms, she strode through all the valleys that she had flown through thousands of times before in her dreams. Terror-stricken that she would fall, lose control or drown in pain – but that was what she was doing now.

She was falling. Worn out by cares, grief and humiliation, Catherine was hitting rock bottom.

'I had no more friends. He said they only wanted to bathe in his glory. His. He couldn't imagine that they might find *me* interesting. He said, "I need you," although he didn't need me at all. He didn't even want me. He wanted to have art to himself. I gave up mine for his love, but that was too little for him. Was I supposed to die to prove to him that he was everything to me? And that he was more than I would ever be?'

And then, as a final thought, Catherine whispered hoarsely, 'Twenty years, Jean. Twenty years without living . . . I spat on my own life and let others spit on it too.'

At some point she started breathing more peacefully. Then she fell asleep. Her body went limp in Perdu's arms.

She too, eh. Twenty years. There are obviously several other ways to ruin your life.

Monsieur Perdu knew that it was his turn. Now he would have to hit rock bottom.

In the living room, on his old white-painted kitchen table, lay Manon's letter. It was a sad consolation to hear that he hadn't been the only one wasting time.

He wondered briefly what would have happened if Catherine had met him at twenty-one instead of Monsieur Le P.

He wondered for a long time whether he was ready for the letter.

Of course he wasn't.

He broke the seal, sniffed the paper, drank it in. Closed his eyes and lowered his head for a moment.

Then Monsieur Perdu sat down on the bistro chair and began to read Manon's twenty-one-year-old letter to him.

CHAPTER 12

Bonnieux, 30 August, 1992

I've already written to you a thousand times, Jean, and every time I had to begin with one and the same word, because it is the truest of all: 'Beloved'.

Beloved Jean, my so beloved, distant Jean.

I've done something very stupid. I didn't tell you why I left you, and now I regret both things – having left you and not saying why.

Please read on, do not burn me. I didn't leave you because I didn't want to stay with you.

I wanted to – far more than what is now happening to me instead.

Jean, I'm dying. Very soon – at Christmas, they predict.

I really wished you would hate me when I left.

I can see you shaking your head, mon amour. But I wanted to do what love thought right, and doesn't it say do what is good for the other person? I thought it would be good if you forgot me in your rage. If you don't grieve, don't worry; don't know anything about my death. Cut, anger, over – and move on.

But I was wrong. It won't work. I have to tell you what happened to me, to you, to us. It is both beautiful and terrible at the same time; it is too much for a short letter. We'll talk it all over when you get here.

That, then, is my request to you, Jean: come to me.

I'm so scared of dying.

But that can wait until you get here.

I love you.

Manon

PS: If you do not want to come because your feelings aren't strong enough, I'll accept it. You owe me nothing, no compassion either.

PPS: The doctors won't let me travel any more. Luc is expecting you.

Monsieur Perdu sat in the dark, feeling battered and bruised.

His whole chest contracted.

This can't be happening.

Every time he blinked he saw himself, but as the man he had been twenty-one years earlier. How he had sat stiffly at this same table and refused to open the letter.

Impossible.

Surely she couldn't have . . .?

★　★　★

92

She had betrayed him twice. She had left him. Then she had died. He had been so sure of that. He had built his entire life since on that assumption.

He felt like throwing up. Now he had to face up to the fact that it was *he* who had betrayed her. Manon had waited in vain for him to come to her while she . . .

No. Please, please – no.

He had messed everything up.

The letter, the PS – it must have seemed to her that his feelings weren't strong enough. As if Jean Perdu had never loved Manon enough to fulfil this wild wish – her final, earnest, most ardent wish.

And with this realisation his shame knew no boundaries.

He saw her before him in the hours and hours of the weeks following the letter, waiting for a car to pull up outside her house and for Jean to knock on her door.

Summer passed, autumn painted frost on the fallen leaves, winter swept the trees bare. Still he hadn't come.

He slapped his hands to his face, but would rather have slapped himself in the face.

And now it's too late.

Fingers shaking uncontrollably, Monsieur Perdu folded up the fragile letter, which miraculously preserved her scent, and pushed it back into the envelope. Then he buttoned up his shirt with grim concentration and groped for his shoes. He tidied his hair in the mirror formed by the darkened windowpane.

Jump out, you vile idiot. That would solve things.

When he looked up, he saw Catherine leaning against the door frame.

'I was her . . .,' he began, indicating the letter. 'She was my . . .' He couldn't find the words. 'But things turned out completely differently.'

What was the word for it?

'Love?' asked Catherine after a while.

He nodded.

That's right. That was the word.

'That's good.'

'It's too late,' he said.

It's destroying everything. It's destroying me.

'It seems that she . . .'

Say it.

'. . . . left me for love's sake. Yes, for love's sake. Left me.'

'Will you see each other again?' asked Catherine.

'No. She's dead. Manon has been dead a long time. But all these years I refused to accept it.'

He shut his eyes so as not to see Catherine, not to see how he was hurting her.

'And I loved her. So much that I stopped living when she went away. She died, but all I could think of was how mean she'd been to me. I was a stupid man. And forgive me, Catherine, for I still am. I can't even talk about it properly. I should go before I hurt you any more, right?'

'Of course you can go. And you're not hurting

me. That's life, and we're not fourteen any more. We turn peculiar when we don't have anyone left to love. And old emotions always linger for a while among the new ones. That's just how humans are,' whispered Catherine, calm and collected.

She stared at the kitchen table, which had set everything off.

'I wish my husband had left me for love's sake. That's the best way to be left.'

Perdu walked stiffly over to Catherine and awkwardly embraced her, even though it felt incredibly strange.

CHAPTER 13

He did one hundred press-ups while the coffee pot spluttered away. After a first sip of coffee he forced himself to do two hundred sit-ups until his muscles sang.

He took a cold and hot shower, and shaved, cutting himself often and deeply. He waited until the blood ceased to flow, ironed a white shirt and put on a tie. He shoved a few banknotes into his trouser pocket and draped his jacket over his arm.

He didn't look at Catherine's door as he went out. His body was yearning desperately for her embrace.

And then? I console myself, she consoles herself, and in the end we're like two used towels.

He took out the book orders his neighbours had stuck in his letterbox, stepped out of the building and greeted Thierry, who was wiping the dew from the café tables.

He ate his cheese omelette without really noticing or even tasting it, because he was concentrating hard on the morning paper.

'What's up?' asked Thierry, laying a hand on Perdu's shoulder.

His gesture was so playful and so friendly that Monsieur Perdu had to force himself not to grab Thierry and shake him.

How did she die? What from? Did it hurt? Did she call out for me? Did she watch the door every day? Why was I so proud?

Why did things turn out like this? What punishment do I deserve? Would it be best to kill myself, to do the right thing for once?

Perdu stared at the book reviews and read them with effortful, frantic concentration, willing himself not to miss a single word, opinion or snippet of information. He underlined things, jotted down comments and forgot what he was reading.

He started again.

He didn't even look up when Thierry said, 'That car, it's been there half the night. Is someone asleep in it? More people looking for that writer?'

'For Max Jordan?' asked Perdu.

May that boy not act so stupidly.

He slipped hurriedly away from his table as Thierry walked over to the car.

When death came knocking, she was scared. And she wanted me to protect her. But I wasn't there. I was too busy pitying myself.

Perdu felt sick.

Manon. Her hands. There was something so alive about her letter, her scent and her handwriting. I miss her so much.

I hate myself. I hate her!

Why did she let herself die? There has to be some misunderstanding. She must still be alive somewhere.

He ran to the toilet and threw up.

It wasn't a peaceful Sunday.

He swept the gangway and carried the books he'd refused to sell over the past few days back to their places, where they fitted to within a millimetre. He put a new roll of paper in the till. He didn't know what to do with his hands.

If I can get through today, I can get through the rest of my days too.

He served an Italian: 'I recently saw a book with a raven wearing glasses on the cover. Has it already been translated?'

He let his picture be taken with a tourist couple, took orders from Syria for some books that were critical of Islam, sold compression stockings to a Spanish lady, and filled Kafka's and Lindgren's bowls.

While the cats roamed around the boat, Perdu flicked through a supplier's catalogue that advertised place mats featuring the most famous six-word stories from Hemingway to Murakami – alongside salt, pepper and spice shakers shaped like the heads of Schiller, Goethe, Colette, Balzac and Virginia Woolf, which dispensed salt, pepper or sugar from the partings in their hair.

What's the point of that?

'The huge non-book bestseller: new bookmarks for every bookshop. With an exclusive offer of

Hesse's *Stages* – the cult bookend for your poetry department.'

Do you know what? That does it. You can stuff your crime-novel toilet paper. And Hesse's Stages – *'In all beginnings dwells a magic force' – as shelf decorations. Honestly, that does it!*

The bookseller stared out the window at the Seine, at the glittering waves, at the curve of the sky.

It really is pretty.

Was Manon cross that she had to leave me that way? Because I am who I am, and there was no other choice? Like talking to me, for example. Asking me for help. Telling me the truth.

'Am I a man who's not up to that? What kind of man am I anyway?' he cried.

Jean Perdu snapped the catalogue shut, rolled it up and stuck it in the back pocket of his grey trousers.

It was as though for the last twenty-one years his life had been leading up to this precise moment when it became clear to him what he had to do, what he should have done from the start, even without Manon's letter.

Down in the engine room, Monsieur Perdu opened his fastidiously tidy toolbox, took out the battery-powered screwdriver, put the bit in his shirt pocket and went out to the gangway. There he laid down the catalogue on the metal plank, worked the bit into the tool and, one by one, began to loosen the large screws that held the gangway to the underside of the embankment.

Finally, he also undid the pipe leading to the harbour's freshwater tank, pulled the plug out of the landing stage's distribution board and cast off the ropes that had bound the *Literary Apothecary* to the bank for two decades.

Perdu gave the gangway a few powerful kicks to release it finally from the ground. He raised the plank, pushed it into the entrance of the book barge, jumped after it and closed the hatch.

Perdu walked to the wheelhouse in the stern, shot a thought in the direction of Rue Montagnard – 'Forgive me, Catherine' – and turned the ignition key to preheat.

Then, after a passionate ten-second countdown, Perdu turned the key a notch further.

The engine started without hesitation.

'Monsieur Perdu! Monsieur Perdu! Hello! Wait for me!'

He looked over his shoulder.

Jordan? Yes, it really was Jordan! Along with his earmuffs he was wearing sunglasses that Perdu identified as Madame Bomme's glittery bug-eyed shades.

Jordan ran towards the book barge, a kit bag slung over his shoulder and bouncing with every step as various other bags dangled from his arms. He was being pursued by a couple with cameras.

'Where are you going?' Jordan shouted in a panicky voice.

'Away from here!' Perdu shouted back.

'Great – I want to come!'

Jordan hurled his luggage aboard when *Lulu* was already a metre from the bank, shaking and trembling with the unfamiliar vibrations. Half of the bags fell in the water, including Jordan's pouch with his mobile and wallet inside.

The engine spluttered, and the exhaust discharged a cloud of black diesel smoke. Half the river was veiled in a blue haze. Monsieur Perdu saw the harbourmaster striding towards them, cursing.

He pushed the throttle to full speed.

The writer launched himself into his run-up.

'No!' cried Perdu. 'No, Monsieur Jordan, no way! I really must . . .'

CHAPTER 14

'. . . beg you!'

Jean Perdu watched as Max Jordan stood up, rubbed his knee, looked back at where the rest of his things floated on the surface of the water for a second before sinking – and then limped to the wheelhouse with a beaming smile.

'Hello,' said the hunted author cheerily. 'Do you travel on this boat too?'

Perdu rolled his eyes. He'd tear a strip off Max Jordan later and then politely chuck him overboard. Now he had to concentrate on all the things heading his way: sightseeing vessels, working barges, houseboats, birds, flies and spray. What were the rules again? Who had priority, and how fast was he allowed to go? And what did the yellow diamonds on the bottom of the bridge mean?

Max was looking at him as if he were waiting for something.

'Jordan, take care of the cats and the books. And make some coffee. Meanwhile, I'll try not to kill anyone with this thing.'

'What? Whom do you want to kill? The cats?' the author asked with a blank look.

'Now take those things off,' Perdu pointed to Jordan's earmuffs, 'and make us some coffee.'

By the time Max Jordan placed a tin cup full of strong coffee in the holder beside the tyre-sized wheel, Perdu had grown more accustomed to the vibrations and to navigating upstream. He hadn't steered the barge in a long time. Simply nosing this thing along the river – the length of three shipping containers – was so discreet. The book barge cut quietly through the water.

He was so scared and yet so thrilled. He wanted to sing and scream. His fingers clutched the wheel. What he was doing was mad, it was daft; it was . . . *fan-tas-tic*!

'Where did you learn to drive a cargo boat and all this?' asked the writer, gesturing in awe at the navigation instruments.

'My father showed me. I was twelve. When I was sixteen, I did the Inland Waterways Helmsman's Certificate because I thought one day I'd be transporting coal to the north.'

And become a big, calm man who never needs to arrive to be happy. My God, how quickly life hurries on.

'Really? My father didn't even show me how to make paper boats.'

Paris passed by like a film reel. The Pont Neuf, Notre Dame, the Arsenal Harbour.

'That was a perfect 007 escape. Milk and sugar,

Mr Bond?' asked Jordan. 'So what made you do it, anyway?'

'What do you mean? And no sugar, Miss Moneypenny.'

'I mean sending your life up in flames. Scramming. Doing a Huckleberry Finn on his raft, a Ford Prefect, a—'

'A woman.'

'A woman? I didn't think you were so interested in women.'

'In most, I'm not. Only in one. And in her case a lot. I want to see her.'

'Oh. Great. Why didn't you take the bus?'

'Do you think only people in books do crazy things?'

'No. I'm just thinking that I can't swim and that you were a kid the last time you drove a monster like this. And I'm thinking about the fact that you arranged the five tins of cat food in alphabetical order. You're probably insane. My God! Were you really twelve once? An actual small boy? Incredible! You seem as if you've always been so . . .'

'So?'

'So grown-up. So . . . controlled. So totally in command.'

If only he knew what an amateur I am.

'I wouldn't have made it to the station. I'd have had too much time to think things over on the way there, Monsieur Jordan. I would have come up with reasons not to go. And I wouldn't have gone through with it. Then I'd be standing up there' – he indicated some girls on bikes waving to them from one of the bridges over the Seine – 'and stay where I've always been. I wouldn't have budged one centimetre from my normal routine. It's shit, but it's safe.'

'You said "shit".'

'So what?'

'Excellent. Now I'm a lot less worried about the ABC in your fridge.'

Perdu reached for his coffee. Wouldn't Max Jordan worry a whole lot more when he began to suspect that the woman Jean Perdu had suddenly dropped everything for had been dead for twenty-one years? Perdu imagined himself telling Jordan. Soon. If only he knew how to.

'How about you?' he asked. 'What's driving you away, Monsieur?'

'I want to . . . look for a story,' Jordan falteringly explained. 'Because . . . I've nothing left inside. I don't want to go home until I've found it. In fact, I only came to the embankment to say good-bye, and then you cast off. May I please come with you? May I?'

He looked at Perdu with such hope in his eyes that for the time being Perdu shelved his plans to set Max Jordan ashore at their next port of call and wish him luck.

With the world ahead, and an unwanted life astern, suddenly he felt once more like the boy he had indeed been – even if that must barely seem possible from Max Jordan's youthful perspective.

In fact, Jean did feel as he had when he was twelve. When he had seldom been lonely, but liked to be alone or with Vijaya, the weedy son of the Indian mathematician's family next door; when he had been enough of a kid to believe that his night-time dreams were an alternative real world and a place of trial. He had once even believed that his dreams contained tasks that would move him up a rung in his waking life if he managed to accomplish them.

'Find the path out of the maze! Learn to fly! Vanquish the hound of hell! Succeed and when you wake up, a wish will come true.'

At the time he had believed in the power of his wishes, which were naturally associated with the offer of forgoing something precious or important.

'Please get my parents to look at each other again over breakfast! I'll give an eye for it to happen, the left one. I need the right one to steer a barge.'

Yes, that's how he had bargained when he was still a boy and had not been so . . . How had Jordan put it? So controlled? He had also written letters to God and sealed them with blood from his thumb. Now, only about a thousand years too late, he stood at the wheel of a gigantic boat and sensed for the first time in a long time that he did indeed have desires.

Perdu let slip a 'Ha!' and stood up a little straighter.

Jordan twiddled the knobs of the radio until he had found VNF Seine's navigation radio, which controlled the river traffic. 'A repeat announcement for the two comedians who smoked out Champs-Élysées harbour. Greetings from the harbourmaster. Starboard is the side where your thumb's on the left.'

'Do they mean us?' asked Jordan.

'Who cares,' said Monsieur Perdu dismissively.

They gave each other a wry grin.

'What did you want to be when you were a boy, Monsieur . . . um . . . Jordan?'

'A boy? You mean, like, yesterday?' Max laughed cockily, before falling into a deep silence.

'I wanted to be a man my father would take seriously. And an interpreter of dreams, which more or less ruled out the former,' he said eventually.

Perdu cleared his throat. 'Chart a course to Avignon for us, Monsieur. Find a nice canal route to the south, one that will maybe bring us . . . significant dreams.' Perdu gestured towards a stack of charts. The maps showed a dense network of navigable blue channels, canals, marinas and locks.

Jordan gave him a questioning glance, and Monsieur Perdu opened the throttle. Eyes firmly on the water, he said: 'Sanary says that you have to travel south by water to find answers to your dreams. He says too that you find yourself again there, but only if you get lost on the way – completely lost. Through love. Through longing. Through fear. Down south they listen to the sea in order to understand that laughing and crying sound the same, and that the soul sometimes needs to cry to be happy.'

A bird awoke inside his chest, and it cautiously spread its wings, amazed to find that it was still alive. It wanted out. It wanted to burst from his chest, taking his heart with it, and soar up into the sky.

'I'm coming,' muttered Jean Perdu. 'I'm coming, Manon.'

MANON'S TRAVEL DIARY

On My Way Into Life, Between Avignon and Lyons

30 July 1986

It was a miracle that they didn't all climb aboard with me. It was irritating enough that they (my parents, Aunt 'women-don't-need-men' Julia, my cousins 'I'm-too-fat' Daphne and 'I'm-always-so-tired' Nicolette) came down to our house from their thyme-scented hills and accompanied me to Avignon to see me actually get on the fast train from Marseilles to Paris. I suspected them all of merely wanting to go to a proper town and visit the cinema again and buy themselves a few Prince records.

Luc didn't come with me. He was worried I wouldn't go if he was at the station. And he's right: I can tell at a distance how he is simply from the way he stands or sits and holds his shoulders and head. He is a southern Frenchman to his marrow; his soul is fire and wine, he's never cold-blooded, he can't do anything without feeling, he's never indifferent. People say that most people in Paris are indifferent to most things.

I'm standing at the window of the express train and feel both young and grown-up at once. It's the first time I'm truly bidding farewell to the land of my birth. Indeed, I'm seeing it for the first time as I move away from it, mile by mile. The light-drenched sky, the calls of the cicadas from the hundred-year-old trees, the winds wrestling over every almond leaf. The heat like a fever. The golden quivering and sparkling of the air when the sun goes down and turns the steep mountains and their perching villages shades of pink and honey. And the land keeps on giving – it will not stop growing for our benefit. It forces rosemary and thyme through the stones, the cherries almost burst out of their skins, and the swollen lime seeds smell like girls' laughter when the harvest boys come to them in the shade of the plane trees. The rivers gleam like fine turquoise threads winding through the craggy rocks, and to the south sparkles a sea of such piercing blue, as blue as the speckles on the skin of black olives when one has made love under one of those trees. The land constantly presses on us humans, comes mercilessly close. Thorns. Rocks. Scent. Papa says that Provence created humans from the trees and the bright rocks and springs, and called them Frenchmen. They are woody and malleable, stony and strong; they speak from deep within their strata and boil over as fast as a pan of water on the stove.

I can already feel the heat subsiding, the sky sinking lower and losing its cobalt streaks. I see the contours of the land growing softer and weaker the further north we go. The cold, cynical north! Can you feel love?

Maman is naturally afraid that something might happen to me in Paris. She isn't so much thinking that I might be torn to pieces by one of the Lebanese Revolutionary Faction bombs that have gone off in the Galeries Lafayette and on the Champs-Élysées; a man, more like. Or, perish the thought, a woman. One of those Saint-Germain intellectuals, who have everything in their heads and not a feeling to speak of, and who could give me a taste for life in a draughty artists' household, where it is, as always, the women who end up rinsing the creative gentlemen's paintbrushes.

I think that Maman is worried that I might discover something far away from Bonnieux and its Atlas cedars, Vermentino vines and pinky twilights that might jeopardise my future life. I heard her weeping with despair out in the summer kitchen last night; she's afraid for me.

People say that Parisians are fiercely competitive about everything, and men charm women with their coldness. Every woman wants to net herself a man and turn his icy defences into passion. Every woman, especially women from the south. That's what Daphne says, and I think she's crazy. Diets obviously make you hallucinate.

Papa is ever the self-controlled Provençal. What can city people offer you? is what he says. I love him when he has one of his five-minute fits of humanism and sees Provence as the cradle of French national culture. He mumbles his Occitan expressions and thinks it's wonderful that every last olive farmer and unwashed tomato grower has been speaking the language of artists, philosophers, musicians and young people for four hundred years. Unlike Parisians, who think only their educated classes deserve to be creative and cosmopolitan. Oh, Papa! Plato with a field spade, and so intolerant towards the intolerant.

I'll miss the spiciness of his breath and the warmth of his embrace. And his voice – rolling thunder on the horizon.

I know that I'll miss the mountains and the mistral that sweeps and washes the vineyards . . . I've brought a little bag of soil and a bunch of herbs with me. Along with a nectarine stone I've sucked clean, and a pebble that I can put under my tongue when I thirst for the springs of home, like Pagnol.

Will I miss Luc? He was always there; I've never missed him before. I'll enjoy pining for him. I don't know the pull that Cousin I'm-too-fat Daphne spoke of, meaningfully omitting words: 'It's as if a man stuck his anchor into your breast, your stomach, between your legs; and when he's not there, the chains pull and tug.' It sounded horrible, and yet she was grinning as she said it.

How might it feel to want a man like that? And do I sink the same barbs into him, or do men find it easier to forget? Did Daphne read that in one of her awful novels?

I know all about men, but nothing about man. What is a man like when he's with a woman? Does he know at twenty how he wants to love her at sixty, because he knows exactly how he's going to think and act and live career-wise at sixty?

I'll come back in a year's time, and Luc and I will get married, like the birds. And then we'll make wine and children, year after year. I'm free this year and in the future too. Luc won't ask questions if I come home late from time to time, and if, in the years that follow, I go off to Paris or somewhere else on my own. That was his gift to me when we got engaged: a free marriage. That's how he is.

Papa wouldn't understand him – freedom from faithfulness, for love's sake? 'Rain isn't enough for all the land either,' he would say; love is the rain, man is the land. And what are we women? 'You cultivate the man and he flourishes in your hands; that's the power of women.'

I don't yet know whether I want Luc's gift of rain. It's big; maybe I'm too small for it.

And do I want to reciprocate? Luc said he didn't insist on that, nor was it a condition.

I am the daughter of a tall, strong tree. My timber forms a ship, but it is anchorless, flagless. I set sail for the shade and the light; I drink the wind and forget all ports. To hell with freedom, gifted or seized; if in doubt, always endure alone.

Oh, and I should mention one last thing before my inner Marianne rips off her tunic again and roars more words of freedom. I did indeed get to know the man who saw me crying and writing my travel diary. In the train compartment. He saw my tears, and I hid them and the babyish 'I-want-it-back' feeling that overcomes me as soon as I leave my little valley behind . . .

He asked whether I was badly homesick.

'It could be lovesickness, couldn't it?' I asked him.

'Homesickness is lovesickness, only worse.'

He's tall for a Frenchman. A bookseller. His teeth are white and his smile friendly; his eyes are green – the green of herbs. They're almost the same colour as the cedar outside my bedroom in Bonnieux. Grape-red mouth, hair as thick and strong as sprigs of rosemary.

His name's Jean. He's in the process of converting a Flemish working barge; he wants to plant books on it, he says, 'paper boats for the soul'. He explained that he wants to make it into an apothecary, a *pharmacie littéraire,* to treat all the emotions for which no other remedy exists.

Homesickness, for example. In his opinion there are various kinds: a desire for shelter, family nostalgia, a fear of separation or a yearning for love.

'The yearning to have something good to love soon: a place, a person, a particular bed.'

He says it in such a way that it doesn't sound silly; it sounds logical.

Jean promised to give me books that would alleviate my homesickness. He said it as though he were talking about a half-magical, yet nonetheless official form of medicine.

He seems like a white raven, clever and strong and floating above reality. He is like some great proud bird watching over the world.

No, I wasn't precise enough. He didn't promise to give me books – he says he cannot stand promises. He suggested it. 'I can help you. If you want to cry some more or stop, or laugh so you cry less; I will help you.'

I feel like kissing him to see whether he can do more than talk and know things; whether he can feel and believe as well.

And how high it can fly, this white raven that sees everything inside me.

CHAPTER 15

'I'm hungry,' said Max.

'Have we got enough fresh water?' asked Max.

'I want to have a go at steering!' demanded Max.

'Haven't we got any fishing rods on board?' grizzled Max.

'I feel somehow castrated without a telephone and credit cards. Don't you?' sighed Max.

'No. You can clean the boat,' replied Perdu. 'It's meditation in motion.'

'Cleaning? Really? Look, here come some more Swedish sailors,' said the writer. 'They always cruise down the middle of the river as though they invented it. The English are different; they give the impression of being the only ones who belong here and everyone else should really be applauding them and waving little flags on the banks. You know, Napoléon's plans to invade their island still rankle with them.'

He lowered the binoculars. 'Have we got a national ensign on our rear?'

'Stern, Max. A ship's back side is called the stern.'

The further they had ploughed their way up the winding Seine, the more excited Max had grown – and the calmer Jean Perdu had become.

The river wound its way in stately loops through woods and parks. The banks were lined with grand, rambling grounds surrounding houses that hinted at old money and family secrets.

'Have a look in the trunk near the tools for an ensign and a French *tricolore* pennant,' Perdu instructed Jordan. 'And dig out the pegs and the mallet, because we'll need them to moor if we don't find a harbour.'

'Oh, I see. And how am I supposed to know how to moor?'

'Um, it's explained in a book about houseboat holidays.'

'Fishing too?'

'That's in the section marked "Survival in the Provinces for City Dwellers".'

'And where's the cleaning bucket? In a book as well?' Max gave a little grunt of laughter and pushed his earmuffs back over his ears.

Perdu saw a group of canoeists ahead and gave a warning blast of the ship's horn. The sound was deep and loud, and it coursed through his chest and stomach – directly under his belly button, and from there deeper still.

'Oh,' whispered Monsieur Perdu.

He tugged on the horn lever again.

Only a man could invent that.

The blast and its vibrations brought back the

119

feeling of Catherine's skin beneath his fingers. How her skin had enveloped the deltoid muscles on top of the shoulder. Soft, warm and smooth. And round. For a moment the memory of Catherine made Jean feel dizzy.

Caressing women, steering ships, running away.

Billions of cells seemed to wake up inside him, blink sleepily, stretch and say: 'Hey! We've missed this. More, please. And step on it!'

Starboard to the right, port to the left, channel marked by coloured buoys: his hands still knew, and navigated between them. And women are the smart ones, because they didn't oppose feeling and thinking, and loved without limits – yes, he knew that in his gut.

And watch out for the eddies coming up to a lock.

Watch out for women who always want to be weak. They won't let a man get away with any weakness.

But the skipper has the last word.

Or his wife.

Finding new moorings? Parking this thing was about as easy as silencing your night-time thoughts. Nah! This evening he would simply head towards a particularly long and indulgent quay, manoeuvre the rudder gently, if he could find it, and then? Maybe he should aim for an embankment instead.

Or just keep on going until the end of my life.

A group of women peered at him from a carefully tended garden on the bank. One of them waved. Very occasionally a working barge or a Flemish cargo vessel, one of *Lulu*'s ancient forebears, would come towards them, its phlegmatic captain relaxing with his feet up and steering the large, smooth-turning wheel with one thumb.

Then all of a sudden civilization ceased. After Melun they plunged into the green of summer.

How good it smelled! So pure, so fresh and so clean.

Yet there was something else that was completely unlike Paris. Something very specific was missing, something Perdu had grown so accustomed to that its absence gave him slight dizziness and caused a humming in his ears.

Immense relief swept through him when he realised what it was. There was no rush of cars, no roar of the metro, no buzz of air conditioners. None of the whirr and grumble of millions of machines and transmissions and lifts and escalators. There were no sounds of reversing lorries, trains braking or heels on gravel and stone. None of the bass-driven music from the yobs two houses down, the crackle of skateboards, the chatter of scooters.

It was a Sunday quietness of the kind Perdu had first experienced this ripely and fully when his father and mother had taken him to see relatives in Brittany. There, somewhere between Pont-Aven and Kerdruc, the silence had struck him as the essence of life, hiding itself away from city dwellers at the end of the world in Finistère. Paris had seemed to him like a giant machine that droned and boomed away to produce a world of illusion. It put people to sleep with laboratory-made scents that imitated nature, and lulled them with sounds, artificial light and fake oxygen – as in E. M. Forster's books, which he had loved as a boy. When Forster's literary 'machine' breaks down one day, people who have so far only communicated via their screens die from the sudden silence, the pure sunlight and the intensity of their own, unfiltered sensations. They die from an overload of life.

That was exactly how Jean Perdu felt now, overrun by hyperintensive perceptions he had never experienced in the city. How his lungs hurt when he took a deep breath! How his ears popped in the unfamiliar liberty of peace. How his eyes were restored by the sight of living shapes. The fragrance of the river, the silken air, the vaulted open space above his head.

He had last experienced such tranquillity and freedom when Manon and he had ridden through the Camargue late one pastel-blue summer. Even so, the days had been as glowing and hot as a stove plate. Already by night, though, the stalks in the meadows and the woods by the swampy lakes sipped dew. The air was steeped in the aromas of autumn and the salt from the salt pans. It smelled of the campfires of the Roma and the Sinti, who lived in summer sites tucked away among bull pastures, flamingo colonies and old forgotten orchards.

Jean and Manon rode on two lean, sure-footed white horses to the deserted beaches among isolated lakes and along small, winding roads that petered out in the woods. Only these horses, native to the Camargue and able to eat with their muzzles underwater, could find their way in the endless, waterlogged emptiness.

Such desolate vastness, such distant quietness.

'Do you remember, Jean? You and me. Adam and Eve at the end of the world?'

How laughter-filled Manon's voice could be. Laughter-filled, melting chocolate.

Yes, it was as though they had discovered an alien world at the end of their own, which for the last two thousand years had remained unbeset by man and his mania for transforming the countryside into cities, streets and supermarkets.

Not a single tall tree, no hills, no houses. Only sky, and beneath that one's own skull as the sole boundary. They saw wild horses passing in herds. Herons and wild geese angled for fish, and snakes pursued green lizards. They sensed all the prayers of thousands of walkers, which the Rhône had carried down from its source under the glacier into this vast delta, and which now flitted about between the broom, the willows and scrubby trees.

The mornings were so fresh and innocent that they rendered him speechless with gratitude to be alive. Every day he had swum in the Mediterranean by the light of the setting sun; he had run, naked and howling, up and down the fine, white sand beaches; and had felt at one with himself and with this natural emptiness – so full of strength.

Manon had been full of genuine admiration for how he had swum and grasped for fish and caught some. They had begun to cast off civilization. Jean let his beard grow, and Manon's hair dangled over her breasts as she rode naked on her good-natured, sensible mount with its small ears. They were both baked brown as chestnuts, and Jean enjoyed the sweet-and-sour tang on her skin when they made love in the evenings in the still-warm sand beside the crackling driftwood fire. He tasted the salt of the sea, the salt of her sweat, the salt of the delta meadows, where river and sea flowed together like lovers.

When he approached the black fuzz between her thighs, Jean was met by the hypnotic aroma of femininity and life. Manon smelled of the mare she was riding so tightly and masterfully – it was the aroma of freedom. She bore the scent of a mixture of oriental spices and the sweetness of flowers and honey; she smelled of woman!

She had whispered and sighed his name unremittingly; she had wrapped the letters in a stream of breath wreathed in lust.

'Jean! Jean!'

In those nights he had been more of a man than ever before. She had opened up completely for him, pressed herself against him, his mouth, his being, his cock. And in her open eyes, which held his gaze, there was always the reflection of the moon – first a crescent, then a semicircle and finally a full, red disc.

They had spent half a lunar journey in the Camargue; they had gone wild, turned into Adam and Eve in the hut of reeds. They were refugees and explorers, and he had never asked whom Manon had had to deceive in order to dream their dreams there at the end of the earth among the bulls, flamingos and horses.

At night only her breathing had saturated the absolute silence beneath the starry sky. Manon's sweet, regular, deep breathing.

She was the world breathing.

It was only when Monsieur Perdu had let go of this image of Manon sleeping and breathing at the wild, foreign, southern frontier – let go as slowly as one might release a paper boat onto water – that he noticed he had been staring ahead with wide-open eyes the whole time – and that he could remember his lover without breaking down.

CHAPTER 16

'Oh, will you please take those earmuffs off, Jordan. Listen to how quiet it is.'

'Shh! Not so loud! And don't call me Jordan – it'd be better if I gave myself a code name.'

'Oh yes. What?'

'I am now Jean, Jean Perdu.'

'With all due respect: I am Jean Perdu.'

'Yeah, brilliant, wasn't it? Shouldn't we be on first-name terms?'

'No, we shouldn't.'

Jordan pushed his earmuffs back, then sniffed.

'It smells of fish spawn here.'

'Can you smell it with your ears?'

'What happens if I fall into the fish spawn and get eaten up by a horde of underdeveloped catfish?'

'Monsieur Jordan, most people only fall overboard if they try to pee over the railing when drunk. Use the toilet and you'll survive. And anyway, catfish don't eat people.'

'Oh yeah? Where does it say that? In another book? You know as well as I do that what people write in books is only the truth they've discovered at their desks. I mean, the earth used to be a disc that hung around in space like a forgotten dining-hall tray.' Max Jordan stretched, and his stomach rumbled loudly and reproachfully. 'We should get something to eat.'

'In the fridge you'll find—'

'Mainly cat food. Heart and chicken – no thanks.'

'Don't forget the tin of white beans.' They really needed to go shopping quickly, but how? Perdu barely had any cash in the register, and Jordan's cards were floating in the Seine. Nevertheless, the water in the tanks would be sufficient for the toilet, the sink and the shower. He also had two crates of mineral water left. They wouldn't make it all the way down south on that, though.

Monsieur Perdu sighed. A few minutes ago he'd been feeling like a buccaneer; now he was a rookie.

'I'm an excavator!' Jordan said triumphantly, as he emerged soon afterwards from *Lulu*'s book-filled belly into the wheelhouse with a pile of volumes and a long cardboard tube under his arm. 'What we have here is a navigation test book containing every traffic sign a bored European bureaucrat can dream up.' He slammed the book down by the wheel. 'There's a book of knots too. I'll take that one. And look at this: a rear . . . sorry . . . stern pennant as well as – wait for it! – an ensign!'

He proudly held up the cardboard tube and slid a large rolled-up flag out of it.

It was a black-and-gold bird with outspread wings. On closer viewing, one could see a stylised book with the spine forming the bird's body and the cover and pages, its wings. The paper bird had an eagle's head and wore an eye patch like a pirate's. It was sewed onto oxblood-red fabric.

'So? Is this our flag or what?'

Jean Perdu felt a powerful pang to the left of his breastbone. He doubled over.

'What's up now?' asked Max Jordan in alarm. 'Are you having a heart attack? If you are, please don't tell me to look up in a book how to insert a catheter!'

Perdu had to laugh despite himself.

'It's all right,' he panted. 'It's only . . . surprise. Give me a second.'

Jean tried to swallow his way through the pain.

He stroked the filigree threads, the fabric and the book bird's beak – and then its single eye.

Manon had backstitched this flag for the book barge's inauguration at the same time as she had been working on her Provençal bridal quilt. Her fingers and eyes had glided across the fabric – this fabric.

Manon. Is this the only thing I have left of you?

'Why are you marrying this wine man?'

'His name is Luc and he's my best friend.'

'Vijaya's my best friend, but that doesn't mean I want to marry him.'

'I love Luc and it'll be wonderful to be married to him. He lets me be who I am in everything, no strings attached.'

'You could marry *me*, and that'd be wonderful too.'

Manon had lowered her sewing; the bird's eye was only half filled in.

'I was already part of Luc's life plan before you even knew we'd be on the same train.'

'And you don't want him to suffer a change of plan.'

'No, Jean. No. *I* don't want to suffer. I'd miss Luc. His lack of demands. I want him. I want you. I want the north and the south. I want life with all it involves. I've opted against the "or" and for the "and". Luc allows me every "and". Could you do that if we were man and wife? If there was someone else, a second Jean, a Luc or two or . . .'

'I'd prefer to have you all to myself.'

'Oh, Jean. What I want is selfish, I know. I can only ask you to stay with me. I need you so I can survive.'

'Your whole life long, Manon?'

'My whole life long, Jean.'

'That'll do me.'

As if to seal the pact, she had stuck the needle into the skin of her thumb and soaked the material behind the bird's eye.

Maybe it was only sex, though.

That had been his fear: that he only meant sex to her.

Yet it was never 'only sex' when they slept together. It was the conquest of the world. It was a fervent prayer. They recognised themselves for what they were – their souls, their bodies, their yearning for life, their fear of death. It was a celebration of life.

Now Perdu could breathe more deeply again.

'Yes, that's our flag, Jordan. It's perfect. Raise it in the bow where everyone can see it. Up front. And the *tricolore* here in the stern. And hurry up.'

While Max leaned towards the stern to find out which of the cables slapping in the wind was the one for raising the national flag, and then traipsed through the bookshop to the bow, Perdu felt the heat rising behind his eyes. Yet he knew he mustn't cry.

Max attached the ensign and pulled it higher and higher.

With every tug, Perdu's heart clenched more and more tightly.

The ensign was now fluttering proudly in their slipstream. The book bird was flying.

Forgive me, Manon. Forgive me.

I was young, stupid and vain.

'Uh-oh. The cops are coming!' shouted Max Jordan.

CHAPTER 17

The patrol boat was closing in on them. Perdu eased back the throttle as the manoeuvrable motorboat came alongside and tied up to Lulu's cleats.

'Do you think they'll put us in a cell together?' asked Max.

'I'll have to apply for witness protection,' said Max.

'Maybe my publisher sent them?' fretted Max.

'You really should go and clean the windows or practise a few knots,' muttered Perdu.

A dashing policeman in a pair of aviator sunglasses jumped on board and clambered swiftly up to the wheelhouse.

'*Bonjour, Messieurs.* Seine River Office, Champagne district. I'm Brigadier Levec,' he reeled off. It was clear from his voice that he loved his title.

Perdu was almost counting on this Brigadier Levec reporting him for having dropped out of his own life without permission.

'Unfortunately, you haven't affixed your French Waterways Authority disc in a visible position. And please show me the mandatory life jackets. Thank you.'

'I'll go and clean the windows,' said Jordan.

A quarter of an hour, a warning and a notification of a fine later, Monsieur Perdu had emptied out the cash register money and the change from his pocket onto the table for a disc to be allowed to navigate on French inland waters, a set of fluorescent life jackets, which were compulsory when passing through the locks on the Rhône, and a certified copy of the FWA guidelines. There wasn't enough.

'So,' said Brigadier Levec. 'What are we going to do now?'

Was that a satisfied glint in his eye?

'Would you . . . um . . . do you by any chance like reading?' asked Perdu, noticing that he was mumbling with embarrassment.

'Of course. I don't approve of the silly habit of lumping men who read together with weaklings and effeminate men,' the river policeman answered, as he made to tickle Kafka, who trotted away, tail in the air.

'Then may I offer you a book . . . or several to make up the balance?'

'Hmm. I'd take them for the life jackets. But what do we do about the fine? And how do you mean to pay the mooring fees? I'm not sure that marina owners are . . . bookworms.' Brigadier Levec had a think. 'Follow the Dutch. They have a nose for a free lunch and will know where you can moor without charge.'

As they walked through *Lulu*'s belly and along

the bookshelves so that Levec could choose his balance of payment, the brigadier turned to Max, who was polishing the window by the reading chair and avoiding looking directly at the policeman: 'Hey, aren't you that famous writer?'

'Me? No. Definitely not. I'm . . . er,' Jordan cast a quick glance at Perdu, 'his son and a completely normal sports sock salesman.'

Perdu stared at him. Had Jordan just gone and got himself adopted?

Levec picked up *Night* from a pile. The policeman scrutinised Max's picture on the cover.

'Sure?'

'Okay, maybe I am.'

Levec raised his shoulders in understanding.

'Course you are. You must have lots of female fans.'

Max fiddled with his earmuffs, which he was wearing around his neck. 'I don't know,' he said. 'Maybe.'

'Well, my ex-fiancée loved your book. She was always going on about it. Sorry – I mean of course the book by that guy you look like. Perhaps you could write his name in here for me?'

Max nodded.

'For Frédéric,' Levec dictated, 'with great affection.'

Max gritted his teeth and wrote what he'd been asked to.

'Wonderful,' said Levec and beamed at Perdu. 'Is your son going to pay the fine too?'

Jean Perdu nodded. 'Of course. He's a good boy.'

After Max had pulled out his pockets to reveal a few notes of small denomination and some coins, they were both broke. With a sigh Levec took some recent publications – 'For my colleagues' – and a recipe book, *Cooking for the Single Man*.

'Wait a minute,' said Perdu, then, after a quick search, handed him Romain Gary's autobiography from the Love for Dummies section.

'What's this for?'

'You mean what's it *against*, dear Brigadier,' Perdu corrected him gently. 'It's against the disappointment of knowing that no woman will ever love us as much as the one who gave birth to us.'

Levec blushed and quickly ducked out of the book barge.

'Thank you,' whispered Max.

As the policemen cast off, Perdu was more convinced than ever that novels about dropouts and river adventurers left out such minor inconveniences as tax discs and life jacket fines.

'Do you think he'll keep it a secret that I'm here?' asked Jordan as the police boat headed off.

'Please, Jordan. What is so terrible about talking to a few fans or the press?'

'They might ask what I'm working on.'

'So what? Tell them the truth. Tell them that you're thinking it over, you're taking your time, you're digging for a story and that you'll let them know when you've found one.'

Jordan looked as though he'd never considered this.

'I rang my father the day before yesterday. doesn't read much, you know, only sports papers. I told him about the translations, the royalties and the fact that I've sold nearly half a million books. I told him I could help him because his pension isn't so great. Do you know what my father asked?'

Monsieur Perdu waited.

'If I was finally going to get a proper job. And he'd heard that I'd written a perverted story. Half the neighbourhood was casting aspersions on him under their breath. Did I have any idea of the harm I'd done him with my crazy ideas.'

Max looked tremendously hurt and lost.

Monsieur Perdu felt an unaccustomed urge to hold him close. When he went ahead and did just that, it took him two attempts before he worked out where to put his arms. He pulled Max Jordan cautiously against his shoulder. They stood there stiffly, leaning towards each other, their knees slightly bent.

Then Perdu whispered into Jordan's ear: 'Your father is a small-hearted ignoramus.'

Max flinched, but Perdu held him in an iron grip. He spoke quietly, as though he were confiding a secret in the young man: 'He deserves to imagine people gossiping about him. Instead, they're probably talking about you, and they're wondering how someone like your father can have such an amazing, magnificent son – maybe his greatest achievement.'

Max swallowed hard.

His voice was reedy as he whispered back, 'My

id he didn't mean it; he just couldn't
s love. Every time he swore at me and
ne was showing his great love for me.'

rdu seized his young companion by the
shoulders, looked him in the eye and said more
emphatically, 'Monsieur Jordan. Max. Your mother
lied because she wanted to console you, but it's
ridiculous to interpret abuse as love. Do you know
what my mother used to say?'

'Don't play with those grubby kids?'

'Oh no, she was never elitist. She said that far
too many women are the accomplices of cruel,
indifferent men. They lie for these men. They lie
to their own children. Because their fathers treated
them exactly the same way. These women always
retain some hope that love is hiding behind the
cruelty, so that the anguish doesn't drive them
mad. Truth is, though, Max, there's no love there.'

Max wiped a tear from the corner of his eye.

'Some fathers cannot love their children. They
find them annoying. Or uninteresting. Or unsettling. They're irritated by their children because
they've turned out differently than they had
expected. They're irritated because the children
were the wife's wish to patch up the marriage when
there was nothing left to patch up, her means of
forcing a loving marriage where there was no love.
And such fathers take it out on the children.
Whatever they do, their fathers will be nasty and
mean to them.'

'Please stop.'

'And the children, the delicate, little, yearning children,' Perdu continued more softly, because he was terribly moved by Max's inner turmoil, 'do everything they can to be loved. Everything. They think that it must somehow be their fault that their father cannot love them. But Max,' and here Perdu lifted Jordan's chin, 'it has nothing to do with them. You already discovered that in your wonderful novel. We cannot decide to love. We cannot compel anyone to love us. There's no secret recipe, only love itself. And we are at its mercy – there's nothing we can do.'

Max was crying now, sobbing uncontrollably, and he sank to his knees and put his arms around Monsieur Perdu's legs.

'Now, now,' the latter murmured. 'It's okay. Want to have a go at steering?'

Max dug his fingers into his trouser legs. 'No! I want to smoke! I want to get drunk! I want to find myself at last! I want to write! I want to decide who loves me and who doesn't. I want to determine whether love hurts, I want to kiss women, I want—'

'Yes, Max. Shh. It's okay. We'll tie up; we'll get ourselves something to smoke and drink; and the other stuff with women – we'll see about that other stuff.'

Perdu pulled the young man to his feet. Max leaned against him and soaked his ironed shirt with tears and saliva.

'It makes you sick!' he sobbed.

'You're right, it does. But please be sick into the water, Monsieur, and not on the deck; otherwise you'll have to mop it clean again.'

Max Jordan's sobs were interspersed with laughter. He cried and laughed as Perdu held him in his arms.

A tremor ran through the book barge and the rear deck hit the bank with a loud thump, throwing the men first against the piano and then to the floor. Books rained down from the shelves.

Max gave a 'hmpf' as a fat volume fell on his stomach.

'Take 'our knee out o' my 'outh,' Perdu requested.

Then he looked out the window, and he didn't like what he saw.

'We're drifting downstream!'

CHAPTER 18

Perdu steered the barge, which the current had pushed sideways, valiantly away from the bank. Unfortunately, *Lulu*'s stern swung out as he did this, leaving the long barge jammed across the river like a cork in a bottle, and in the crossfire of honking ships whose channel it was blocking. A British narrow boat, one of the two-metre-wide but very long houseboats, narrowly avoided crashing into *Lulu*'s midriff.

'Landlubbers! Guttersnipes! Slime eels!' the British shouted over from their dark-green houseboat.

'Monarchists! Atheists! Crust cutters!' Max called back in a voice that was shrill from crying and blew his nose a few times to give his words extra force.

When Perdu had turned the *Literary Apothecary* around far enough so that they were no longer stuck across the river but facing in the right direction, they heard applause. It came from three women in striped tops on a rented houseboat.

'Ahoy, you book paramedics. Doing some crazy cruising there!'

Perdu pulled on the lever that controlled the

horn and greeted the ladies' boat with three blasts. The women waved as they nonchalantly overtook the book barge.

'Follow those ladies, *mon capitaine*. Then we have to turn right at Saint-Mammès. Or starboard, as they say,' Max commented. He hid his eyes, red from crying, behind Madame Bomme's glittery sunglasses. 'When we get there, we'll find a branch of my bank and do some shopping. The mice are so hungry they're hanging themselves in your alphabetical cupboard.'

'Today's Sunday.'

'Oh. Well, expect more mouse suicides in that case.'

They tacitly agreed to act as though that moment of desperation had never taken place.

The more the day tended towards night, the greater the number of chattering birds that winged their way across the sky – grey geese, ducks and oystercatchers heading for their roosts on the sandbanks and the riverside. Perdu was fascinated by the thousand varieties of green he saw. All of this had been hiding all this time, and so close to Paris?

The men were approaching Saint-Mammès.

'Good grief,' murmured Perdu. 'There's a lot going on here.'

Boats of all sizes sporting pennants in dozens of national colours were packed side by side into the marina. Innumerable people were having meals on their boats – and without exception they were all staring at the big book barge.

Perdu was tempted to open up the throttle.

Max Jordan studied the map. 'You can travel in all directions from here: north to Scandinavia, south to the Mediterranean, east and up to Germany.' He looked over at the marina.

'It's like reversing into a parking space outside the only café in town at the height of summer with everyone watching – even the queen of the ball, her rich fiancé and his gang.'

'Thanks, that makes me feel a lot more relaxed.'

Perdu steered *Lulu* gradually towards the harbour at the lowest possible speed.

All he needed was a space, a very big space.

And he found it. Right at the end of the harbour, where only one boat was moored. A dark-green British narrow boat.

He succeeded at the second attempt, and they only briefly bumped against the English boat, relatively gently.

An angry man stormed out of the cabin brandishing a half-empty wine glass. The other half of the wine had landed on his dressing gown. Along with the potatoes. And the sauce.

'What the devil have we done to make you keep attacking us like this?' he shouted.

'Sorry,' called Perdu. 'We . . . um . . . you don't like reading by any chance?'

Max took the book of knots out onto the landing stage. There he tried to tie up the boat with stern lines and a forward spring around the mooring posts, as explained by the book's illustrations. He took a long time over it and refused any assistance.

In the meantime, Perdu picked out a handful of novels in English and offered them to the Briton. He flicked through them and gave Perdu a brisk handshake.

'What did you give him?' whispered Max.

'Some literary relaxation from the library of moderately intense emotions,' Perdu murmured back. 'Nothing cools anger like a nice splatter book, where the blood almost spurts off the page.'

As Perdu and Jordan walked along the pontoon towards the harbour office, they felt like boys who had kissed a girl for the first time and had come through it with their lives intact and an unbelievable thrill.

The harbourmaster, a man with leathery skin like an iguana's, showed them where the charging points, the fresh water supply and the waste tank were. He also demanded fifteen euros as an advance on the mooring fee. There was no option: Perdu had to smash the little porcelain kitten he kept on his register for tips; the odd coin had found its way through the slit between its ears.

'Your son can go ahead and empty your toilet tank – it's free of charge.'

Perdu let out a deep sigh. 'Sure. My . . . *son* particularly likes doing the toilet.'

Jordan threw him a less-than-friendly look.

Jean looked after Max as he set off with the

harbourmaster to connect the pipes to the waste tank. What a spring there was in young Jordan's step! He had all his hair – and he could presumably eat vast quantities without worrying about his tummy or his hips. But did he realise that he still had a whole lifetime ahead of him to commit some monumental mistakes?

Oh no, I wouldn't want to be twenty-one again, thought Jean – or only with the same knowledge he had today.

Oh, dammit. Nobody would ever wise up if they hadn't at some stage been young and stupid.

Yet the more he thought about all the things he no longer possessed compared with Jordan, the more fretful he became. It was as if the years had trickled through his fingers like water – the older he got, the quicker it went. And before he knew it, he'd need tablets for high blood pressure and a flat on the ground floor.

Jean had to think of Vijaya, his childhood friend. His life had been very similar to Perdu's – until he lost his love and the other found it.

In the summer month when Manon had left Perdu, Vijaya had found his future wife, Kiraii, in a car accident; he had driven around the Place de la Concorde for hours at walking pace, not daring to cross the lanes thick with traffic to exit the roundabout. Kiraii was a worldly wise, warm-hearted and determined woman with firm ideas of how she wanted to live. Vijaya had found it easy to step into her life. The short space of time from

9 a.m. to 6 p.m. sufficed for his own plans: he remained a director of scientific research, specialising in the structure and reactivity of human cells and their sensory receptors. He wanted to know why a person felt love when he or she ate something specific, why smells conjured up long-buried childhood memories, why one grew fearful of feelings, what made one feel disgust for slime and spiders, and how the body's cells behaved when a human was human.

'So you're searching for the soul,' Perdu had said during one of their nocturnal phone calls at the time.

'No, sir. I'm searching for the mechanism. It's all about action and reaction. Aging, fear and sex all govern your ability to feel. You drink a coffee, and I can explain why you like the taste. You fall in love, and I'll tell you why your brain acts like an obsessional neurotic's,' Vijaya had explained to Perdu.

Kiraii had proposed to the shy biologist, and Perdu's friend had mumbled yes, stunned to the core by his luck. He must surely have thought of his sensory receptors, spinning like disco balls. He moved to America with the pregnant Kiraii, and sent Perdu regular photos of his twin sons – first as prints, then as email attachments. They were sporty, candid-looking young men who smiled at the camera with a hint of mischief, and they resembled their mother, Kiraii. They were Max's age.

144

How differently Vijaya had spent these twenty years!

Max, writer, earmuff wearer and future interpreter of dreams. My decreed 'son.' Am I so old I look like a father? And . . . what would be so bad about that?

Here, in the middle of the river marina, Monsieur Perdu felt an enormous longing for a family, for someone who would remember him with fondness, for a chance to go back to the moment he'd decided not to read the letter.

And you denied Manon exactly the thing you long for: you refused to remember her, to speak her name, to think of her every day with affection and love. Instead you banished her. Shame on you, Jean Perdu. Shame on you for choosing fear.

'Fear transforms your body like an inept sculptor does a perfect block of stone,' Perdu heard Vijaya's voice say inside him. 'It's just that you're chipped away at from within, and no one sees how many splinters and layers have been taken off you. You become ever thinner and more brittle inside, until even the slightest emotion bowls you over. One hug, and you think you're going to shatter and be lost.'

If Jordan ever needed a piece of fatherly advice, Perdu would tell him: 'Never listen to fear! Fear makes you stupid.'

CHAPTER 19

'What now?' asked Max Jordan after they had done some reconnaissance.

Both the little food shop at the marina and the *crêperie* at the neighbouring campsite had refused to accept books as currency. Their suppliers worked; they didn't read.

'White beans with heart and chicken,' Perdu said.

'Oh no. I'd have to have a lobotomy to enjoy white beans.'

Max let his eyes wander over the marina. Everywhere people were sitting out on deck, eating, drinking and engaging in lively conversation.

'We'll have to crash someone's party,' he decided. 'I'll wangle us an invitation. Maybe that nice British gent?'

'Certainly not. That's sponging. That's . . .'

But Max was already on his way towards one particular houseboat.

'Ahoy, ladies!' he called. 'Our food supplies unfortunately fell in the water, and the catfish ate them. You couldn't spare a lump of cheese for two lonely travellers, could you?'

Perdu was so ashamed he wished the ground

would open up and swallow him. You co[...]
around chatting up women like that! Esp[...]
when you needed help. It wasn't . . . *right.*

'Jordan,' he hissed and grabbed the young ma[...]
by the sleeve of his blue shirt. 'Please, I don't like
this. We shouldn't disturb the ladies.'

Max gave him the kind of look people had
always given Jean and Vijaya when they were
young. The two of them had been as happy
among books as two apples on a tree, but around
people, and women and girls in particular, the
teenagers were shy to the point of being tongue-
tied. Parties were a torment – and talking to girls
equivalent to hara-kiri.

'Look, Monsieur Perdu. We want some dinner
and we'll pay them back with our amusing company
and some harmless flirting.'

With a grin, he studied Perdu's face. 'Remember
what that is? Or is it buried in a book where it
can't bother you?'

Jean didn't answer. It seemed inconceivable to
young men that women could drive you to despair.
Growing older and gaining deeper knowledge of
women only made things worse. The flaws a
woman could find in a man were many. She would
start with the state of your shoes and work her
way up to your inattentive ears – and it didn't stop
there.

The things he had heard as he sat in on the
clinic he ran for parents! Women would giggle
with their friends for years about a man who

the right way or wore the wrong
...ould mock his teeth and his hair
...e proposal.

beans are delicious,' said Perdu.
it. When did you last go on a

...ineteen ninety-two.' Or the day before yesterday,
but Perdu didn't know whether dinner with Catherine
qualified as a 'date'. Or more. Or less.

'Nineteen ninety-two? The year I was born.
That's incredible.' Jordan thought for a second.
'Okay. I promise it won't be a date. We're going
to dinner with some intelligent women. All you
need is to have a couple of compliments and some
topics that will appeal to women up your sleeve.
That shouldn't be too hard for a bookseller like
you. Throw in the odd literary reference.'

'All right, fine,' said Perdu. He straddled the low
fence, hurried into a nearby field and dashed back
with an armful of summer flowers.

'Here's a different kind of reference.'

The three women in Breton jerseys were Anke,
Corinna and Ida, all Germans in their mid-forties
who loved books. Their French was sketchy and
they were travelling the waterways 'to forget', as
Corinna put it.

'Really? Forget what? Not men, by any chance?'
asked Max.

'Not all men. One particular man,' said Ida. Her
mouth, framed in her freckled face like a twenties
film star's, opened in laughter, but only for a

couple of heartbeats. Under her ginger curls her eyes brimmed with both sorrow and hope.

Anke was stirring a Provençal risotto. The aroma of mushrooms filled the small galley as the men sat out on *Baloo*'s afterdeck with Ida and Corinna, drinking red wine from a three-litre box and a bottle of mineral-tasting local Auxerrois.

Jean admitted that he understood German, every book-seller's first language. So they conversed in a merry mishmash; he answered in French and asked them questions in a colourful combination of sounds that bore at least some relation to German.

It was as if he had passed through a gate of fear and had realised to his surprise that behind it lay not a gaping chasm, but other doors, bright hallways and inviting rooms. He tilted his head back and what he saw above him moved him deeply: the sky. It was unencumbered by houses, telegraph poles and lights, and scattered with dense clusters of sparkling stars of every size and intensity. The lights were so profuse that it looked as if a meteor shower had rained down on the roof of the heavens. It was a sight no Parisian could ever witness without leaving the city.

And there was the Milky Way. Perdu had first glimpsed this smeary veil of stars as a boy, bundled up warmly in a jacket and blanket in a buttercup meadow near the Brittany coast. He had stared up into the blue-black night sky for hours while his parents tried once more to save their marriage at a Breton *fest-noz* party in Pont-Aven. Every time there was a shooting star, Jean Perdu made a wish that Lirabelle Bernier and Joaquin Perdu might again laugh with each other rather than at each other, that they would dance a gavotte to the sound of the bagpipes, the violin and the bandoneon instead of standing stony-faced, arms crossed, on the edge of the dance floor.

Young Jean had gazed out into the depths of space, watching in raptures as the heavens continued to turn. He had felt safe, ensconced in the heart of that endless summer night. For those few hours Jean Perdu had grasped life's secrets and purposes. He had been at peace with himself, everything in its rightful place. He had known that nothing ever ends, that everything in life flows into everything else and that he could do no wrong.

As a man, he had only once felt as intensely: with Manon.

Manon and he had sought out the stars, venturing further and further from the cities into the darkest corner of Provence. In the mountains around Sault they discovered remote farmsteads that were hidden away in stone sinkholes and rocky ravines bristling with thyme bushes. Only there did the summer night sky display itself in full clarity and depth.

'Did you know we're all children of the stars?' Manon had asked, her warm lips snug to his ear so as not to break the mountain silence.

'When the stars imploded billions of years ago,

iron and silver, gold and carbon came raining down. And the iron from that stardust is in us today – in our mitochondria. Mothers pass on the stars and their iron to their children. Who knows, Jean, you and I might be made of the dust from one and the same star, and maybe we recognised each other by its light. We were searching for each other. We are star seekers.'

He had looked up and wondered if they could see the light of the dead star that lived on inside them.

Manon and he had chosen one twinkling celestial dot – a star that was still shining, although it had conceivably disappeared long ago.

'Death means nothing, Jean. We'll forever be what we once were for each other.'

The celestial pearls were reflected in the Yonne River. Dancing on the river, each star rocked alone, making gentle contact only when the waves met and, for the briefest instant, two dots of light came together.

Jean could no longer find their star.

When Perdu glanced at Ida and noticed that she was watching him, they were not man and woman but two travellers, each on a specific quest.

Perdu saw Ida's pain flickering in her eyes, saw that the red-haired woman was struggling to embrace a new future that felt even now like a second choice. She had been abandoned, or had left before she was rejected. The presence of the person who had been her pole star, and for whom she'd presumably forsworn many things, lingered over her smile like a veil.

All of us preserve time. We preserve the old versions of the people who have left us. And under our skin, under the layer of wrinkles and experience and laughter, we, too, are old versions of ourselves. Directly below the surface, we are our former selves: the former child, the former lover, the former daughter.

Ida was not looking for comfort on these rivers; she was looking for herself, for her place in this new, unfamiliar, second-class future. On her own.

'And you?' her face asked. 'And you, stranger?'

Perdu knew only that he wanted to reach Manon to ask her forgiveness for his vain and foolish act.

Then Ida suddenly said quietly, 'I really didn't want to be free. I didn't want to have to build a new life; I was fine as I was. Maybe I didn't love my husband the way people love in books. But it wasn't bad. Not bad is good enough. It is enough to stay. Not to cheat. Not to have any regrets. No, I don't regret the small love of my life.'

Anke and Corinna gazed tenderly at their friend, and Corinna asked, 'Is that an answer to my question yesterday about why you hadn't left him long ago if he wasn't your big love?'

Small love. Big love. Wasn't it terrible that love came in several sizes?

When Jean looked at Ida, who had no regrets about her previous life, he hesitated, but went ahead and asked: 'And . . . what did *he* think of your time together?'

'Our small love wasn't enough for him after twenty-five years. He's found his big love now. She's seventeen years younger than me and very flexible: she can polish her toenails holding the brush in her mouth.'

Corinna and Anke snorted with laughter, and Ida joined in.

Later they had a game of cards. At midnight a radio station started to play swing: the Benny Goodman Sextet's cheerful 'Bei Mir Bist Du Schoen,' dreamy 'Cape Cod' and then Louis Armstrong's melancholy 'We Have All the Time in the World'.

Max Jordan danced with Ida – or at least shuffled his feet – and Corinna and Anke danced with each other. Jean stuck to his chair.

The last time he had heard these songs Manon was still alive.

What a terrible thought: 'She was still alive.'

When Ida noticed Perdu battling for composure, she whispered something to Max and stepped away from him.

'Come on,' she said to Jean, opening her arms to him. He was glad he did not to have to confront these familiar tunes, and the many memories they evoked, on his own.

He remained bewildered that Manon was gone, while the songs, the books and life itself simply carried on.

How could they?

How could it all just . . . carry on?

How afraid he was of death – and life. Of all the days without Manon that lay ahead.

Every song conjured up images of Manon walking and lying and reading, dancing by herself, dancing for him. He saw her sleeping and dreaming and stealing his favourite cheese from his plate.

'Is that why you wanted to spend the rest of your life without music? Oh, Jean! You loved music so much. You sang for me when I was scared of falling asleep and missing out on time with you. You composed songs on my fingers and toes and nose. You're musical to the core, Jean – how could you kill yourself like this?'

Yes, how could he. Practice, that's how.

Jean felt the wind's caress and heard the women's laughter. He was slightly tipsy – and overwhelmed with silent gratitude to Ida for holding him.

Manon loved me. And together we watched the stars above.

CHAPTER 20

He dreamed he was awake.

He was on the book barge, but everything around him kept changing. The wheel shattered, the windows misted up, the rudders failed. The air was thick, as though he were wading through rice pudding. And Perdu again lost his way in the maze of watery tunnels. The boat creaked and ripped apart.

Manon was standing by his side.

'But you're dead,' he groaned.

'Am I really?' she asked. 'What a shame.'

The ship broke up, and he plunged into the water.

'Manon!' he screamed. She watched as he fought against the current, against a whirlpool that had formed in the black water. She watched him. She didn't reach out to him, just watched him drown.

He sank and sank.

But he didn't wake up.

Very deliberately, he breathed in and out – and in and out again.

I can breathe underwater!

Then he touched the bottom.

At that moment Monsieur Perdu woke up. He was lying on his side, and opening his eyes he saw a halo of light dancing over Lindgren's red-and-white fur. The cat was lounging next to his feet. She got up, stretched and then, purring, meandered up to Jean's face and tickled him with her whiskers. 'So?' her expression seemed to say. 'What did I tell you?' Her purring was as soft as the distant hum of a boat engine.

He remembered waking with this same anxious amazement once as a boy, the first time he had dreamed of flying. He had jumped off a rooftop and sailed with outspread arms into a castle court-yard. And he had found out that if he wanted to fly, he first had to jump.

He climbed out on deck. Mist drifted, as white as cobwebs, over the river, and steam rose from the nearby meadows. The light was still young, the day had just been born. He revelled in the sight of so much sky and in the huge variety of colours around him. The white mist, grey outlines, subtle pinks and milky orange.

A sleepy silence lay over the craft in the marina. Over on the *Baloo* all was quiet.

Jean Perdu crept down to check on Max. The author had bedded down among the books on one of the reading couches in the section that Perdu had christened How to Become a Real Person. One book was by the divorce therapist Sophie Marcelline, a colleague of his regular Friday customer, the therapist Eric Lanson. Sophie's advice on relationship troubles was a month's mourning for every year the couple had been together, and two months for each year of friendship when friends fell out. And for those who left us for good – the dead – 'a lifetime, because our love for our dearly departed goes on forever. We miss them until the very last day of our lives.'

Beside the sleeping Max, who was curled up like a little boy, knees tucked into his chest, mouth pursed into a surprised pout, lay Sanary's *Southern Lights*. Perdu picked up the slim volume. Max had underlined certain sentences in pencil and jotted some questions in the margins; he had read the book as a book ought to be read.

Reading – an endless journey; a long, indeed never-ending journey that made one more temperate as well as more loving and kind. Max had set out on that journey. With each book he would absorb more of the world, things and people.

Perdu began leafing through the book. He had loved this particular passage too: 'Love is a house. Everything in a house should be used – nothing mothballed or "spared". Only if we fully inhabit a house, shunning no room and no door, are we truly alive. Arguing and touching each other tenderly are both important; so are holding each other tight and pushing the other away. We must use absolutely every one of love's rooms. If not, ghosts and rumours will thrive. Neglected rooms and houses can become treacherous and foul . . .'

Does love resent my refusal to open the door to that room and . . . do what exactly? What should I do? Build a shrine to Manon? Bid her farewell? What? Tell me, what am I meant to do?

Jean Perdu replaced the book next to the sleeping Max. After a while, he pushed the hair from the young man's brow.

Then he quietly picked out a few books. Using them as currency didn't come easily to him, for he knew their true worth. A bookseller never forgets that books are a very recent means of expression in the broad sweep of history, capable of changing the world and toppling tyrants.

Whenever Monsieur Perdu looked at a book, he did not see it purely in terms of a story, retail price and an essential balm for the soul; he saw freedom on wings of paper.

A little later he borrowed a bike from Anke, Ida and Corinna and rode out to the nearest village along winding, empty, narrow roads, past fields, paddocks and pastures.

At the *boulangerie* on the church square a cheerful, ruddy-cheeked baker's daughter was taking baguettes and croissants out of the oven.

She looked happy to be where she was: in a small bakery that saw boaters in summer and farmers, winemakers, tradesmen, butchers and city dropouts from Burgundy, the Ardennes and the Champagne region the rest of the year. Now and then a dance at the mill, harvest festivals, cooking contests and local history societies; a spot of cleaning and laundry for the artists who lived in converted sheds and stables dotted around the area – this was life in the peace of the countryside beneath glittering stars and red summer moons.

Could that be sufficient for a fulfilling existence?

Perdu took a deep breath when he stepped into the old-fashioned shop. He had no choice but to make his customary offer.

'*Bonjour, Mademoiselle.* Excuse me for asking, but do you like reading?' After some haggling, she 'sold' him a newspaper, stamps and a few post-cards of the marina at Saint-Mammès, as well as some baguettes and croissants, in exchange for a single book: *The Enchanted April,* about four English ladies who run away to an Italian paradise.

'That covers my costs,' she innocently assured him. Then she opened the book, held it to her nose and took a long sniff of the pages. Her face reappeared, glowing with contentment.

'It smells of *crêpes*, I think.' She stowed the book away in her apron pocket. 'My father says that reading makes you impudent.' She smiled apologetically.

Jean sat down by the church fountain and tore into a warm croissant. How it steamed, how fragrant was its soft, golden inside. He ate slowly and watched the village awaken.

Reading makes you impudent. Oh yes, unknown father, so it does.

Perdu wrote a few cautious lines to Catherine.

Fully aware that Madame Rosalette would read the card anyway, he decided that he might as well address it to everyone.

> Dear Catherine, dear Mme. Rosalette (New hairstyle? Wonderful! Mocha?), my esteemed Mme Bomme and all at number 27,
> Until further notice, please order your books from Voltaire et plus. I haven't abandoned or forgotten you, but there are a few incomplete chapters I need to read first . . . and finish. I'm off to tame my ghosts. JP

Was that too sparse, not flashy enough?

His thoughts raced over the fields and the river to Paris, to Catherine's laughter and her moans of pleasure. He felt a sudden flood of emotion. He was struggling to identify the source of this surge of longing to be touched, of this yearning for physical contact, nakedness and warmth under shared covers; a longing for friendship, for a home and a place where he could stay and be fulfilled. Did it come from Manon? Or Catherine? He was ashamed when he allowed them to intermingle in his mind. And yet: it had done him so much good to be with Catherine. Should he stop himself? Was that wrong?

I wanted never to need anyone again. I'm such a coward.

Monsieur Perdu cycled back, flanked by buzzards and larks that hung high in the air and hovered on the breeze over the wheat fields. He felt the wind through his shirt.

He felt he was returning to the barge a different man from the one who had set out an hour earlier.

He hung on the handlebars of Ida's bike a bag containing warm croissants, a bunch of freshly picked red poppies and three copies of *Night*, in which Max had written lengthy dedications before going to bed.

Then he made coffee in the pot in his galley, fed the cats, checked the humidity in the bookshop (satisfactory) and the oil level (near critical), and prepared *Lulu* for cast-off.

As the book barge slid out onto the pristine river, Perdu saw Ida appear on the aft deck of the *Baloo*. He waved until he had rounded a bend. He wished with all his heart that Ida would one day find a big love to make up for losing her small one.

He calmly steered the ship into the morning light. The coolness in the air gave way to the silky warmth of summer.

'Did you know that Bram Stoker dreamed up his *Dracula*?' Jean Perdu asked an hour later, full of cheer, as Max reached gratefully for a mug.

'Dreamed of Dracula? Where are we – in Transylvania?'

'On the Canal du Loing heading towards the Canal de Briare. We're following the Bourbonnais route you chose, which will take us to the Mediterranean.' Perdu sipped his coffee. 'All because of some crab salad. Stoker had eaten some rotten crab and contracted food poisoning. Between bouts of sickness he had his first dreams about the lord of the vampires. They marked the end of his creative slump.'

'Really? Well, I didn't dream up a bestseller,' mumbled Max, dunking his croissant in his coffee, making sure not to let a single crumb escape. 'I wanted to read my book, but the letters kept sliding off the page.' Then he perked up. 'Do you think an attack of indigestion would help me come up with a story?'

'Who knows?'

'*Don Quixote* started out as a nightmare before it became a classic. Did *you* dream of anything useful?'

'That I could breathe underwater.'

'Wow. You know what that means?'

'That I can breathe underwater in my dreams.'

Max curled his top lip into an Elvis smile, then said solemnly, 'No. It means you're no longer choked by your emotions. Especially not down there.'

'"Down there"? Where's that from? The 1905 Good Housewives calendar?'

'Nope. From the *1992 Compendium of Dream Interpretation.* That was my bible. My mother blacked out the bad words with a marker. I used it to interpret everyone's dreams: my parents', the neighbours', my classmates' – I knew Freud inside out.'

Jordan was doing a few stretches and tai chi exercises. 'It got me into trouble, particularly when

I interpreted the headmistress's dream about horses. I'm telling you, women and horses are something else.'

'That's what my father always says.'

Perdu recalled that when he was getting to know Manon, he had had dreams in which she turned into a female eagle. He tried to catch and tame her. He would chase her into the water because when her wings were wet, she couldn't escape.

We are immortal in the dreams of our loved ones. And our dead live on after their deaths in our dreams. Dreams are the interface between the worlds, between time and space.

As Max stuck his head out into the breeze to blow the sleep from his eyes, Perdu said, 'Look, that's our first lock up ahead.'

'What? That baby's bath next to the dollhouse all covered in flowers? We'll never fit in there.'

'Just you wait and see.'

'We're too long.'

'This is a *péniche* and smaller than the Freycinet standard all French locks are built to.'

'Not this one. It's too narrow.'

'We're 5.04 metres wide, which leaves at least 6 centimetres, 3 to the right and 3 to the left.'

'I feel sick.'

'Imagine how I feel. Because you're going to operate the locks.'

The two men looked at each other and burst out laughing.

★　★　★

The lock-keeper impatiently beckoned them forward. His dog planted its legs wide and snarled at the boat; meanwhile, the lock-keeper's wife brought out some freshly baked plum tart and let them keep the plate in return for the latest John Irving.

'And a kiss from the young writer there.'

'Give her another book, Perdu, I beg you,' Jordan hissed. 'That woman's got a beard.'

She insisted on a peck on the cheek.

The lock-keeper called his wife an ogress while their shaggy blond dog barked himself hoarse and peed on Max's hand as he held on to the ladder. In return, the exasperated lock-keeper's wife berated her husband for being a show-off and an amateur janitor. He irritably shouted, 'Bring her in!'

Wind the left lock gate shut, walk around, wind the right lock gate shut. Walk forward, open the upper lock barriers on both sides – water runs in. Open the right lock gate, walk around, open the top left one.

'Take her out now!' The lock-keeper was stern and could probably bark this order in twelve different languages.

'How many locks left before the Rhône?'

'About a hundred and fifty. Why do you want to know, Jordan?'

'We should take the canal between Champagne and Burgundy on the way back.'

Way back? thought Perdu. *There is no way back.*

CHAPTER 21

The Loing Canal ran level with the surrounding countryside. They saw the occasional single-minded cyclist, dozing angler or lonely jogger on the towpath. Meadows where sturdy white Charolais cattle grazed and fields of sunflowers alternated with lush woodland. Sometimes a car driver would give them a friendly honk of his horn. The small villages they passed had good moorings, many of them free of charge and vying for boats to tie up so that the crew would spend their money in the local shops.

Then the landscape changed. The canal was higher now, and they could look down into people's gardens.

By the time they had entered the Champagne region with its many fisheries, Max was operating the locks almost like an old pro. An increasing number of side channels flowed off from the canal into lakes. Gulls rose shrieking from patches of reeds and clumps of bulrushes and wheeled inquisitively over the waterborne *Literary Apothecary*.

'What's the next major mooring place?' asked Perdu.

'Montargis. The canal flows right through the town centre.' Max flicked through the house-boating book. 'The flower-filled town where pralines were invented. We should look for a bank there. I'd kill for a piece of chocolate.'

And I'd do the same for some detergent and a fresh shirt.

Max had washed their shirts with liquid hand soap, so they both smelled of rose potpourri.

Then a thought struck Perdu. 'Montargis? We should pay a visit to P. D. Olson first.'

'Olson? *The* P. D. Olson? Do you know him too?'

'Know' was too strong a word. Jean Perdu had been a young bookseller when Per David Olson was being talked about as a potential Nobel laureate for literature – along with Philip Roth and Alice Munro.

How old would Olson be now? Eighty-two? He'd moved to France thirty years ago. *La grande nation* appealed to this descendant of a Viking clan a lot more than his American homeland did.

'A nation that has less than a thousand years of culture to look back on, no myths, no superstition, no collective memories, values or sense of shame; nothing but pseudo-Christian warrior morals, deviant wheat, an amoral arms lobby, and rampant sexist racism' – those were the words of a *New York Times* article in which he had laid into the United States before leaving the country.

However, the most interesting thing about P. D. Olson was that his was one of eleven names on

166

Jean Perdu's list of possible authors of Sanary's *Southern Lights*. And P.D. lived in Cepoy, a village on the canal just this side of Montargis.

'So what do we do? Ring his doorbell and say, "Hi, P.D., old buddy, did you write *Southern Lights*?"'

'Exactly. What else?'

Max puffed out his cheeks. 'Well, any normal person would write an email,' he said.

Jean Perdu had to restrain himself from making a remark that smacked of 'we had to walk to school uphill both ways, and things were still better than now.'

In place of a harbour, Cepoy had two large iron rings in the grass, through which they pulled the *Literary Apothecary*'s ropes taut.

Soon afterwards the owner of the waterside youth hostel – a sunburned man with a red bulge on the back of his neck – directed them to the old rectory where P. D. Olson lived.

They knocked on the door, and it was opened by a woman straight out of a Pieter Bruegel painting. A flat face, hair like coarse flax on the spindle, a white lace collar on a plain grey smock. She said neither 'Hello' nor 'What do you want?' nor even 'We don't buy from door-to-door salesmen'; she simply opened the door and waited in silence – a silence as hard as stone.

'*Bonjour, Madame*. We'd like to see Monsieur Olson,' said Perdu after a pause.

'He doesn't know we're coming,' added Max.

'We've come by boat from Paris. Unfortunately, we don't have a phone.'

'Or any money.'

Perdu elbowed Max in the ribs. 'But that's not why we've come.'

'Is he at home?'

'I'm a bookseller and we met at a book fair once. In Frankfurt, in 1985.'

'I'm an interpreter of dreams. And an author. Max Jordan. Pleased to meet you. You wouldn't have any leftovers from yesterday's casserole? All we have on our boat is a tin of white beans and some Whiskas.'

'Plead all you like, gentlemen, but there'll be no forgiveness and no casserole,' they heard a voice say. 'Margareta has been deaf since her fiancé threw himself off a church tower. She tried to save him and got caught up in the midday bell ringing. She lip-reads only with people she knows. Damn church! Heaps misery on any who haven't already given up hope.'

Before them stood the notorious critic of America: P. D. Olson, a stunted Viking in a pair of rough cord trousers, a collarless shirt and a stripy waistcoat.

'Monsieur Olson, we do apologise for ambushing you like this, but we have an urgent question we—'

'Yes, yes. Of course, everything's urgent in Paris, but it's not the same here, gentlemen. Here time cuts its own cloth. Here the enemies of mankind toil in vain. Let's have a little drink and make

168

acquaintances first,' he said, inviting in his two visitors.

'The enemies of mankind?' Max said under his breath. He was obviously concerned that they might have run into a madman.

'You're regarded as a legend,' he tried by way of conversation when Olson had taken a hat from the coat-rack and they were striding along beside him towards the *bar tabac*.

'Don't call me a legend, young man. It makes me sound like a corpse.'

Max said nothing, and Jean Perdu decided to follow his example.

As Olson preceded them through the village, his gait betraying a stroke sometime in the past, he said, 'Look around! People here have been fighting for their homeland for centuries! Over there – do you see how the trees have been planted and the roofs tiled? See how the main roads give the village a wide berth? All part of a strategy that was centuries in the making. Nobody here thinks of the present.'

He greeted a man who came clattering past in a Renault with a goat in the passenger seat.

'Here they work and think for the future, always for those who will come after them. And then their descendants do the same. This land will be destroyed only if one generation stops thinking of the next and tries to change everything now.'

They reached the *bar tabac*. Inside, a TV over the bar was showing a horse race. Olson ordered three small glasses of red wine.

'A bet, the backwoods and a little booze. What more does a man need?' he said with pleasure.

'Anyway, we've got a question—' Max began.

'Easy, son,' said Olson. 'You smell of potpourri and look like a DJ with those earmuffs on. But I know you – you've written something. Dangerous truths. Not a bad start.' He clinked glasses with Jordan.

Max glowed with pride. Perdu felt a stab of jealousy.

'And you? Are you the literary apothecary?' Olson said, turning to him. 'What ailments do you prescribe my books for?'

'For retired husband syndrome,' Perdu answered, more pointedly than he had intended.

Olson stared at him. 'Aha. And how does that work?'

'When, after his retirement, a husband gets under a woman's feet so much that she feels like killing him, she can read your books and she'll feel like killing you instead. Your books are lightning conductors.'

Max looked perplexed. Olson pinned Perdu with his gaze – and erupted into gales of laughter.

'God, that brings it all back! My father was always getting in my mother's way and criticising her. Why do you have to peel the potatoes before cooking them? Welcome home, dear, I've done a little tidying in the fridge. Terrible. He'd been a workaholic and didn't have any hobbies. Fairly soon the boredom and lost dignity made him want to die, but my mum wouldn't let him. She kept sending him out with the grandchildren, to DIY courses and into the garden. I think she'd have ended up in jail for murder.' Olson chuckled. 'We men become a pain if our job's the only thing we were ever good at.' He drained his wine in three long swigs.

'Okay, drink up,' he said, leaving six euros on the counter. 'We're off.'

And because they hoped he would answer their question once he'd had a chance to listen, they, too, knocked back their wine and followed P.D. outside.

In a few minutes they reached the old schoolhouse. The playground was full of cars with registration numbers from all over the Loire region and from as far afield as Orléans and Chartres.

Olson marched purposefully towards the sports hall.

They entered and suddenly found themselves in central Buenos Aires.

Along the left-hand wall: the men. On the chairs to the right: the women. In the centre: the dance floor. At the front, where the climbing rings hung: a tango band. At the end where they were standing: a bar, behind which a short, very rotund man with bulging biceps and a bushy black moustache was serving drinks.

P. D. Olson turned and called over his shoulder, 'Dance! Both of you. Afterwards I'll answer whatever questions you like.'

A few seconds later, as the old man strode confidently across the dance floor towards a young woman with a severe ponytail and a slit skirt, he was utterly transformed into a lithe, ageless *tanguero* who pressed the young woman tightly to him and guided her gracefully around the hall.

While Max gawked at this unsuspected world, Monsieur Perdu grasped right away where he was. He had read about places like this in a book by Jac. Toes: secret tango *milongas* in school halls, gymnasiums or deserted barns. There dancers of all levels and ages and every nationality would meet up; some would drive hundreds of miles to savour these few hours. One thing united them: they had to keep their passion for the tango a secret from jealous partners and families who greeted these depraved, suggestive, frivolous moves with disgust and rigid, pinch-mouthed embarrassment. No one had a clue where the *tangueras* were at this time of the afternoon. They thought they were playing sport or attending a course, at a meeting or at the shops, in the sauna, out in the fields or at home. Yet they were dancing for their lives; they were dancing for life itself.

Few did it to meet their mistresses or lovers, for tango was not about that: it was about everything.

MANON'S TRAVEL DIARY

On the Way to Bonnieux

11 April 1987

For eight months I've known that I'm a very different woman from the girl who came to the north last August and was so scared that I wouldn't be capable of loving – twice.

It still comes as a huge shock to me to discover that love doesn't need to be restricted to one person to be true.

In May I'll marry Luc, beneath a thousand blossoms and amid the sweet scent that a new beginning and confidence bring.

I shall not break up with Jean; I shall, however, leave it up to him whether he does so with me, the voracious want-it-all.

Am I so terrified of transience that I need to experience everything immediately, just in case I'm struck down tomorrow?

Marriage. Yes? No? To question that would be to call everything into question.

I wish I were the light in Provence when the sun goes down. Then I could be everywhere, in every living thing. It would be who I am, and no one would hate me for it.

I must arrange my face before I arrive in Avignon. I hope it's Papa picking me up, not Luc, not Maman. Whenever I spend time in Paris, my features seek to adapt to the expressions urban creatures wear as they jostle past each other in the streets, as though oblivious to the fact that they're not alone. They are faces that say: 'Me? I don't want anything. I don't need anything. Nothing impresses me, nothing shocks me, surprises or even pleases me. Pleasure is for simpletons from the suburbs and from stinking cowsheds. They can be pleased. The likes of us have more important matters to attend to.'

But it's not my indifferent face that's the problem; it's my ninth face.

Maman says I've added it to my other ones. She has known my every gesture and facial expression since I entered this world as a wrinkly little grub. But Paris has transformed my face from my hair parting to the tip of my chin.

She must have noticed the last time I came home, while I was thinking of Jean, his mouth, his laugh, his 'you've got to read this, it'll do you good'.

'I'd be scared to have you for a rival,' she said. She was stunned that she'd blurted it out.

We've always dealt with truths in that direct, clear way. I learned as a girl that the best type of relationship was 'clear as mountain water'. I was taught that difficult thoughts lost their poison when spoken aloud.

I don't think that's always true.

My 'ninth face' unsettles Maman. I know what she means. I've seen it in Jean's mirror as he rubbed my back with a warm towel. Every time we see each other he takes a part of me out and warms it up so I don't wither like a frost-damaged lemon tree. He would be a father hen. My new face is sensual, but it hides behind a mask of self-control, which only makes it seem spookier to Maman.

Maman's still anxious for me. Her anxiety is practically infectious, and I think that should something happen to me, I want to have lived as intensely as possible up to that point, and I don't want to hear anyone complain.

She asks little, and I tell a lot – I give virtually a blow-by-blow account of my weeks in the capital and I hide Jean behind a beaded curtain of tinkling, brightly coloured, transparent minutiae, detail upon detail. Clear as mountain water.

'Paris has taken you further from us and closer to yourself, hasn't it?' says Maman, and when she says 'Paris', she knows I know she's got a man's name in mind, but I'm not prepared to tell her.

I never will be.

I am so foreign to myself. It's as if Jean had peeled back a shell to reveal a deeper, truer self who is reaching out to me with a mocking grin.

'So?' it says. 'Did you really think you were a woman without qualities?' (Jean says that quoting Musil's *The Man Without Qualities* is not a sign of intelligence, merely of a well-trained memory.)

But what exactly is happening to us?

This damned freedom! It means I have to be as silent as a tree stump about what I am up to while my family and Luc mistakenly imagine me in a seminar at the Sorbonne or working hard in the evenings. It means I have to control myself, destroy and hide myself in Bonnieux, and not expect anyone to take my confession or listen to the truth of my secret life.

I feel as if I'm sitting on top of Mount Ventoux, exposed to the sun, the rain and the horizon. I can see further and breathe more freely than ever before; but I am stripped of my defences. To be free is to lose one's certainty, says Jean.

But do I really know what I'm losing?

And do I really know what he's giving up by choosing me? He says he wants no other woman but me. It's enough that I'm leading two lives; he didn't want to do the same. Each time he makes things easy for me I could weep with gratitude. Never a reproach, barely a tricky question; he makes me feel that I'm a gift, not simply a bad person who makes too many demands on life.

If I confided in someone back home, he or she would be forced to lie with me and keep it secret and silent. I need to make it difficult for myself, not for others: those are the rules for the fallen.

Not once have I mentioned Jean's name. I'm worried that the way I say it could allow Maman, Papa or Luc to see straight through me.

Maybe each of them in their own way would show understanding. Maman, because she knows a woman's longings. They are there in all of us, even as small girls when we can hardly see over the table in the corner of the kitchen, and spend our time chatting to our long-suffering soft toys and wise ponies.

Papa, because he knows the animal lust that lurks inside us, would understand the wild, nourishing side to my behaviour; perhaps he would even recognise the biological instinct – like a potato's urge to germinate. (I'll ask him for help if I don't know what to do. Or Mamapapa, as Sanary wrote in a book that Jean read aloud to me.)

Luc would understand because he knows me, because it was his decision to stay with me even knowing I needed more. He always stands by his decisions: what's right is right, even if it hurts or later turns out to be wrong.

But what happens if I tell him about Jean, and thirty years from now he admits how badly I hurt him when I couldn't keep my mouth shut?

I know my future husband – he would spend many horrible hours and nights. He would look at me and see the other man over my shoulder. He would sleep with me and think: Is she thinking of him? Is it good, is it better with him? Whenever I talked to a man at the village fete or the Bastille Day procession, would he wonder: Is he the next one? When will she finally be satisfied? He would come to terms with it all on his own and wouldn't breathe a word of reproach to me. What was it he said? 'This is the only life we have. I want to spend mine with you, but without impeding yours.'

For Luc's sake too I must keep my mouth shut.

And for my sake – I want Jean all to myself.

I hate wanting all of this – it's more than I bargained for . . .

Oh, merciless freedom, you continue to overwhelm me! You demand that I challenge myself and feel ashamed, and yet continue to feel so outrageously proud to live a life full of my desires.

How I will enjoy looking back on all our experiences when I am old and can no longer touch my toes!

Those nights when we lay in the grass in the fort at Buoux, searching the stars. Those weeks when we turned wild in the Camargue. Oh, and those fabulous evenings when Jean introduced me to a life with books as we sprawled naked on the divan with Castor the cat, and Jean used my backside as a book rest. I didn't know there was such an infinite number of thoughts and marvels, and so much knowledge to be had. The world's rulers should be forced to take a reader's licence. Only when they have read five thousand – no, make that ten thousand – books will they be anywhere near qualified to understand humans and how they behave. I often felt better, no longer so bad, fake and unfaithful, when Jean read me bits where good people did nasty things out of love or necessity or their hunger for life.

'Did you think you were the only one, Manon?' he asked – and yes, it really did feel that awful, as if I were the only one unable to rein in my appetite.

Often when we've finished making love and haven't yet started again, Jean tells me about a book that he's read, wants to read or wants me to read. He calls books freedoms. And homes too. They preserve all the good words that we so seldom use.

Leniency. Kindness. Contradiction. Forbearance.

He knows so much; he is a man who

knows what it means to love selflessly. He lives when he loves. His confidence falters when he's loved. Is that why he feels so awkward? He has no idea what is where in his body! Grief, anxiety, laughter – where does it all come from? I'd press my fist into his tummy: 'Do your butterflies live here?' I'd blow under his belly button: 'Virility there?' I'd put my fingers to his neck: 'Tears here?' His body can be frozen, paralysed.

One evening we went out dancing. *Tango argentino*. A disaster! Jean was embarrassed and shunted me around, a little this way and a little that, practising the steps he'd learned in dance classes, but only using his hands. He was there, but he was not in control of his own body.

Impossible – not him, not this man! He wasn't like men from the north, from Picardy, Normandy or Lorraine, who suffer from a great sterility of the soul, though there are many women in Paris who find that erotic – as if it were a sexual challenge to elicit the tiniest of emotions from a man! That kind of woman imagines that somewhere within this coldness is a blazing passion that will spur him on to throw her over his shoulder and pin her to the floor. We had to break off. We went home, had a drink and tiptoed round the truth. He was exceptionally tender as, naked, we played like a tom and his puss. My despair knew no bounds. If I couldn't dance with him, then what?

I am my body. My pussy glistens when I feel desire, my chest perspires when I'm humiliated, and my fingers tingle with fear of my own courage; they quiver when I'm primed to protect and defend. When I ought to be afraid of real things, though – like the knot they found in my armpit and want to remove with a biopsy – I feel both bewildered and calm. My bewilderment makes me want to keep busy; but I'm calm, so calm that I don't wish to read serious books or listen to grand, sweeping music. All I want to do is sit here and watch the trickle of autumn light onto the red-golden leaves; I want to clean the fireplace; I want to lie down and sleep, exhausted by all these puzzling, insubstantial, ridiculous, fleeting thoughts. Yes, when I feel afraid I want to go to sleep – the soul's refuge from panic.

But what about him? When Jean dances, his body is a clothes stand with a shirt, trousers and a jacket hanging from it.

I stood up, he followed me, I slapped him.

A burning in my hand, a fire as though I'd reached into the embers.

'Hey!' he said. 'What's that for?'

I slapped him again; I had hot coals in my fingers now.

'Stop thinking! Feel!' I screamed at him.

I went over to the record player and put the 'Libertango' on for us. Accordion playing like the lashing of a whip, like blows from a riding crop or the crackling of branches in the fire. Piazzolla, driving the violins up into the heights.

'No, I—'

'Yes. Dance with me. Dance the way you feel! How do you feel?'

'I'm furious! You hit me, Manon!'

'Then dance furiously! Find the instrument in the piece that reflects your emotions and follow it! Grab me with the fury you feel for me!'

No sooner had I spoken these words than he seized me and pushed me up against the wall with both arms above my head, his grip firm, very firm. The violins wailed. We danced naked; he had chosen the violin as the instrument of his emotions. His rage turned to desire, then to tenderness, and when I bit and scratched him, resisted his lead and refused to take his hand – my lover became a *tanguero*. He returned to his body.

While I leaned against him, heart to heart, and he was making me feel what he felt for me, I saw our shadows dancing across the wall, across the walls of the Lavender Room. They were dancing in the window frame, they were dancing as one, and Castor the tomcat observed us and our shadows from the top of the wardrobe.

From that evening on we always danced tango – naked at first because it made the swaying and the coaxing and the holding easier. We danced, our hands on our own hearts. And then at some point we switched and laid our hand on the other's heart.

Tango is a truth drug. It lays bare your problems and your complexes, but also the strengths you hide from others so as not to vex them. It shows what a couple can be for each other, how they can listen to each other. People who only want to listen to themselves will hate tango.

Jean couldn't help feeling rather than escaping into abstract thoughts about dancing. He felt me: the fine hairs between my legs, my breasts. Never in all my life has my body felt so feminine as during those hours when Jean and I danced and then made love on the divan, on the floor, sitting on the chair, everywhere. He said, 'You are the source from which I flow when you are here, and I run dry when you leave.'

From then on we danced our way through the tango bars of Paris. Jean learned to transmit the energy from his body to mine and to show me which tango he wanted from me – and we learned the Spanish spoken in Argentina. Or at least the quiet poems and verses that a *tanguero* whispers to his *tanguera* to get her ready for . . . tango. The delicious, inexplicable games we began to play: we learned to address each other formally in the bedroom – and this polite address sometimes allowed us to request some very rude things.

Oh, Luc! With him I am differently – or less – desperate. But less natural too. From the very beginning I never lied to Jean. To Luc I don't express my desire for him to be harsher or more tender, more courageous or more playful. I'm ashamed because I want more than he can give. Or who knows:

maybe he could if only I asked for it? But how?

'Even when you dance with another woman, never betray the tango by holding back,' we were told by Gitano, a tango teacher at one of the bars.

He also proclaimed that Jean loved me, and I loved Jean. Gitano could see it in every step we took: we were one being. Maybe that's not so far from the truth?

I need to be with Jean because he's the male part of me. We look at each other and see the same thing.

Luc is the man whom I stand beside, and we look in the same direction. Unlike the tango teacher, we never talk about love.

Only the pure and the free may say, 'I love you'. Romeo and Juliet. But not Romeo, Juliet and Stephen.

We're in a constant race against time. We have to do everything at once; otherwise we'll get nothing done. We sleep together and talk about books at the same time, and in between we eat and are silent and argue and make up, dance and read aloud, sing and look for our lucky star – all at great speed. I long for next summer when Jean will come to Provence and we will search the stars.

I can see the Palais des Papes, glinting

golden in the sun. That light again, at last; at last, people who don't act as though no one else exists, not in lifts or in the street or on the bus. At last, fresh apricots from the tree again.

Oh, Avignon. I used to wonder why this city with its sinister palace, always cold and shady-looking, is so full of secret passages and trapdoors. Now I know. This restless lust has been with us since the dawn of mankind. Bowers, private rooms, theatre boxes, corn mazes – all designed for one and the same game!

Everyone knows this game is going on, but pretends it isn't, or at least is far away, harmless and unreal.

Yeah, really.

I can feel the burning shame in my cheeks; I can feel the longing in my knees; and the lie nestles between my shoulder blades and scrapes them sore.

Dear Mamapapa, please, don't make me have to choose between them.

And make the pea-sized lump in my armpit be just one of the grains of chalk that come trickling out of the taps up there in Valensole, home of the lavender and the world's most incorruptible cats.

CHAPTER 22

Monsieur Perdu sensed eyes brushing over him from under mascaraed lashes. If he caught, held and returned a woman's gaze, he would already be entangled in the *cabeceo*, the silent exchange of glances that was the currency of every tango negotiation: an 'invitation with the eyes'.

'Look down at the floor, Jordan. Don't look directly at a woman,' he whispered. 'If your eyes linger, she'll assume you're asking her whether you may invite her to dance. Can you dance *tango argentino*?'

'I was handy at freestyle fan routines.'

'*Tango argentino* is very similar. There are very few fixed step sequences. You touch chests, heart to heart, and then you listen to how the woman wants to be led.'

'Listen? But nobody's saying a word.'

It was true: none of the women or men or the couples on the dance floor were wasting their breath on talking, and yet they were so eloquent: 'Lead me more tightly! Not so fast! Give me some room! Let me entice you! Let's play!'

The women corrected the men: here a rub of the calf with the back of the shoe – 'Concentrate!'; there a stylised eight on the floor – 'I'm a princess!'

At other *milongas*, men would employ all their powers of persuasion during the four-dance sequence to arouse their partners' passion. In soft Spanish a man would whisper in his partner's ear, to her neck and into her hair, where the breath stirred the skin: 'I'm crazy for your tango. You're driving me wild with your dancing. My heart will set yours free to sing.'

Here, though, there were no tango whisperers. Here, everything was done with the eyes.

'Men run their eyes discreetly around the room,' said Perdu, whispering the rules of *cabeceo* to Max.

'How do you know all of this? From a—'

'No. Not from a book. Listen. Cast your eyes around slowly, but not too slowly. That's how you seek out the person with whom you want to dance the next *tanda* – the set of four pieces of music – or check if someone wants to dance with you. You ask them with a long, direct gaze. If it's answered, maybe with a nod or a half-smile, then you may consider your invitation accepted. If she looks away it means "No, thank you".'

'That's good,' Max said quietly. 'That "No, thank you" is so quiet that nobody has to worry about being embarrassed.'

'Exactly. It's a gallant gesture when you stand up to fetch your partner. On the way over you have time to make sure that she really did mean you . . . and not the man diagonally behind you.'

'What about after the dance? Do I invite her for a drink?'

'No. You escort her back to her seat, thank her and go back to the men's side. Tango doesn't commit you to anything. For three or four songs you share your yearnings, hopes and desires. Some people say it's like sex, only better – and more frequent. But then it's over. It would be totally improper to dance more than one *tanda* with a woman. It's considered bad manners.'

They watched the couples under lowered eyelids. After a while Perdu gestured with his chin to a woman who might have been anywhere between her early fifties and her late sixties. Black hair with some grey streaks, tied at the nape of her neck like a flamenco dancer's; a dress that looked new; three wedding rings on one finger. She had the poise of a ballerina and the slender, firm, supple figure of a young briar. A splendid dancer, secure and precise, and yet charitable enough to make up for her partner's lack of movement or meekness, disguising the man's flaws with her grace. She made everything look easy.

'She'll be your dance partner, Jordan.'

'Her? She's much too good. I'm scared!'

'Remember the feeling. Someday you'll want to write about it, and then it'll be good to know how the fear feels and to go ahead and dance all the same.'

As Max tried, half in panic, half pluckily, to attract the proud briar queen's gaze, Jean weaved his way to the bar, ordered a thimbleful of pastis in a glass and topped it up with the water. He was . . . excited. Extremely excited.

As though he were about to step out on stage.

How frantic he had been whenever he was due to meet Manon! His trembling fingers turned shaving into a bloodbath. He could never decide how to dress, wanting to look strong and slender and elegant and cool all at once. That was when he started running and doing weights to get himself in good shape for her.

Jean Perdu took a sip of pastis.

'*Grazie*,' he said on a hunch.

'*Prego, Signor Capitano*,' said the small, round, moustachioed bartender in a singsong Neapolitan accent.

'You flatter me. I'm not really a captain—'

'Oh yes, you are. Cuneo can see.'

Chart music was spilling out of the loudspeakers: the *cortina*, time for a change of partners. In thirty seconds the band would launch into the next *tanda*.

Perdu saw the briar dancer take pity and allow a pale Max, head held high, to lead her out into the middle of the dance floor. Within a few steps she bore herself like an empress, and this did something in turn to Max, who till then had merely been clinging to her outstretched arm. He took off his earmuffs and tossed them aside. He looked taller now, his shoulders broader, his chest puffed out like a torero's.

She shot Perdu a quick look with her bright, clear-blue eyes. Her gaze was young, her eyes were old, and her body sang the sweet, passionate song of the tango, beyond all notion of time. Perdu had tasted the *saudade* of life, a soft, warm feeling of sorrow – for everything, for nothing.

'Saudade': *a yearning for one's childhood, when the days would merge into one another and the passing of time was of no consequence. It is the sense of being loved in a way that will never come again. It is a unique experience of abandon. It is everything that words cannot capture.*

He should include it in his encyclopedia of emotions.

At that moment, P. D. Olson came over to the bar. The moment his feet and legs were no longer dancing, he reverted to walking like an old man.

'You have to dance the things you cannot explain,' Perdu said under his breath.

'And you have to write the things you cannot express,' the old novelist thundered.

As the band launched into 'Por una Cabeza', the briar dancer bent into Max's chest, her lips whispering incantations, and her hand, foot and hips subtly correcting his posture; she created the impression that he was leading her.

Jordan danced the tango, wide-eyed at first and then, following a whispered instruction, with lowered lids. Soon they looked like a well-grooved couple, the stranger and the young man.

P. D. nodded to Cuneo, the chubby barman, who advanced towards the dance floor. He seemed to grow lighter as he walked – light and wondrously gallant in his restrained, deferential movements. His dancing partner was taller than he was, and yet she moulded herself to him, brimming with trust.

P. D. Olson leaned closer to Perdu and whispered, 'What a magnificent literary figure this Salvatore Cuneo is. He came to Provence as a harvest worker, to pick cherries, peaches, apricots – anything that requires delicate handling. He worked with Russians and Moroccans and Algerians, then spent a night with a young river pilot. She disappeared back to her barge the next day. Something to do with the moon. Ever since, Cuneo has been scouring the rivers for her. It's been twenty years. He works awhile here, awhile there, and he can now turn his hand to almost anything – especially cooking. But he can also paint, repair a fuel tank and cast horo-scopes; whatever you need done, he can do it. And if he can't, he learns in a flash. The man's a genius in the guise of a Neapolitan *pizzaiolo*.' P. D. Olson shook his head. 'Twenty years. Imagine that! And for a woman!'

'Why not? Can you think of a better cause?'

'You would say that, John Lost.'

'What? What did you call me, Olson?'

'You heard. Jean Perdu, John Lost, Giovanni Perduto . . . I've dreamed about you on occasion.'

'Did you write *Southern Lights*?'

'Have you danced?'

Jean Perdu downed the rest of his pastis.

Then he turned and surveyed the women in the room. Some looked away; others held his gaze . . . and one shot a glance at him. She was in her mid-twenties. Short hair, a small bust, firm muscles between her upper arms and her shoulders, and eyes blazing with a boundless hunger, as well as the boldness to assuage that hunger.

Perdu nodded to her. She stood up without a smile and walked halfway towards him – halfway minus exactly one step. She wanted to wrench that final step from him. She waited, a raging cat, coiled to pounce.

At the same instant the band finished its first song; and Monsieur Perdu strode towards the hungry cat woman.

Her face said 'Let battle commence!'

Her mouth demanded 'Subjugate me if you can, but don't you dare humiliate me. And woe betide you if you're too timid to challenge me. I'm soft, but I only feel that softness in the heat of passion. And I can protect myself!' said her small, firm hand, the quivering tension that held her body upright, and her thighs, which melded themselves to his.

She pressed against him from chest to toe – but when the first notes rang out, Jean transmitted his energy to her with a thrust of his solar plexus. He eased her down further and further until they both had one knee bent and the other leg stretched out to one side.

A murmur ran through the line of women, but it immediately ceased when Perdu pulled the young woman up, winding her free leg quickly and smoothly around his knee. The backs of their knees kissed gently. They were entwined as closely as otherwise only naked lovers could be.

Jean throbbed with long-dormant power. Could he still do it? Could he return to a body he had not used for so long? 'Don't think, Jean! Feel!'

Yes, Manon.

Manon had taught him not to think during love-making, foreplay, dancing and conversations about emotions. She'd called him 'typically northern' because he tried to hide his bad moods from her behind stock phrases and a poker face, because he paid too much attention to what was proper during sex. And because he would pull and push Manon across the dance floor like a shopping trolley instead of dancing the way he wanted to – as the impetus of his will, reactions and desire dictated.

Manon had cracked open this stiff outer casing like a nut, with her hands, her bare hands, her bare fingers, her bare legs . . .

She freed me from my misanthropy, silence and inhibitions. From my compulsion to only make the right moves.

They say that men who are at one with their bodies can sense and smell when a woman wants more from life than she is getting. The girl in his arms longed for a stranger, for a permanent traveller: he could smell it as he felt her heart beating against his chest. The unknown man who rides into town and gives her one night of adventure, laying at her feet all the things she cannot find in this village, lost among silent wheat fields and ancient woodlands. This is her only means of protest, of ensuring she does not become bitter in this rural idyll where only land, family and offspring matter, never her, never her alone.

Jean Perdu gave the young woman what she desired. He held her the way no young carpenter, winemaker or forester ever would. He danced with her body and with her womanhood unlike any of the people for whom she was plain 'Marie, the daughter of the old blacksmith who shoes our nags'.

Jean put the full force of his body, breath and concentration into every gesture. He whispered to her in the language of tango, which Manon and he had learned and murmured to each other in bed. They had addressed each other formally, the way traditional elderly married couples in Spain had in days gone by, and whispered lascivious words to each other.

Everything merged into one – the past, the present, this young woman and the other one called Manon; the young man he had once been, with no inkling of the man he could become; the not-yet-old but nonetheless older man, who had nearly forgotten what it was like to desire and to hold a woman in his arms.

And here he was in the arms of a cat woman who loved to fight, be vanquished and then return to the fray.

Manon, Manon, this is how you danced. With the hunger to make something entirely your own, without the burden of your family and the land of your ancestors on your shoulders. Just you; no future, you and the tango. You and I, your lips, my lips, your tongue, my skin, my life, your life.

As the third song, the 'Libertango', struck up, the fire escape doors burst open.

'Here they are, the swines!' Perdu heard an incensed male voice shout.

CHAPTER 23

Five men barged their way through the door. The women screamed.

The first intruder was already tearing Cuneo's partner from his arms and making as if to slap her. The burly Italian caught his arm, upon which a second man threw himself at Cuneo and punched him in the stomach, allowing the other to drag the woman away.

'Betrayed,' hissed P. D. Olson, as he and Jean Perdu guided the cat woman away from the frenzied mob of men, who reeked of alcohol.

'That's my father,' she gasped, turning ghostly pale, and pointing to an axe-wielding maniac with eyes that were too close together.

'Don't look at him! Go out that door ahead of me!' ordered Perdu.

Max was fending off a pair of furious guys who saw Cuneo as the instigator of their wives', daughters' and sisters' satanic sex games. Salvatore Cuneo had a split lip. Max kicked one of the assailants in the knee, and threw the other on his back with a kung fu move. Then he hurried back to the briar dancer, who was standing motionless and proud amid the chaos. Max bowed and kissed her hand with a flourish.

'I'd like to thank you, queen of this incomplete night, for the most wonderful dance of my life.'

'Hurry up or it will be your last,' called P. D., seizing Max's arm.

Perdu saw the queen smile as she watched Max go. She picked up his earmuffs and clutched them to her heart.

Jordan, Perdu, P. D., the cat woman and Cuneo ran outside and over to a battered blue Renault. Cuneo squeezed his barrel belly in behind the wheel, a panting P. D. piled into the passenger seat, and Max, Jean and the young woman crawled onto the load bed at the back, alongside a toolbox, a leather suitcase, a bottle carrier with spices, various kinds of vinegar and bunches of herbs, and mountains of textbooks on various subjects. They were thrown higgledy-piggledy as Cuneo put his foot to the floor, pursued by the irate, fist-shaking mob that had chased the strangers out into the car park, no longer prepared to put up with their womenfolk's secret urge to dance.

'Dumb hicks!' spat P. D. Olson, tossing a reference book on butterflies into the back. 'They're so small-minded they think we're a bunch of swingers who start off dancing fully clothed and then strip. That would look fairly repulsive – all those shrunken balls, pot bellies and skinny little grandpa legs.'

The cat woman snorted, and Max and Cuneo

laughed too – the exaggerated laughter of people who have evaded danger by the skin of their teeth.

'Wait, sorry but . . . can we stop at a bank anyway?' Max asked in a pleading voice as they raced hell-for-leather back to the boat along Cepoy's main street.

'Only if you're looking to sing castrato,' P. D. huffed.

They soon pulled up at the book barge. Lindgren and Kafka were lazing by the window in the early evening sun, studiously ignoring an excitable couple of crows that were croaking insults at them from a twisted apple tree.

Perdu noticed Cuneo's longing glance at the barge.

'I don't think it's safe for you to stay here,' he said to the Italian.

Cuneo sighed. 'You wouldn't believe how many times I've heard those words before, Capitano.'

'Come with us. We're on our way to Provence,' said Perdu.

'That damn letter splicer told you my story, *si*? About me travelling the rivers in search of a *signorina* who has stolen my heart?'

'Sure did. The Yank spilled the beans again. So what? I'm old and I'm going to die soon anyway – a bit of mischief is all that'll keep me alive. At least I didn't post it on Facebook.'

'You're on Facebook?' Max asked in disbelief. He had picked some apples and was cradling them in his shirt.

'Yeah. And? Just because it's like tapping on the walls of a prison cell?' Old Olson snickered. 'Of course I am. How else am I supposed to find out what people are up to or that village lynch mobs can suddenly recruit members worldwide?'

'Right. Okay,' said Max. 'I'll send you a friend request.'

'You do that, sonny. I'm on the internet every last Friday in the month, from eleven to three.'

'You still owe us an answer,' said Perdu. 'After all, both of us danced. Well? And give us a straight answer – I can't stand lies. Did you write *Southern Lights*? Are you Sanary?'

Olson turned his wrinkled face to the sun. He took off his ridiculous hat and swept his white hair back.

'Me? Sanary? What makes you think that?'

'Technique. The words.'

'Ah, I know what you mean! "The great Mamapapa." Wonderful. The personification of everybody's longing for the ultimate caregiver, the mothering father. Or "rose love", blooming and fragrant, but without thorns, which is to misconstrue the nature of the rose. Magnificent, every word of it. But not mine, sad to say. Sanary has no regard for conventions, but I consider him a great philanthropist. Which is not a claim I can make for myself. I don't like people much, although I also get diarrhoea if I have to respect social etiquette. No, my dear John Lost – it's not me. And that is the unfortunate truth.'

201

P. D. struggled out of the car and hobbled around to the other side.

'Listen, Cuneo. I'll look after your old jalopy until you come back. Or don't come back, who knows.'

Cuneo was undecided, but when Max picked up his books and bottle carrier and hauled them over to the boat, Cuneo grabbed the toolbox and the leather suitcase too.

'Capitano Perduto, may I come aboard?'

'Please do. I would be honoured, Signor Cuneo.'

As Max prepared to cast off, the cat woman leaned on the Renault's bonnet, her expression inscrutable, and Perdu shook P. D. Olson's hand in farewell.

'Did you really dream about me? Or was that idle talk?' he asked.

Per David Olson gave a roguish smile. 'A world of words is never real. I read that once in a book by a German called Gerlach, Gunter Gerlach. Not for dimwits.' He thought for a second. 'Head for Cuisery, on the Seille River. Maybe you'll find Sanary there. If she's alive.'

'She?' asked Perdu.

'Hey, what do I know? I always imagine that anything interesting is female. Don't you?' Olson grinned and eased himself carefully into Cuneo's old car. He waited there for the young woman to join him.

She, meanwhile, clasped Perdu in her arms.

'You owe me something too,' she said huskily and sealed Perdu's lips with a kiss.

It was the first time a woman had kissed him in twenty years, and even in his wildest dreams Jean could not have imagined how intoxicating it was.

She sucked him in, and her tongue briefly met his. Then, eyes blazing, she thrust Jean away.

'Even if I did desire you, what business is that of yours?' said her angry, proud gaze.

Hallelujah. What did I do to earn that?

'Cuisery?' asked Max. 'What's that?'

'Paradise,' said Perdu.

CHAPTER 24

Cuneo took up quarters in the second cabin, and then declared the galley his private territory. The burly man with the receding hairline extracted spices, oils and blends from his suitcase and bottle carrier, and arranged them alongside a formidable battery of home-made mixtures used to spice up dishes, to enhance dips or simply 'to sniff and be happy'.

Noting Perdu's sceptical expression, he asked: 'Something wrong?'

'No, Signor Cuneo. It's just . . .'

It's just that I'm not used to such nice aromas. They're too good. Too unbearably good. And not 'happy'.

'I once knew a woman,' Cuneo began, as he continued to order his things and carefully check his knives, 'who wept when she smelled roses. Another woman found it incredibly erotic when I baked *pâté en croûte*. Aromas do funny things to the soul.'

Pâté happiness, thought Perdu. Under P. Or under L for the Language of Aromas. Would he really include all this in his encyclopedia of emotions one day?

How about starting tomorrow? No – how about right now?!

All he needed was a pen and paper, and then someday, letter by letter, he would have achieved his dream. Would, should, could . . .

Now. It is only ever now. So do it, you coward. Breathe underwater at last.

'For me it's lavender,' he admitted hesitantly.

'Do you have to weep, or the opposite?'

'Both. It's the scent of my greatest failure – and happiness.'

Now Cuneo shook some pebbles out of a plastic bag and arranged them on the sideboard.

'This is *my* failure and *my* happiness,' he declared, unbidden. 'Time. It rubs the rough edges that hurt us smooth. Because I tend to forget that, I've kept a pebble from every river I've ever travelled.'

The Canal du Loing had merged into the Canal de Briare on one of the most spectacular sections of the Route Bourbonnais, through a trough-shaped aqueduct that carried the canal over a turbulent and unnavigable stretch of the Loire. They had dropped anchor in the marina at Briare, which was so resplendent with flowers that dozens of painters were sitting on the banks, attempting to capture the scene.

The marina looked like a miniature Saint-Tropez. They saw a host of expensive yachts and people strolling along the promenades. The *Literary Apothecary* was the largest boat there, and a number of hobby yachtsmen sauntered up to stare at her, inspect the conversion work and cast an eye over the crew. Perdu knew how odd they looked. Not merely like rookies, but something far worse: *amateurs*.

An undaunted Cuneo asked every visitor whether he or she had spotted a cargo vessel called *Moonlight* on their travels. A Swiss couple, who had been cruising around Europe on a Luxe motor barge for thirty years, thought they remembered it. Maybe ten years back. Or was it twelve?

When Cuneo's thoughts turned to dinner, he found the larder full of air, and only cat food and the aforementioned white beans in the fridge.

'We have no money, Signor Cuneo, and no supplies,' Perdu started to explain. He told him about their impetuous departure from Paris and their various mishaps.

'Most river-goers are glad to lend a hand, and I've got some savings,' was the Neapolitan's comment. 'I could give you something towards the fare.'

'That's very noble of you,' said Perdu, 'but it's out of the question. We have to earn some money somehow.'

'Isn't that woman waiting for you?' said Max Jordan in all innocence. 'We shouldn't waste too much time.'

'She's not expecting me. We've got all the time in the world,' said Perdu hastily, dismissing the question.

Oh yes, we have all the time in the world. Oh, Manon, do you remember that basement bar, Louis Armstrong and us?

'A surprise visit? That's so romantic . . . but fairly risky.'

'If you don't take any risks, life will pass you by,' Cuneo chipped in. 'But let's get back to the subject of money.' Perdu gave him a grateful smile.

Cuneo and Perdu studied the waterways map, and the Italian marked a few villages. 'I know some people here in Apremont-sur-Allier, the other side of Nevers. Javier is often looking for help repairing gravestones. And I worked as a private chef in Fleury once . . . for a painter in Digoin . . . And here in Saint-Satur, if she's got over the fact that she and I didn't, um . . .' He blushed. 'Some of them are bound to help us out with food or fuel. Or they'll know where there are jobs to be had.'

'Do you know anyone in Cuisery?'

'The book town on the Seille River? Never been there. But maybe I'll find what I'm looking for there.'

'The woman.'

'Yes, the woman.' Cuneo took a deep breath. 'Women like her don't come along that often, you know. Maybe only once every two hundred years. She's everything a man could dream of. Beautiful, clever, wise, considerate, passionate – absolutely everything.'

Amazing, thought Perdu. I could never talk about Manon that way. Talking about her would mean sharing her. It would mean owning up, and he couldn't yet bring himself to do that.

'So the big question,' Max mused, 'is how to earn a quick buck. I'm telling you right now that I'd make a terrible gigolo.'

Cuneo glanced around. 'What about the books?' he asked tentatively. 'Do you plan to keep them all?'

Why hadn't he thought of it himself?

Cuneo went off into Briare to buy fruit, vegetables and meat with his own money and talked a wily angler into giving him his day's catch. Jean opened the book barge, and Max went off to drum up some business. He strolled around the marina and the village calling out: 'Books for sale! All the latest releases. Entertaining, smart and cheap – books, glorious books!'

Whenever he passed a table of women, he would announce: 'Reading makes you beautiful, reading makes you rich, reading makes you slim!' In between times he posted himself outside Le Petit St Trop restaurant and cried: 'Feeling unloved? We have the book for you. Having trouble with your skipper? We've got the book for that too! Caught a fish, but don't know how to gut it? Our books know everything about everything.'

Some passers-by recognised the author from newspaper pictures, others turned away in irritation, and a handful did make their way to the *Literary Apothecary* for advice.

And so Max, Jean and Salvatore Cuneo earned

their first euros. A tall, dark monk from Rogny also presented them with a few pots of honey and jars of herbs in exchange for Perdu's non-fiction titles on agnosticism.

'What on earth is he going to do with them?'

'Bury them,' Cuneo reckoned.

Having asked the harbourmaster about the *Moonlight* cargo ship, he bought a few more herb seedlings from him, and using timber from some bookshelves, speedily created a kitchen garden on the afterdeck, much to the delight of Kafka and Lindgren, who made a mad dash for the mint. The cats were soon chasing each other around the boat, their tails bristling like scrubbing brushes.

That evening Cuneo, sporting a flowery apron and matching oven gloves, brought in their meal.

'Gentlemen, a variation on the ratatouille so demeaned by the tourist industry: *bohémienne de legumes*,' Salvatore explained, setting down the dish on the makeshift table out on deck. The dish turned out to be finely diced roasted red vegetables, seasoned with a generous pinch of thyme, pressed into a mould, then skilfully turned out onto a plate and drizzled with the finest olive oil. It was accompanied by lamb cutlets, which Cuneo had passed three times over the open flame, and a snow-white, melt-in-the-mouth garlic flan.

Something strange happened when Perdu took his first bite. Images seemed to explode inside his head.

'This is unbelievable, Salvatore. You cook the way Marcel Pagnol writes.'

'Ah, Pagnol. A good man. He knew that you can only really see with your tongue. And your nose and your stomach,' said Cuneo with an appreciative sigh. Then, between two mouthfuls, he added, 'Capitano Perduto, I'm a firm believer that you have to taste a country's soul to understand it and to grasp its people. And by soul I mean what grows there, what its people see and smell and touch every day, what travels through them and shapes them from the inside out.'

'Like pasta shapes the Italians?' Max asked as he chewed.

'Watch what you say, Massimo. Pasta makes women *bellissima*!' said Cuneo, enthusiastically tracing a voluptuous female figure in the air with his hands.

They ate and they laughed. The sun went down to their right, the moon came up to their left; they were enfolded in the luxurious scent of the harbour flowers. The cats explored the surrounding area, and later they kept the men company from their vantage point on top of an overturned book crate.

Jean Perdu was overcome by an unfamiliar sense of tranquillity.

Can eating heal you?

With every bite of food steeped in the herbs and oils of Provence he seemed to absorb a little more of the land that lay ahead; it was as if he were eating the surrounding countryside. Already

210

he could taste the wild banks of the Loire, covered in forests and vineyards.

He slept peacefully that night. Kafka and Lindgren watched over his sleep, the tomcat stretched out by the door, Lindgren by his shoulder. Occasionally Jean would feel paws patting his cheek, as if to check that he was still alive.

The next morning they decided to stay a little longer in Briare. It was a popular base and meeting point, and the houseboating season had begun. New canal boats arrived almost every hour, bringing potential book buyers.

Max offered to share his few remaining clothes with Jean, who had set out with only the shirt, grey trousers, jacket and jumper he was wearing. For the time being, clothing was not high on their list of essential purchases.

Perdu found himself wearing jeans and a faded shirt for the first time in what felt like centuries. He barely recognised the man he glimpsed in the mirror. The three-day beard, the slight tan he had caught at the wheel, the airy clothes . . . He no longer looked so uptight or older than his years, though not exactly much younger either.

Max had started to draw an ironic pencil moustache on his upper lip and combed his hair back to cultivate a gleaming, black pirate ponytail. Every morning he practised kung fu and tai chi out on the rear deck in only a light pair of trousers. At lunchtime and in the evening he read aloud to

Cuneo while the latter prepared the meals. Cuneo would often request stories by women authors.

'Women tell you more about the world. Men only tell you about themselves.'

They were now keeping the *Literary Apothecary* open late into the night. The days were getting warmer.

Children from the nearby villages and the other boats would hang out for hours in *Lulu*'s belly, reading the adventures of Harry Potter, Kalle Blomquist, the Famous Five and the Warrior Cats, or Greg's diary. Perdu frequently had to suppress a smile at the sight of Max sitting on the floor in the middle of a circle of children, his long legs folded and a book on his lap. His reading aloud was constantly improving, and his stories were more like radio plays. Perdu suspected that these small children, listening with eyes wide and in rapt concentration, would one day grow up to need reading, with its accompanying sense of wonder and the feeling of having a film running inside your head, as much as they needed air to breathe.

He sold books by weight to anyone under fourteen: two kilos for ten euros.

'Aren't we running at a loss?' asked Max.

Perdu shrugged his shoulders. 'Financially speaking, yes. But it's well known that reading makes people impudent, and tomorrow's world is going to need some people who aren't shy to speak their minds, don't you think?'

Giggling teenagers would crowd into the erotica

corner and then fall suspiciously silent. Perdu made sure to approach noisily so that they had time to pry their lips from each other's and hide their flushed faces behind a harmless book.

Max often lured customers aboard by playing the piano.

Perdu got into the habit of posting a card to Catherine every day, and collecting new entries for his encyclopedia of minor and moderate emotions in a notebook, for the benefit of the next generation of literary pharmacists.

Each evening he would sit down in the stern and look up at the sky. The Milky Way was always there, and every now and then a shooting star would race past. The frogs gave a cappella concerts and the crickets joined in with a chirp, all to the background beat of lines slapping softly against masts and the occasional chime of a ship's bell.

New feelings surged through his body. It was only fair that Catherine should hear about them, for she was the one who had set everything in motion. He was still waiting to see what kind of man this would make him.

Catherine, today Max understood that a novel is like a garden where the reader must spend time in order to bloom. I feel strangely paternal when I look at Max. Regards, Perduto.

Catherine, for three seconds when I woke up this morning I had the insight that you are a sculptor of souls, a woman who tames fear. Your hands are turning a stone back into a man. John Lost, menhir.

Catherine, rivers are not like the sea. The sea demands, while rivers give. Here we are, stocking up on content-ment, peace, melancholia and the glass-smooth calm of evening that rounds off the day in grey-blue tones. I have kept the sea horse you fashioned out of bread, the one with the peppercorn eyes. It desperately needs a companion. In the humble opinion of Jeanno P.

Catherine, river people only really arrive when they're afloat. They love books about desert islands. River people would feel nauseated if they knew where they were going to moor the next day. Someone who understands them is J. P. from P., currently of no fixed address.

Perdu had discovered another thing above the rivers – stars that breathed. One day they shone brightly, the next they were pale, then bright again. And this had nothing to do with the haze or with his reading glasses, but with the fact that he no longer simply stared at his own feet.

It looked as though they were breathing to some never-ending slow, deep rhythm. They breathed and watched as the world came and went. Some stars had seen the dinosaurs and the Neanderthals; they had seen the pyramids rise and Columbus discover America. For them, the earth was one more island world in the immeasurable ocean of outer space, its inhabitants microscopically small.

CHAPTER 25

At the end of their first week in Briare, a man from the council told them on the quiet that they'd either have to register as a seasonal trader or move on. He happened to be addicted to American thrillers.

'But from now on, watch out where you moor – by definition French bureaucracy has no blind spots.'

Equipped with food, power, water and the names and mobile numbers of a handful of friendly people living along the waterways, they swung out of the marina and into a side canal of the Loire. Soon they were passing châteaux, dense woods redolent with the scent of resin, and vineyards growing Sauvignon and Pinot Noir grapes to make Sancerre and Pouilly-Fumé wines.

The further south they went, the warmer the summer weather. From time to time they would meet a boat with women in bikinis stretched out on deck.

In the river meadows, alders, brambles and wild vines formed a magical jungle, dappled with shimmering, greenish light and spangled with twirling forest particles. Marshy pools lay sparkling among the elderberries and leaning beeches.

Cuneo pulled one fish after another from the murmuring waters, and they sighted herons, ospreys and swifts on the long, shallow, sandy shoals. Here and there, beavers peeked out of the bushes as they hunted for river rats. An ancient and lush France unfolded before their eyes, luxuriant, grand, leafy and remote.

One night they tied up beside an overgrown pasture. It was silent. There was not even the burbling of water, and no sound of traffic was to be heard. They were completely alone, aside from a few owls that sent the occasional call scooting over the water.

After a candlelit dinner they dragged blankets and cushions out onto the deck and lay there – three men, head to head, in a three-pointed star.

The Milky Way was a streak of light, a vapour trail of planets overhead. The silence was almost overpowering, and the blue depths of the night sky seemed to suck them in.

Max conjured forth a thin joint.

'I protest in the strongest terms,' said Jean in a relaxed drawl.

'Aye aye, skipper. Message received. A Dutch guy gave it to me because he didn't have any money to buy the Houellebecq.'

Max lit the reefer.

Cuneo sniffed. 'Smells like burned sage.'

He accepted the joint clumsily and took a short, cautious toke.

'Ugh. Like licking a Christmas tree.'

'You have to draw it into your lungs and hold it there for as long as possible,' Max advised him. Cuneo followed his instructions.

'Holy *balsamico*!' He coughed.

Jean took one gentle drag and let the smoke roll around his palate. Part of him was afraid of losing control; part of him longed for exactly that. Even now it seemed as though a dam of time, habit and petrified fear were preventing his grief from gushing forth. He felt as if there were stone tears inside him that left no room for anything else.

He had not yet confessed to Max or Cuneo that the woman for whom he had cast off from Paris had long since turned to dust. Nor had he confessed that he was ashamed, and that it was shame driving him on. But he had no idea what he was supposed to do when he reached Bonnieux or what he hoped to find there.

Inner peace? He had a long way to go to even merit it.

Oh well, a second drag couldn't do any harm.

The smoke was searingly hot. This time he sucked it in deep. Jean felt as though an ocean of heavy air were pressing down on him. It was as silent as the marine depths. Even the owls made no sound.

'Super starry,' mumbled Cuneo, tripping over his tongue.

'We must be flying above the sky. The earth is a discus, yeah that's what it is,' said Max by way of explanation.

'Or a platter of cold meats,' hiccupped Cuneo.

Max and he snorted. They laughed, and their voices echoed across the river and frightened the baby hares in the undergrowth into pressing themselves, hearts thumping, deeper into their sleepy hollows.

The night dew settled on Jean's eyelids. He didn't laugh.

'So, Cuneo, this woman you're looking for: what was she like?' asked Max when their laughter had subsided.

'Beautiful. Young. And extremely brown from all the sun,' answered Cuneo.

He paused. 'Apart from you-know-where. There she was as white as cream.' He sighed. 'And tasted every bit as sweet.'

They saw shooting stars flare up here and there, flash across their field of vision, and fade away.

'Love's follies are the sweetest. But you pay most dearly for them,' Cuneo whispered and pulled his blanket up to his chin. 'Little ones and big ones alike.' He sighed again. 'It was only one night. Vivette was engaged at the time, but all that meant was that no man should touch her, especially not a man like me.'

'What, a foreigner?' asked Max.

'No, Massimo, that wasn't the problem. A river man – we were taboo.'

Cuneo took another toke and passed the joint on.

'Vivette came over me like a fever – and I've still got it today. My blood boils at the thought of her. Her face stares out at me from every shadow and from every ray of sun on the water. I dream about her, but each night reduces the number of days we might spend together.'

'I feel somehow terribly old and parched,' Max said. 'All these passions you two feel! One of you has been searching for his one-night stand for twenty years, and the other sets off at a moment's notice to . . .' Max broke off.

In the pause after these words Jean felt a jolt at the very edges of his grass-clouded consciousness. What was it that Max had just stopped himself from saying? But Max carried on talking, and Jean let it go.

'I don't even know what I *ought* to want. I've never been that deeply in love with a woman. I've always focused on what . . . what she is *not*. One was pretty, but a snob about people who earned less than her father. Another was nice, but took forever to get a joke. And another girl was unbelievably beautiful, but she started weeping when she took her clothes off – I've no idea why – so I preferred not to sleep with her. I wrapped her up in my biggest jumper instead and hugged her all night long. I tell you, women love to snuggle and spoon, but all the man gets is a dead arm and a bursting bladder.'

Perdu took another drag.

'Your princess is somewhere too, Massimo,' said Cuneo with conviction.

'So where is she?' asked Max.

'Maybe you're searching for her already and you simply don't know that you're on your way to finding her,' whispered Jean.

That was how it had been with him and Manon. He had got on the train from Marseilles that morning with no idea that half an hour later he would find the woman who would shake his life to its foundations and topple all the pillars holding it up. He had been twenty-four, barely older than Max was now. He had had only five years of stolen hours with Manon, but he had paid for what amounted to those few days with two decades of pain, longing and loneliness.

'But I'll be damned if those few hours weren't worth it.'

'What did you say, Capitano?'

'Nothing, I was merely thinking. Can you hear my thoughts now? You'll both walk the plank.'

His travelling companions chuckled.

The silence of the country night seemed to grow increasingly surreal, drawing the men away from the present.

'What about your love, Capitano?' asked Cuneo. 'What's her name?'

Jean said nothing for a long time.

'*Scusami*, I didn't mean to . . .'

'Manon. Her name is Manon.'

'She must be beautiful.'

'As beautiful as a cherry tree in spring.'

It was so easy to close his eyes and answer the difficult questions Cuneo asked in his mellow, kindly voice.

'And clever, *si*?'

'She knows me better than I know myself. She . . . taught me to feel. And to dance. And loving her was easy.'

'Was?' a voice asked, yet so softly that Perdu was unsure whether it came from Max, Salvatore or his own inner censor.

'She's my home. And she's my laughter. She's . . .'

He fell silent. Dead. He couldn't say it. He was so scared of the grief that lurked behind the word.

'And what will you say to her when you meet?'

Jean wrestled with himself, then opted for the only truth that concurred with his silence about Manon's death.

'Forgive me.'

Cuneo ceased his questions.

'I envy you so much,' said Max. 'You live out your love and your longings, however crazy they may be. I, on the other hand, feel like a waste. I breathe, my heart beats, the blood pumps through my veins. But my writing's going nowhere. The world is falling to pieces, and I'm whining like a pair of punctured bellows. Life's not fair.'

'Death alone awaits us all,' said Perdu coolly.

'That's true democracy,' added Cuneo.

'Well, I think death's politically overrated,' said Max. He handed the end of the joint to Jean.

'Is it really the case that men choose their beloved according to whether she looks like their mother?' asked Cuneo.

'Hmm,' said Perdu and thought of Lirabelle Bernier.

'*Si, certo!* In that case I'd have to look for someone who's always calling me an imposition and slaps me when I'm reading or use words she doesn't understand,' said Cuneo with a bittersweet laugh.

'And I'd have one who only in her mid-fifties learns to say no and to eat something she actually likes rather than whatever's cheapest,' Max admitted.

Cuneo stubbed out the roll-up.

'Hey, Salvo,' asked Max when they had almost fallen asleep. 'May I write your story?'

'Don't you dare, *amico*,' was Salvatore's reply. 'Kindly come up with your own *storia*, young Massimo. If you take mine, I'll have none left of my own.'

Max gave a deep sigh. 'Oh, okay,' he muttered drowsily. 'Do the two of you at least have a couple of words for me? You know, a favourite word or two? To send me to sleep?'

Cuneo smacked his lips. 'Like milk soufflé? Pasta kiss?'

'I like words that sound like the things they describe,' whispered Perdu. His eyes were closed. 'Evening breeze. Night runner. Summer child. Defiance: I see a little girl in pretend armour, fighting off all the things she doesn't want to be.

Well behaved and thin and quiet – no way! Lady Defiance, a lone knight against the dark forces of reason.'

'Some words can cut you,' mumbled Cuneo, 'like razor blades in your ear and on your tongue. Discipline. Drill. Or reason.'

'"Reason" is the word on everyone's lips, so it's no wonder others can hardly make it through,' Max complained. Then he laughed: 'Imagine if you had to buy beautiful words before you could use them.'

'Some people with verbal diarrhoea would soon be broke.'

'And the rich would call the shots because they'd buy up all the important words.'

'And "I love you" would cost the most.'

'And twice as much if it's not used sincerely.'

'The poor would have to steal words. Or play charades rather than speak.'

'We should all do that anyway. Loving is a verb, so . . . do it. Less talk and more action. Right?'

Crikey, dope does amazing things.

Not long afterwards Salvo and Max rolled themselves out of their blankets and slipped away to their berths belowdecks.

Before Max Jordan disappeared, he glanced back at Perdu one last time.

'What is it, Monsieur?' Perdu asked sleepily. 'Want another word to take to bed with you?'

'Me? . . . No. I just wanted to say . . . I really like you. Whatever . . .'

Max looked as if he wanted to add something, but didn't know how.

'I like you too, Monsieur Jordan. A lot, in fact. I'd be delighted to be your friend. Monsieur Max.'

The two men looked at each other. The only light on their faces came from the moon; Max's eyes were in darkness.

'Yes,' whispered the young man. 'Yes . . . Jean. I'll gladly be your friend. I'll try to be a good one.'

Perdu didn't understand the last bit, but put it down to the grass.

When Perdu was alone, he simply lay there. The fragrance of the night was beginning to change. From somewhere a scent wafted over to him . . . was it lavender?

Something quaked inside him.

He remembered that he had felt the same about the scent of lavender as a young man, even before he had met Manon. A shock wave. As though his heart knew even then that at some point far in the future this scent would be associated with longing. With pain. With love. With a woman.

He took a deep breath and let this memory sweep through him from head to toe. Yes, maybe he had sensed long ago, at Max's age, the shock wave Manon would soon send through his life.

Jean Perdu took the flag that Manon had sewn down from the prow and smoothed it out. Then he kneeled and laid his eye on the book bird's eye, on the spot where the drop of Manon's blood had dried into a dark stain.

We're nights apart, Manon.

As he kneeled there with his head tilted, he whispered:

> Nights and days and countries and oceans.
>   Thousands of lives have come and gone,
>   and you are waiting for me.
> In a room somewhere, next door.
> Knowing and loving me.
> In my mind you still love me.
> You are the fear that cuts stone inside me.
> You are the life that awaits expectantly
>   inside me.
> You are the death I fear.
> You happened to me, and I withheld my
>   words from you. My sorrow. My memories.
> Your place inside me and all our time
>   together.
> I lost our star.
> Do you forgive me?
> Manon?

CHAPTER 26

'Max! Another chamber of horrors ahead!' Jordan dragged himself out on deck. 'Want to bet that the lock-keeper's mutt pees on my hand again, like the ones at the last thousand locks or so? My fingers are all bloody from winding these damn handles and opening the lock paddles. Will these gentle hands ever be able to caress another vowel?' Reproachfully, Max held out red hands dotted with tiny suppurating blisters.

Having passed countless pastures from which cattle descended into the shallow waters to cool off, and the imposing castles of former royal mistresses, they were now approaching the La Grange lock shortly before Sancerre.

The wine-growing village sat on top of a hill that was visible from afar and signalled the southern limit of the twenty-kilometre-long Loire Valley nature reserve.

Weeping willows trailed their branches in the water like playful fingers. The book barge entered the embrace of shifting green walls that seemed to close in around them.

It was true that a jittery dog had barked at them at every lock that day. And every yapping dog had peed unerringly on the precise bollard to which Max tied the two ropes that held the book barge steady in the lock while the water flowed in and drained out again. This time Max let the two lines slide from his fingertips onto the deck.

'Don't worry, Capitano! Cuneo will take care of the lock.'

The short-legged Italian set the ingredients for the evening meal to one side, clambered up the ladder in his flowery apron, pulling on his brightly coloured oven gloves when he reached the top, and swung the mooring line back and forth like a snake. The dog retreated in the face of this rope boa constrictor and trotted sullenly away.

Cuneo then twisted the iron rod with one hand to open the paddle regulating the inflow; his tensed muscles bulged under his striped short-sleeved shirt. He sang 'Que Sera, Sera' in a gondolier's tenor as he worked, and winked at the delighted lock-keeper's wife while her husband wasn't looking. He handed the man a can of beer as they sailed past. This earned Salvatore a smile and the tip-off that there was a dance at Sancerre that evening, and that the harbourmaster at the next harbour had run out of diesel. He also replied in the negative to Cuneo's most important question: the cargo boat *Moonlight* had not passed this way in a long time. Last seen towards the end of Mitterrand's lifetime, or thereabouts.

Perdu watched Cuneo's reaction as he received this news.

The guy had been hearing the same word for a week now: 'No no no.' They had asked lock-keepers, harbourmasters, skippers, even customers who beckoned to the *Literary Apothecary* from the bank. The Italian would thank them, his face impassive. He must have an unquenchable flame of hope burning inside him. Or did he simply keep on looking out of habit?

Habit is a vain and treacherous goddess. She lets nothing disrupt her rule. She smothers one desire after another: the desire to travel, the desire for a better job or a new love. She stops us from living as we would like, because habit prevents us from asking ourselves whether we continue to enjoy doing what we do.

Cuneo joined Perdu at the wheel.

'Aye, Capitano. I lost my love. What about the boy?' he asked. 'What has he lost?'

The two men looked over at Max, who was leaning on the railing and staring at the water, his thoughts apparently far, far away.

Max was talking less and had given up playing the piano.

I'll try to be a good friend, he had said to Perdu. What had he meant by 'try'?

'He's lost his muse, Signor Salvatore. Max made a pact with her and gave up his normal life. But his muse has gone. Now he doesn't have a life – either a normal one or an artistic one. And so he's on a quest to find her.'

'*Si, capisco*. Maybe he didn't love his muse enough? If so, he'll have to ask for her hand all over again.'

Could writers marry their muses afresh? Should Max, Cuneo and he dance naked and chanting around a fire of vine twigs in the middle of a wildflower meadow?

'What are muses like? Are they like kitty cats?' asked Cuneo. 'They don't like people grovelling for their love. Or are they like dogs? Can he make the muse jealous by making love with another girl?'

Before Jean Perdu could reply that muses were like horses, they heard Max yell something.

'A deer! There. In the water!'

It was true: ahead of them, an utterly exhausted young doe was flailing in the middle of the canal. It panicked when it caught sight of the *péniche* looming up behind it.

It tried again and again to find a foothold on the bank, but the smooth, vertical walls of the man-made canal made escape from the lethal waters impossible.

Max was already hanging out over the railing, trying to rescue the exhausted animal with the life buoy.

'Leave it, Massimo. You'll fall in.'

'We have to help it! It won't make it out on its own – it's drowning!'

Max now formed a lasso with one of the mooring lines and threw it repeatedly in the direction of the deer. But the animal panicked and writhed even more, disappeared underwater and then resurfaced.

The complete fear in the deer's eyes touched off something inside Perdu.

'Keep calm,' he beseeched the animal. 'Keep calm, trust us, trust us . . . Trust us.' He throttled back *Lulu*'s engine and threw the barge into reverse, though it would continue to glide for another dozen metres.

The deer was already level with the middle of the boat.

It struggled more and more desperately with each splash of the rope and the life buoy on the water. The animal twisted its slight young head towards them, its brown eyes wide with panic and dread.

And then it screamed, making a sound somewhere between a hoarse whimper and a plaintive cry.

Cuneo was whipping off his shoes and shirt, readying himself to dive into the canal.

The deer screamed and screamed.

Perdu feverishly assessed the options. Should they tie up? Perhaps they could grab hold of it from the land and pull it out of the water.

He steered the boat towards the bank and heard the side scrape along the canal wall.

The deer kept on screaming the same shrill, desperate call. Its movements were growing ever wearier, and its efforts to gain a grip on the bank with its front legs were flagging. It couldn't find one.

Cuneo stood by the railing in his underpants. He must have realised that he wouldn't be able to help the little doe if he was unable to climb out of the canal himself. And *Lulu*'s hull was too high to heave the struggling deer aboard or to clamber up the emergency ladder with it in his arms.

When they finally managed to moor, Max and Jean leaped onto the bank and raced back through the undergrowth towards the deer. In the meantime, it had pushed away from their bank and was attempting to reach the far side.

'Why won't it let us help it?' whispered Max, tears running down his cheeks. 'Come here!' he croaked. 'Come here, you stupid bloody animal!'

All they could do was watch.

The deer mewled and whimpered as it tried to scale the far bank. Then it even stopped doing that. It slid back into the water.

The men watched in silence as the deer struggled merely to keep its head above water. Again and again it glanced at them and tried to paddle away from them. Its fearful gaze, full of distrust and defiance, pierced Perdu to the bone.

The deer gave one final desperate, lingering scream. Then the screaming ceased.

It went under.

'Oh, God, please,' whispered Max.

When it reappeared, it was floating on its side, head below the water, and front legs twitching. The sun shone, the midges danced, and somewhere in the woods a bird trilled. The deer's body turned in lifeless circles.

The tears trickled down Max's face. He lowered himself into the water and swam out to the corpse.

Jean and Salvatore watched Max pull the deer's limp body along behind him until he reached Perdu's bank. Max raised the slender, wet body into the air with unsuspected strength until Jean was able to grasp it. He was barely able to lift it out onto the bank.

The deer smelled of brackish water and leaf litter, and carried the aroma of an alien, ancient world far from the city. Its wet fur was bristly. As Perdu laid the deer carefully beside him on the sun-warmed ground, with its small head on his lap, he hoped that by some miracle the deer would shake itself, stand up on wobbly legs and dart off into the bushes.

Jean ran his fingers over the young animal's chest. He stroked its back, then its head, as though his mere touch might break the spell. He felt the remaining warmth in its spare frame.

'Please,' he begged softly. 'Please.'

Over and over he caressed the head on his lap.

The deer's hazel eyes stared glassily past him.

Max was swimming on his back with his arms spread wide.

On deck Cuneo had his face in his hands.

None of the men dared look at the others.

CHAPTER 27

Without a word they motored south through Burgundy along the side canal of the Loire, through mighty green cathedral-vaults of trees that arched over the canal. Some vineyards were so large that the rows of vines seemed to stretch off to the horizon. Everywhere flowers were blooming; the locks and bridges were bright with them.

The three men ate in silence, sold books to customers on the banks in silence, and avoided one another. That evening they read, each in his own corner of the boat. The bemused cats wandered from one to the other, but even they could not tear the men from their wilful isolation. Head nudges, intense stares and questioning meows elicited no response.

The deer's death had scattered the three-man star. Now each man drifted alone through time – the hideous mazes of time.

Jean spent a long time pondering the lined school notebook he was using for his encyclopedia of emotions. He stared out of the window without noticing how the sky was ablaze with every colour from red to orange. Thinking felt like wading through treacle.

The next evening they passed Nevers and after a brief, tense discussion – 'Why not Nevers? We can sell some books there.' 'There are enough bookshops in Nevers, but no one who can sell us diesel' – they tied up minutes before the locks closed for the night near a tiny village called Apremont-sur-Allier, which nestled on a bend in the Allier River. Cuneo knew some people there – a sculptor and his family who lived in an isolated house between the village and the river.

From here, in the 'Garden of France', it wasn't far to Digoin and the turn-off onto the Canal du Centre, which would carry them towards the Rhône and thence along the Seille to Cuisery, the town of books.

Kafka and Lindgren scampered off into the riverside woods to hunt. Seconds later a flurry of birds exploded from the trees.

As the three men walked through the village, Jean felt as though they had stepped back into the fifteenth century. The tall trees with their broad canopies, the many unpaved lanes, the smattering of houses built of yellow sandstone, pinkish earth and red tiles, even the flowers in the farm gardens and the ivy sprouting over the buildings – it all combined to suggest that they had entered a bygone France of knights and witches. There was a small castle perched above this erstwhile village of stonemasons and builders, its walls shining golden red in the rays of the sinking sun. Only the modern bicycles of touring cyclists picnicking on the banks of the Allier spoiled the impression.

'A bit bloody twee, this place,' griped Max.

Passing behind an ancient squat round tower, they crossed a garden of flowers, which were blooming in such myriad pinks and reds and whites that the sight and scent made Jean dizzy. Enormous wisterias bowed over the paths, and a lake was dominated by a lonely pagoda, which could only be reached via stepping-stones.

'Do any real people actually live here, or are they all movie extras?' Max asked. 'What's it meant to be? A picture postcard for American tourists?'

'Yes, Max, people do live here. The kind who resist reality a little more than others do. And no, Apremont isn't for Americans; it's for the pursuit of beauty,' answered Cuneo.

He parted the branches of a large rhododendron bush to reveal a concealed door in a high old stone wall. He pushed it open and they stepped into a spacious garden with a well-tended lawn leading to a splendid manor house with tall casement windows, a turret, two wings and a terrace.

Jean felt awkward and out of place. It had been a long time since he'd last been to someone's home. As they drew closer, they heard the tinkle of a piano and peals of laughter and, crossing the garden, Perdu caught sight of a woman sitting on a chair under a copper beech, dressed in nothing but a stylish old hat and painting a canvas. Near her a young man in an old-fashioned English summer suit was sitting at a piano on wheels.

'Hey! You with the pretty mouth! Can you play the piano?' the naked woman called when she spotted the three men.

Max blushed – and nodded.

'Then play me something; paints love to dance. My brother doesn't know a B from a B-flat.'

Max wedged himself in between the stool and the piano on wheels, and tried not to gawk at the woman's breasts – especially as she had only one, the left one. A fine red line on the right-hand side betrayed where its round, full young twin had once been.

'Take a good look to satisfy your curiosity,' she said. She took off her hat and exhibited herself to him: a bald skull covered in sprouting fuzz, a cancer-damaged body fighting its way back to life.

'Do you have a favourite song?' asked Max, after he'd swallowed his embarrassment, fascination and pity.

'I do, Mr Pretty Lips. Lots. Thousands of them!' She leaned forward, whispered something to Max, donned her hat again and dipped her brush expectantly in the red paste on her palette.

'I'm ready,' she said. 'And call me Elaïa!'

'Fly Me to the Moon' struck up soon after. Max played a wonderful jazz rendition of the song while the artist waved her paintbrush about to the stream of music.

'She's Javier's daughter,' whispered Cuneo to

Perdu. 'She's been battling cancer since she was a girl. I'm pleased to see she's obviously still winning.'

'No way! It can't be true! You think you can just turn up out of the blue, after all this time?'

A woman of about Jean's age came running over from the terrace and flew into Cuneo's arms. Her eyes sparkled with laughter.

'You bloody pasta twizzler! Look who's turned up, Javier – the stone stroker!'

A man in threadbare coarse corduroy trousers and a checked shirt emerged from the house, which, as Jean noticed upon closer inspection, was by no means as grand as it appeared from a distance. Its glory days of golden chandeliers and a dozen servants must have lain many decades in the past.

Now the woman with the laughing eyes turned to Perdu.

'Hello,' she said. 'Welcome to the Flintstones'!'

'Hello,' Jean Perdu began, 'my name's—'

'Oh, forget about names. There's no need for them here. Here we can call ourselves whatever we want. Or by what we're good at. Are you especially good at anything? Or are you something special?'

Her dark-brown eyes scattered sparks.

'I'm the stone stroker!' called Cuneo. He was familiar with this game.

'I'm . . .' began Perdu.

'Don't listen to him, Zelda. He's a soul reader, that's what he is,' said Cuneo. 'And his name's

Jean and he'll supply you with any book it takes to get you sleeping well again.'

He spun around when Zelda's husband tapped him on the shoulder.

The lady of the manor studied Perdu more intently.

'Is that right?' she asked. 'Can you do that? That would make you a miracle worker.'

There were marks of sadness around her laughing mouth.

Perdu's gaze roamed around the garden and settled on Elaia.

Max was now pounding out a tearaway version of 'Hit the Road, Jack' for Javier and Zelda's sick daughter.

Zelda must be tired, thought Perdu, tired of having death share this beautiful house with them for so long.

'Have you . . . given it a name?' he asked.

'It?'

'The thing that lives and sleeps in Elaia's body – or only pretends to sleep.'

Zelda ran her hand over Perdu's unshaved cheeks.

'You know all about death, huh?' She gave a sad smile. 'It – the cancer – is called Lupo. That's the name Elaia gave it when she was nine. Lupo, like the cartoon dog. She imagined that they lived together in her body like housemates. She respects the fact that it sometimes demands more attention. That way, she says, she can rest easier than if she imagines it wants to destroy her. What on earth would destroy its own home?'

Zelda smiled lovingly as she gazed at her daughter. 'Lupo's been living with us for more than twenty years. I get the impression that he's starting to feel old and tired too.'

She suddenly turned away from Jean to flash a glance at Cuneo, as though she regretted her candour.

'Your turn. Where have you been, have you found Vivette, and are you staying the night? Tell me everything. And help me with the cooking,' she commanded to the Neapolitan, linking arms with him and leading him off to the house. Javier laid his left arm around the Italian's shoulders, and Elaia's brother, Leon, followed along behind.

Jean felt superfluous. He wandered idly around the garden. He discovered a weathered stone bench in the deeper shadows under a beech tree in a corner of the garden. No one could see him here, but he could see everything. He could see the house and he watched the lights come on one by one and its inhabitants moving around the rooms. He saw Cuneo at work with Zelda in the large kitchen, and Javier appeared to be asking the occasional question as he and Leon sat smoking at the dining table.

Max had ceased playing the piano. Elaia and he were chatting quietly. And then they kissed.

Shortly afterwards Elaia drew Max after her into the depths of the house. A candle flared in a bay window. Jean could see Elaia's shadow kneeling over Max, holding his hands to the spot where her heart beat as she bent over him. Jean observed her stealing a night on which Lupo had no claim.

Max was still lying there when Elaia waltzed out of the room into the kitchen in a long T-shirt. Perdu saw her take a seat on the bench next to her father.

Max soon stumbled into the kitchen too. He lent a hand setting the table and opened the wine. From his hiding-place Perdu could see how Elaia looked at Max when his back was turned. She pulled a mischievous face as she did so, as though it were all some big prank. He cast her a shy, doe-eyed smile when she wasn't looking.

'Please don't fall in love with a dying woman, Max. It's almost unbearable,' whispered Jean.

He felt something constrict in his chest. It wormed its way up his throat and spilled out of his mouth.

A deep, shuddering sob.

How it screamed. How the deer screamed! Oh, Manon.

And then they came: the tears. He just about managed to lean against the beech tree and press his hands against the sides of the trunk for support.

He whimpered, he wept. Jean Perdu wept like never before. He clung to the tree. He broke out in a sweat. He heard the sounds coming from his mouth, and it was as if a dam had ruptured. He had no idea how long it lasted. Minutes? Quarter of an hour? Longer?

He wept into his hands with deep, desperate sobs until suddenly they stopped; it was as though he had cut open a sore and pressed out the infection inside. All that was left was an exhausted emptiness – and warmth, an unknown warmth that might have been produced by an engine fuelled by tears. It was this that made Perdu stand up and stride across the garden, faster and faster until he was running, straight into the large kitchen.

They hadn't started eating yet, and this caused him a strange, fleeting sense of joy, because these strangers had waited for him, because he wasn't superfluous.

'And of course, like a painting, good pâté can—' Cuneo was raving. Halfway through his sentence, he and his audience looked up in amazement.

'There you are!' Max said. 'Where were you hiding?'

'Max. Salvo. I've got to tell you something,' Jean blurted.

CHAPTER 28

aying those words. Actually saying them and listening to how they sounded. How the sentence hung there in Zelda and Javier's kitchen, among the salad bowls and glasses of red wine. And what it meant.

'She's dead.'

It meant that he was alone.

It meant that death made no exceptions.

He felt a small hand grip his.

Elaia.

She drew him down onto the bench. His knees were trembling. Jean looked first at Cuneo and then at Max, right in the eye.

'I don't need to hurry,' he said, 'because Manon's been dead for twenty-one years already.'

'*Dio mio*,' Cuneo gasped.

Max took an audible breath, then reached into his shirt pocket. He pulled out a twice-folded news-paper cutting, and slid it across the table to Jean.

'I found it back in Briare. It was in Proust.'

Jean opened the slip of paper.

The death announcement.

He had pushed it into the first available book at

the *Literary Apothecary,* put it back on the shelf at random and then, after a while, forgotten which it was and where it might have ended up among the thousands of books.

He flattened the piece of paper, folded it again and put it in his pocket.

'But you didn't say anything. You knew I'd left you in the dark. No, let's call a spade a spade: you knew I'd lied to you. But you didn't say that you knew I was lying to you. And to myself. Until . . .'

Until I was ready.

Jordan shrugged his shoulders slightly.

'Of course,' he said quietly. 'What else.'

The grandfather clock ticked in the hallway.

'Thank you . . . *Max,*' whispered Perdu. 'Thank you. You're a good friend.'

He got to his feet, as did Max, and they fell into each other's arms across the table. It was awkward and uncomfortable, but as Jean embraced Max he felt relief at last.

They had found each other again.

Jean felt fresh tears welling up.

'She's dead, Max. Oh, God!' he said in a choked whisper to Max's neck, and the young man gripped Perdu even more firmly. He put his knee on the table and moved the plates, glasses and dishes carefully aside to give Jean a very strong, very tight hug.

Jean Perdu wept again.

Zelda stifled a quiet sob before it left her mouth.

Elaia looked at Max with infinite tenderness as

243

she wiped away her own rolling tears. Her father had leaned back to follow the drama, fiddling with his beard with one hand and twiddling his cigarette between the fingers of his other.

Cuneo kept his eyes riveted to his plate.

'All right,' Perdu whispered after his violent sobbing fit, 'all right. It's fine. Really. I need a drink.'

He breathed out loudly. Bizarrely he felt like laughing first, kissing Zelda next, and then dancing with Elaia.

He had barred himself from mourning because . . . because he had never officially been part of Manon's life. Because there was nobody to mourn with him. Because he was alone, totally alone, with the burden of his love.

Until today.

Max got down from the table, everyone rearranged a plate or a glass, and cutlery clattered on the tiles. Javier said, 'Okay then, I'll open another bottle.'

The atmosphere was beginning to be upbeat until . . .

'Wait,' Cuneo requested very quietly.

'What?'

'I said, please wait a second.'

Salvatore stared fixedly at his plate. Water was dripping from his chin into the salad dressing.

'Capitano. *Mio caro* Massimo. Dear Zelda, Javier, my friend. Little Elaia, dear little Elaia.'

'And Lupo,' the young woman whispered.

'I too have a . . . confession to make.'

His chin was resting on his bulky chest.

'It's like this . . . *Ecco:* Vivette is the girl I loved, and for the past twenty-one years, I've been scouring every river in France, every marina, every harbour for her.'

Everyone nodded.

'And?' Max asked tentatively.

'And . . . she's married to the mayor of Latour and has been for twenty years. She has two sons and an unbelievable, gigantic triple backside. I found her fifteen years ago.'

'Oh,' Zelda sighed.

'She remembered me, but only after she'd mistaken me for Mario, Giovanni and Arnaud in turn.'

Javier leaned forward. His eyes flashed. He was now pulling very quietly on his cigarette.

Zelda smiled nervously. 'Surely you're joking?'

'No, Zelda. I carried on regardless, looking for the Vivette I'd met on the river one summer's night many years ago. Even when I'd long since found the real Vivette. *Because* I'd found the real Vivette I had to carry on looking for her. It's—'

'Sick,' Javier cut him off sharply.

'Papa!' cried Elaia in horror.

'Javier, my friend, I'm so—'

'Friend? You lied to me and to my wife! Here, in my house. You came to us seven years ago and served us up your . . . your pack of lies. We gave you work, we trusted you, for God's sake!'

'Let me explain why.'

'You used your little romantic comedy to wheedle compassion out of us. It's nauseating.'

'Please stop shouting,' Jean said sternly. 'He certainly didn't do it to spite you. Can't you see how hard this is for him?'

'I can shout as much as I like. And it's no surprise you understand him. You don't seem to be right in the head either, what with that dead woman of yours.'

'You've gone too far, Monsieur,' snapped Max. 'I'd better leave.'

'No, Cuneo, please. Javier's on edge. We're waiting for some laboratory results about Lupo.'

'I'm not on edge, I'm disgusted, Zelda. Disgusted.'

'The three of us are leaving. Right now,' said Perdu.

'Good riddance,' hissed Javier.

Jean stood up. So did Max.

'Salvo?'

Only now did Cuneo look up, streaming tears and bottomless sadness from his eyes.

'Thank you very much for your hospitality, Madame Zelda,' said Perdu.

She gave him a thin, despairing smile.

'Best of luck with Lupo, Mademoiselle Elaia. I am very, very sorry for what you're going through. From the depths of my heart,' he said, turning to the sick girl. 'And I hope for your sake, Monsieur Javier, that your wonderful wife goes on loving you and that one day you realise how precious that is. Good-bye.'

It was clear from Javier's expression that he wanted to punch Perdu.

Elaia ran after the men across the dark, silent garden. Her footsteps in the damp night-time grass were the only sound apart from the chirping of the crickets. Elaia walked alongside Max in her bare feet. He took her gently by the hand.

As they stood by the boat, Cuneo said hoarsely: 'Thanks for the . . . lift. With your permission, Giovanni Perduto, I'll pack my stuff and leave.'

'No need to stand on your dignity and slip off into the night, Salvo,' Perdu replied serenely.

He climbed up the ship's ladder, and Cuneo followed him hesitantly.

When they had struck the flag from the prow, Perdu asked with a little laugh: 'A gigantic triple backside? What the hell's that?'

Cuneo answered uncertainly: 'Well, imagine a triple chin . . . on someone's backside.'

'No, I'd rather not,' snorted Perdu, barely stifling a chuckle.

'You're not taking this seriously,' Cuneo complained. 'Just imagine if the love of your life turned out to be an illusion. With a horse's backside, a horse's teeth and a brain that was presumably reeling from kenophobia.'

'A fear of empty spaces? Scary.'

They smiled shyly at each other.

'Loving or not loving should be like coffee or tea; people should be allowed to decide. How else are we to get over all our dead and the women we've lost?' Cuneo whispered dejectedly.

'Maybe we shouldn't.'

'You think so? Not get over it, but . . . then? What then? What task do the departed want us to do?'

That was the question that Jean Perdu had been unable to answer for all these years.

Until now. Now he knew.

'To carry them within us – that is our task. We carry them all inside us, all our dead and shattered loves. Only they make us whole. If we begin to forget or cast aside those we've lost, then . . . then we are no longer present either.'

Jean looked at the Allier River, glittering in the moonlight.

'All the love, all the dead, all the people we've known. They are the rivers that feed our sea of souls. If we refuse to remember them, that sea will dry up too.'

He felt an overwhelming inner thirst to seize life with both hands before time sped past even faster. He didn't want to die of thirst; he wanted to be as wide and free as the sea – full and deep. He longed for friends. He wanted to love. He wanted to feel the marks that Manon had left inside him. He still wanted to feel her coursing through him, mingling with him. Manon had changed him forever – why deny it? That was how he had become the man whom Catherine had allowed to approach her.

Jean Perdu suddenly realised that Catherine could never take Manon's place. She took her own place. No worse, no better: simply different.

He longed to show Catherine the full expanse of his sea!

The men watched Max and Elaia kiss.

Jean knew they wouldn't mention their lies and illusions again. The essential had been said.

CHAPTER 29

Aweek had passed. Hesitantly, cautiously, they had confided the major events of their lives to each other: Salvatore was the 'imposition' of an 'accident' between his cleaning lady mother and a married teacher during a free period; Jean was the child of a quarrelsome relationship between an occasional craftsman and an aristocratic academic; Max, a final attempt by a chronic people pleaser and a pedant, worn down by expectation and disappointment, to save their sclerotic marriage.

They had sold books, read to children and had the piano tuned in exchange for a few novels. They had sung and laughed. From a public telephone Jean had rung his parents – and number 27 too.

No one had picked up, even though he had let it ring twenty-six times.

He had asked his father what it had felt like to go all of a sudden from being a lover to a father.

Joaquin Perdu had said nothing for an unusually long time, then Jean heard him sniff. 'Well, Jeanno . . . having a child is like casting off your own

250

childhood forever. It's as if it's only then that you really grasp what it means to be a man. You're scared too that all your weaknesses will be laid bare, because fatherhood demands more than you can give . . . I always felt I had to earn your love, because I loved you so, so much.'

At that they had both sniffed.

'Why are you asking, Jeanno? Do you mean to say you—'

'No.'

Unfortunately. A Max and a daughter, a little Lady Defiance, would have been nice. Would, could, should.

Jean felt as though the tears he had shed by the Allier had created some space inside him. He could fill those initial gaps with fragrances, caresses, his father's love . . . and Catherine. He could also squeeze in his affection for Max and Cuneo as well as the beauty of the landscape; he had found beneath the sorrow a place where emotion and happiness could live alongside tenderness and the realisation that he was lovable after all.

They reached the Saône via the Canal du Centre, and there they sailed into the eye of a storm. Between Dijon and Lyons, the Burgundy sky came crowding down, growling and black, repeatedly split by lightning.

Tchaikovsky's piano concertos illuminated the murky darkness in *Lulu*'s belly like a spark in the belly of Jonah's whale. Max braced his feet resolutely against the frame of the piano, and conjured ballads, waltzes and scherzi from the keyboard while the boat careened along on the cresting waves of the Saône.

Perdu had never heard Tchaikovsky like this: accompanied by the trumpets and violins of the storm and underpinned by the groaning and pumping of the engine, and the creaking of the timbers as the wind buffeted the boat's vulnerable waist and tried to drive her against the bank. Books rained down from the bookcases, Lindgren lay under a screwed-down sofa, and through a tear in the armchair's upholstery Kafka, ears flattened, observed the volumes slip-sliding around.

As Jean Perdu navigated up the Seille, a tributary of the Saône, the view ahead was reminiscent of a giant steamed-up laundry. He could smell the air – it was electric; he could smell the foaming, green water; he could feel the wheel twisting in his calloused hands – and he was delighted to be alive. To be alive now, right now!

He was even enjoying the storm, force 5 on the Beaufort scale.

Out of the corner of his eye, as the boat bucked and dipped between two buffeting waves, he spied the woman.

She was wearing a see-through plastic rain cape and carrying an umbrella like a London stockbroker's. She was gazing out over reeds pressed low by the gusty wind. She raised her hand in greeting before (he could barely believe it, but it was actually happening) unzipping her cape, tossing it aside, turning around and spreading her arms, the open umbrella in her right hand.

Then, arms outstretched like the statue of Christ on Rio de Janeiro's Corcovado, she let herself topple backwards into the heaving river.

'What the . . .?' hissed Perdu. 'Salvo! Woman overboard!' he cried, and the Italian came barrelling out of the galley.

'*Che?* What have you been drinking?' he cried, but Perdu merely pointed to the body now rising and sinking in the whipped-up water. And to the umbrella.

The Neapolitan stared at the foaming river. The umbrella sank.

Cuneo's teeth were grinding.

He made a grab for the mooring lines and the lifebuoy.

'Bring us in closer!' he ordered. 'Massimo!' he called. 'Get off the piano! I need you here, right now . . . *subito*!'

While Perdu wrestled the book barge nearer to the bank, Cuneo took up a position beside the railing, tied the rope to the lifebelt and braced his short, pudgy legs against the boards. Then he hurled the lifebelt with all his might towards the bundle in the water. He handed the other end of the rope to the watching Max, who had turned as white as a sheet.

'When I get hold of her, you pull. Pull like a carthorse, boy!'

He kicked off his shoes and dived headlong into the river. Streaks of lightning rent the sky.

Max and Perdu watched Cuneo swim through the ravening water with powerful crawl strokes.

'Shit, shit, shit!' Max pulled his anorak sleeves well down over his hands and gripped the rope again.

Perdu dropped anchor with a rattle. The barge pitched and tossed as if it were being thrown about inside a washing machine.

Cuneo reached the woman and put his arms around her.

Perdu and Max tugged on the rope and heaved them both aboard. Cuneo's moustache was dripping; the woman's heart-shaped face was framed by sopping, ruddy-brown hair like curly seaweed.

Perdu dashed to the wheelhouse, but as he reached for the radio to call the emergency doctor, he felt Cuneo's heavy wet hand on his shoulder.

'Don't! The woman doesn't want you to. She'll be all right as it is. I'll take care of her – she needs drying off and warming up.' Perdu trusted Cuneo's words and asked no further questions.

Sometime after they had hauled anchor, Perdu saw Cuisery marina emerge from the mist and steered *Lulu* into the harbour. Amid the lashing rain and waves Max and he tied boat to pontoon.

'We've got to get off!' cried Max over the whistling and wailing of the wind. 'The boat's going to take one hell of a battering!'

'I'm not going to leave the books and the cats all alone!' Perdu called back. The water was running into his ears, down his neck and up his sleeves. 'And anyway, I'm the *capitano*, and a skipper doesn't abandon his ship.'

'Aye aye! Then I'm not going anywhere either.'

The boat groaned, as though they both had a screw loose.

Having set up camp in Perdu's cabin, Cuneo had helped peel the castaway out of her clothes. The woman with the heart-shaped face was lying naked under a huge heap of blankets with a blissful expression on her face. The Italian had decked himself out in his white tracksuit, which made him look ever so slightly silly.

He kneeled down beside her and fed her Provençal *pistou*. He spooned the garlic, basil and almond paste straight into a cup and diluted it with clear flavoursome vegetable broth.

She smiled at him between two sips.

'So it's Salvo. Salvatore Cuneo, from Naples,' she said.

'*Si.*'

'I'm Samantha.'

'And you're gorgeous,' said Salvo.

'Is it . . . is it not too bad out there?' she asked. Her eyes were really very large and deepest, darkest blue.

'Nah!' Max shot back. 'Huh, what do you mean?'

'A light shower. There's a little moisture about,' Cuneo reassured her.

'I could read something aloud,' Perdu suggested.

'Or we could sing a song,' added Max. 'In the round.'

'Or cook,' suggested Cuneo. 'Do you like daube, a stew made with *herbes de Provence*?'

She nodded. 'And beef cheeks too, right?'

'So what's the problem?' asked Max.

'Life. The water. Tinned whorlfish.'

The three men stared at her, completely baffled.

On first appraisal Perdu thought that this Samantha might say and do some mad things, but she neither appeared nor was in fact mad. She was just . . . peculiar.

'Three times nine, I'd say,' he replied. 'What are whorlfish, though?'

'Did you fall into the water *on purpose*?' asked Max.

'On purpose? Yes, of course,' Samantha answered. 'Who goes for a walk on a day like today and accidentally falls in backwards? Now that would be stupid! No, you need to plan this kind of thing.'

'So you were depressed, and you wanted to, um . . .?'

'Oh no, is that how it looked?'

Genuinely bewildered, she turned her heart-shaped face to each of the three men.

'Practise pushing up the daisies? Send myself over the Styx? Die? Nooo. Why on earth would I do that? No, no. I like being alive, even if it's occasionally a real struggle and fairly pointless in the grand scheme of things. No. I wanted to know what it felt like to jump into the river in this weather. The river looked so interesting, like soup gone wild. I wanted to know if I'd feel afraid in that soup or if my fear would tell me something important.'

Cuneo nodded as if he understood exactly what she meant.

'And what was it supposed to tell you?' Max asked. 'Something like God is dead, long live extreme sports?'

'No, I merely wanted to see if a different way of living my life might occur to me. When it comes down to it, you only regret the things you didn't do. That's what they say, isn't it?'

The three men nodded.

'Anyway, I didn't want to wind up frustrated. I mean, who wants to bite the dust with the depressing thought that you've run out of time to do the really important things?'

'All right,' said Jean. 'Naturally, we can bring our desires into sharper focus. But I'm not sure that really requires jumping into a river.'

Cuneo gave Samantha a rapturous smile, and ran his fingers repeatedly over the tips of his moustache.

'Hallelujah,' he muttered, and passed her the *pistou*.

'And something important did occur to me as the waves tossed me about and I felt like the last raisin in the cake mix. I realised what I was missing,' she announced.

And took a spoonful of soup.

And another spoonful.

And . . . yes . . . another spoonful.

They waited spellbound for the punch line.

'I want to kiss a man again, and this time do it properly,' said the woman after she had scraped the very last spoonful out of the pot. Then she gave a belch of pleasure, reached for Cuneo's hand, laid it under her cheek and closed her eyes. 'After I've had some sleep,' she managed to mumble.

'At your service,' whispered Cuneo with a slightly glazed expression.

No answer. A smile, that was all. She was soon asleep and snoring like a snuffly little terrier. The three perplexed men looked on. Max laughed to himself and gave a double thumbs-up. Cuneo tried to find a more comfortable sitting position so as not to disturb the stranger's dreams; her head lay on his large hand like a cat on a cushion.

CHAPTER 30

While the storm raged over the town of books and the Seille, cutting swaths through the woods, flipping cars onto their roofs and sending farmhouses up in flames, the male trio did their best to play it cool.

'So why is Cuisery paradise, as you said about three thousand years ago?' Max asked Jean quietly.

'Oh, Cuisery! An avid reader will lose his heart here. The whole village is crazy about books – or crazy full stop – but that's not unusual. Virtually every shop is a bookshop, a printer's, a book-binder's, a publisher's, and many of the houses are artists' workshops. The place is buzzing with creativity and imagination.'

'You wouldn't think so right now,' Max com-mented. The wind was whistling around the barge, rattling anything that wasn't nailed down. The cats had bedded down on top of Samantha. Lindgren was nestling by her neck, and Kafka was lying in the hollow between her thighs. Their poses said 'She belongs to us now.'

'Every bookseller in Cuisery specialises in some-thing. You can find everything here – and when I say everything, I mean everything,' explained Perdu.

In a previous life, when he was still a Parisian bookseller, he had contacted some of the rare book dealers – for example when a wealthy customer from Hong Kong, London or Washington decided he had to own a Hemingway first edition worth a hundred thousand euros, complete with buckskin binding and an inscription from Hemingway to his dear old friend Otto 'Toby' Bruce. Or a book from Salvador Dalí's personal library – one the master had supposedly read before having his surrealist melting-clock dreams.

'So do they have palm leaves too?' asked Cuneo. He was still kneeling beside Samantha, supporting her face.

'No. There's science fiction, the fantastic and fantasy – yes, specialists do make a distinction – as well as—'

'Palm leaves? What's that supposed to mean?' Max wanted to know.

Perdu groaned. 'Nothing,' he said hurriedly.

'Never heard of the library of destiny? Of,' the Italian was whispering now, 'the book of life?'

'Nyom, nyom,' Samantha murmured.

Jean Perdu knew the legend too. The magical Book of Books, the great memory of mankind, which had been written by seven supernatural, all-seeing wise men five thousand years earlier. Legend had it that those seven Rishis had discovered these ethereal books, which described the entire past and future of the world, the script for all life, drawn up by beings that existed beyond such constraints as time and space. The Rishis supposedly interpreted the destinies of several million people and far-reaching historical events from those supernatural books and transcribed them onto marble or stone tablets, or even palm leaves.

Salvo Cuneo's eyes lit up. 'Imagine, Massimo. Your life is described in that palm-leaf library, on your own slender frond; every single detail of your birth, your death and everything in between: whom you'll love, whom you'll marry, your career; absolutely everything – even your past life.'

'Pfff . . . king of the road,' escaped from Samantha's lips.

'Your whole life and past life on a beer mat. Very plausible,' muttered Perdu.

During his life as a bookseller, Jean Perdu had been forced to chase away several collectors who had wished to acquire these so-called Akashic Records, whatever the price.

'Really?' said Max. 'Hey, guys, maybe I was Balzac.'

'Maybe you were a tiny cannelloni too.'

'And you can find out about your death as well. Not the exact day, but the month and the year. And it doesn't hide how you'll die either,' added Cuneo.

'No, I think I'll do without,' Max said doubtfully. 'What's the point of knowing the date of your own death? I'd spend the rest of my life out of my mind with fear. No thanks. What I'd like is some hope that eternity's on my side.'

Perdu cleared his throat. 'To return to Cuisery: most of the 1,641 inhabitants do something involving the printed word; the others take care of the visitors. They say the booksellers' fraternities and sororities have woven a dense web of international contacts based on a parallel communications network. They don't even use the internet – the book elders guard their knowledge so closely it would be lost when one of their members died.'

'Mmm,' sighed Samantha.

'To ensure that doesn't happen, each of them selects at least one successor, into whose ear he will pour his vast knowledge of books. They know mystical tales about the writing of famous works, secret editions, original manuscripts, the Women's Bible . . .'

'Cool,' said Max.

'. . . . or books that tell a very different story between the lines,' Perdu continued in a low, conspiratorial tone of voice. 'They say there's a woman in Cuisery who knows the real endings of many famous works because she collects their final drafts and the drafts before that. She knows the original ending of *Romeo and Juliet*, the one where they both survive, marry and have children.'

'Yuck.' Max was appalled. 'Romeo and Juliet survive and have kids? That ruins all the drama.'

'I like it,' said Cuneo. 'I've always felt sorry for little *Julia*.'

'And does any of them know who Sanary is?' asked Max.

Jean Perdu certainly hoped so. He had written a postcard from Digoin to the president of Cuisery's book guild, Samy Le Trequesser, to say that he was on his way.

At two in the morning, utterly spent, they fell asleep to the rocking of the waves that had grown gentler as the storm subsided.

When they awoke, the new day glittered with harmless, freshly rinsed sunshine, as though the previous night had never happened. The storm was gone – and so was Samantha.

Cuneo looked down, nonplussed, at his empty hand, then waved it at the other two.

'Is it happening all over again? Why do I only find women on the waterways?' he complained. 'I've barely recovered from the last one.'

'Oh right. You've only had fifteen years,' grinned Max.

'Women,' grumbled Cuneo. 'Couldn't she at least write her number on the mirror in lipstick!'

'I'll fetch some croissants,' Max announced.

'I'll come with you, *amico*, to look for the sleep singer,' said Cuneo.

'What? Neither of you knows his way around. I'll go,' Perdu butted in.

In the end all three of them went.

As they made their way from the small marina across the campsite and through the town gate to the bakery, an orc came towards them carrying an armful of baguettes. It was accompanied by an elf dressed up as Legolas, its eyes glued to its iPhone.

Perdu encountered a group of Harry Potters arguing at the top of their voices with a troop of Night's Watch members outside the blue-painted front of *La Découverte* bookshop. Two ladies in vampire costumes rode towards them on mountain bikes, shooting Max hungry looks, and two Douglas Adams fans were emerging from the church in dressing gowns with towels slung over their shoulders.

'A convention!' cried Max.

'A what?' asked Cuneo, staring after the orc.

'A fantasy convention. The village is packed with people dressed up as their favourite author or character. Wicked.'

'Like – Moby Dick, the whale?' asked Cuneo.

Perdu and Cuneo gaped at creatures that seemed to have sprung from Middle Earth or Winterfell. Such is the power of books.

Cuneo asked which book each costumed figure came from, and Max gave him the lowdown, glowing with excitement. Yet even he had to pass when a woman in a scarlet leather coat and white bucket-top boots came walking towards them.

Perdu explained, 'Gentlemen, that lady isn't in fancy dress; she's the medium who speaks to Colette and George Sand. How she does it, she doesn't say. She claims to meet them in time-travel dreams.'

There was room in Cuisery for anything remotely associated with literature. There was a doctor who specialised in literary schizophrenia. He was consulted by people whose alter ego was a reincarnation of Dostoyevsky or the German mystic Hildegard von Bingen. Some of his patients had become entangled in their many pseudonyms.

Perdu directed his steps towards the home of Samy Le Trequesser, the chairman of the Cuisery guild and supporters' association. A word from Le Trequesser would open doors so that he might talk to booksellers about Sanary. Le Trequesser lived above the old printer's shop.

'Will the book boss give us a password or something?' asked Max. He could hardly tear himself away from the book displays outside every other shop.

'More like "something".'

Cuneo kept stopping to read the bistro menus and jot the details down in his recipe book. They were in the Bresse region, which boasted that it was the cradle of innovative French cuisine.

They gave their names at the printer's shop and, after waiting awhile in the chairman's office, they got a real surprise: Samy Le Trequesser was not a chairman – she was a chairwoman.

CHAPTER 31

Facing them across a desk that appeared to have been assembled from driftwood sat the woman Salvo had fished out of the Seille the previous evening.

Samy was Samantha. She was wearing a white linen dress. She also had on hobbit feet, huge and extremely hairy ones.

'So,' asked Samy, crossing her shapely legs and giving one hobbit foot a delightful waggle, 'how can I help you?'

'Um, yes. I'm looking for the author of a specific book. The name's a pseudonym, a cryptic one, and—'

'Are you better now?' Cuneo interrupted.

'Yes, fine.' Samy flashed Salvo a smile. 'And thank you, Salvo, for saying that I can kiss you before I grow old. I haven't been able to get it off my mind since.'

'Can you buy those furry feet in Cuisery?' Max wanted to know.

'Anyway, getting back to the book *Southern Lights*—'

'Yes, at Eden. It's a leisure cum info cum tourist

cum rip-off centre, and it sells hobbit feet, orc ears, slit stomachs . . .'

'The author might be a woman—'

'I want to cook for you, Signora Samantha. And it's no trouble if you feel like taking a swim first.'

'I think I'll get myself some hobbit feet too. As slippers. Wow, that would really freak out Kafka.'

Perdu looked out the window, struggling to keep his composure.

'Will you all shut up? Sanary! *Southern Lights*! I want to know who the real author is! Please!'

It had come out louder than he'd intended. Max and Cuneo looked at Jean in surprise, but Samy had leaned back in her seat as though she were beginning to enjoy this.

'I've spent twenty years looking for him. Or her. The book . . . it's . . .' Jean Perdu was trying his best to find the right words, but all he could see was light sparkling on a river. 'That book is like the woman I used to love. It leads to her. It's liquid love. It's the dose of love I could more or less bear, and yet nevertheless feel. It's like a straw I've been breathing through for the last twenty years.'

Jean ran his hand over his face.

But that wasn't the whole truth; no longer the only truth.

'It helped me to survive. I don't need the book any more, because now I can . . . breathe on my own again. But I would like to say thank you.'

Max looked at him with great respect and astonishment.

Samy's face had broken into a broad grin.

'A book for catching your breath. I understand.'

She looked out the window. More and more fictional characters were gathering in the streets outside.

'I didn't expect someone like you to ever come along,' she said with a sigh.

Jean sensed his back muscles tensing.

'Of course you're not the first, but there haven't been many of you. The others all left with the riddle unsolved; none of them asked the right questions. Asking questions is an art.'

Samy did not avert her eyes from the window, along whose frame short lengths of driftwood dangled from fine threads. If one looked at the flotsam for a while it coalesced into a leaping fish. Or a face, an angel with one wing . . .

'Most people only ask questions so they can listen to themselves talk. Or hear something they are able to cope with, but please, nothing that might get the better of them. "Do you love me?" is one of those questions. There should be a total ban on it.'

She tapped her hobbit feet together.

'Ask your question,' she ordered.

'Do I . . . do I get only one?' asked Perdu.

Samy smiled warmly.

'Of course not. You don't get just one, you get as many as you like. But you have to phrase them so that you receive a yes-or-no answer.'

'So you know him?'

'No.'

'The right question means *every word* has to be right,' Max emphasized and elbowed Jean excitedly in the ribs.

Perdu corrected himself: 'So you know *her*?'

'Yes.'

Samy looked kindly at Max. 'I see, Monsieur Jordan, that you have grasped the art of questioning. The right questions can make a person very happy. How's your next book coming along? Your second, isn't it? The curse of the second book, all that expectation. You should leave yourself a good twenty years. The best time would be when everyone's forgotten about you for a while, then you'll be free.'

Max's ears burned red.

'Next question, soul reader.'

'Is it Brigitte Caron?'

'Heavens no!'

'But Sanary is alive?'

Samy smiled. 'Oh yes!'

'Can you . . . introduce me to her?'

Samy thought this over.

'Yes.'

'How?'

'That wasn't a yes-no question,' Max reminded him.

'Well, I'm cooking bouillabaisse today,' Cuneo broke in. 'I'll pick you up at half past seven. That way you and Capitano Perduto can carry on playing "yes-no-don't know". *Sì?* You're not engaged, by some bad luck? Fancy coming on a little boat trip?'

Samy looked from one man to the next.

'Yes and no and yes,' she said decisively. 'So, that's everything cleared up. Now if you'll excuse me, I have to go out and greet those wonderful creatures and say a few nice words in a language invented by Tolkien. I've practised, but I sound like Chewbacca making a New Year's speech.'

Samy stood up, and they all took another good look at her superlative hobbit-foot slippers.

She turned to face them one last time as she reached the door.

'Max, did you know that when a star is born, it takes a year for it to reach its full size? Then it spends millions of years busily burning up. Strange, eh? Have you ever tried to invent a new language? Or a few new words? I'd be delighted if France's most famous living author under thirty were to offer me a new word this evening. Deal?'

Her dark-blue eyes sparkled.

And a little bomb exploded in Max's imagination, showering his secret inner garden with seeds.

When Salvo Cuneo, dressed in his finest checked shirt, jeans and patent-leather shoes, arrived to pick Samy up from the printer's that evening, she was standing by the door with three suitcases, a potted fern and her rain cape draped over her arm.

'I really hope you're going to take me with you, Salvo, although of course your invitation meant

something different. I've lived here long enough,'
she said by way of greeting. 'Nearly ten years. One
whole stage, as Hesse says. Now it's time to head
south to learn to breathe anew, to see the sea and
to kiss a man again. Goodness, I'm approaching
my late fifties. I'm entering the prime of my life.'

Cuneo stared directly into the book woman's
dark-blue eyes.

'The offer stands, Signora Samy Le Trequesser,'
he said. 'I am at your service.'

'I haven't forgotten, Salvatore Cuneo from
Naples.'

He called a car to transport her packed belongings to the boat.

'Ahem . . . would I be right in thinking,' asked a
perplexed Perdu, as Salvo lugged the suitcases over
the gangway a little later, 'that you haven't only
come for dinner, but you're moving in as well?'

'You would, my dear. May I? For a little while?
Until you cast off and toss me overboard?'

'Of course. There's a free sofa over by the
children's books,' said Max.

'May I have a say?' asked Perdu.

'Why? Are you going to say something other than
yes?'

'Um, no.'

'Thank you.' Samy was visibly moved. 'You'll
hardly hear a peep from me. I honestly only sing
in my sleep.'

On the postcard Perdu wrote Catherine that

night were the phrases Max had invented that afternoon so he could present them to Samy at dinner.

Samy found them so beautiful that she kept repeating them to herself, rolling their sounds back and forth on her tongue like a crumb of cake.

Star salt (the stars' reflection in a river)
Sun cradle (the sea)
Lemon kiss (everyone knew exactly what
   this meant!)
Family anchor (the dinner table)
Heart notcher (your first lover)
Veil of time (you spin around in the sandpit
   to find you are old and wet your pants
   when you laugh)
Dreamside
Wishableness

This last word was Samy's new favourite.

'We all live in wishableness,' she said. 'Each in a different kind.'

CHAPTER 32

'The Rhône is a nightmare, to put it mildly,' said Max and pointed to the nuclear power station. It was the seventeenth one they'd passed since the point where the Saône meets the Rhône near Lyons. Fast-breeder reactors alternated with vineyards and motorways. Cuneo had given up on fishing.

They had wandered around Cuisery and its literary catacombs for a further three days. Now they were approaching Provence; they recognised the chalky hills near Orange that reared up like the gateway to southern France.

The sky was in flux. It had begun to take on the deep-blue glow of the air above the Mediterranean at the height of summer, when the water and the heavens reflect and intensify each other.

'Like layers of puff pastry, blue upon blue upon blue. The land of blue pastries,' murmured Max.

He had discovered a delicious addiction to forming combinations of words and images; he would play tag with words.

Occasionally Max would get his word games all mixed up, and Samy would chortle lustily.

Her laugh was like the honking of a flying crane, thought Jean.

Cuneo was absolutely besotted with Samy, even though she hadn't yet taken him up on his offer. She wanted Perdu to solve the mystery first.

She would often sit in the wheelhouse, playing yes-no-don't know with Perdu.

'Does Sanary have kids?'

'No.'

'A husband?'

'No.'

'Two?'

She laughed like an entire flock of cranes.

'Did she ever write a second book?'

'Nooo,' said Samy, drawing it out. 'Unfortunately.'

'Did she write *Southern Lights* when she was happy?'

A long silence.

Perdu let the landscape float past as Samy contemplated her answer.

After Orange, they quickly left Châteauneuf-du-Pape behind. They would be in Avignon in time for dinner, and from the ancient Papal City Jean could hire a car and within an hour be in the town of Bonnieux in the Luberon.

Too quick, he thought. Should I – to use Max's words – ring Luc's doorbell and say, 'Hello, Basset, you old wine whisperer, I used to be your wife's lover.'

'Between yes and no,' Samy answered. 'Difficult question. We don't generally lie around for days wallowing in our happiness like roast beef in gravy, do we? Happiness is so short-lived. How long have you ever been genuinely happy in one stretch?'

Jean considered this.

'About four hours. I was driving from Paris to Mazan. I wanted to see my sweetheart, and we'd arranged to meet at a small hotel called Le Siècle, opposite the church. I was happy then. For the whole journey. I sang. I imagined her whole body and I sang to it.'

'Four hours? That's so terribly beautiful.'

'Yes. I was happier in those four hours than during the four days that followed. But looking back I'm happy to have had those four days too.' Jean faltered. 'Do we only decide in retrospect that we've been happy? Don't we notice when we're happy, or do we realise only much later that we were?'

Samy sighed. 'That really would be stupid.'

Musing over belatedly discovered happiness, Jean steered them swiftly and safely down the Rhône, which in these parts resembled a major maritime route. There was no one standing on the bank, waving to them to come and sell them books. The locks were fully automatic and handled dozens of ships at a time. Their languid canal days were well and truly over.

The closer Jean got to Manon country, the more his time with Manon occupied his thoughts. How it had felt to touch her.

As though she could read his mind, Samy mused

aloud: 'Isn't it amazing how physical love is? Our body is better at recalling what it felt like to touch someone than our brain is at remembering the things that person said.' She blew on the fine hairs on her lower arm. 'I remember my father mainly in terms of his body. How he smelled and how he walked. How it felt to lay my head on his shoulder or put my hand in his. Almost the only thing I can recall of his voice is how he used to say, "My little Sasa". I miss the warmth of his body and I'm still furious that he'll never come to the telephone again, even though I've got important things to tell him. God, it makes me mad! But I miss his body most. Where he always used to sit in his armchair there's nothing but air. Stupid, empty air.'

Perdu nodded. 'The trouble is that so many people, most of them women, think they have to have a perfect body to be loved. But all it has to do is be capable of loving – and being loved,' he added.

'Oh, Jean, please tell that to the world,' laughed Samy and passed him the on-board microphone. 'We are loved if we love, another truth we always seem to forget. Have you noticed that most people prefer to be loved, and will do anything it takes? Diet, rake in the money, wear scarlet underwear. If only they loved with the same energy; hallelujah, the world would be so wonderful and so free of tummy-tuck tights.'

Jean joined in with her laughter. He thought of

276

Catherine. When they'd come together, they had both been too delicate and too vulnerable, and they had hankered more to be loved, rather than having the strength and the courage to love. Loving requires so much courage and so little expectation. Would he ever be able to love someone properly again?

Does Catherine even read my cards?

Samy was a good listener, taking everything in and playing it back to him. She told him that she used to be a teacher in Melchnau, in Switzerland; a sleep researcher in Zurich; and a technical draughtsperson for wind farms in the Atlantic. She had reared goats in the Vaucluse and made cheese.

And she had an innate flaw: she could not lie. She could say nothing or refuse to answer, but she was incapable of telling a deliberate lie.

'Imagine what that's like in today's world,' she said. 'It got me into such trouble as a girl. Everyone thought I was a nasty little brat who revelled in being rude. The waiter in a posh restaurant asks, "Did you enjoy your meal?" and I reply, "No, not at all." The mother of a classmate asks after a birthday party, "So, little Samy, did you have a good time?" and I honestly try to squeeze a yes out of myself, but all I can manage is, "No, it was horrid, and your breath stinks from all that red wine you drink!"'

Perdu chuckled. It's amazing how close you are to your essential self as a kid, he thought, and how far from it you drift the more you strive to be loved.

'I fell out of a tree when I was thirteen, and as I was being examined in one of those tubes, they spotted something: my brain has no lie-making machine. I can't write fantastical parables – unless, of course, I were to bump into a unicorn sometime soon. I can only talk about things I've experienced firsthand. I'm the kind of person who'd have to get into the pan with the potatoes in order to give my opinion on chips.'

Just then Cuneo brought them some homemade lavender ice cream. It had a tangy yet floral flavour.

The woman with no aptitude for lying watched the Neapolitan walk away.

'He's short, fat and, objectively speaking, not the most obvious choice of pin-up boy. But he's smart, strong and he can probably do whatever's necessary for a life of love. I think he's the most beautiful man I will ever kiss,' said Samy. 'It's strange that magnificent, good-hearted people like him don't receive more love. Do their looks disguise their character so well that nobody notices how open their soul, their being and their prin-ciples are to love and kindness?'

She took a long, languid breath. 'Strangely, I was never loved either. I used to think it was because of the way I look. Then I thought to myself: why do I always end up in places where every man I meet already has a wife? The cheese producers in the Vaucluse . . . My word, what a bunch of old foxes! They see a woman as a tall two-legged goat that does the washing. You can consider yourself blessed if they even say hello.'

Samy licked her ice cream dreamily.

'I think – and correct me if I'm getting too carried away with my ideas about the global sister-hood – that first there is the love in which we think with our knickers. I know all about that. It's fun for about fifteen minutes. Second, there's logical love, the type we create in our heads; I've experienced that too. You look for men who objec-tively suit your set-up or who won't upset your life plans too much, but you don't feel any magic. And third, there's the love that comes from your chest or your solar plexus, or somewhere in between. That's the type I want. It's got to have the magic that sets my lifeblood alight, right down to the tiniest little globule. What do you think?' She stuck out her tongue at him. It was purple from the ice cream.

Jean Perdu thought he now knew the question he needed to ask.

'Samy?' he asked.

'What, Jeanno?'

She spoke differently, but that was always the case: the way an author wrote was the true sound of her heart and soul.

'You wrote *Southern Lights*, didn't you?'

CHAPTER 33

It was surely no coincidence that the sun chose that very moment to break through between two banks of cloud and cast a ray into Samy's eyes, like a finger pointing down from the heavens. It illuminated them – two blazing candles.

Samy's face came alive.

'Yes,' she admitted quietly, then said, more loudly: 'Yes.'

'Yes!' she cried, laughing and weeping, throwing her arms up. 'And this book was meant to bring me my man, Jeanno! Someone who loves me from the place between his chest and his belly button. I wanted him to find me because he'd been hunting for me, because he'd dreamed of me, because he enjoys everything I am and needs none of the things that I'm not. You know what, though, Jean Perdu?'

She could not stop crying and laughing.

'You found me – but you're not the one.'

She turned around.

'That chap in his flowery apron, with those nice, firm bunched muscles. With his moustache, which will tickle me: *he's* the one. You brought him to me. Together you and *Southern Lights* brought him. By pure magic.'

Her joy infected Jean. She was right, as wishable as that might sound: he had read *Southern Lights*, he had stopped in Cepoy, met Salvo and from there . . . hey presto, they had arrived here.

Samy wiped her tear-salted face. 'I had to write my book. You had to read it. You had to endure and suffer in order to get into your boat and set off at last. Let us believe that's how it came about. Okay?'

'Of course, Samy. I believe it. Some books were written for a single person: *Southern Lights* was for me.' He mustered his courage. 'I only survived till now because of your book,' he confessed. 'I understood your every thought. It was as if you knew me before I knew myself.'

Sanary-Samy clapped her hands to her mouth.

'That's so uncanny, Jean. Those are the most wonderful words I've ever heard.'

She threw her arms around him.

She kissed him left and right and then again on the cheeks, the forehead and the nose. After each kiss she said, 'I'm telling you: never again will I write to summon love. Do you know how long I've waited? More than twenty years, dammit! And now you'll have to excuse me: I'm going to kiss my man – and I'm going to do it properly. That's the final part of the experiment. But I probably won't be in much of a mood this evening if it doesn't work out.'

281

She hugged Jean tightly once more.

'Crikey, I'm scared! It's horrid! But so wonderful. I'm alive. How about you? Did you feel it, right now?'

She disappeared down into the belly of the barge.

Jean caught a 'Yoo-hoo, Salvo . . .'

Jean Perdu realised with astonishment that he had – and it felt great.

MANON'S TRAVEL DIARY

Paris

August 1992

You're asleep.

I see you, and I'm no longer so ashamed that I simply want to bury myself in salty sand because one man can never be everything to me. I've stopped berating myself as I have done for the last five cobalt-blue summers. And we had relatively few days together in total: adding them all up, Jean Ravenfeather, I come to half a year in which we breathed the same air – 169 days, just enough to string a double pearl necklace, one pearl for each day.

However, the days and nights away from you – as far away as a vapour trail in the sky – when I thought of you and looked forward to seeing you, they count too. Double and threefold, in elation and guilt. Seen that way, it

283

actually felt like fifteen years, time to try out several lives. I dreamed up so many different scenarios.

I've often wondered, did I do wrong, make the wrong choice? Would it have been a 'proper' life, alone with Luc, or with someone else entirely? Or was I dealt a good hand of opportunities but played it badly?

There are no wrongs and no rights in life, though. And there's no reason to ask myself that now anyway: why one man was never enough for me.

There were so many answers.

Such as hunger for life!

And desire, such red-hot, restless, sticky-wet desire.

Such as letting me live before I grow wrinkled and grey, a half-inhabited house at the end of the road.

Such as Paris.

Such as your running into me, like a ship colliding with an island. (Ha-ha. That was my it's-not-my-fault-it-was-fate phase.)

Such as does Luc really love me enough to put up with this?

Such as I'm worthless, I'm bad, so it doesn't matter what I do.

Oh, and of course I can only be with one if I'm with the other. Both of you,

Luc and Jean, husband and lover, south and north, love and sex, earth and sky, body and spirit, country and city. You are the two things I need to be whole.

Breathe in, breathe out, and in between: live at last.

So three-sided spheres do exist.

But all those answers are now redundant. Now the main question is an entirely different one:

When?

When will I tell you what's happening to me?

Never.

Never, never, never and never. Or at any moment, when I touch your shoulder, which is poking, as always, out of the covers you've rolled yourself in. If I touched you, you'd wake immediately and ask, 'What's the matter? What's up, cat girl?'

I wish you'd wake up and save me.

Wake up!

Why should you? I've lied to you too well.

When will I leave you?

Soon.

Not tonight – I can't. It feels as if I'd need a thousand attempts to break loose from you, to turn on my heel and never look back, to actually manage it once.

I leave in stages. I count along, telling myself: 1,000 more kisses . . . 418 more kisses . . . 10 more . . . 4 more. I've set the last 3 aside. Like three sugared almonds for good luck.

Everything is counting down. Sleeping together. Laughing together. Our last dances are upon us.

Incidentally, you really can scream with your heart; but it's incredibly painful.

And speaking of pain, it makes the world smaller. Now I see only you and me and Luc, and that which has grown between the three of us. Each of us has played our part. Now I'll try to rescue what can be rescued. I don't want to brood on punishment; misfortune comes equally to all.

When will I give up?

Only afterwards, I hope.

I still want to see whether my salvage bid succeeds.

The doctors have offered me ibuprofen and opiates, which they say affect only the brain, interrupting the electronic signals running through the lymph glands between my armpits, my lungs and my head.

Some days that means I no longer dream in pictures; on others I detect aromas that remind me of the past – way back in the past, when I wore knee socks. Or else things smell very different: faeces like flowers, wine like burning tyres. A kiss like death.

But I want to be completely sure for the child, so I do without. Sometimes the pain is so bad that I lose my words and cannot reach you. Then I lie to you. I write down the sentences I mean to say to you and read them out loud. When the pain comes, I am incapable of capturing the letters inside my head. A mush of letters, overcooked letters: alphabet soup.

On occasion, it hurt me that you let yourself be lied to; on occasion, I was livid with you for even walking into my life. But never enough to make me hate you.

Jean, I don't know what to do. I don't know whether to wake you up and beg you to help me. Whether to tear out these pages – or copy them and post them to you. Then. Or never. I'm writing so that I can think more clearly.

Whichever way, I'm losing the ability to speak about anything else.

More than ever I use my body to talk to you. This weary, sick, southern wood, with one last tender green shoot sprouting from it; it can voice the most basic desires at least.

Love me.

Hold me.

Stroke me.

Panic flowering, Papa used to say. Great trees blossom one final time before they die, pumping all their sap into their last remaining cancer-free shoot.

Not long ago you said how beautiful I am.

I'm on the cusp of my panic flowering.

One night recently Vijaya rang from New York. You were still on the barge, selling the latest edition of *Southern Lights*. You would love everyone to read that small, strange, beautiful book. You said once that it didn't lie. No sophistication, no embellishments. Only truth.

Vijaya has new bosses: two oddball cellular scientists. They think it is the body, rather than the brain, that determines a person's soul and character. They say it is the billions of other cells. What happens to them happens to the soul.

Pain, for example, he said: it reverses the polarity of the cells. It starts after only three days: arousal cells become pain cells, sensory cells become fear cells, coordination cells become pin-cushions. Eventually tenderness only causes hurt; every breeze, every musical vibration, every approaching shadow triggers fear. And pain feeds hungrily on every movement and every muscle, breeding millions of new pain receptors. Your insides are completely transformed and replaced, but it is invisible from the outside.

By the end you want no one ever to touch you again, Vijaya says. You grow lonely.

Pain is a cancer of the soul, says your oldest friend. He says it like a scientist; he doesn't consider the nausea such words will trigger in non-scientists. He is fore-telling everything that will happen to me.

Pain makes the body dull and your mind with it, as your Vijaya knows. You forget; you can no longer think logic-ally, only in panic. And all your healthy thoughts fall into the furrows the pain gouges into your brain. All your hopes. Eventually you too fall in and are gone, your entire self swallowed up by pain and panic.

When will I die?

In purely statistical terms, it's certain that I will.

I was planning to eat the traditional thirteen Christmas desserts. Maman is in charge of the biscuits and the mousse, Papa will contribute the four fruit delicacies, Luc will polish the finest nuts. Three tablecloths, three candelabras, three hunks of broken bread: one piece for the living sitting at the table, one for the happiness to come, and one for the poor and the dead to share. I'm scared that I'll be fighting for crumbs with the down and out by then.

Luc has implored me to undergo the therapy.

Quite apart from the fact that the odds are as lousy as betting on a horse, a part of me would die anyway; a gravestone would have to be ordered anyway, Mass read and the handkerchiefs ironed.

Will I feel the gravestone's weight?

Papa understands. When I told him why I don't want chemo, he went to the barn and wept. I was fairly convinced he was going to hack off one of his arms.

Maman: petrified. She looks like a petrified olive tree; her chin is gnarled and hard, her eyes are like two chips of bark. She wonders what she has done wrong, why she was unable to turn her first deathly premonition into a bad dream, or into motherly love, which worries her more than the worries merit.

'I knew that death was waiting in Paris, that godforsaken city.' But she can't bring herself to blame me. Ultimately she blames herself. Being hard on herself enables her to carry on and to prepare my last room according to my exact wishes.

You are lying there now like a dancer doing a pirouette. One leg stretched out, the other pulled up. One arm above your head, the other almost braced against your side.

You always looked at me as though I were unique. In five years, not once did you look at me with anger or indifference. How did you manage it?

Castor is staring at me. We two-legged creatures must seem very strange to cats.

I feel crushed by the eternity that awaits me.

Sometimes – but it is a truly evil thought – just sometimes I wished there were someone I love who would go before me. To show me that I can make it too.

Sometimes I thought that you had to go before me so I could do it too, certain that you are waiting for me.

Adieu, Jean Perdu.

I envy you for all the years you still have left to live.

I shall go into my last room and from there into the garden. Yes, that is how it will be. I shall stride through tall, inviting French windows and straight into the sunset. And then . . . then I shall become light, and then I can be everywhere.

That would be my nature; I would be there always, every evening.

CHAPTER 34

The travellers spent a heady evening together. Salvo served pot after pot of mussels, Max played the piano, and they took turns dancing with Samy out on deck.

Later the four of them enjoyed the view of Avignon and the Saint Bénézet Bridge, which had been immortalised in song. July showed itself in all its splendour; even after sundown, the air was a velvety 28 degrees.

Shortly before midnight Jean raised his glass.

'Thank you,' he said. 'For friendship. For truth. And for this unbelievably delicious meal.'

They all raised their glasses. Their clinking sounded like a bell tolling for the end of their journey together.

Despite this, Samy said with glowing cheeks: 'By the way, I'm happy now,' and half an hour later: 'I still am'; and another two hours later . . . well, she probably said it in many other ways that did not require words, but neither Max nor Jean heard her. Deciding not to cramp Samy and Salvo's style, the two men left the couple on *Lulu* for the first of what, hopefully, would be many thousands of nights and ambled through the nearest gate into the old part of Avignon.

The narrow streets were thronged with aimless wanderers. The summer heat had naturally postponed activity till the late hours. Max and Jean bought ice cream on the square in front of the magnificent city hall, and watched buskers juggle with fire, perform acrobatic dances and amuse their audiences in the cafés and bistros with their slapstick comedy. This city didn't appeal to Jean; it seemed to him like a hypocritical whore, living off her past papal glories.

Max caught the rapidly melting ice cream on his tongue. With his mouth half full, he said in a deliberately casual tone: 'I'm going to write children's books. I've got a couple of ideas.'

Jean glanced at him out of the corner of his eye.

So this is Max's moment, he thought. This is the moment he starts to become the man he will one day be.

'May I hear them?' he requested, rousing himself from his affectionate astonishment at being allowed to share in this instant.

'Whew, I thought you were never going to ask.'

Max pulled his notebook from his back pocket and read aloud: 'The old master magician was wondering when a brave girl might finally come along and dig him up from the garden where he had lain forgotten under the strawberries for a century and a half . . .'

Max gazed at Perdu dreamily.

'Or the story of the little cow?'

'Little cow?'

'Yeah, the holy cow that always has to take the blame. I imagine that even the holy cow used to be a young calf once, before people started saying, "Holy cow, *what* did you say you want to be? A writer?"' Max grinned. 'And another one about Claire, a girl who swaps bodies with her kitty cat. Then there's . . .'

The future hero of children's bedtimes, Jean mused as he listened to Max's marvellous storylines.

'. . . and the one where little Bruno complains to the guardians of heaven about the family they lumbered him with . . .'

As Max continued, Jean savoured a sensation that was like delicate flowers unfolding inside his heart. He was so fond of this young man! His quirks, his eyes, his laughter.

'. . . and when people's shadows go back to straighten their owners' childhoods out a bit . . .'

Wonderful, thought Jean. I'll send *my* shadow back in time to straighten *my* life out. How tempting. How sadly impossible.

They arrived back at the barge in the dead of the night, an hour before dawn came stealing across the sky.

While Max took himself off to his corner, noted down a few thoughts and then fell asleep, Jean Perdu paced slowly around his book barge, which was swaying gently in the current. The cats pattered along beside him, their eyes trained closely on the tall man; they sensed impending farewells.

Again and again Jean's fingers met thin air as he ran them along the rows of books, caressing their spines. He knew precisely where each book had stood before it had been sold, the same way we know the houses and fields on the streets where we grew up – and continue to see them, long after they have made way for a motorway or a shopping centre.

He had always felt that books created a force field around him. He had discovered the whole world on his barge – every emotion and place and era. He had never had to travel; his conversations with books had been sufficient . . . until finally he prized them more highly than people. They were less threatening.

He sat down in the armchair on the low dais and gazed out at the water through the wide window. The two cats leaped onto his lap.

'Now you won't be able to stand up,' said their bodies, growing heavier and warmer. 'Now you have to stay.'

So this had been his life. Eighty feet by fifteen. He had started building it all when he was Max's age: the barge, the collection for his 'soul pharmacy', his reputation, this anchor chain. Day after day he had forged and tempered it, link by link – and shackled himself with it.

But it somehow no longer felt right. Were his life a photo album, the random snaps would have all been alike; they would always show him on this boat, with a book in his hand, his hair alone growing more silvery and thinner. At the back would be a picture of him with a searching, pleading look on his wrinkled old face.

No, he didn't want to end up like that, wondering if it was all over. There was only one solution, a radical one that shattered his chains.

He had to leave the barge. Leave it for good.

The thought made him feel nauseated . . . but then, as he took a few deep breaths and imagined life without *Lulu*, relieved.

His guilty conscience stirred immediately. Rid himself of the *Literary Apothecary*, as if she were a troublesome lover?

'She's no trouble,' mumbled Perdu.

The cats purred under his stroking hands.

'What am I going to do with the three of you?' he said dolefully.

Somewhere nearby Samy was singing in her sleep. And a picture formed in his mind: maybe he didn't have to leave the barge an orphan, or search high and low for a buyer.

'Would Cuneo feel at home here?' he asked the cats on his lap. They nuzzled his hand.

It was said that their purring could patch a pail of broken bones back together and revive a fossilised soul; yet when their work was done, cats would go their own way without a backwards glance. They loved without reticence, no strings attached – but no promises either.

Hesse's *Stages* came to Perdu's mind. Most people were familiar with the first line, of course: 'In all beginnings dwells a magic force . . .' but very few people knew the ending: 'For guarding us and helping us to live.' And hardly anyone realised that Hesse wasn't talking about new beginnings.

He meant a readiness to bid farewell.

Farewell to old habits.

Farewell to illusions.

Farewell to a long-expired life, in which one was nothing but a husk, rustled by the occasional sigh.

CHAPTER 35

The day greeted Jean and Max for their late breakfast with 34-degree heat – and a surprise from Samy, who had already been out shopping with Cuneo and had bought them all prepaid mobile phones.

Perdu studied the one she pushed across the table to him between the croissants and cups of coffee with scepticism. He needed his reading glasses to make out the numbers.

'These things have been around for twenty years; you can trust them,' Max mocked him.

'I've saved our numbers for you,' Samy instructed Jean. 'And I want you to ring us. Even if you're fine or don't know how to poach an egg. Or if you're bored and tempted to jump out of a window to feel real again.'

Jean was touched by Samy's earnestness. 'Thank you,' he said awkwardly.

He was overawed by her open, fearless affection. Was this why people liked friendship so much? Tiny Samy almost vanished in his embrace.

'I, um . . . I'd like to give you something,' Perdu

rejoined. Sheepishly he pushed the keys to the barge over to Cuneo.

'My esteemed world's worst liar and greatest cook west of Italy, I must travel without my boat from now on. Therefore and herewith, I give *Lulu* into your hands. Always keep a corner free for cats and for writers in search of a story. Do you accept? You don't have to, but if you do, I'd be delighted to know you are looking after my boat. On a permanent loan, so to speak, so . . .'

'No! It's your job, your office, your soul surgery, your getaway and your home. You *are* the book barge, you stupid nerd. You can't give something like this away to strangers, however much they'd love to take it!' yelled Samy.

They all stared at Samantha in bewilderment.

'Sorry,' she mumbled. 'I . . . eh . . . I mean what I said. It's not on. Swap a mobile phone for a book barge? No way! How distressing!' She let out a stifled giggle.

'This inability to lie seems a real gift in life,' Max remarked. 'And by the way, before anyone asks me: No, I don't need a boat, but I would be grateful for a lift in your car, Jean.'

Cuneo had tears in his eyes.

'Alas, alas,' was all he could say. 'Alas, Capitano. Alas, everything. I'm . . . *cazzo* . . . and all the rest.'

They discussed at length the pros and cons of the matter. The more Cuneo and Samy appeared to hesitate, the harder Jean argued his case. Max kept his counsel, except once when he asked: 'Don't they call this hara-kiri or something?'

Perdu ignored him. He felt that it had to be done, but it took him half the morning to convince Samy and Cuneo.

Solemnly and visibly moved, the Italian said at last: 'Fine, Capitano. We'll look after your boat until you want it back. It doesn't matter when: the day after tomorrow, in a year or thirty years from now. And cats and writers will always be welcome.'

They sealed the pact with an emotional group hug. Samy let go of Jean last and stared at him fondly.

'My favourite reader,' she said with a smile. 'I couldn't have dreamed of anyone better.'

Max and Jean packed their belongings in Max's kit bag and a few large shopping bags, and stepped ashore. Other than his clothes, all Perdu took with him were the first pages of his book: *The Great Encyclopedia of Small Emotions*.

Perdu felt nothing at all as Cuneo started the engine and steered *Lulu* expertly out into midstream. He could hear and see Max beside him, but it seemed as though Max were drifting away too, like the book barge. Max waved with both arms, shouting *'Ciao'* and *'Salut'*; Perdu, by contrast, could not even muster the energy to raise his hand.

He gazed after his book barge until it had vanished around a bend in the river. He stared after it when it was long gone, waiting for the numbness to subside so he could feel again. When he was finally ready to turn around, he found Max sitting quietly on a bench, waiting for him.

'Let's go,' said Perdu, his voice rough and dry.

For the first time in five weeks they withdrew money in Avignon from branches of their banks, though this required dozens of phone calls, faxed signatures for comparison and close examination of their passports. Then they rented a small milk-white car at the train station and set off for the Luberon.

They took a minor road southeast from Avignon. It was only thirty miles to Bonnieux. Max gazed raptly out of the open windows. To the left and the right fields of sunflowers, lush green carpets of vines and rows of lavender bushes painted the land a mosaic of colours. Yellow, dark-green and purple, spanned by a saturated blue sky dotted with white cushions of cloud.

Far away on the horizon they could make out the Big Luberon and the Little Luberon – a great, long table mountain with a matching stool to its right.

The sun was beating down on the land, eating into earth and flesh, flooding the fields and towns with its imperious brilliance.

'We need straw hats,' Max groaned languidly, 'and linen trousers.'

'We need deodorant and sun cream,' Perdu snapped in reply.

It was obvious that Max was in his element. He slipped into this landscape like the right piece into a jigsaw puzzle. Unlike Jean. Everything he saw seemed strangely remote and foreign to him. He still felt numb.

Villages were perched like crowns on top of the green hills. Beige sandstone and light roof tiles to ward off the heat. Majestic birds of prey patrolled the air. The roads were narrow and empty.

Manon had seen these mountains, hills and colourful fields. She had felt this mild air; she had known these hundred-year-old trees in whose dense canopies cicadas crouched, producing a constant clicking that sounded to Jean's ears like: 'What? What? What?'

What are you doing here? What are you looking for here? What do you feel here?

Nothing.

This country made no impression on Jean.

They were already passing Ménerbes with its curry-coloured rocks, and approaching the Calavon valley and Bonnieux among vineyards and farmsteads.

'Bonnieux rises in a stack between the Grand Luberon and the Petit Luberon. Like a five-layered cake,' Manon had told Perdu. 'At the very top, the old church and the hundred-year-old cedars and the most scenic cemetery in the Luberon. Down at the bottom, the winegrowers, the fruit farmers and the holiday homes. And between them three layers of houses and restaurants. All connected by steep paths and stairs, which explains why all

the village girls have such gorgeous, strong calves.'
She had shown Jean hers, and he had kissed them.

'I think it's beautiful around here,' said Max.

They bumped along dirt tracks, curved around
a sunflower field, drove through a vineyard – and
were forced to admit that they had absolutely no
idea where they were. Jean pulled over onto the
verge.

'It should be somewhere near here, Le Petit St
Jean,' muttered Max, staring at the map.

The cicadas chirped. Now it sounded more like:
'Hee hee hee hee hee.' Other than that it was so
quiet that only the soft ticking of the cooling
engine troubled the deep silence of the countryside.

Then there was the juddering of a fast-
approaching tractor. It emerged from one of the
vineyards at speed. They'd never seen a tractor
like this before – it was extremely narrow, and
its tyres were thin but very tall to allow it to race
between the rows of vines.

Behind the wheel sat a young man in a baseball
cap, sunglasses, cutoff jeans and a faded white T-shirt;
he acknowledged them with a nod as he rumbled
past. Max waved frantically, and the tractor pulled
up a few yards further along the track. Max ran
over.

'Excuse me, Monsieur!' Jean heard Max call over
the noise of the engine. 'Where can we find a house
called "Le Petit St Jean", belonging to Brigitte
Bonnet?'

The man cut the engine, took off his baseball cap and sunglasses, and wiped his lower arm across his face as a cascade of long, chocolate-brown hair fell over his shoulders.

'Oh. *Pardonnez-moi*, pardon me, Mademoiselle. I thought you were a, er . . . man,' Jean heard a distraught Max croak.

'I bet you imagine women trussed up in tight dresses, not driving tractors,' the stranger said coolly, piling her hair back under her cap.

'Or pregnant, barefoot and chained to the stove,' Max added.

The stranger hesitated – then broke into peals of laughter.

As Jean craned his neck to get a better look at the two of them, the young woman had already put her large dark glasses back on and was explaining the way to Max: the Bonnets' property lay on the far side of the vineyard, and they simply had to drive around it on the right.

'*Merci, Mademoiselle.*'

The rest of Max's words were swallowed up in the howl of the throttle. Perdu could see only the bottom half of her face now – her lips twitched into an amused smile. Then she pressed the accelerator to the floor and rattled away, whipping up a small cloud of dust as she went.

'It's really beautiful around here,' said Max as he got back into the car. Jean thought there was a glow about him.

'Something happen?' he asked.

'With that woman?' Max said with a laugh that was a little too loud and a little high-pitched. 'Well, in a nutshell, straight ahead, that's the way, so . . . anyway, she looked terrific.' Max was as happy as a cuddly toy rabbit, Jean thought. 'Dirty, sweaty, but really cute. Like chocolate on top of the fridge. Other than that, no, otherwise . . . nothing happened. Nice tractor. Why do you ask?' Max looked befuddled.

'No reason,' Jean lied.

A few minutes later they found Le Petit St Jean, an early-eighteenth-century farmhouse, something out of a picture book: watery-grey stone; tall, narrow windows; a garden in such full and extravagant bloom that it looked as if it had been painted. In an internet café Max had come across www. luberonweb.com, and through it he had found Madame Bonnet, who had one of the last vacancies in the area. She rented out a room in her converted dovecote, her *pigeonnier*, breakfast included.

Brigitte Bonnet – a petite crop-haired woman in her late fifties – was waiting for them with a warm smile and a basket full of freshly picked apricots. She was dressed in a man's vest and light-green Bermuda shorts, her outfit topped off with a floppy hat. Madame Bonnet was tanned as brown as a nut, and her eyes shone a liquid blue.

Her apricots were covered with sweet, soft fuzz, and her converted dovecote turned out to be a twelve-foot-square hideaway with a washtub, a toilet the size of a cupboard, a few hooks by way of a wardrobe, and an uncomfortably narrow bed.

'Where's the second bed?' asked Jean.

'Oh, Messieurs, there's only one. Aren't you a couple?'

'I'll sleep outside,' Max swiftly suggested.

The dovecote was small but wonderful, and the view from its high windows stretched as far as the Valensole plateau. The building stood in the middle of a huge fruit and lavender garden with a gravel terrace and a broad stone wall that resembled the remains of a castle. A small, welcoming fountain burbled away next to the dovecote. One could cool a bottle of wine in it and sit on the wall, legs dangling, gazing out over orchards, fields of vegetables and vineyards far down the valley, which seemed devoid of any roads or other farms. The site had been chosen by someone with a keen eye for a view.

Max jumped up onto the broad wall and looked out over the plain, one hand shielding his eyes from the sun. If he concentrated, he could hear a tractor engine and see a small cloud of dust moving steadily from left to right, and then back from right to left.

More lavender bushes, roses and fruit trees had been planted around the dovecote's terrace, and two chairs with comfy, brightly coloured cushions stood at a mosaic table beneath a generous parasol. Here Madame Bonnet served the two men a bulbous, ice-cold bottle of Orangina each and, by way of greeting, some chilled *bong veng*, as she pronounced *bon vin* in her Provençal accent – a shimmering pale-yellow wine.

'This is a *bong veng* from here, a Luc Basset,' she chattered. 'The estate was founded in the seventeenth century. It's just the other side of the D36, a fifteen-minute walk. Their *Manon XVII* won a gold medal this year.'

'Excuse me, their what? *Manon?*' asked Perdu in shock.

Max had the presence of mind to intervene and thank their flustered hostess profusely. Max studied the wine label as Brigitte Bonnet sauntered away between the magnificent borders, stopping here and there to pick something. There was a printed drawing of a face above the word 'Manon' – a gentle frame of curls, the ghost of a smile and large, intense eyes directed at the viewer.

'That's your Manon?' asked Max in astonishment.

Jean nodded initially, then shook his head. No, of course this wasn't Manon, much less *his* Manon. His Manon was dead and lovely, and she lived on only in his dreams. But now, without warning, she was staring out at him from this wine bottle.

He took the bottle from Max's hand and ran his finger gently over the drawing of Manon's face. Her hair. Her cheek. Her chin, mouth, neck. He used to touch her in all those places, but . . .

Only now came the tremors. They began in his knees and continued upward, sending a sizzling and a quaking through the inside of his tummy and chest, before advancing along his arms and fingers, and taking hold of his lips and eyelids. His circulation was on the point of collapse.

His voice was flat as he whispered, 'She loved the sound apricots make as you pick them. You need to take them gently between your thumb and two fingers, twist them a little and they go *knck*. Her cat was called Miaow. In winter Miaow would sleep on Manon's head like a hat. Manon said she had inherited her father's toes – toes with a shapely waist. Manon loved her father dearly. And she loved pancakes filled with Banon cheese and lavender honey. And she would sometimes laugh in her dreams when she was asleep, Max. She was married to Luc, whereas I was merely her lover. Luc Basset, the vigneron.'

Jean looked up. He set down the wine bottle on the mosaic table with trembling hands. He would have preferred to hurl it against the wall, had it not been for his irrational fear of shattering Manon's face.

He could barely stand it; he could barely stand *himself*. He was in one of the most picturesque places on earth, with a friend who had become his son and confidant. He had burned his bridges behind him and sailed south on water and tears.

Only to discover that he still wasn't ready.

In his head he was standing in the hallway of his flat, trapped behind a bookcase.

Had he imagined that simply coming here would miraculously resolve everything? That he could leave

309

his torment behind on the waterways, and trade his unwept tears for a dead woman's absolution? That he had come far enough to earn redemption?

Yes, he had.

But it wasn't that easy.

It's never that easy.

He reached out angrily and gave the bottle a violent spin. He didn't want Manon giving him that look any more. No. He couldn't face her like this. Not as this non-person whose heart drifted, unmoored, lest he love and lose his beloved again.

When Max slipped a hand into his, Jean clutched it tightly. Very tightly.

CHAPTER 36

The silky southern air streamed through the car. Jean had wound down all the windows of the clapped-out Renault 5. Gérard Bonnet, Brigitte's husband, had lent him this one after they had dropped off the rental car in Apt.

The right door was blue, the left one red, and the rest of the old banger was a rusty-beige colour. Perdu had set out in this car with a small travel bag. He had driven via Bonnieux to Lourmarin, and then via Pertuis to Aix. From there he had taken the fastest route south to the sea. Marseilles was resplendent and proud, spread out on the bay down below – the great city where Africa, Europe and Asia kissed and did battle. The port lay like a glittering, breathing organism in the summer twilight as he came out of the hills on the motorway near Vitrolles.

To his right the white houses of the city. To his left the blue of sky and water. The view took his breath away.

The sea.

How it sparkled.

'Hello, sea,' whispered Jean Perdu. The view

311

tugged at him as though the water had pierced his heart with a harpoon and was slowly reeling him in on strong ropes.

The water. The sky. White vapour trails in the blue above, white bow waves on the blue below.

Oh yes, he was going to head into this boundless blue. Along the cliffs, and on and on and on. Until he shook off the trembling that still plagued him. Did it come from abandoning *Lulu*? Did it come from abandoning the hope that he had emerged from the sorrow?

Jean Perdu wanted to carry on driving until he was sure. He wanted to find a place where he could hole up like a wounded animal.

Heal. I have to heal. He hadn't known that when he'd left Paris.

He switched the radio on before he could be overwhelmed by the thought of everything he hadn't known.

'If you were to describe one event that made you who you are, what would it be? Give me a call, and tell me and everyone listening in the Var area.'

The woman presenter with the friendly *mousse-au-chocolat* voice gave a phone number, then she put on some music. A slow track. Like rolling waves. The occasional melancholy sigh of an electric guitar. Drums murmuring like surf on the shore. 'Albatross' by Fleetwood Mac: a song that made Jean Perdu think of gulls wheeling in the

312

setting sun, and of driftwood fires flickering on a beach at the edge of the world.

As Jean drove along the motorway through the warm summer air above Marseilles, and wondered what his event might have been, 'Margot from Aubagne' told listeners about the moment when she began to become herself.

'It was the birth of my first child, my daughter. She's called Fleur. Thirty-six hours in labour. Who'd have thought that pain could bring such joy, such peace? I felt an incredible sense of release. All at once everything had a meaning, and I wasn't scared of dying any more. I had given life, and pain was the path to joy.'

For an instant Jean could understand this Margot from Aubagne. Nonetheless, he was a man. What it felt like to share one's body with another for nine months remained a mystery to him; he would never be able to understand how part of himself could be passed on to a child and leave him forever.

He entered the long tunnel under Marseilles' cathedral, but he had radio reception anyway.

The next caller was Gil from Marseilles. He had a rough, hard, working-class accent.

'I became myself when my son died,' he said falteringly, 'because grief showed me what's important in life. That's what grief does. In the beginning it's always there. You wake up and it's there. It's with you all day, everywhere you go. It's with you in the evening; it won't leave you alone at night. It grabs you by the throat and shakes you. But it keeps you warm. One day it might go, but not forever. It drops by from time to time. And then, eventually . . . all of a sudden I knew what was important – grief showed me. Love is important. Good food. And standing tall and not saying yes when you should say no.'

More music. Jean left Marseilles behind.

Did I think I was the only one grieving, the only one knocked sideways by it? Oh, Manon. I had no one I could talk to about you.

He thought back to the trivial event that had caused him to cast off from Paris: seeing Hesse's *Stages* made into novelty bookends; that deeply personal poem of human understanding . . . used for marketing purposes.

He vaguely grasped that he could not afford to skip a stage in his mourning. But which one had he reached? Was he still in the end stage? Had he already reached a new beginning? Or was he falling, losing his footing? He turned the radio off. Soon he saw the exit for Cassis and got in the lane.

He left the motorway, still deep in thought, and reaching Cassis a little later, he wound his way noisily up its steep streets. An abundance of holidaymakers, inflatable plastic animals; elsewhere, ladies in evening dresses and diamond earrings. A large poster in front of an expensive-looking beach restaurant advertised a 'Bali buffet'.

I don't belong here.

Perdu thought of Eric Lanson, the therapist from

Paris's administrative district who loved reading fantasy novels and had tried to amuse Perdu with a spot of literary psychoanalysis. He could have talked to Lanson about his grief and his fear! The therapist had sent Jean a postcard from Bali once. There, death was the culmination of life; it was celebrated with dancing, gamelan concerts and seafood feasts. Jean found himself wondering what Max would have to say about that kind of festival. Something mildly disrespectful, without doubt; something humorous.

Max had said two things to Jean during their good-byes. First, that one had to gaze upon the dead, cremate them and bury their ashes – and then begin to tell their story.

'Remain silent about the dead, and they'll never leave you in peace.'

Second, that he thought the area around Bonnieux was *extremely* beautiful and he was going to stay in the dovecote and write. Jean Perdu guessed that a certain red tractor had played a part in this decision.

But what did it mean – that one had to tell the story of the dead?

Perdu cleared his throat and announced to the empty car: 'Her words were so natural. Manon showed her feelings, always. She loved the tango. She drank from life as if it were champagne and faced it in the same spirit: she knew that life is special.'

He felt a deep sorrow welling up inside him.

He had wept more in the last two weeks than in the previous twenty years. But the tears were all for Manon, every last one, and he was no longer ashamed of them.

Perdu had raced up the steep streets of Cassis. He left Cap Canaille and its spectacular red cliffs behind to his left, and drove on through small hills and pine forests along the old, windy coastal road from Marseilles to Cannes. Villages merged into one another, rows of houses blurred across town boundaries, palms alternated with pines, flowers and rocks. La Ciotat. Le Liouquet. And then Les Lecques.

Spotting a car park beside a path down to the beach, Jean swung spontaneously out of the smooth stream of vehicles. He was hungry.

The little town's sweeping waterfront, comprising weather-beaten old villas and pragmatic new hotel complexes, was bustling with families. They were strolling on the beach and the promenade, and eating in restaurants and bistros that had opened their sliding windows wide onto the sea view. A few well-tanned boys were playing Frisbee in the surf, and a flotilla of white one-man training dinghies bobbed up and down beyond the line of yellow marker buoys and the lighthouse.

Jean found a seat at the counter of the L'Équateur beach bar, which was two yards back from the sand and ten yards from the gentle breakers. Large blue parasols fluttered in the wind over shiny tables, which were tightly clustered, as was the case all over Provence in the high season, when restaurants packed diners in like sardines. Perdu enjoyed an unrivalled view from the bar.

He kept his eyes on the sea as he ate mussels in a rich herb and cream sauce from a deep black pot, and washed them down with some mineral water and a glass of dry white Bandol wine. The water was light blue in the late sunshine.

At sunset it elected to turn dark turquoise. The sand went from light blonde to dark flax and then slate grey. The women walking past became more excitable, their skirts shorter, their laughter more expectant. An open-air disco had been set up on the breakwater, and it was there that mixed groups of three or four girls, dressed in skimpy dresses or jean shorts, and guys wearing shirts that rippled on their shiny, tanned shoulders, were heading.

Perdu gazed after the young women and men. In their impatient, hurrying gait he recognised the young's unbridled lust for new experience, their striving towards places with the whiff of adventure about them. Erotic adventures! Laughter, freedom, dancing into the early hours, barefoot in the cool sand, heat in their loins. And kisses, forever engraved on the memory.

At sunset Saint-Cyr and Les Lecques were transformed into one big party area. Summer life in the south. These were the hours carried over from the hot afternoon, when the blood stood weary and thick in the veins.

★　　★　　★

The steep tongue of land dotted with houses and pines to Jean's left gleamed a rusty gold colour; the horizon was delineated in orange-blue, and the sea swelled sweet and salty.

For a few minutes, as he reached the bottom of his pot of mussels, and sifted idly through the remnants of briny cream sauce and blue-black shimmering shards of mussel shell, sea, sky and land took on the same shade of blue: a cool grey-blue that tinted the air, his wine glass, the white walls and the promenade, and briefly turned people into chattering stone sculptures.

A blond surfer dude cleared away Perdu's pot and plate of shells, and smoothly set down a bowl of warm water for Perdu to wash his hands in.

'Would you like dessert?' It sounded friendly, but there was a hint of 'if you don't, then please leave, because we can get another two sittings in.'

It had felt good, nonetheless. He had eaten the sea and drunk it in with his eyes. He had yearned for this, and the trembling inside him had subsided a little.

Perdu left the rest of his wine, tossed a banknote onto the plate with the bill and walked to his patchwork Renault 5. He drove on along the coast road with the taste of creamy salt on his lips.

When he lost sight of the sea, he took the next right off the main road. He soon spotted the water again, a glinting ribbon in the bright moonlight among the pines, cypresses, windswept evergreens and houses, hotels and villas. He drove along empty lanes through a pretty residential area. Colourful, stately villas. He didn't know where he was, but he knew that this was where he wanted to wake up the next morning and swim. It was time to look for a guesthouse, or a stretch of sand where he could make a campfire and sleep under the stars.

As Perdu was rolling down the Boulevard Frédéric Mistral, the Renault started to make a whistling *woooeeeh* sound. This ended in a hissing bang, and the engine spluttered and died. Channelling the last momentum from the descent, Perdu steered the car to the edge of the road, where the Renault issued its final breath. There was not so much as an electronic click as Jean turned the key in the ignition. The car obviously wanted to stay here too.

Monsieur Perdu got out and looked around.

Below him he spied a small bathing beach and above it villas and blocks of flats, which appeared to condense into a town half a mile from where he stood. Over this scene flickered a friendly peach-coloured glow. He fetched his small bag out of the car and marched off.

There was a soothing peacefulness in the air. No open-air disco. No traffic. Yes, even the sea swell was quieter here.

After a ten-minute walk he reached an odd square tower, around which someone had built a hotel more than a hundred years ago – and he realised where he was.

Of all places! How fitting.

He stepped reverently onto the quayside and closed his eyes to take in the smell. Salt. Open spaces. Freshness.

He opened his eyes again. The old fishing port. Dozens of coloured boats rocking on the glossy blue water. Sparkling white yachts further out. The houses – none higher than four storeys, their façades painted in pastel shades.

This charming old seafarers' village: daylight made the colours blossom; by night it was lit by the wide starry sky, and in the evening by the soft rosy light of old-fashioned lanterns. Over there the market with its yellow-and-red awnings under lush plane trees. Around them, soothed by the sun and the sea, people reclined dreamily in their chairs at countless tables in old bars and new cafés.

This town had seen and harboured many a fugitive before him.

Sanary-sur-Mer.

CHAPTER 37

To: Catherine [surname of the famous Le
P.-You-Know-Who],
  27 Rue Montagnard, 75011 Paris
  Sanary-sur-Mer, August

Faraway Catherine,
The sea has sparkled in twenty-seven
colours so far. Today, a mix of blue and
green: petrol, the women in the shops call
it. They should know, but I call it wet
turquoise.
The sea can cry out to you, Catherine.
It can scratch at you with catlike swipes. It
can snuggle up to you and stroke you;
it can be as smooth as a mirror, and the
next moment it rages, luring surfers into
its crashing waves. It is different every day,
and the gulls screech like little kids
on stormy days and like heralds of glory on
sunny ones. 'Fine! Fine! Fine!' they call.
Sanary's beauty could kill you, and you
wouldn't go willingly.
My bachelor days in the *belle bleue* – my

blue room in André's Beau Séjour guest-house – ended soon after 14 July. I no longer need to stuff my clothes inside my bed linen and visit Madame Pauline wearing the expression of a pleading son-in-law, or haul my bundle to the launderette behind the shopping centre in Six-Fours-les-Plages; I have a washing machine now. It was payday at the bookshop. MM – Madame Minou Monfrère, the owner and doyenne of the town's booksellers – is happy with me; I don't get in the way, she says. Fair enough. The first boss I've ever had put me in charge of children's books, encyclopedias and the classics, and asked me to stock up on books by writers who fled the Nazis to live here in exile. I do everything she says, and it feels strangely good not to have to bear any responsibility.

I've found a home too – for my washing machine and me.

It's up on a hill above the harbour, behind the Notre-Dame-de-la-Pitié chapel, but overlooking Portissol, the tiny bathing beach where the holidaymakers lie towel to towel. Some old Parisian flats are bigger than this house – but not as nice.

Its colour varies from flamingo red to curry-powder yellow. From one of the bedrooms all you can see is a palm, a pine tree, a lot of flowers and the back of the little chapel, and further along, beyond the hibiscus, the sea. Gauguin would have adored the colour combination: pink and petrol, rose and wet turquoise. I'm starting to learn to stand on my own two feet here, Catherine.

In lieu of rent I've been renovating the flamingo-curry house since I moved; it too belongs to André and his wife, Pauline. They don't have the time to work on it themselves or any children of their own they could cajole into doing it. Their nine-room guesthouse, the Beau Séjour, is booked all summer.

I miss the blue room, number three on the first floor, and André's raucous voice, his breakfasts and his quiet garden with its roof of green leaves. There's a touch of my father about André. He cooks for his half-board guests, Pauline plays solitaire, or tarot if the occasional old lady requests her to, and she makes sure that there's always a good atmosphere. I generally see her smoking and tutting as she lays down the cards on the plastic table. She has offered to tell my fortune. Should I take her up on it?

Their cleaning ladies – Aimée, blond, fat, very loud and very funny, and Sülüm, tiny, thin, hard, a shrivelled olive, discordant laughter pouring from her toothless mouth

– carry their buckets of washing water with the handles slung over their arms, as Parisian women do their Vuitton and Chanel bags. I often see Aimée in church, the one by the harbour. She sings and she has tears in her eyes as she does so. The services here are very human. The altar boys are young, wear those white nightshirts and have winning smiles. Sanary shows few signs of the general phoniness of many tourist destinations in the south.

Everyone should sing like Aimée: weeping with happiness. I've started to belt out some tunes in the shower again while pretending to hop about to the rhythm of the faulty showerhead's jets. Yet sometimes it still feels as if I'm sewed up in my own skin, as if I'm living in an invisible box that keeps me in and everyone else out. In such moments even my own voice strikes me as superfluous.

I'm building a shade roof over the terrace, for however reliable the sun is here, it is like an aristocrat's drawing room: warm and safe, cosseting and luxurious; and yet when the heat continues for too long, it can become oppressive, threatening and suffocating. Between two and five in the afternoon, sometimes until seven, nobody in Sanary ventures outdoors. They prefer to retreat to the coolest part of the house, lie naked on the cellar tiles and wait for the beauty and the furnace outside finally to take pity on them. I put damp towels around my head and on my back.

From the kitchen terrace that I am building, you can see the bright house fronts between the ship's masts in the harbour, but the main features are the gleaming white yachts and the lighthouse at the end of the breakwater, from where the fire service shoot their thundering pyrotechnics into the sky on Bastille Day. You can see the sweeping hills and mountains opposite, with Toulon and Hyères beyond. Lots of little white houses scattered along the rocky outcrops.

Only if you stand on tiptoes can you see old Saint-Nazaire's square watchtower. The Hôtel de la Tour is built around it, a plain cube in which several exiled German writers survived the terrors of the war years. The Manns, the Feuchtwangers, Brecht. The Bondys, Toller. One Zweig, and the other too. Wolff, Seghers and Massary. Fritzi – what a wonderful name for a woman.

(I'm sorry, Catherine, this has turned into a bit of a lecture! Paper is patient; authors never are.)

At the end of July, when my *pétanque* game had finally progressed beyond that of an unwelcome novice, a small, rotund Neapolitan appeared around the corner of Quai Wilson near the old harbour, panama on his head, whiskers quivering like the cat that got the cream, and a woman on his arm, the warmth of whose heart shone in her expression. Cuneo and Samy! They stayed for a week, having left the barge in the custody of the Cuisery council. Book-crazed *Lulu* in her rightful place – among her own kind.

Where from, why, how come? Effusive greetings.

'Why do you never turn your mobile on, you paper ass?' roared Samy. Well, they had found me, even without it. Via Max, and then Madame Rosalette, of course, as unselfish as ever with the results of her espionage. She had analysed the postmarks on the letters that I sent you and located me in Sanary long ago. How would friends and lovers get by without the concierges of this world? Who knows, maybe each of us has a specific role in the great book of life. Some of us love particularly well; others look after lovers particularly well.

Of course, I know why I'd forgotten all about my phone: I've spent too long living in a world of paper. I'm feeling my way with these gadgets.

Cuneo gave me a hand with the masonry

for four days and tried to teach me to regard cooking as being similar to lovemaking. His extraordinary lessons – master classes, really – began at the market, where the sales-women are surrounded by head-high piles of tomatoes, beans, melons, fruit, garlic, three types of radishes, raspberries, potatoes and onions. We ate salted caramel ice cream in the ice-cream parlour by the children's merry-go-round. Lightly salted, burned and sweet, creamy and cold. I've never eaten more perfect ice cream, and now I eat it every day (and sometimes even at night).

Cuneo taught me to see with my hands. He showed me how to recognise what needs to be handled how. He taught me to smell and to tell which ingredients were good together and what I could cook with them by their aromas. He put a cup of ground coffee in my fridge to absorb all the odours that didn't belong there. We braised, steamed, fried and grilled fish.

If you ask me to cook for you again, I'll charm you with all the tricks I've picked up.

My little big friend Samy left me with one final scrap of wisdom. For once she didn't shout – she tends to shout. She gave me a hug as I sat there, staring at the sea and counting the colours, and whispered very quietly to me: 'Do you know that there's a halfway world between each ending and each new beginning? It's called the hurting time, Jean Perdu. It's a bog; it's where your dreams and worries and forgotten plans gather. Your steps are heavier during that time. Don't underestimate the transition, Jeanno, between farewell and new departure. Give yourself the time you need. Some thresholds are too wide to be taken in one stride.'

Since then I have often thought about what Samy called the hurting time and the halfway world, about the threshold that you have to cross between farewell and new departure. I wonder whether my threshold starts here . . . or whether it began twenty years ago.

Have you experienced that hurting time too? Is being lovelorn like mourning someone? Do you mind my asking these questions?

Sanary must be one of the only places in France where the locals smile when I recommend a German author. In a way they are proud that they provided a safe haven to various prominent German writers under the dictatorship. However, too few of the exiles' houses have been preserved. Only six or seven; the Manns' house was rebuilt. The bookshops seldom stock their works, even though dozens of them sought refuge here. I'm expanding that section in our shop, and MM has given me free rein.

She has also recommended me to the town dignitaries – imagine that. Monsieur Bernhard, the mayor, a tall, well-groomed silver fox, loves leading the parade of fire engines on Bastille Day. They show off every piece of equipment they've got, Catherine: tankers, jeeps, even a bicycle and some boats on trailers. A splendid display, and the youngsters march along behind, proud and relaxed. On the other hand, the mayor's library is a miserable medicine cabinet. Sonorous names including Camus, Baudelaire and Balzac, all leather-bound, so visitors think: 'Oh! Montesquieu! And Proust! How dull.'

I've suggested to the mayor that he read what he wants to read rather than what he thinks will impress people, and that he give up arranging his books according to the colour of the binding, or in alphabetical order or by genre. He should group them by theme instead. Everything about Italy in one corner: cookbooks, whodunnits by Donna Leon, novels, illustrated books, essays on Leonardo, religious treatises by Assisi, anything. Everything about the sea in another corner – from Hemingway to sharks, fish poems and fish recipes.

He thinks I'm smarter than I really am.

There's one spot I really love in MM's bookshop. Right next to the encyclopedias, a quiet spot where only the occasional little girl will peek in and furtively look something up because her parents have fobbed her off by saying, 'You're too young for that. I'll explain it to you when you're older.' Personally, I don't believe that any question is too big; you simply have to tailor your answers.

I install myself in this corner on the step-ladder, put on an intelligent face and simply sit and breathe. That's all.

From my hideaway I can see, mirrored in the open glass door, the sky and a strip of sea in the distance. This view makes everything appear lovelier and softer, even though it's almost inconceivable that anything here could be more beautiful than it already is. Sanary is the last place on the coast between Marseilles and Toulon, among all the towns made up of little white boxes, where life continues even when there are no more tourists. Naturally, everything is geared towards them from June to August, and it's impossible to get a table for dinner if you haven't reserved. When the guests have gone home, they don't leave empty, draughty houses and deserted supermarket car parks behind them. Life always goes on here. The lanes are narrow, the houses are colourful and small. The residents stick together, and the fishermen sell gigantic fish from their boats at daybreak. This little town could be in the Luberon; it is neighbourly, peculiar and proud. But the Luberon has become the 21st arrondissement of Paris. Sanary is a nostalgic place.

I play *pétanque* every night, not at the *boulodrome*, but on Quai Wilson. They leave the floodlights on until an hour before midnight. It's where the sedate (some would say old) men play, and there's not a lot of conversation.

It's the prettiest spot in Sanary. You can see the sea, the town, the lights, the *boules*, the boats. You're in the thick of things, yet it's peaceful. No applause, just the occasional low 'Aah!'; the click of *boule* on *boule*; and when the striker, who is also my new dentist, hits, a cry of 'Peng!' My father would love it.

Lately I've often pictured myself playing with my father. And talking. Laughing. Oh, Catherine, there is so much more for us to discuss and laugh about.

Where did the last twenty years go?

The south is a vivid blue, Catherine.

Your colour is missing here. It would make everything shine all the more brightly.

Jean

CHAPTER 38

Perdu went swimming every morning before the heat set in, and every evening shortly before sunset. He had discovered that this was the only way he could flush the sorrow out of his system and let it flow away, bit by bit.

He had tried praying in church, of course. Singing too. He had hiked through Sanary's hilly hinterland. He had recited Manon's story loudly, in the kitchen and on his dawn walks; he had shouted her name to the gulls and the buzzards. But only occasionally did it help.

Hurting time.

The sorrow often arrived and took hold of him as he was falling asleep. Just when he was relaxed and drifting off – it came. He lay in the dark and wept bitterly; and at that moment the world felt reduced to the size of his bedroom, lonely and devoid of all comfort. In those instants he was afraid that he would never be able to smile again and that his pain would never, ever cease. In those gloomy hours a thousand different 'what ifs' swirled around in his head and his heart. That his father might die while he was playing *boules*. That his mother would start to squabble with the television set and waste away with grief. He was afraid that Catherine was reading his letters to her girlfriends and that they were laughing at them together. He was afraid that he was destined to mourn over and over for people he loved.

How should he endure that for the rest of his life? How could anyone endure it?

He wished he could prop his fearful self up in a corner like a broom and walk away.

The sea was the first thing he had found that was large enough to absorb his sorrow.

After a serious workout, Perdu would drift on his back, his feet pointing towards the beach. There, on the waves, with the water spilling through his outspread fingers, he drew up from the depths of his memory every hour he had spent with Manon. He examined each one until he no longer felt any regret that it was past, then he let it go.

So Jean let the waves rock him, raise him up and pass him on. And slowly, infinitely slowly, he began to trust. Not the sea, far from it; no one should make that mistake! Jean Perdu trusted himself again. He wouldn't go under; he wouldn't drown in his emotions.

And each time he abandoned himself to the sea another small grain of fear trickled out of him. It was his way of praying.

The whole of July, the whole of August.

One morning the sea was gentle and calm. Jean swam out further than ever before. Finally, a long way from the shore, he surrendered to the delicious sensation of being able to relax after his exertions. He felt warm and serene inside.

Maybe he fell asleep. Maybe he was daydreaming. The water drew back as he sank, and the sea turned to warm air and soft grass. He caught the scent of a fresh, velvety breeze, of cherries and May weather. Sparrows hopped about on the arms of a deckchair.

She was sitting there. Manon. She smiled tenderly at Jean.

'What are you doing here?'

Rather than answer her, Jean walked towards her, went down on his knees and embraced her. He laid his head on her shoulder, as though he longed to crawl inside her.

Manon ruffled his hair. She hadn't aged, not a single day. She was as young and radiant as the Manon he had last seen one August evening twenty-one years earlier. She smelled warm and alive.

'I'm sorry I abandoned you. I was very stupid.'

'Of course you were, Jean,' she whispered gently.

Something changed. It was as though he could see himself through Manon's eyes. As though he were hovering above his body and could look back through time at every episode of his strange life. He counted two, three, five versions of himself – each at a different age.

There – how embarrassing! One Perdu, bending

over the map jigsaw and destroying it as soon as it was finished, then piecing it back together again.

The next Perdu, alone in his spartan kitchen, staring at the bleak wall, a naked bulb hanging above his head; chewing on shrink-wrapped cheese and sliced bread from a plastic bag. He denied himself the food he liked to avoid triggering any emotions.

And the next Perdu, turning his back on women. Their smiles. Their questions. 'What are your plans for this evening?' or 'Will you give me a call?' Their sympathy when they sensed with the antenna only women possess for such things that he had a great, sad hole inside. But their touchiness too, their lack of understanding for the fact that he was incapable of separating sex from love.

And another change came over him.

Now Jean thought that he could feel himself pushing up into the sky like a tree. He was simultaneously tumbling like a butterfly and diving like a buzzard from a mountaintop. He felt the wind streaming through his chest feathers – he was flying! Powerful strokes drove him down towards the seabed: he could breathe underwater.

A mysterious, overwhelming upsurge of energy swept through him. He finally understood what was going on inside him . . .

When he awoke, the waves had almost carried him back to the shore.

That morning, for some unfathomable reason,

he wasn't sad after his swim and his daydream. He was angry. Furious!

Yes, he had seen her. Yes, she had shown him what a hideous life he had chosen, how painful was the loneliness he endured because he didn't have the courage to trust someone again. To trust someone entirely because in love there is no other way.

He was more furious than he had been in Bonnieux when Manon's face had stared out at him from the label on the bottle of local wine. Angrier than he had ever been before.

'*Merde!*' he roared at the surf. 'You stupid, stupid, stupid cow – why did you have to go and die in the prime of life!'

Two women joggers were gawking at him from the tarmac beach path. He was embarrassed, but only for a second.

'What are you looking at?' he barked. He was brimming with a blazing, roaring fury.

'Why didn't you simply ring me like any normal person would have? What was the point of not telling me you were sick? How could you, Manon? How could you sleep next to me all those nights and *say nothing*? *Merde*, you stupid . . . you . . . God!'

He didn't know where to direct his rage. He wanted to punch something. He kneeled down and pummelled the sand and shovelled it behind him with both hands. He shovelled. And raged.

And shovelled some more. But it wasn't enough. He stood up and ran into the water; he thrashed at the waves with his fists and hands, both together, one after the other. The salt water splashed into his eyes. It stung. He punched and punched.

'Why did you do it? Why?' It didn't matter whom he was asking – himself, Manon, death; it made no difference. He was raging. 'I thought we knew each other, I thought you were on my side, I thought . . .'

His fury hardened. It sank into the sea between two waves; it became flotsam and would be washed up elsewhere to make someone else furious – furious that death could break in at any moment and ruin a life.

Jean sensed the stones under his bare feet and noticed that he was shivering.

'I wish you'd told me, Manon,' he said, calmer now, breathless and deflated. Disappointed.

The sea rolled in, imperturbably.

The weeping stopped. He still thought of particular moments with Manon; he continued to perform his aquatic prayers. Afterwards, however, he simply sat, let his skin dry in the morning sun and enjoyed the shivering. Yes, he enjoyed walking back along the fringe of the water in bare feet, and enjoyed buying his first espresso of the day and drinking it, his hair still wet, while he observed the sea and its colours.

Perdu cooked, swam, drank very little, kept a

regular sleep routine and met up with the other *boules* players every day. He continued to write letters. He worked on *The Great Encyclopedia of Small Emotions*, and in the evenings he worked at the bookshop, selling books to people in beach shorts.

He had altered his method of matching books to readers. He often asked, 'How would you like to feel when you go to sleep?' Most of his customers wanted to feel light and safe.

He asked others to tell him about their favourite things. Cooks loved their knives. Estate agents loved the jangle made by a bunch of keys. Dentists loved the flicker of fear in their patients' eyes; Perdu had guessed as much.

Most often he asked, 'How should the book taste? Of ice cream? Spicy, meaty? Or like a chilled rosé?' Food and books were closely related. He discovered this in Sanary, and it earned him the nickname 'the book epicure'.

He finished renovating the little house in the second half of August. He shared it with a morose, stripy stray tomcat, which never meowed, never purred and would only visit in the evening. It could be relied on to stretch out next to his bed and glower at the door. From this position the cat would guard the sleeping Perdu.

He tried to call it Olson, but because the animal bared its fangs at this name, he settled on Psst.

★   ★   ★

Jean Perdu didn't wish to leave a woman guessing about his feelings again – even if he himself could only guess at what his feelings were. He was still in the in-between zone, and any new beginning lay shrouded in mist. He couldn't say where he would be at the same time the next year. All he knew was that he must continue along this path until he found its destination. So he'd written to Catherine, as he had begun to do while on the waterways and since he had been in Sanary – every three days in fact.

Samy had counselled him: 'Try your phone for once. Amazing little device, I'm telling you.'

So one evening he picked up the mobile and dialled a number in Paris. Catherine needed to know who he was: a man caught between darkness and light. You become someone else when your loved ones die.

'Number 27. Hello? Who's there? Say something!'

'Madame Rosalette . . . Had your hair dyed recently?' he asked hesitantly.

'Oh! Monsieur Perdu, how . . .'

'Do you know Madame Catherine's number?'

'Of course I do. I know every number in the building, every single one. Now, Madame Gulliver upstairs . . .'

'Could you give me it?'

'Madame Gulliver's? What on earth for?'

'No, *chère Madame*. Catherine's.'

'Oh. Yes. You write to her a lot, don't you? I know

because Madame carries the letters around with her. They fell out of her bag once. I couldn't help seeing. It was the day Monsieur Goldenberg . . .'

He chose not to press her to give him the number, and instead allowed Madame Rosalette's gossip to wash over him. Gossip about Madame Gulliver, whose new coral-red mules made an awful showy clatter on the stairs. About Kofi, who had decided to study political science. About Madame Bomme, who'd had a successful eye operation and no longer needed a magnifying glass for reading. And Madame Violette's balcony concert: wonderful! Someone had shot a – what's it called? – a video and put it on that internet thing, and other people had clacked on it a lot or something, and now Madame Violette was famous.

'Clicked?'

'That's what I said.'

And, oh yes, Madame Bernard had converted the attic and wanted to let some artist move in. And his fiancé. His fiancé! How about a sea horse while he was at it?

Perdu held the mobile away from his ear so that she wouldn't hear his laughter. As Madame Rosalette nattered on and on, Jean could think of only one thing: Catherine kept his letters and carried them around with her. Fa-bu-lous, as the concierge would say.

After what felt like hours she finally dictated Catherine's number to him.

'We all miss you, Monsieur,' Madame Rosalette said. 'I hope you're no longer so terribly sad?'

He clenched his fist around the phone.

'Not any more. Thank you,' he said.

'Don't mention it,' Madame Rosalette said quietly before she hung up.

He tapped in Catherine's number and, closing his eyes, raised the mobile phone to his ear. It rang once, twice . . .

'Hello?'

'Um . . . it's me.'

It's me? Crumbs, how was she supposed to know who 'it's me' was, for goodness' sake?

'Jean?'

'Yes.'

'Oh my God.'

He heard Catherine gasp and put the phone down. She blew her nose and came back on the line.

'I didn't expect you to ring.'

'Should I hang up?'

'Don't you dare!'

He smiled. From her silence he figured that she must be smiling too.

'How . . .'

'What . . .'

They'd spoken at the same time. They laughed.

'What are you reading at the moment?' he asked softly.

'The books you gave me. For the fifth time, I think. I haven't washed the dress I wore on our evening together either. There's still a hint of your aftershave on it, you know, and each sentence in the books tells me something new every time, and I put the dress under my cheek at night so I can smell you.'

Then she said nothing; nor did he, surprised by the happiness that suddenly came over him.

They listened wordlessly to each other, and he felt very close to Catherine, as though Paris were directly next to his ear. All he would have to do was open his eyes and he would be sitting by her green front door, listening for her breath.

'Jean?'

'Yes, Catherine.'

'It's getting better, isn't it?'

'Yes. It's getting better.'

'And yes, being lovesick is like being in mourning. Because you die, because your future dies and you with it . . . There is a hurting time. It lasts for so long.'

'But it gets better. I know that now.'

Her silence felt good.

'I can't stop thinking that we didn't kiss each other on the mouth,' she whispered hastily.

Distraught, he said nothing.

'Talk to you tomorrow,' she said and hung up.

That must mean he could ring her again?

He sat there in the dark kitchen, a crooked smile on his lips.

CHAPTER 39

By the end of August he saw that his body had become toned. He had to tighten his belt a couple of notches, and his shirt stretched tight over his biceps.

He studied himself in the mirror as he dressed and saw in the reflection a very different man from the one he had been in Paris. Tanned, fit, erect, his dark, silver-streaked hair longer and swept casually back. The pirate beard; the loosely buttoned, washed-out linen shirt. He was fifty.

Nearly fifty-one.

Jean stepped up to the mirror. There were more lines on his face from exposure to the sun; more laugh lines too. He guessed that some of the freckles weren't freckles but age spots. But it didn't matter – he was alive. That was all that counted.

The sun had turned his body a healthy, shimmering shade of brown, which made his green eyes all the more luminous. His boss MM thought he looked like a noble rogue with his three-day beard. Only his reading glasses detracted from this impression.

★   ★   ★

MM had taken him aside one Saturday evening. Business was quiet. A fresh wave of holiday home renters had just arrived, and they were dazzled by late summer's sweet delights; they had other things on their mind than to visit a bookshop. They would come in a week or two to buy the obligatory post-cards before they left for home.

'How about you?' MM asked. 'What does your favourite book taste of? Which book is your salvation in this evil world?' She said it with a chuckle: her girlfriends found the book epicure fascinating and wanted to know more.

He never had any trouble getting to sleep in Sanary. His favourite book would have to taste of new potatoes sprinkled with rosemary – his first meal with Catherine.

But which is my salvation? He almost burst out laughing when he realised the answer.

'Books can do many things, but not everything. We have to live the important things, not read them. I have to . . . experience my book.'

MM gave him a broad, flashing smile.

'It's a shame that your heart is blind to women like me.'

'And the others too, Madame.'

'Yes, that's some consolation,' she said. 'A small one.'

In the afternoons, when the heat rose to dangerous levels, Perdu would lie motionless on his bed in nothing but a pair of shorts, with wet towels on his forehead, chest and feet. The terrace door was open, and the curtains swayed listlessly in the breeze. He let the warm wind caress his body as he dozed.

It was good to be back in his body. To feel that his flesh was sensitive and alive again. Not numb, limp, unused – an adversary. Perdu had got used to thinking with his body, as though he could stroll around inside his soul and peer into every room.

Yes, the grief lived on in his chest. When it came, it constricted his lungs, cut off his breathing and the universe faded to a narrow sliver. But he wasn't scared of it any more. When it came, he let it flow through him.

Fear occupied his throat too, but it took up less space if he breathed out slowly and calmly. With every breath he could make the fear smaller and crumple it up, and he imagined throwing it to Psst so that the cat could toy with the ball of anxiety and chase it out of the house.

Joy danced in his solar plexus, and he let it dance. He thought of Samy and Cuneo, and of Max's hilarious letters, in which one name cropped up more and more frequently: Vic. The tractor girl. In his mind he saw Max running around the Luberon after a wine-red tractor, and he couldn't help laughing.

Amazingly, love had settled on Jean's tongue. It tasted of the hollow at the base of Catherine's throat.

Jean had to smile. Here, in the light and warmth of the south, something else had returned. Vitality. Sensation. Desire.

Some days, as he sat looking out to sea or reading on a wall beside the harbour, the mere warmth of the sun was enough to fill him with a pleasant, urgent, restless tension. Down there too, his body was shaking off its sorrow.

He hadn't slept with a woman for two decades. Now he felt an intense yearning to do so.

Jean let his thoughts wander to Catherine. He could still feel her under his hands – the familiar sensation of touching her hair, her skin, her muscles. He pictured what her thighs would feel like. Her breasts. How she would look at him, gasping. How their skin and their selves would meet, press belly against belly, joy to joy. He imagined every detail.

'I'm back,' he whispered.

He went about his life, eating and swimming and selling books and spinning laundry in his new washing machine. Then, all of a sudden, something inside him took a step forward.

Unexpectedly. At the end of the holidays, on 28 August.

He was eating his lunchtime salad and wondering whether he should light a candle for Manon at the Notre-Dame-de-la-Pitié chapel, or swim out from Portissol as usual. But suddenly he noticed that his inner turmoil had ceased. So had the burning sensation, and everything else that brought tears of dismay and loss to his eyes.

He stood up and went out anxiously onto the

346

terrace. Was it possible? Was it really possible? Or was grief playing tricks on him and readying itself to rush in through the front door again?

He had reached the bottom of his soul's sour, sad tribulations. He had dug and dug and dug. And suddenly – there was a chink of light.

He rushed inside to the sideboard, where he always kept a pen and paper. He scribbled:

Catherine,

I don't know if it'll work out or if we can avoid hurting each other. Probably not, because we're human.

However, what I do know now, now that this moment I have craved has arrived, is that it's easier to fall asleep with you in my life. And to wake up. And to love.

I want to cook for you when hunger has blackened your mood. Any kind of hunger: hunger for life, hunger for love, hunger for light, sea, travel, reading and sleep too.

I want to rub cream into your hands when you've touched too many rough stones. In my dreams you are a rescuer of stones, capable of seeing through layers of stone and detecting the rivers of the heart that flow underneath.

I want to watch you as you walk along a sandy path, turn and wait for me.

I want all the little things and the big things too. I want to have arguments with you and explode into laughter halfway through; I want to pour cocoa into your favourite mug on a cold day; and after partying with wonderful friends I want to hold the passenger door open while you climb happily into the car.

I want to hold you at night and feel you press your small bottom against my warm tummy.

I want to do a thousand little and big things with you, with us – you, me, together, you as a part of me and me as a part of you.

Catherine, please. Come! Come soon!

Come to me!

The reality of love is better than its reputation.

Jean

PS: Truthfully!

CHAPTER 40

On 4 September Jean set off early so that his regular stroll along Rue de la Colline and around the fishing port would bring him to the bookshop on time.

Autumn was on its way, bringing visitors who preferred to build castles out of books rather than sand. This had always been his favourite time of year: new publications spelled new friendships, new insights and new adventures.

The blinding light of midsummer grew milder with the approach of autumn – mellower. Autumn shielded Sanary from its parched hinterland like a screen.

He breakfasted alternately at the Lyon, the Nautique and the Marine on the harbour front. The resemblance to the town where Brecht had once performed his mocking songs about the Nazis had naturally faded. And yet he could still detect a whiff of exile. The cafés were welcome islets of entertainment in his solitary life with Psst; they were something of a surrogate family, a hint of Paris. They were a confessional box and a news-room where you could find out what was going on behind the scenes in Sanary: how the fishing was holding up despite the algal bloom; how the *boules* players were building up to their autumn tournaments. The players on Quai Wilson had asked him to be a substitute 'pointer'; it was an honour to be asked to step in for a tournament. In the cafés Perdu could be in the middle of town life without anyone caring if he didn't talk or play an active role.

Sometimes he would sit in the corner at the back and speak to his father, Joaquin, on the phone, as he was doing that morning. When Joaquin heard about the tournament in La Ciotat, he was raring to polish his *boules* and set off.

'Please don't,' pleaded Perdu.

'Don't, eh? Well, then. What's her name?'

'Does it always have to be a woman?'

'Same one as before?'

Perdu laughed. Both Perdus laughed.

'Were you keen on tractors when you were a kid?' Jean asked next.

'Jeanno, my lad, I love tractors! Why are you asking?'

'Max has met someone. A tractor girl.'

'A tractor girl? Fantastic. When do we get to see Max again? You're fond of him, aren't you?'

'Hold on, who's we? That new girlfriend of yours who doesn't like cooking?'

'Oh, hobgoblins! Your mother. Madame Bernier and me. And? Speak now or forever hold your peace. I'm allowed to meet up with my ex-wife, aren't I? Well, actually, since the fourteenth of July . . . we've done a bit more than meet up. Of course, she sees things differently. She says we simply had a fling and I shouldn't get my hopes up.' Joaquin Perdu's smoker's laugh descended into a jovial splutter.

'So what?' he said. 'Lirabelle's my best friend. I like the way she smells, and she's never attempted to change me. She's a marvellous cook too – I always feel so much happier with life when I'm there. And you know, Jeanno, the older you get the more you feel like being with someone you can talk to and laugh with.'

His father would presumably have signed up without hesitation to the three things that made you really 'happy' according to Cuneo's worldview.

One: eat well. No junk food, because it only makes you unhappy, lazy and fat.

Two: sleep through the night (thanks to more exercise, less alcohol and positive thoughts).

Three: spend time with people who are friendly and seek to understand you in their own particular way.

Four: have more sex – but that was Samy's addition, and Perdu saw no real reason to tell his father that one.

He often spoke to his mother on his way from a café to the bookshop. He always held the phone up to the wind so that she could hear the sound of the waves and the gulls. That September morning the sea was calm, and Jean asked her,

'I hear Dad's been eating at your place a lot recently.'

'Well, yes. The man doesn't know how to cook, so what am I supposed to do?'

'Dinner and breakfast, though? Overnight too? Doesn't the poor man have his own bed to go to?'

'You say it as if we were up to something obscene.'

'I've never told you I love you, Maman.'

'Oh, my dear, dear child . . .'

Perdu heard her open a box and close it again. He knew this noise, and the box too. It held the tissues. As stylish as ever, Madame Bernier, even when she came over all sentimental.

'I love you too, Jean. I feel as if I've never told you that, only thought it. Is that true?'

It was true, but he said, 'I noticed all the same. You don't have to tell me every few years.'

She laughed and called him a cheeky so-and-so.

Great. Nearly fifty-one, and still a kid.

Lirabelle complained about her ex-husband a bit more, but her tone was affectionate. She grouched about the autumn book releases, but only out of habit.

Everything was the same as ever – yet so very different.

As Jean walked across the quayside towards the bookshop, MM was already rolling the postcard racks out into the open.

'It's going to be a beautiful day!' his boss called

to him. He handed Madame Monfrère a bag of croissants.

'Yes, I think so too.'

Shortly before sunset he retired to his favourite spot in the corner of the shop. The one from where he could observe the door, the reflected sky and a scrap of sea.

And then, in the midst of his thoughts, he saw her. He watched her reflection. She looked as though she were stepping straight out of the clouds and the water. Unbridled joy surged through his veins.

Jean Perdu stood up. His pulse was racing. He was readier than he'd ever been.

Now! he thought. Now the times were converging. He was finally emerging from his period of numbness, of standing still, of hurting. Now.

Catherine was wearing a bluish-grey dress that set off her eyes. She walked with a swing in her stride, upright, her tread firmer than before . . .

Before?

She has made it from the end to the beginning too.

She paused for a second at the counter, as if to get her bearings.

MM asked, 'Are you looking for something in particular, Madame?'

'Yes I am. I've been looking for a long time, but now I've found it. That particular something there,' said Catherine and beamed across the room at

Jean. She walked straight towards him, and, heart pounding, he went to meet her.

'You cannot imagine how long I've been waiting for you to finally ask me to come to you.'

'Honestly?'

'Oh yes. And I'm so hungry,' said Catherine.

Jean Perdu knew exactly what she meant.

That evening they kissed for the first time – after they'd had dinner and enjoyed a wonderful long walk by the sea, long, relaxed chats in the hibiscus garden by the veranda, during which they drank a little wine and a lot of water, and above all enjoyed each other's company.

'This warm air is so comforting,' Catherine said at one point.

It was true: Sanary's sun had sucked the cold out of him and dried all his tears.

'And it gives you courage,' he whispered. 'It gives you the courage to trust.'

In the evening breeze, confused and entranced by their bold faith in life, they kissed.

Jean felt as though it were his very first kiss.

Catherine's lips were soft, and they moved with and fit his perfectly. It was so wonderful to eat, drink, feel and caress her at last . . . and so thrilling.

He wrapped his arms around this woman and kissed and bit her mouth gently; he traced the corners of her mouth with his lips; he kissed his way up her cheeks to her fragrant, delicate temples. He pulled Catherine towards him; he was overflowing with tenderness and relief. Never again would he sleep badly as long as this woman was beside him – never. Never again would loneliness embitter him. He was saved. They stood and held each other.

'Hey?' she said eventually.

'Yes?'

'I looked it up, and the last time I slept with my ex-husband was in 2003. When I was thirty-eight. I think it was an accident.'

'Great. That makes you the more experienced of the two of us.'

They laughed.

How strange, thought Perdu, that one laugh can wipe away so much hardship and suffering. A single laugh. And the years flow together and . . . away.

'I do know one thing, though,' he said. 'Making love on the beach is overrated.'

'Sand in all the places it shouldn't get.'

'Worst of all are the mosquitoes.'

'You don't get many on the beach, do you?'

'You see, Catherine. I don't have a clue.'

'Then I'll show you,' she murmured. Her expression was youthful and reckless as she pulled Jean into the spare bedroom.

He saw a four-legged shadow scuttle away through the moonlight. Psst sat down on the terrace and politely turned his ginger-and-white striped back to them.

I hope she likes my body. I hope I haven't lost my

old vitality. I hope I touch her the way she likes, and I hope . . .

'Stop thinking, Jean Perdu!' Catherine ordered tenderly.

'Can you tell?'

'You're easy to analyse, darling,' she whispered. 'My lover. Oh, I wanted you so . . . and you . . .'

They continued in whispers, but their sentences had no beginning and no ending.

Slowly he peeled off Catherine's dress. Underneath she was naked apart from her plain white knickers.

She unbuttoned his shirt, buried her face in his throat and chest, and drank in his scent. Her breath tickled him, and no, he didn't need to worry about his vitality, because it was there when he saw the flash of the white, cotton triangle in the dark and felt her body move in his hands.

They savoured the whole of September in Sanary-sur-Mer. Eventually Jean had drunk his fill of southern light. He had been lost and he had found himself again. The hurting time was over.

Now he could go to Bonnieux and complete this stage.

CHAPTER 41

By the time Catherine and Jean left Sanary, the fishing village had become their home away from home. Small enough to fit snugly into their hearts, big enough to protect them, beautiful enough to be a permanent touchstone as they got to know each other. Sanary stood for happiness, peace and quiet; it stood for the first stirrings of empathy with someone who was still a stranger, someone you loved without being able to say why. Who are you, how would you, how do you feel, and what is the arc of your moods over an hour, a day, a few weeks? These things they discovered with ease in their heart-sized home. It was during the quiet hours that Jean and Catherine grew close, and so they tended to avoid loud, busy places such as fairs, the market, the theatre and readings.

September bathed their calm, intense period of getting-to-love-each-other in a spectrum of tones from yellow to mauve and gold to violet. The bougainvilleas, the rough sea, the painted houses by the harbour that oozed pride and history, the crunchy golden gravel of the *boules* area: this was the landscape in which their affection, friendship and deep understanding of each other could thrive.

And they always took it slowly with each other.

The more important a thing is, the slower it should be done, Jean would often think as they began to caress each other. They kissed lingeringly, undressed slowly and left themselves time to stretch out, and even more time to flow together. This careful, focused concentration on the other called forth an especially intense physical, spiritual and emotional passion from their bodies, a feeling of being touched all over.

Each time he slept with Catherine, Jean Perdu drew closer to the stream of life again. He had spent twenty years on the far bank of that river, avoiding colours and caresses, scents and music – fossilised, alone and defiantly withdrawn.

And now . . . he was swimming again.

Jean was a man revived because he was in love. He knew a hundred new little things about this woman. For instance, that when Catherine woke in the morning she was still half caught up in her dreams. Occasionally she would flounder in the fog of the blues; what she had seen in the shadows of the night would make her irritable or ashamed or irksome or gloomy for hours on end. This was her daily struggle through the in-between world. Jean discovered that he could chase away the dream-ghosts by brewing Catherine a cup of hot coffee and guiding her down to the sea to drink it.

'Because of your love I'm learning to love myself too,' she said one morning when the sea was still a sleepy shade of grey-blue. 'I have always taken what life has offered me . . . but I've never offered myself anything. I was never any good at looking after myself.' As he pulled her tenderly to him, Jean thought that he felt the same: he was only capable of loving himself because Catherine loved him.

Then came the night when she held him close as a second great wave of anger smashed over him. This time it was anger at himself. He showered insults on himself, crudely and desperately, with the wrath of a man who realises, with terrifying clarity, that he has irrevocably wasted a part of his life, and the time remaining is all too short. Catherine didn't stop him, she didn't mollify him, she didn't turn away.

Then peace flooded through him. Because that short time would still be enough. Because a few days could contain a lifetime.

Now to Bonnieux, the site of his distant past, a past that was still embedded deep within Jean, though it was no longer the only room in his emotional household. At last he had a present with which to counter it.

That's why it feels easier to return, thought Jean, as Catherine and he took the narrow, rocky pass from Lourmarin – in Perdu's opinion, this town was like a leech, sucking the blood of tourists – to

Bonnieux. They overtook cyclists as they drove, and heard the crack of hunters' guns in the craggy mountains. The occasional near-leafless tree cast a tattered shadow; otherwise the sun bleached out every colour. After the relentless motion of the sea, the inert bulk of the Luberon mountains made a stark, inhospitable impression on Jean. He was looking forward to seeing Max. Really looking forward to it. Max had booked them a big room under the roof in Madame Bonnet's ivy-clad home, formerly a Resistance hideout.

When Catherine and Jean had put their luggage in their room, Max came over and led them to his dovecote. He had prepared a refreshing picnic of wine, fruit, ham and baguette on the broad wall by the fountain. It was the season for truffles and literature. The countryside was redolent of wild herbs, and glowed in autumnal rust reds and wine yellows.

Max was brown, Jean thought. Brown and looking much more of a man.

After two and a half months alone in the Luberon, he seemed at home, as if he had always been a southerner at heart. But Jean thought he also seemed very tired.

'Who sleeps when the earth is dancing?' Max mumbled cryptically when Jean brought it up.

Max told him that Madame had hired him without further ado as a 'general dogsbody' during his 'sickness'. She and her husband, Gérard, were over sixty, and the property, with its three holiday houses and flats, was too big for them to contemplate growing old there on their own. They grew vegetables, fruit and a few vines; Max lent them a hand in return for board and lodging. His dovecote was piled high with notes, stories and drafts. He wrote at night and in the morning until noon. From late afternoon onward he helped out around the bounteous estate, doing anything that Gérard asked him to do: cutting vines, weeding, picking fruit; mending roofs; sowing and harvesting; loading the delivery van and driving to market with Gérard; looking for mottled mushrooms; cleaning truffles; shaking fig trees; pruning cypresses into the shape of standing stones; cleaning the pools; and fetching bread for the bed-and-breakfast guests.

'I've learned to drive a tractor too and I can recognise the call of every toad in the pool,' he announced to Jean with a self-deprecating grin.

The sun, the winds and shuffling around on his knees over the Provence soil had changed Max's youthful city face into that of a man.

'Sickness?' Jean enquired as Max, having finished his account, poured them glasses of white Ventoux wine. 'What sickness? You didn't mention that in your letters.'

Max turned red beneath his tan and became a little fidgety.

'The sickness a man catches when he's deeply in love,' he confessed. 'Sleeping badly, nightmares, not being able to think straight. Not being able to

361

read or write or eat. Brigitte and Gérard obviously couldn't stand by any longer so they prescribed me some activities to stop my mind from going to pot. That's why I'm working for them: it helps me too. We don't mention money, and that suits me just fine.'

'The woman on the red tractor?' Jean asked.

Max nodded, then took a deep breath as though he were building up to an announcement.

'That's right. The woman on the red tractor. That's a good cue, because there's something about her I have to te—'

'The mistral's coming!' Madame Bonnet called to them anxiously, interrupting Max's confession. In shorts and a man's shirt as always, and carrying a basket of fruit, the small, wiry woman came towards them and pointed to the spinning windmills planted in the ground beside a lavender bed. For now it was merely a breeze tugging at the stems, but the sky was bright and the colour of deep-blue ink. The clouds had been swept away, and the horizon appeared to have closed in on them. Mount Ventoux and the Cévennes stood out, sharp and clear – a typical sign that the strong northwesterly wind was rising.

They greeted each other, then Brigitte enquired, 'Do you know about the effects of the mistral?'

Catherine, Jean and Max looked at each other in bemusement.

'We call it *maestrale*, the ruler. Or *vent du fada*, the wind that drives you mad. Our houses keep a low profile' – she gestured to the layout of her buildings, their shorter sides facing the prevailing wind – 'so that it won't take any notice of them. The weather doesn't just turn cooler; it makes every noise louder, and every movement harder. It'll drive us all crazy for a few days, so it'd be better not to discuss anything too important – you'll only argue.'

'What?' Max said quietly.

Madame Bonnet looked at him with a kindly smile on her nut-brown face.

'Oh yes. The *vent du fada* makes you feel as crazy and stupid and edgy as when you're unsure if your love will be reciprocated. But when it's over, all the cobwebs have been blown away – from the countryside and from your head. Everything's spick-and-span again, and we can start life afresh.'

She took her leave, saying, 'I'll roll up the parasols and tie down the chairs.' Jean turned back to Max and asked, 'What were you about to say before?'

'Um . . . I've forgotten,' Max said quickly. 'Are you hungry?'

They spent the evening at a tiny restaurant in Bonnieux called Un Petit Coin de Cuisine, which had a wonderful view of the valley and of a red-and-gold sunset that gave way to a clear night sky strewn with stars glistening like ice. Tom, the cheerful waiter, served them Provençal pizza on wooden boards, and lamb stew. There, at the wobbly red table in the cosy, stone-vaulted room, Catherine added a new and positive element to the chemical bond between Jean and Max. Her presence spread harmony and warmth. Catherine had a way of looking at people as though she took every word they said seriously. Max told her about himself, about his childhood and unrequited crushes on girls, and how he came to be on the run from noise, which was something he had never told Jean – or, presumably, any other man.

While they were deep in conversation, Jean was able to slip away into his own thoughts. The cemetery lay barely a hundred metres above him on the hill, next to the church; they were separated by only a few thousand tonnes of stone and timidity.

It was only as they started down into the valley through the noticeably stronger wind that Jean wondered whether Max had been saying so much about his childhood to conceal the fact that he didn't wish to say any more about the tractor girl.

Max escorted them to their room.

'You go ahead,' Jean said to Catherine.

Max and he were standing together in the shadows between the main house and the barn. The wind hummed and wailed softly but constantly around the corners.

'Come on, Max. What did you want to tell me?' Jean asked him cautiously.

Jordan was silent.

'Don't we want to wait until the wind's dropped?' he said at last.

364

'Is it that bad?'

'Bad enough for me to wait till you got here before telling you. But not . . . fatal. I hope.'

'Tell me, Max, tell me, otherwise my imagination will get the better of me. Please.'

I'll imagine, for instance, that Manon is still alive and was merely playing a trick on me.

Max nodded. The mistral hummed.

'Manon's husband, Luc Basset, married again three years after Manon's death. Mila, a well-known local chef,' Max began. 'Manon's father gave him the vineyard as a wedding present. They produce white and red wines. They're . . . very popular. So is Mila's restaurant.'

Jean Perdu felt a sharp pang of jealousy.

Together Luc and Mila had a vineyard, an estate, a popular restaurant, maybe a garden. They had sunny, flower-filled Provence, and someone to whom they could confide all their concerns; Luc's luck had simply repeated itself. Or maybe not simply, but at that moment Jean couldn't muster the will to form a more balanced opinion.

'How lovely,' he muttered, more sarcastically than he meant to.

Max snorted. 'What did you expect? That Luc would flagellate himself, never look at another woman and wait, on a diet of dry bread, shrivelled olives and garlic, for death to come?'

'What's that supposed to mean?'

'You tell me,' Max hissed back. 'To each his own way of mourning. The wine man chose the "new wife" option. So what? Do we blame him? Should he have done . . . what you did?'

A blaze of indignation shot through Perdu.

'I could punch you right now, Max.'

'I know,' Max replied. 'But I also know that afterwards we'll still be able to grow old together, you daft git.'

'It's the mistral,' said Madame Bonnet, who had heard them arguing and crunched grimly past them across the gravel towards the main house.

'Sorry,' Jean muttered.

'Me too. Damn wind.'

They fell silent again. The wind might have been merely a convenient excuse.

'Are you still going to go and see Luc?'

'Yes, of course.'

'I've been meaning to tell you something ever since you got here.'

And when Max revealed what had been making him feel so ill for the past few weeks, Jean was sure that he must have misheard him amid the buzzing and jeering of the wind. Yes, that must be it, because what he heard was so wonderful and yet so terrible that it could hardly be true.

CHAPTER 42

ax served himself another helping of the aromatic scrambled eggs with truffle that Brigitte Bonnet had cooked them for breakfast. In keeping with Provençal tradition, she had placed nine fresh unbroken eggs in a Kilner jar with an early winter truffle for the eggs to absorb its fragrance. Only three days later did she carefully scramble the eggs and garnish them with a few wafer-thin slices of truffle. The taste was sensual, wild, almost earthy and meaty.

What a lavish last meal for a condemned man, it occurred to Jean. Today, he feared, would be the hardest and longest day of his life.

He ate as though he were praying. He didn't speak; he relished everything with quiet concentration so as to have a reserve to fall back on in the coming hours.

Aside from the scrambled eggs there were two varieties of juicy Cavaillon melon, white and orange; full-flavoured coffee with steaming-hot, sugared milk in large flowery mugs; and home-made plum and lavender jam, freshly baked baguette and buttery croissants, which Max had fetched, as always, from Bonnieux on his wheezing scooter.

Jean looked up from his plate. Up there was Bonnieux's old Romanesque church. Alongside it the cemetery wall, blazing hot in the sun's rays. Stone crosses reared into the sky. He recalled the promise he had broken.

I'd like you to die before me.

Her body had embraced his as she gasped, 'Promise! Promise me!'

He had promised.

Now he was sure: Manon had known then that he wouldn't be able to keep his oath.

I don't want you to have to walk to my grave on your own.

Now he would have to walk that path alone after all.

After breakfast, the three of them set out on their pilgrimage, through cypress groves and orchards, vegetable fields and vineyards.

After a quarter of an hour the Basset winery – a long, three-storey, soft-yellow manor house, flanked by tall, spreading chestnut trees, copper beeches and oaks – came glittering into view through the rows of vines.

Perdu gazed uneasily at the splendid building. The wind was teasing the bushes and trees.

Something stirred inside him. Not envy, not jealousy, not last night's indignation. Rather . . .

It often turns out very differently to how you feared.

Warmth. Yes, he felt a detached warmth – towards the place and towards the people who had named their wine *Manon* and dedicated themselves to restoring their own happiness.

Max was smart enough to keep quiet that morning.

Jean reached for Catherine's hand.

'Thank you,' he said. She understood what he meant.

There was a new hangar to the right of the winery – for trailers, large and small tractors, and for the special vineyard tractor, the one with the tall, narrow wheels.

Two legs in work overalls poked out from beneath one of the tractors, and some imaginative swearwords and the clink of tools could be heard spilling forth from under the machine.

'Hi, Victoria!' called Max, his voice a mixture of cheeriness and despondency.

'Oh, Mister Napkin Man,' a young female voice could be heard saying.

A second later the tractor girl rolled out from under the vehicle. She wiped an embarrassed hand over her expressive face, but only succeeded in making things worse by smudging the dirt and oil stains.

Jean had steeled himself, but still it was bad.

A twenty-year-old Manon stood before him. No make-up, her hair longer, her body more androgynous.

And of course she didn't really resemble Manon;

when Perdu looked closely at this captivating, athletic, self-assured girl, the picture went fuzzy. Nine times he didn't see her, but the tenth time there was Manon, looking out of the unfamiliar young face.

Victoria's entire attention was focused on Max as she ran her eyes over him from top to bottom, scrutinising his work shoes, his threadbare trousers and his washed-out shirt. There was a hint of acknowledgment in her gaze. She nodded appreciatively.

'You call Max "Napkin Man"?' asked Catherine, hiding her amusement.

'Yeah,' said Vic. 'That's precisely the kind of guy he used to be. Used a napkin, took the metro instead of walking, had only seen dogs in special holdalls, and so on.'

'You have to excuse the young lady. Out here in the sticks, they only learn manners in the run-up to their wedding,' Max taunted her fondly.

'Which, as everyone knows, is the key event in any Parisian woman's life,' she countered.

'Preferably more than one,' Max said with a grin.

Vic shot him a complicit smile.

The journey is over when you begin to love, thought Jean, as the two youngsters feasted their eyes on each other.

'Did you want to see Papa?' said Vic, abruptly breaking the spell.

Max nodded with a glazed look in his eye, Jean nodded uneasily, but Catherine said with a smile, 'Yes, sort of.'

'I'll take you to the main house.'

She didn't walk like Manon either, it struck Perdu, as they followed her under soaring plane trees from which crickets chirped.

The young woman looked around at them.

'By the way, I'm the red wine: Victoria. The white's my mother, Manon. The vineyards used to belong to her.'

Jean felt for Catherine's hand. It pressed his briefly.

Max's eyes were glued to Victoria as she skipped up the stairs two at a time in front of them, but he suddenly stopped and tugged Jean back by the arm.

'One thing I didn't mention last night is that this is the woman I'm going to marry,' Max said with calm sincerity. 'Even if she turns out to be your daughter.'

Oh God. Mine?

Victoria gestured for them to come inside and pointed to the wine-tasting room. Had she overheard? There was an edge to her smile: Marry me? A napkin man like you? Only if you seriously up your game.

Aloud she said, 'The old cellars are through there to the left; that's where we store the *Victoria*. The *Manon* is matured in the vaults under the apricot orchard. I'll fetch my father. He'll show you around the winery. Wait here in the tasting room. Whom shall I . . . announce?' Vic concluded with a cheerful flourish. She flashed Max a smile, a smile that seemed to radiate out from her entire body.

'Jean Perdu. From Paris. The bookseller,' said Jean Perdu.

'Jean Perdu, the bookseller from Paris,' Victoria repeated contentedly, then disappeared.

Catherine, Jean and Max heard her bound up some creaking steps, walk along a corridor and speak to someone. Speak for some time, question, answer, question, answer. Her steps coming back down, equally lithe and carefree.

'He'll be with you right away,' said Victoria, poking her head into the room, smiling, fleetingly turning into Manon, and then disappearing again.

Jean heard Luc walking up and down upstairs, opening a cupboard or a drawer.

Jean stood there while the mistral gathered speed, tore at the building's shutters, raced through the leaves of the towering chestnut trees and heaped dry soil between the vines.

He stood there until Max made himself scarce and went after Victoria; until Catherine rubbed his shoulder and whispered, 'I'll be waiting in the bistro, and I love you whatever happens,' and set off to visit Mila's domain of the farm.

Jean waited as he heard Luc's footsteps approaching across the squeaking floorboards, creaking stairs and tiled floor of the winery. Only then did Perdu turn to the door. Any moment now he would be face-to-face with Manon's husband. The man whose wife he had loved.

Jean hadn't considered for one second what he was going to say to Luc.

CHAPTER 43

Luc was the same height as he was. Almond-coloured hair, dulled by the sun; short, but in need of a trim. Intelligent light-brown eyes bordered by many tiny wrinkles. A tall, slender tree in jeans and a faded blue shirt, a body shaped by its dealings with soil, fruit and stone.

Perdu immediately saw what had appealed to Manon.

Luc Basset possessed an obvious dependability combined with sensitivity and virility. A virility that could not be measured in money, success and wittiness, but in strength, stamina and the ability to care for a family, a house, a piece of land. Such men were bound to the land of their ancestors; selling, leasing or even granting a new son-in-law a piece of it was equivalent to having an organ removed.

'Weatherproof' would have been Lirabelle's comment on Luc. 'You're a different person if you've been warmed by open fires rather than by central heating as a child, if you've climbed trees instead of cycling on the pavement with a helmet on, if you've played outside rather than sitting in front of the television.' That was why she would send Jean out into the rain at their relatives' in Brittany and heat his bathwater in a kettle over the fire. Hot water had never felt so good since.

What was it that reminded Jean of that boiling kettle when he looked at Luc? It was because Manon's husband was every bit as intense, alive and authentic as it. Luc's sturdy shoulders, his work-hardened arms; his whole bearing said, 'I will not bend.' This man looked at him with his dark eyes, studying Jean's face, examining his body and fingers. They did not shake hands.

'Yes?' Luc asked instead from the doorway. A deep, measured voice.

'I'm Jean Perdu. I'm the man your wife, Manon, lived with in Paris. Up until . . . twenty-one years ago. For five years.'

'I know,' Luc said steadily. 'She told me when she knew she was dying.'

The two men stared at each other, and for one crazy moment Perdu thought they were going to hug. Only they could understand each other's pain.

'I've come to ask for forgiveness.'

A smile flickered across the vintner's face.

'Ask whom?'

'Manon. Only Manon. As her husband . . . you couldn't possibly forgive me for loving your wife. Or for being the other man.'

Luc's eyes narrowed. He stared very intently at Perdu.

Did he wonder whether Manon had liked feeling

these hands? Did he wonder whether Jean had been capable of loving his wife as well as he had?

'Why have you only come now?' Luc asked slowly.

'I didn't read the letter at the time.'

'My God,' Luc said in surprise. 'Why not?'

This was the hardest part.

'I expected it to contain only the kind of things women usually write when they're sick of their lovers,' said Perdu. 'Refusing was the only way to preserve my dignity.'

It was so, so hard to say these words.

And now, at last, pour your hate on me, please.

Luc gave himself time. He paced up and down the wine-tasting room. At last he spoke again, this time to Jean's back.

'It must have been terrible – when you did read the letter, and realised that you'd been wrong the whole time, that they weren't the usual words. "Let's stay friends" and that sort of rubbish. That's what you expected, right? "It's not your fault, it's mine . . . I hope you find someone who deserves you . . ." But this was totally different.'

Jean hadn't reckoned on such empathy. He was beginning to understand why Manon had married Luc. And not him.

'It was hell,' he admitted. He wanted to say more, much more. But it was choking him. The idea that Manon had stared at a door that never opened. He didn't look around at Luc. His eyes burned with tears of shame.

It was then that he felt Luc's hand on his shoulder.

Luc turned Jean to face him. He looked him in the eyes, searching them, exposing his own grief to Jean.

They stood a mere yard apart as their eyes spoke the unspeakable. Jean saw sorrow and tenderness, anger and understanding. He saw that Luc was wondering what they should do now, but he also noticed his readiness to endure whatever might happen.

I wish I'd known Luc earlier.

They could have grieved together. After the hatred and the jealousy.

'I have to ask this now,' said Jean. 'I haven't been able to get it out of my head since I saw her. Is . . . is Victoria . . .?'

'She's our daughter. Manon was three months pregnant when she went back to Paris; Victoria was conceived in the spring. Manon already knew she was sick, but she kept it to herself. She decided in favour of the child and against the cancer therapy when the doctors assured her that the baby stood a chance.'

Luc's voice was quavering now too.

'Manon chose certain death on her own. She told me only when it was too late . . . too late to give up the baby and to attempt to cure her. She kept her cancer secret from me until her letter to you, Jean. She said that she was so ashamed, and it was her just deserts for loving twice in one lifetime. My God! As if love were a crime . . . Why did she have to be so hard on herself? Why?'

The two men stood there and though neither cried, they both watched the other man struggle for breath, swallow hard, grit his teeth and try not to sink without a trace.

'Do you want to know the rest?' Luc asked after a while.

Jean nodded. 'Yes, please,' he said. 'Please – I want to know everything. And Luc . . . I'm sorry. I never meant to steal someone else's love. I'm sorry I didn't resist and . . .'

'Forget it!' Luc said wildly, fierily. 'I don't hold it against you. Of course I felt like the forgotten man whenever she was in Paris. And when she was with me, I came to life again as her lover and your rival, and all of a sudden you were the one who was being cheated on. Yet that was all part of life . . . and, strange as it may seem to some people, it wasn't unforgivable.'

Luc slammed his fist into his other palm. His face was flushed with such turmoil that Jean feared the other man might hurl him against the wall at any moment.

'I'm so sad that Manon had to make things so hard for herself. My love would have been sufficient for her and you, I swear, just as hers would have been for you and me. She never robbed me of anything. Why didn't she forgive herself? It wouldn't have been easy between you and me and her and whoever else. But life is never easy, and there are a thousand ways to live it. She needn't have feared – we'd have found a way. There's a path up every mountain, every one.'

Did Luc truly believe that? Could anyone feel so intensely and be so full of love for others?

'Come on!' Luc ordered him.

He led Perdu along the corridor, right, left, another corridor, and then . . .

A light-brown door. Manon's husband collected himself before pushing a key into the lock, turning it and pushing down the brass handle with his large, dependable hand.

'This was the room where Manon died,' he said in a rasping voice.

The room wasn't very big, but it was bathed in light. It looked as though it were still used. A tall wooden cabinet, a bureau, a chair with one of Manon's shirts draped over it. An armchair, flanked by a small table with an open book on it. The room was lived in; not like the one he had left behind in Paris – the bleak, tired, sad room in which he had locked away their memories and their love.

It was as if this room's occupant had popped outside for a second. A wide door led out onto a stone terrace and a garden full of horse chestnut trees, bougainvilleas, almond, rose and apricot trees. A white cat was weaving its way between them.

Jean looked at the bed. It was covered with the bright patchwork quilt that Manon had sewed before her wedding at his place, in Paris;

along with the flag with the book bird emblazoned on it.

Luc followed Jean's gaze.

'She died in that bed. Christmas Eve 1992. She asked me whether she would make it through the night. I said yes.'

He turned to Perdu. Luc's eyes were very dark now, his face riven with pain; all control had deserted him. His voice was cracked, choked and distressed as he blurted, 'I said yes. It was the only time I ever lied to my wife.'

Before he knew what he was doing, Perdu reached out to pull Luc to him. The other man didn't resist. Sighing 'Oh, God!' he returned Jean's embrace.

'Whatever you meant to each other, it was not spoiled by what I meant to her. She never wanted to be without you, never.'

'I never lied to Manon,' mumbled Luc, as if he hadn't heard what Jean had said. 'Never. Never.'

Jean Perdu held Luc as convulsions racked his body. Luc didn't weep, Luc didn't speak. He just shook endlessly in Jean's arms.

Shamefully, Jean dug up Christmas Eve 1992 from his memory. He had got drunk, staggered through Paris, sworn at the Seine. And while he was occupied with those trivial, trifling things, Manon had been fighting, fighting to the bitter end. And she had lost.

I didn't feel it when she died. No wrench. No earthquake. No bolt of lightning. Nothing.

Luc recovered his composure in Jean's embrace.

'Manon's diary. She told me to give it to you if you ever came,' he said in a reedy voice. 'That was her wish. She continued to hope beyond death.'

Hesitantly they let go of each other. Luc sat down on the divan. He reached over to the bedside table and opened the drawer.

Jean recognised the notebook immediately. Manon had been writing in it when they first met in the train to Paris. As she wept at leaving the south she loved so much. And she would often note things in it at night when she couldn't sleep, after they had made love.

Luc got up and handed the book to Jean. He took it, but the stocky vintner's fingers clung to it for a moment.

'And I need to give you this from me,' he said calmly.

Jean had foreseen it – and knew he mustn't duck. So he simply closed his eyes.

Luc's fist struck him between lip and chin. Not too hard, but hard enough to knock the wind out of Jean, blur his vision and send him reeling against the wall.

Luc's apologetic voice reached him from somewhere. 'Please don't think that it was because you slept with her. I knew when I married her that one man could never be everything to Manon.' Luc offered Jean his hand. 'It's more because you didn't come to her when you should have.'

Fleetingly, everything blended into one.

His forbidden, lifeless room in Rue Montagnard.

The warm, bright room where Manon had died. Luc's hand in his.

And all of a sudden the memory was there.

Jean *had* felt something when Manon died.

In the days leading up to Christmas, when he was often drunk and on the brink of sleep, in that confused state he had heard her talking. Scattered words he couldn't understand: 'friends' windows', 'coloured crayon', 'southern light' and 'raven'.

He stood there in Manon's room, her diary in his hand, and had a premonition that he would find these words inside. All of a sudden he felt a great inner peace, and the welcome pain of the deserved blow stung his face.

'Can you eat with that?' Luc asked sheepishly, pointing to Perdu's chin. 'Mila's made lemon chicken.'

Jean nodded.

He no longer needed to ask why Luc had dedicated a wine to Manon. He understood.

MANON'S TRAVEL DIARY

Bonnieux

24 December 1992

Maman has made the thirteen desserts. Different kinds of nut, different kinds of fruit, raisins, nougat in two different colours, oil cake, butter cake with cinnamon milk.

Victoria is lying in her cradle, with rosy cheeks and sparklingly inquisitive eyes. She looks like her father.

Luc no longer blames me for the fact that I am going and Victoria is staying behind, and not the other way round.

She will be a southern light of great radiance.

I ask Luc to give this book to Jean to read if he should ever come, at some stage, whenever that might be.

I don't have the strength to explain everything in a good-bye letter.

My little southern light. I only had

forty-eight days with Vicci, and yet I dreamed of many years and saw so many lives that await my daughter.

Maman is writing these final words for me, for I no longer have the strength even to hold a pen. I have struggled this far so that I can eat the thirteen desserts myself, and not the bread of the dead.

Thinking takes me a long time.

The words have dwindled. Moved out, all of them.

Into the wide world. Many coloured crayons among pencils. Lots of lights in the dark.

Everyone loves one another, me included. Everyone is brave and deeply in love with the baby.

(My daughter wants to hold her daughter. Manon and Victoria lie there together, and the twigs crackle in the fireplace. Luc comes in and puts his arms around his two girls. Manon has signalled that she wants me to write something else. My hand holding the pen is ice-cold. My husband brings me some warm brandy, but my fingers don't feel the warmth.)

Dear Victoria, my daughter, my beauty. It was so easy to sacrifice myself for you. That's life: laugh about it, you'll be loved, forever.

As for the rest, daughter, about my life in Paris, read this and be cautious with your judgement.

(Manon has blanks. I write only what she whispers now. She winces when a door opens somewhere. She is still waiting for him, the man from Paris. She is still hoping.)

Why didn't Jean come?
Too much pain?
Yes. Too much pain.
Pain makes a man stupid. And a stupid man is more easily afraid.
The cancer of life, that's what my raven had.

(My daughter is disintegrating before my eyes. I write and try not to weep. She asks whether she will live through the night. I lie to her and say yes. She says I'm lying, like Luc.
She briefly dozes off. Luc takes the baby. Manon wakes up.)
He received the letter, says good old Madame Rosalette. She'll watch out for him, as much as she can, as much as he lets her. I tell her: Proud! Stupid! Pain!
And she adds that he has smashed his

furniture and gone numb. Numb to everything. He's almost dead, she says.

That makes two of us.

(Here my daughter laughs.)

Maman has secretly written some words she shouldn't have.

Won't show me.

We're still jockeying for position, even on the home straight.

So what? What else are we supposed to do? Wait silently in our Sunday best for the reaper to swing?

(She laughs again and coughs. Outside, the snow has turned the Atlas cedars the colour of a burial shroud. Dear God, you are everything I hate, because you are taking my daughter before her time and leaving me to grieve with her child. Is that your idea of how things ought to be? Replacing dead cats with kittens, dead daughters with granddaughters?)

Shouldn't we carry on living the same way until the last, because that is what vexes death the most – to see us drinking life to the final draft?

(Here, my daughter coughs, and twenty minutes pass before she next speaks. She gropes for words.

Sugar, she says, but it's not the right one. She gets annoyed.

Tango, she whispers.

Friends' windows, she shouts.

I know what she means: French windows.)

Jean. Luc. Both. The two of you.

In the end. I'm only going next door.

To the end of the corridor, into my favourite room.

And from there, out into the garden. And there I will become light and go wherever I want.

I sit out there sometimes in the evening, and look at the house we lived in together.

I see you, Luc, my beloved husband, roaming through some rooms, and I see you, Jean, in the others.

You're searching for me.

I'm no longer in the sealed rooms, of course.

Look at me! Out here.

Raise your eyes, I'm here!

Think of me and call my name!

None of this is any less real because I am gone.

Death doesn't matter.
It makes no difference to life.
We will always remain what we were
to one another.

Manon's signature was ghostly and feeble. More than twenty years later Jean Perdu bent over the scrawled letters and kissed them.

CHAPTER 44

On the third day, without any warning, the mistral stopped. That was how it always went. It had tugged at the curtains, rearranged the strewn plastic bags into new patterns, made dogs bark and brought people to tears.

Now it was gone, having taken with it the dust, the spent heat and the fatigue. The countryside had also cast out the tourists, who were too fast, too frantic and too eager to invade the local towns. The Luberon swung back into its accustomed rhythm, one determined purely by the cycles of nature. Flowering, sowing, mating, waiting, being patient, harvesting and doing the right thing at the right time, without hesitation.

The warmth returned, but it was the mellow, genial warmth of autumn that rejoiced at the thought of evening thunderstorms and the cool of morning, which had been sorely lacking during the searing summer months, leaving the land thirsty.

The higher Jean Perdu climbed up the steep, rutted sandstone path, the quieter it became. The crickets, the cicadas and the faint lament of the wind were his only company as he scaled the massive hill on which Bonnieux's church sat. He was carrying Manon's diary and an open but loosely recorked bottle of Luc's wine.

His gait was the one the steep, uneven path demanded, stooped like a penitent, with small steps, aches creeping up his calves and along his legs, back and head. Passing the church, whose steps vaguely resembled a stone ladder, and the cedars, he reached the top.

The view made him dizzy. The landscape lay fanned out far, far below. The day was bright after the mistral had bled the sky of its colour, and the horizon was virtually white where Jean imagined Avignon to be. He saw sand-coloured houses, scattered like dice on the green and red and yellow patchwork, as in an old painting. Long rows of vines, ripe and juicy, lined up like soldiers. Huge, faded squares of lavender. Green, brown and saffron-coloured fields, and among them the swaying, waving green of trees. The countryside was so beautiful, the view so majestic; anyone with a soul could not fail to be subjugated by it.

This Calvary, with its thick walls, solid tombs and stone crosses, seemed to be the bottom-most step to heaven. God must be secretly sitting here, gazing out from this bright summit; only he and the dead were granted the enjoyment of this solemn, sweeping panorama.

Head bowed and heart pounding, Jean crossed the coarse gravel to the iron gate.

The enclosure was long and narrow. It was laid out on two terraces, each with two rows of graves. Weathered ochre shrines to the dead and grey-black marble tombs on the top terrace, the same on the lower level. Gravestones the height of doors and the width of beds, many crowned with defiant crosses. Mostly family graves, deep deathly homes with room for centuries of grief.

Cropped, slender cypresses stood among the graves, casting no shadow. Everything here was naked and bare; there was no shelter anywhere.

Slowly, still breathless, Perdu paced along the first row and read the names. Porcelain flowers and stylised stone books stood on the large graves, polished and adorned with photos or short verses. Some were decorated with small figurines depicting the hobby of the deceased. One man, Bruno, in a hunting outfit, an Irish setter at his side. Another grave had a hand of playing cards on it. The next featured the outline of an island, Gomera, obviously the dead person's favourite spot. Stone dressers with photos, cards and well-fastened trinkets on them. Bonnieux's living sent the dead on their way with a host of tidings.

The decorations reminded Perdu of Clara Violette. She would cover her Pleyel grand piano with knick-knacks, and he had to clear them away before her balcony concerts.

Perdu suddenly realised that he missed the

residents of 27 Rue Montagnard. Was it possible that all those years he had been surrounded by friends, but had never truly appreciated it?

In the middle of the second row, with a view of the valley, Jean found Manon. She lay next to her father, Arnoul Morello.

At least she's not alone in there.

He sank to his knees, rested his cheek on the stone and placed his arms around the sides, as though he were trying to embrace the sarcophagus.

The marble was cool despite the sun glinting off it.

The crickets chirped.

The wind moaned.

Perdu waited to feel something. To feel *her*. But all his senses could discern was the sweat running down his back, the blood beating painfully in his ears, and the sharp gravel under his knees.

He opened his eyes again and stared at her name – Manon Basset (née Morello) – at the dates – 1967–1992 – and at her framed black-and-white photo.

But nothing happened.

She isn't here.

A gust of wind ruffled a cypress.

She isn't here!

He got to his feet, baffled and disappointed.

'Where are you?' he whispered into the wind.

The family grave was piled high with porcelain flowers, cat figurines and a sculpture of an open book. Some of the sculptures held photos, lots of pictures of Manon that Perdu had never seen before.

Her wedding photos, with writing below: 'With love and no regrets, Luc.'

Another, showing Manon holding her cat, read: 'The door out onto the terrace is always open – Maman.'

A third: 'I came because you went – Victoria.'

Jean reached out carefully to touch the sculpture that looked like an open book, and read the inscription. 'Death doesn't matter. We will always remain what we were to one another.'

Jean read the lines again, this time out loud. They were the words Manon had spoken in Buoux as they searched for their star among the dark mountains.

He ran his hand over the grave.

But she isn't here.

Manon wasn't in there, shut away in stone, surrounded by earth and dismal solitude. Not for one instant had she descended into the crypt to her abandoned body.

'Where are you?' he asked once more.

He went over to the stone parapet and looked out at the broad, sumptuous Calavon valley below. Everything was so tiny. It was as though he were one of the circling buzzards. He sniffed the air. Breathed in every molecule, then out again. He felt the warmth and heard the wind playing in the Atlas cedars. He could even make out Manon's vineyard.

Next to one of the cypresses, near the hoses for watering the flowers, a broad flight of steps led to the upper terrace. Jean sat down on them, removed the cork from the bottle of *Manon XV* white wine, and poured some into the glass he had brought. He took a tentative sip. He smelled the wine; it had a cheering aroma. The *Manon* tasted of honey and pale fruit, of a tender sigh before sliding into sleep. A vibrant, contradictory wine, a wine brimming with love.

Fantastic work, Luc.

He set the glass down beside him on the stone steps and opened Manon's diary. He had dipped into it repeatedly over the previous days and nights while Max, Catherine and Victoria had been working in the vines. Some passages he knew by heart; others had surprised him. Some things had hurt him, and much of what was written had filled him with gratitude. He had had no idea of how much he had meant to Manon. He used to long for it to be so, but only now that he had made peace with himself and was newly in love did he learn the truth. And it healed old wounds.

Now, though, he searched for an entry she had written during her wait.

I have already lived long enough, Manon had written in late autumn, *on an autumn day like today. I have lived and loved, I have had the best of this world. Why cry over the ending? Why cling to what remains? The advantage of dying is that you stop being afraid of it. There is a sense of peacefulness too.*

He leafed forward through the pages. Now came the entries that broke his heart with compassion. The ones where she spoke of the fear that flooded through her body in waves, the nights when Manon would wake up in the silent darkness and hear death creeping closer. The night too, when she was heavily pregnant and had run into Luc's room, where he held her until morning, forcing himself not to cry.

And then did, in the shower, where he thought she couldn't hear him.

She had heard, of course.

Again and again, Manon expressed her disbelief at Luc's strength. He had fed and washed her, had watched her dwindling away, with the exception of her pregnant tummy.

Perdu drank another glass before he went on reading.

> My child is feeding on me. It takes my healthy flesh. My tummy is rosy, plump and alive. There must be a litter of tiny cats in there, it's that frisky. The rest of me is a thousand years older: grey and putrid and brittle like one of those crispbreads northerners are always eating. My girl will eat buttery, shiny, golden croissants. She will be victorious – victorious over death. We shall thumb our noses at it, this child and I. I would like to call her Victoria.

How Manon loved her unborn baby! How she nourished it with the love that burned so exceptionally brightly within her.

No wonder Victoria is so strong, he thought. *Manon gave herself entirely to her.*

He flicked back to that August night when Manon had decided to leave him.

You are lying there now like a dancer doing a pirouette. One leg stretched out, the other pulled up. One arm above your head, the other almost braced against your side.

You always looked at me as though I were unique. In five years, not once did you look at me with anger or indifference. How did you manage it?

Castor is staring at me. We two-legged creatures must seem very strange to cats.

I feel crushed by the eternity that awaits me.

Sometimes – but it is a truly evil thought – just sometimes I wished there were someone I love who would go before me. To show me that I can make it too.

Sometimes I thought that you had to go before me so I could do it too, certain that you are waiting for me . . .

Adieu, Jean Perdu.

I envy you for all the years you still have left to live.

I shall go into my last room and from there into the garden. Yes, that is how it will be. I shall stride through tall, inviting French windows and straight into the sunset. And then . . . then I shall become light, and then I can be everywhere.

That would be my nature; I would be there always, every evening.

Jean Perdu poured himself another glass of wine.

The sun was slowly sinking. Its pinkish light settled over the land, painting the houses gold, and making his wine glass and the windows of the farms down below glitter like diamonds.

Then it happened: the air began to glow.

Like billions of dissipating droplets, sparkling and dancing, a veil of light descended on the valley, the mountains and him; the light seemed to be laughing. Never in his whole life, never before, had Jean Perdu seen such a sunset.

He took another sip as the clouds revealed themselves in a multitude of colours, from cherry and raspberry to peach and honeydew. Then, at last, Jean Perdu understood.

She is here.

There!

Manon's soul, Manon's energy, Manon's whole disembodied essence filled the land and the wind; yes, she was everywhere and in everything; she sparkled and manifested herself to him in every form she had taken on . . .

. . . *because everything is within us. And nothing dies away.*

Jean Perdu laughed, but his heart ached so much that he fell silent and turned his attention inwards, where his laughter danced on.

You're right, Manon.

It is all still there. The times we spent together are immortal, imperishable, and life never stops.

The death of our loved ones is merely a threshold between an ending and a new beginning.

Jean breathed deeply in and slowly out again.

He would invite Catherine to explore this next stage, this next life, with him – the new, bright days after a long, dark night that had commenced twenty-one years earlier.

'Good-bye, Manon Morello, good-bye,' whispered Jean Perdu. 'It was wonderful to have known you.'

The sun sank behind the hills of the Vaucluse, and the sky glowed with molten fire.

Only when the colours had paled and the world had turned to shadow did Perdu drain his glass of *Manon* to the last drop.

EPILOGUE

It was the second time they had eaten the thirteen desserts together on Christmas Eve, laying three extra places for the dead, for the living and for good fortune in the year to come. Three seats were always left empty at the long table in Luc Basset's house.

They had listened to the 'Ritual of the Ashes', the Occitan prayer of the dead, which Victoria read to them beside the open fire in the kitchen. She had asked to read it on this anniversary, for her mother's sake and for hers: it was a message from the dead woman to her beloved.

'Am the bark that carries you to me,' Vic began in her clear voice. 'Am salt on your numbed lips, am the aroma and the essence of every food . . . Am startled dawn and garrulous sundown. Am a dauntless island, fleeing the sea. Am what you find and what slowly releases me. Am the positive boundary of your solitude.'

At these final words Vic started to cry. So did Jean and Catherine, who were holding hands; and Joaquin Albert Perdu and Lirabelle Bernier, occasionally known as Perdu, who were testing out a truce as lovers and companions in Bonnieux. Austere northerners, whom little moved to tears otherwise – certainly not words.

They had grown very fond of Max, their so-called adopted grandson, and of the Basset family, to whom their lives were bound by love, death and grief. For a few days around Christmas, this unusual mix of emotions brought Perdu's parents together – in bed, at the table and for a shared car journey. Throughout the rest of the year Jean continued to be treated over the telephone to his mother's moaning about her ex-husband – 'that social dyslexic' – and to his father's jocular complaints about the professor.

Catherine suspected that the old couple's sniping was their way of warming up before they fell into each other's passionate arms on Bastille Day, Christmas and, more recently, even Perdu's birthday.

The elder Perdus and Jean and Catherine spent the period from 23 December to Twelfth Night in Bonnieux. They passed the days between the years with eating, laughing and talking, interspersed with long walks and wine-tasting sessions, female chatter and male silence. Now a new era was drawing near – again.

The late-winter blooming of the peach trees, when the approaching spring decorates the fruit trees along the Rhône with flowers, is the sign of new beginnings in Provence. Max and Vic had chosen this season of white and red blossoms for their wedding. She had made him woo her for twelve months before she would grant him his first kiss – but things had moved fast from then on.

Max's first children's book was published soon after: *The Magician in the Garden – A Heroic Book for Children.*

It dumbfounded the critics, upset parents and enthralled children and teenagers, who were amused by how worked up figures of authority were over the book. This was because it urged youngsters to challenge everything that grown-ups reacted to with the words: 'You mustn't do that!'

Catherine and Jean had combed Provence for an atelier until they finally found one. The main stumbling block had never been the premises themselves, but rather the fact that she wanted the countryside around to be an exact reflection of her and Jean's inner landscapes. They eventually found a barn adjoining a charming, slightly rundown Provençal farmhouse between Sault and Mazan, with a lavender field to the right of it, a mountain to the left and an uninterrupted view of vineyards and Mount Ventoux out the front. Behind it lay an orchard for their two cats, Rodin and Némirovsky, to patrol.

'It's like coming home,' Catherine had announced to Jean, as with great satisfaction she paid over the majority of the divorce proceeds she had received from the lawyer.

Her sculptures were almost double human size. It

was as though Catherine could detect beings trapped in the stone, as though she could see through the unhewn blocks into their soul, hear their cries and feel their hearts beating. Catherine would then begin to chisel them free.

Not all of her creations were likeable.

Hatred. Suffering. Forbearance. The soul reader.

Hang on!

It really was. From a block the size of a banana crate Catherine had released two hands that were forming a shape. Were these seeking, finding fingers reading, caressing or touching words? To whom did they belong? Were they pulling something out, or reaching in?

If you pressed your face to the stone, you could sense that a concealed, bricked-up wall was opening inside yourself. The entrance . . . to a room?

'Everybody has an inner room where demons lurk. Only when we open it and face up to it are we free,' said Catherine.

Jean Perdu looked after her in Provence and in Paris, when the two of them stayed in his old flat in Rue Montagnard. He made sure that Catherine ate and slept well, got together with her girlfriends and cast off her cobwebs of dreams in the morning.

They made love often, with the same concentrated languidness. He knew every inch of her, every perfect and imperfect spot. He stroked and caressed each of those imperfections until her body believed that for him she was the most beautiful woman alive.

When he wasn't working part-time at the bookshop in Banon, Perdu went hunting. While Catherine was in Paris or sculpting alone on the farm, giving courses, selling art, filing, sanding and correcting, he went prospecting for the world's most exciting books – in school libraries, concealed among the bequests of gnarled old teachers and blathering fruit growers, in forgotten Aladdin's caves, and unfurnished homemade bunkers dating from the Cold War.

Perdu had launched his trade in unique books with a facsimile of Sanary's handwritten manuscript, which had come into his possession by a roundabout route. Samy had insisted that her pseudonym must remain a secret.

With the help of Claudine Gulliver, the auctioneer's registrar from the fifth floor at 27 Rue Montagnard, Perdu soon found a wealthy collector for this singular work. However, it was Perdu's subjecting the man to an emotional test before he would sell him the book that had established his reputation as an eccentric book lover, whom even a substantial sum could not persuade to sell to the wrong person. Sometimes dozens of collectors would come clamouring for a book, but Perdu would select the person who struck him as that volume's ideal friend, lover or patient; the money was secondary.

Perdu travelled from Istanbul to Stockholm, and from Lisbon to Hong Kong, unearthing the most precious, most intelligent and most dangerous books – as well as special ones for bedtime reading.

Often, as right now, Jean Perdu sits in the farmhouse's summer kitchen, eyes closed, plucking rosemary and lavender flowers, breathing in this most profoundly Provençal fragrance, and writing his *Great Encyclopedia of Small Emotions: A Guide for Booksellers, Lovers and Other Literary Pharmacists.*

He is making an entry under K: 'Kitchen solace – the feeling that a delicious meal is simmering on the kitchen stove, misting up the windows, and that at any moment your lover will sit down to dinner with you and, between mouthfuls, gaze happily into your eyes. (Also known as living.)'

RECIPES

The cuisine of Provence is as diverse as its scenery: fish by the coast, vegetables in the countryside, and in the mountains lamb and a variety of staple dishes containing pulses. One region's cooking is influenced by olive oil, another's is based on wine, and pasta dishes are common along the Italian border. East kisses West in Marseilles with hints of mint, saffron and cumin, and the Vaucluse is a paradise for truffle and confectionery lovers.

Yet many ingredients unite the culinary traditions of the Rhône valley and the Côte d'Azur: thick, flavoursome olive oil; garlic; many varieties of tomato, some sun-dried, for salads, sauces, soups, tarts, pizzas, fillings and so on; goat's cheese from Banon and fresh herbs. Provençal cooks never add more than three of these to their roasts and other dishes, but they use sage or lavender, thyme or rosemary, fennel or winter savoury in large quantities.

The following recipes are typical of the region, and their fragrances and colours have marked its history.

BOHÉMIENNE DE LÉGUMES

*T*his is related to ratatouille but is supplemented with aubergine and enhanced with a basil and tomato sauce. It is generally made with finely chopped vegetables of one colour. The taste of this Provençal vegetable dish depends on the quality and intensity of the ingredients. The vegetables must be 'sun-kissed'; large, flavourless, watery tomatoes will leave the dish tasting bland. The aromas of the fresh herbs are equally essential.

SERVES 6

INGREDIENTS

For the Vegetable Terrine
3 red peppers
3–6 spicy, fruity tomatoes (or one tin of chopped tomatoes)
2 firm aubergines
olive oil
2 large onions
2 small, tasty courgettes
Salt and pepper
Garlic clove, chopped
Fresh thyme

Rosemary (optional)
Bay leaves (optional)

For the Tomato Sauce
500 grams ripe, sweet-and-spicy tomatoes
3 tablespoons mild olive oil
A liberal sprinkling of thyme and basil

PREPARATION

1. *To make the vegetable terrine:* Prepare the vegetables (remove the seeds from the peppers and peel them with a potato peeler; soak the tomatoes in hot water and peel) and dice them finely. Dice the unpeeled aubergines, then fry them in hot oil in a large pan for 10–15 minutes, stirring constantly. Gradually add the other vegetables. When the vegetables are tender, season with salt and pepper, and add the chopped garlic and thyme. Add the rosemary and bay leaves, if desired. Press into a mould.

2. *To make the tomato sauce:* Remove the tomato skins and seeds. In a deep pot over medium heat, heat the oil and gently fry the tomatoes and herbs, reducing them to a thick paste. Season with salt and pepper to taste, and blend.

3. Glaze the vegetable terrine with a drizzle of olive oil, and serve with the tomato sauce. This dish goes well with a fresh baguette and crème fraîche.

PISTOU

*T*his is the Provençal soup that brings the warmth back into Samy's limbs and can raise anyone's spirits. However, it is not the best option for a romantic dinner; read on to find out why.

Almost everyone in Provence has his or her own pistou recipe. The staple ingredients are beans (green, white or red), courgettes, tomatoes, basil and garlic, but everyone gives the soup a particular twist with fresh seasonal vegetables from the garden or the market, such as pumpkin, turnip and celery. Some people like to cook pistou as you would minestrone, whereas others prefer to use small, fat noodles – gobetti, small macaroni or rigate. Near Nice they like to add a little bacon. The dish's magic ingredient, though, is the pistou (which means 'pounded' in Provençal), a tangy green sauce similar to Italian pesto, but without the pine nuts.

SERVES 4

INGREDIENTS

For the Vegetable Soup
200 grams carrots
250 grams courgettes

1 leek (or fresh spring onions)
500 grams potatoes
1 onion
200 grams green beans
4 strong-tasting, sweet tomatoes (or half a tin of peeled tomatoes) Tomato purée to taste
Olive oil
3–4 sprigs each of thyme, winter savoury and rosemary
Salt
1 tin (250 grams) white Italian beans
Pepper

For the Paste
2–3 cloves of garlic
½ teaspoon sea salt
3–4 bunches of fresh basil
25 grams fresh Parmesan (or Pecorino, according to taste), plus more for a garnish (optional)
5 tablespoons finest mild olive oil

PREPARATION
1. *To make the vegetable soup:* Wash and cut the carrots, courgettes, leek, potatoes, onion and green beans into pieces, rounds or cubes. If using tomatoes, soak the tomatoes in hot water, peel them and dice (or if you prefer, use a tin of good-quality tomatoes). Heat the oil in

a large pot over medium heat. Add the vegetables, herbs and tomato purée (if using) and stir continuously for 10 minutes on a gentle heat. Season with salt to taste.

2. Rinse the beans in cold water and pat dry with paper towels, then add them to the pot with the other vegetables. Pour in 1½–2 litres of water, cover and leave to simmer for 30–45 minutes (or until the white beans are soft). Season with salt and pepper.

3. *To make the paste:* Peel and chop the garlic and blend to a smooth paste. In a medium bowl, mix the garlic paste with the salt, basil leaves and Parmesan. Add the olive oil, and mix well.

4. Spoon the *pistou* into four soup bowls. Pour in the hot vegetable soup, and serve. Some people prefer to stir the paste into the soup afterwards. Garnish with a sprinkle of Parmesan cheese, if desired.

LAMB CUTLETS WITH GARLIC FLAN

*T*he success of a lamb dish depends largely on the quality of the meat and the marinade. Should your butcher not prepare marinades, you'll find below a couple of ideas for making a delicious marinade of your own. The meat should be left to marinate overnight.

SERVES 2 TO 3

INGREDIENTS

For the Marinade
2–3 cloves of garlic
A little tomato juice
1 tablespoon fresh rosemary
1 tablespoon dried thyme
2–3 tablespoons runny honey
Pepper
Good-quality olive oil (flavoured with rosemary, garlic, lavender or lemon, say!)
Optional: Dijon mustard, sweet chilli, sweet sherry, balsamic vinegar or a little red wine. Whatever takes your fancy!

For the Lamb Cutlets
1 pound lamb cutlets
4 tablespoons olive oil

For the Garlic Flan
Olive oil
100 grams garlic
115 millilitres milk or cream
Salt and pepper
3 eggs, beaten
Nutmeg

PREPARATION
1. *To make the marinade:* Peel the garlic, chop finely and mix with the tomato juice, herbs, honey, pepper, olive oil and the optional ingredients, if desired. Pour the marinade into a 3-litre freezer bag with the lamb cutlets. Seal the bag, place in a bowl in the refrigerator and leave to marinate for a few hours or overnight.
2. *To prepare the lamb cutlets:* Heat the oil in a griddle on high heat. Add the cutlets and cook them one minute per side. Take the pan off the heat and set aside for 5 minutes to cool. The cutlets should be pink inside. (In case you're interested, the author loves to fry them on a raclette grill – perfection!)
3. *To make the garlic flan:* In a small pot over low heat, heat the oil. Add the freshly

411

peeled cloves of garlic (see Note) and the milk and heat until they are soft. Press through a sieve and season with salt and pepper. Add the beaten eggs and a pinch of nutmeg to taste.

Pour the mixture into a well-greased soufflé mould, and thicken for 20 minutes in a bain-marie. Leave to cool for 10 minutes, and turn out onto a plate.

4. Serve with potatoes brushed with olive oil, oven-fried and sprinkled with rosemary and sea salt.

Note: If you choose dried garlic, it is advisable to blanche it in boiling water for 5 minutes, then press it with a fork before adding it to the milk.

LAVENDER ICE CREAM

*T*he lavender ice cream on sale in the ice-cream shops of Roussillon is indeed the intense purple colour of the flowers; it is often dyed with a few drops of blueberry juice. Locally made blueberry-free ice cream is white with purple speckles.

4 SERVINGS

INGREDIENTS
1–2 teaspoons dried lavender or 2–4 teaspoons lavender flowers (freshly picked or organic), plus lavender flowers for garnish
200 grams sugar
120 millilitres fresh milk
8 egg yolks (organic, if possible)
225 millilitres cream (yoghurt, if you prefer it to be lighter)
1 handful of blueberries for colouring (optional)

PREPARATION
1. In a small bowl, blend the lavender with the sugar, and push through a sieve until you have a fine powder. Dissolve the

lavender powder in the milk until the crystals no longer 'crunch' (you may need to heat the mixture slightly, but avoid boiling). In a separate bowl, beat together the egg yolks and cream (or yoghurt) until smooth. Stir the lavender milk into the egg cream and mix thoroughly. Purée the blueberries and add them to colour the mixture, if desired.

2. Place the mixture in an ice-cream maker, or leave to set in a freezer compartment, stirring occasionally.

3. Garnish with lavender flowers for decoration.

Alternative Recipe for
LAVENDER ICE CREAM WITH LAVENDER SYRUP OR LAVENDER HONEY

4 SERVINGS

INGREDIENTS
5 tablespoons lavender syrup, plus more for garnish
450 millilitres Greek yoghurt
120 millilitres fresh milk
225 millilitres cream
1 handful of blueberries for colouring (optional)
Lavender honey or flowers, for garnish

PREPARATION
1. In a medium bowl, stir the lavender syrup into the yoghurt, add milk and cream, and stir until smooth.
2. Purée the blueberries and add them gradually to colour the mixture, if desired.
3. Place the mixture in an ice-cream maker or a freezer compartment. Garnish with syrup, flowers or lavender honey prior to serving.

THE THIRTEEN DESSERTS

These fourteen desserts all come from Provence, and it has been a tradition to eat them at Christmas for nearly a hundred years. They stand for the thirteen participants at the Last Supper (Jesus and the twelve Apostles), and are served after midnight Mass or at the end of le gros souper, a meal that consists of seven simple vegetarian dishes.

A typical selection for *lei tretze dessèrts*, as they are known in Provençal dialect, would be:

- Raisins (home dried);
- Dried figs (homegrown);
- The obligatory nuts: almonds, hazelnuts and walnuts;
- Dates, to represent the regions where Christ lived and died;
- Four different types of fresh fruit, which may include plums (traditionally from Brignoles), winter pears, melons, apples, oranges, grapes and tangerines;
- Candied fruits;
- Light and dark Turkish honey, white and

black nougat. The light variety is made from hazelnuts, pine nuts and pistachios, and symbolises goodness and purity; the dark or black nougat stands for evil and impurity;

- Fougasse (or fouace), a flat cake made with olive oil (which must be broken, not cut!);
- Oreillettes: light, thin waffles flavoured with lemon zest;
- Roulés: cinnamon-flavoured brioche rolls;
- Ratafia, a mixture of juice and brandy, or cartagène, a sweet fortified wine;
- Calissons d'Aix: sweets similar to marzipan made from almond paste and candied melon;
- Biscotins;
- Marinated goat's cheese.

JEAN PERDU'S EMERGENCY LITERARY PHARMACY FROM ADAMS TO VON ARNIM

Fast-acting medicines for minds and hearts affected by minor or moderate emotional turmoil.

To be taken in easily digestible doses (between five and fifty pages) unless otherwise indicated and if possible, with warm feet and/or with a cat on your lap.

Adams, Douglas. *The Hitchhiker's Guide to the Galaxy: A Trilogy in Five Parts.*

Effective in large doses for treating pathological optimism or a sense of humour failure. Ideal for sauna-goers with exhibitionist tendencies.

Side effects: An aversion to owning things, and a potentially chronic tendency to wear a dressing gown all day.

von Arnim, Elizabeth. *The Enchanted April.*

For indecision and for trusting one's friends.

Side effects: Falling in love with Italy; a yearning for the South; a heightened sense of justice.

Barbery, Muriel. *The Elegance of the Hedgehog.*

An effective cure in large doses for if-such-and-such-happens-ism. Recommended for unacknowledged geniuses, lovers of intellectual films and people who hate bus drivers.

Cervantes, Miguel de. *The Ingenious Gentleman Don Quixote of La Mancha.*

To be taken when your ideals clash with reality.
Side effects: Anxiety about modern technology and about the destructive effects of machines, which we fight as though they were windmills.

Forster, E. M. 'The Machine Stops', a short story first published in *The Oxford and Cambridge Review,* 1909.

Handle with care! Highly effective antidote to internet technocracy and blind faith in iPhones. Also cures an addiction to Facebook and dependency on *The Matrix.*
Directions for use: Small doses only for members of the Pirate Party and web activists!

Gary, Romain. *Promise at Dawn*, trans. John Markham Beach.

For a better understanding of motherly love and protection against nostalgia for one's childhood.
Side effects: Daydreaming; lovesickness.

Gerlach, Gunter. *Frauen von Brücken werfen* (Throwing Women Off Bridges – unpublished in English).

For authors with writer's block and people who think that murders are an overrated feature of crime novels.

Side effects: A loss of your sense of reality; a broadening of the mind.

Hesse, Hermann. 'Stages', a poem, in *The Glass Bead Game*, trans. Richard and Clara Winston.
Cures grief, and inspires you to trust.

Kafka, Franz. 'Investigations of a Dog', a short story in *The Great Wall of China*, trans. Malcolm Parsley.
A remedy for the odd sensation of being generally misunderstood.

Side effects: Pessimism; a longing to stroke a cat.

Kästner, Erich. *Doktor Erich Kästners Lyrische Hausapotheke* (*Dr Erich Kästner's Lyrical Medicine Chest* – unpublished in English).
According to the poetic Dr Kästner, it treats a variety of ailments and disturbances, including know-it-alls, an urge to break up with someone, everyday irritations and the autumn blues.

Lindgren, Astrid. *Pippi Longstocking*, trans. Edna Hurup.
Effective against acquired (rather than innate) pessimism and a fear of miracles.

Side effects: Diminished numeracy skills; singing in the shower.

Martin, George R. R. *A Game of Thrones*. The first in a series of five novels.

Helps one to kick a TV habit and to cope with lovesickness, the hassles of daily life and tedious dreams.

Side effects: Insomnia; unsettling dreams.

Melville, Herman. *Moby-Dick; or, The Whale*.

For vegetarians.

Side effects: A fear of water.

Millet, Catherine. *The Sexual Life of Catherine M.*, trans. Adriana Hunter.

Helps you answer the great question of whether you jumped into a relationship too quickly. NB: Things could always be worse.

Musil, Robert. *The Man Without Qualities*, trans. Sophie Wilkins and Burton Pike.

A book for men who've forgotten what they wanted from life. A remedy for aimlessness.

Side effects: The effects are gradual: after two years, your life will have changed forever. The main risks are that you will alienate all your friends, develop a predisposition to social satire and suffer from recurring dreams.

Nin, Anaïs. *Delta of Venus*.

Will cure listlessness and restore sensuality within days of your starting treatment.

Orwell, George. *Nineteen Eighty-Four.*

Reduces gullibility and apathy. Old home remedy for chronic optimism, but past its sell-by date.

Pearce, Philippa. *Tom's Midnight Garden.*

Effective for those who are unhappy in love. (PS: Sufferers from this particular illness may read anything, as long as there is no mention of love, splatter fiction, thrillers and steam-punk novels.)

Pratchett, Terry. The Discworld Novels. Terry Pratchett published forty novels in the Discworld series, beginning with *The Colour of Magic.*

For the world-weary and the dangerously naïve. Mind-warping stuff, even for novices.

Pullman, Philip. *His Dark Materials* trilogy.

For those who occasionally hear imaginary voices and believe they have an animal soul mate.

Ringelnatz, Joachim. *Kindergebetchen* (*Little Bedtime Prayers* – unpublished in English).

For agnostics who for once are moved to prayer. *Side effects:* Flashbacks to evenings when you were small.

Saramago, José. *Blindness,* trans. Giovanni Pontiero.

Helps you to tackle overwork, to prioritise and to see your purpose in life.

Stoker, Bram. *Dracula.*

Recommended for those susceptible to boring dreams and those who sit, paralysed, by the phone ('Will he ever ring?').

Surre-Garcia, Alem and Françoise Meyruels. *The Ritual of the Ashes.* An Occitan invocation from the dead to the living. The original was published as *Lo libre dels rituals*, 2002.

Helps in cases of recurring grief for a loved one, and as a secular grave-side incantation to be said by people who do not believe in prayer.

Toes, Jac. *De vrije man* (*The Free Man* – unpublished in English).

For tango dancers between *milongas* and for men who are too scared to love.

Side effects: Makes you look again at your relationship.

Twain, Mark. *The Adventures of Tom Sawyer.*

To overcome adult worries and rediscover the child within.

NB: The authors **Sanary** (*Southern Lights*), **P. D. Olson** and **Max Jordan** (*Night*) exist only as characters in this novel.